# THE THREE BOOKS OF SHAMA

## BY

## BENJAMIN KWAKYE

Publisher's information, address:
Cissus World Press, P.O. Box 240865, Milwaukee, WI 53224
www.cissusworldpressbooks.com

ISBN: 978-0-9679511-3-3
First published in the U.S.A by Cissus World Press

Cover art by Philip N. Okoro
First Edition

CISSUS WORLD PRESS BOOKS are published by Dike Okoro, Founding Publisher.

**Other Books by Benjamin Kwakye:**

**Novels**

*The Clothes of Nakedness*
*The Sun by Night*
*The Other Crucifix*
*Legacy of Phantoms*

**Collections**

*Eyes of the Slain Woman (novellas)*
*The Executioner's Confession (short stories)*

**Poetry**

*Scrolls of the Living Night*

For Kristodia
Who broke out like the morning light
And stole love from the circling night.

# THE THREE BOOKS OF SHAMA

## BY

## BENJAMIN KWAKYE

# THE FIRST BOOK OF SHAMA

**CONVERSATIONS WITH THE ABYSS**
**THE FOOL'S TOMATOES**
**THE FIRE OF BEGINNINGS**
**SHADOW OF DEATH**
**ARM OF THE FLESH**

# One

My first birth is the simplest version among the three. No doubt, it is what everyone hopes or would hope for—delivered like any other through my mother's birth canal after a normal incubation and labor. For a long time, this was all I knew of my beginnings and it suited me well, clinging to that wish to be normal, to belong like all others. But, despite this wish, another towering tale would come to eclipse this account of simple origins, suggesting to me that I was different, perhaps not even normal. But I have long rejected the tendency to determine what is normal and what is not, as experience has taught me that everyone bears something in secret that would seem to defy some norm. And as every destination starts from the beginning, I too open my story from the beginning. In so starting, I could expand on the first version of my birth, but since it is so simple and common, no more needs to be said about it. Consider it already told.

I continue with the second, the one that is bolder, fantastic, and fabulous. More interesting. More disturbing. And it is also more convoluted but, over the years, I have managed to piece together some form of coherence from multiple accounts (mainly my parents'). This has not come easily—neither the cohering nor the recounting—and I am retelling it with significant effort, refusing to sift out the pain and disappointments or to augment the joys and achievements. At times, in undertaking this wearying sojourn, I wondered if it wouldn't be best to leave such tedious excavation to the anthropologists of creation myths and offer them the space and time to account for it as fact, fiction, or metaphor. But the story keeps pulling me to it like an enchantress at once offering burning fire and soothing water: Come close and be warmed; come close and be replenished; come close and be scathed; and come close and be parched.

This second version of my birth that I speak of, is it to be trusted? I learned of its details on the eve of a form of pregnancy with a violent labor that birthed a tragedy. In retrospect, I have come to believe that the fear of imminent tragedy compels disclosures that typically remain concealed in the shame-guard of memory, the deep ocean floors of the past. And I have worried that confessions made under such duress can warp the truth; at best, shade it. I am sometimes sure of the excavations of my mind and sometimes I am extremely doubtful. But if I continue in such self-interrogation, I risk going on and on like a forceful wind blowing nowhere. So let me begin. Here it comes. Brace yourself as I sew together what I have heard and what I have observed, licensing my imagination to plug the gaps where there are insufficient details.

Now, then, here is my second birth.

# Two

Papa stood outside by himself in the early morning while the town slept, when waking voices had not begun to drown legacies of night's silence, the silence that steals peace that a good night sleep bestows—those quiet hours that disengage the mind from troubles of the day, teasing it into the dreadful places of its oppressive imaginations. As if the earth had undergone a sweltering shower, thick fog hugged the hills beyond. I could imagine Papa calling to the vaporous horizon, asking for an embrace where he might be relieved of all his worries and fears and where he might levitate into nothingness when the fog dissipated. It was evident that Papa would rather not confront himself, his family or his society as his deep funk had become a life force of its own. Still tormenting him years after his best friend Anan died, the fog of funk that periodically enveloped him wouldn't lift. I had heard many question how one man's death could affect another so deeply, so many years after it happened. However, as I studied my father that morning, I knew there was more to it than his friend's death. There also was the fear for the future as the country flirted with civil war. I was certain his mind was embroiled with questions. What would happen to his children? Would they perish in the slaughter that was consuming the country? He had no answer. No one did. In fact, it would be unfair to expect any, whether man or beast, to respond to such cold questions.

Given these concerns, was this not the best time to reveal the secret he had guarded for so long? The secret....

He would soon make a profound confession to me, more than I thought I needed to know at that time, although in retrospect, it was the perfect time, a time when even the bravest among us worried about mayhem and potential death—our own. And the world is never the same when death gives notice with its macabre telltales of mutilations and murders. Such notice had been served in Kigali and elsewhere, even pre-announced in Butare. What was rational before had become irrational and the normal had become abnormal and vice versa. In fact, I have often thought that Papa had not intended to divulge all that he did, not in the graphic manner he presented events; but, with possible death hovering over us, I believe his will to withhold himself was overwhelmed, simply

9

overran. By looking to the past, with the mistuned echoes of death pervading the country, he must have lost the ability to keep even the ugliest elements of his personal history at bay. No longer would it lie in the comforting distance from where he could leisurely peck on its details from time to time. But if Papa knew exactly what the future was about to deal us, he should have paid more attention to it, and not merely exhumed the mournful bones of the past for his daughter to consume.

That day when he looked from the front of our adobe home to the unresponsive, if promisingly picturesque horizon, and saw the home of his fallen friend that had become desolate, Papa was saddened anew that Anan's life had been so prematurely snuffed by cholera. If sadness were the equivalent of tears, Papa's would flood oceans. He was that inconsolable, even if he soon welcomed the sun's spitting rays descending as though in cruel benevolence. He needed that warmth as a balm for the fever that had seized him, a fever of the spirit that the company of family could hardly cure.

He stayed outside, as the fog began to lift, as the grass, soon bearing the rays of the rising sun, seemed to drink the glory of morning-light. Even the cedar trees in the far distance glowed in the increasing sunbath. By any measure, a beautiful morning was arriving in Butare, yet Papa was sad.

I was worried about my father, given all that was happening in the country, especially as he seemed to take it more gravely than all of us. And it wasn't until his confession that I would understand what Papa meant by "Anan's gifts," which he'd said a number of times before. When he'd first said this, I thought he was referring to the fruits of the tomato garden Anan had helped us start in our backyard, which we had maintained in one form of cultivation or another over the years. Speaking of Anan, both my brother Placide and I loved him. We wept and brooded for long periods when he died, but none of that mourning could match Papa's alternating melancholy and depression.

As the country stood on the precipice of civil war and genocide and signs of genocide glared, I was more determined than ever to help my father end his continual mourning. We needed to focus on the present. If I'd hesitated in the past, the desperate times required more frontal measures, especially in handling the emotional life of one so close. Also, I was now an adult, having just completed my bachelor's degree. I would have to find a way to bring Papa out of his shell of long sorrow. I looked at his forlorn figure outside and decided it would be the wrong time to approach him. I waited.

That evening, he sat in the living room, his eyes closed, his palm rubbing his cheeks, on which the claws of age hung its wrinkles. He'd turned off the TV, preferring to stare at nothing. Next to him on the couch were a stack of books, which Anan had given him, but which remained largely unread, except when I sat next to him and asked him to read to me, and then he would reluctantly read me a few paragraphs. I enjoyed the sound of his voice, its smooth cadence, the measured opening and closing of his mouth, the focus on the pages as he read, and I felt closer to him and perhaps he felt closer to me. When I entered the living room that evening, I saw him stand, remove his sandals, move forward and squash a cockroach that had started a crawl on the wall to his left. Papa sat down again and stared at the TV's blank screen. The room was dark, the light coming in from the dying light from outside falling like strained shadows through the windows.

I turned on the light bulb that hang from the ceiling, sat on the armchair next to my father and asked, "Papa, are you still crying over Uncle Anan?"

"Shama," he said, as if unaware that I had entered the room. He turned his head slowly to look at me, his big eyes suddenly opened wide, his sexagenarian wrinkles more visible, the dark blotches under his eyes deeper, a contrast to the gray of his cropped hair. He pursed his lips and peered at me. "I wasn't crying," he stated.

"Not tears, Papa" I said. "But you haven't stopped mourning ever since Uncle Anan died. It's been so many years, Papa."

My father stayed silent for seconds, then he shook his head slowly in a manner that suggested regret more than disagreement and said, "Anan's gifts."

"I've heard you say that many times, Papa. The tomatoes from the garden are nice and I know Uncle Anan helped us with it, but why do you still say Anan's gifts to this day? Has he left his imprints so deeply, even though he's gone? Does it have anything to do with Nana's visitations?"

11

"Shama," he said. I wanted to hug him as he took a deep breath. "I have struggled with something very important, never thinking it was the right time to reveal it to you. But now my hand is being forced by circumstances. No one knows tomorrow, as they say. I wouldn't want to go to my grave with this secret."

"What are you talking about, Papa? Who is talking about anyone going to his grave?" Although my intentions to encourage my father were as clear as air, I knew my words were just as hollow.

"You are braver than you know, Shama. I've always known that. And though you are my second child, you are the more mature, the stronger of the two. That's why I will tell you this and then we can decide how to tell Placide. I'm not sure he can handle it well, not as well as you will. It may break him apart. But you, you have been through so much and yet you have survived and thrived. Look at how intelligent and beautiful you have become. I have a feeling you can overcome any situation, no matter how difficult."

I'm not sure I agreed with this assessment, but perhaps Papa saw something in me that I didn't.

"I don't follow you, Papa?"

"Come with me," he said. "I will explain."

Papa went to the kitchen to drink banana wine. At first, when Papa drank after they were married, Mama complained, quoting him the Koran, 5:90-91, describing the drink as evil and saying that *khamr* sows enmity among people and turns one away from God and prayer, to which Papa replied that he was a Christian and in his Bible, the first miracle of Jesus was to turn water into wine. Mama stopped complaining after a while, apparently resigned to the reality that Papa wouldn't budge.

Now filled with the wine, Papa led the way outside and I followed dutifully, perplexed that my question would trigger this journey, which seemed to have no preplanned destination as Papa walked in circles. Even after the evening turned into early night, starless and moonless, we walked with no apparent aim for at least twenty minutes. I was getting irritated by the length of the promenade when Papa abruptly sat by a eucalyptus tree and said, "Sit with me." Judging from what Papa would say to me, his twenty-one year old daughter at the time, I concluded he'd drunk the banana wine to summon courage.

12

"People always ask me how Anan's death could make me so sad," Papa said. "They tell me I should let it go, that it's not healthy for me to hold on to the grief this long. What they don't understand is that Anan was more than a friend. He was a brother who gave me gifts so priceless and selfless that I sometimes struggle with its implications. Gifts so priceless...." He paused and licked his lips noisily.

"What gifts, Papa?" I asked to nudge him.

Even under the influence of the wine, he struggled for the courage to continue.

When he continued, I could barely hear the whisper that came from his mouth, as if he had borrowed a new voice from somewhere deep within his body that lacked energy. "Placide," he said. "You."

I wasn't sure I had heard him well. I made him repeat himself.

"We are his gifts?" I asked. "Papa, you are confusing me."

"What I am about to say is heavy, but you now deserve to know the truth. You also need to know that, no matter what, your mother and I love you and your brother more than life itself. You in particular, Shama, you are my very heartbeat."

My heart began to beat abnormally as I suspected my father was about to set loose something burdensome and that I would be expected to carry a portion of that burden. I took an attentive listen as he resumed speaking.

"Yes, Shama," Papa said. "You are Anan's gift to me. And this is how it happened."

# Three

I was already aware that Mama wasn't Papa's first wife. In fact I knew where Mama Ange lived. She was not mentioned in our household. Both Papa and Mama would hush anyone who mentioned her name, as if her sprit was evil hovering-in-wait, ready to respond to a call by name. I'd never appreciated this attitude, as Mama Ange was pleasant and reputedly kind, always eager to offer smiles and pleasant greetings whenever I saw her. She always asked me to give Papa her greetings, but well aware that her name was abolished from all lips in our homestead, I refrained from relaying any such compliments.

After he married Mama Ange, Papa began to worry that God, pulling a humorous prank, had neutralized the creative power of the juices flowing from his loins. Papa confessed how much he'd loved Mama Ange, who was good to him and catered well to his needs and wants—from the breakfast served hot to help recoup the energies expended in the nocturnal hours, the smiles provided frequently in the diurnal interlude, the conversations shared in affectionate tones daylong, to the serenades of twilights and the bodily warmth offered in the long nights of sleepless blissfulness in search of a baby. But family and friends insisted she was a curse after they'd been married for five years without issue.

"If she can't bear children," they said, "then she's a curse."

Papa at first resisted these attempts to sour his affections. How could anyone truly appreciate the love between husband and wife? "She's a blessing," Papa insisted. But the pressure kept building, the voices growing louder and increasingly strident. He shouldn't have budged, Papa said. "I don't know, though, if I'd stood firm, I wouldn't have married your mother and I may not have had you or Placide."

Papa succumbed after nights of worry and days of tormenting thoughts. "I was weak." He told Mama Ange that his decision to divorce her was not by choice.

"Deep inside you," she said "you know, Placide, that you agree with their assessment of me. You do believe that I am a curse."

He wanted to ask for her forgiveness, to urge her to try and understand why his weakness and desire for children trumped whatever reservoir of love he still had for her. But why prolong the pain and delay

14

the expedience of a divorce to please all naysayers? The blow must not be made to tarry. He kept his quiet while Mama Ange left the home, which he'd built with Anan's help.

With Mama Ange gone, Papa mourned her loss for months and then turned his energies in a quest for a successor-wife, which initially took the form of increased church attendance. The man who had attended church once a month now went every Sunday, gaining the applause of Rev. Didier Murenzi. After service, he waited by the bougainvillea in front of the chapel to attract the attention of unattached ladies. When that didn't bear the quick results he craved, he started frequenting the various waterholes he could find in Butare, singing and bonding with other winebibbers. Stripped of all the trappings of marriage and its responsibilities, Papa was determined to establish himself as the most eligible bachelor in town. At least, that was his intention, but his path of imbibing, false swashbuckling and engaging in the inebriated-propositioning of as many women as he could in high reliance on the law of averages only attracted to him characters whose sole purpose was to help him diminish the money he made from his small tea plantation, who were eager to help him spend it but reluctant to commit to lasting relationships. He changed them as frequently as he ate his meals, drawing criticism from his pastor and peers for being irresponsible, especially on account of the ill-reputation he was beginning to acquire. "A good name, once soiled, is hard to repair," the pastor said. Papa also began to tire and despair as all his efforts were going to waste, unfulfilled by the shallow relationships built on the tenuous foundations of nocturnal liaisons. He needed a wife, not companions he found wanting in wifely attributes. They were too old or too young, too quiet or too loud, too uninterested or too inquisitive.

It was at this time of desperation that Anan said to Papa over banana wine, "Let me help you."

Those were the most pleasing words Papa had heard in a long time, given that it came from the man he trusted the most. After all, they'd been friends since childhood, their families living close to each other—or, come to think of it, who was Anan's family? As children, Papa and Anan had met once on the streets in a casual encounter and been drawn to each other and become inseparable, star-crossed friends if ever such existed. Anan

15

never attended any school that Papa knew of, claiming he was home schooled and had all the education he needed when Papa asked him about this. An only child, Anan would come to Papa's house sometimes, but he never invited Papa to his. Once when Papa had asked to see where Anan lived, he'd said that his parents were strict, too strict, and didn't like him inviting friends home. The closest Papa got to seeing Anan's home was from afar, with Anan pointing and saying, "Never get near. My parents are dangerous. They can injure or kill you, and our dog bites whatever can be bitten." Even when he was young, Anan spoke with such confidence that he was unquestionably believable. It was as if he made nothing up, had no time for fancy ideas. And such strength of persuasion and imagery of maimed body under canine onslaught hindered Papa's curiosity. Once or twice he stood a distance from the Anan household and contemplated visiting it, but refrained from doing so. Not once did Papa observe any activity in or around the household, which always stood in the distance, quiet as the catacombs, desolate as a tombstone. What kind of family is this? Papa wondered, although this didn't dissuade him from spending his free time with Anan. Anan himself was sufficient for Papa. He didn't need to know any more about the man. On his seventeenth birthday, Anan declared to Papa that his parents had left the town and left him by himself. These secretive parents formed an unanswered question mark that forever hovered in Papa's mind.

"Weren't you curious that they were just phantoms?" I asked.

"Of course, but in our friendship, as close as we got, such matters were almost irrelevant."

"That is hard to believe, Papa," I said.

"It was what it was," Papa replied with oracular assuredness.

Beyond this unknown, Papa and Anan fostered a relationship that seemed so well balanced: sharing hopes—e.g., how they would each grow up to own large plantations; and mutually condoling each other—e.g., Anan consoling Papa when another kid beat him up or Papa saying kind words when Anan announced how much he missed his parents. These were times Papa preferred to keep in a safe place, returning to them when he needed some refurbishing thought.

And here was Anan offering help after Mama Ange's departure. Why had Papa not consulted with his friend first rather than embark on

16

this path of barren results? Anan wasn't married himself, but he could easily have married judging from the women who thronged to him, each proclaiming she could be his harlot, mother, sister and wife all at once: in other words, attempting to fulfill any feminine need Anan desired, including whatever fantasies he harbored. Not to mention his resume of travels—far and wide he'd traversed land, river and lake (and some said, even sea), meeting people in high societal echelons and building connections that established a wide network of influence. At some point Papa asked Anan how he managed this, but the response was a shrug and a smile and, "It is just so." And a man who was so within reach was at the same time outside of reach.

"You will help me find a wife?" Papa asked, knowing that Anan was capable.

"Of course, that's not a problem."

Having put his faith in Anan, Papa rested soundly that night, assured that his friend would deliver. Anan disappeared and reappeared three days later to invite Papa to his newly built home, a home within easy view of Papa's. "You and I can get even closer now," he'd told Papa.

"I didn't know you were building a house," Papa said. "I saw it being built, but I didn't know it belonged to you."

"I wanted to surprise you," Anan replied. "Now you and I will be even closer."

When they got close to the house, Anan urged Papa to enter the living room alone. "There is a surprise waiting for you," he whispered.

Papa entered the living room with anxious breath. Immediately, he observed a woman sitting in the corner as the smell of burning incense nourished the air. All lights in the room were off and it was lit instead by a number of candles placed in several places so that Papa wasn't sure whether to genuflect in homage to this apparent religious ambiance or begin some manner of oblation to the seated woman. As she was all covered up in body and veiled in the face, Papa kept his distance, judging, wondering, even apprehensive. The woman lifted the veil to allow Papa a full facial view. Papa didn't speak, finding no words to address her. She didn't speak either, walking out in seconds, the veil descending as quickly as it had ascended.

"That's your next wife," Anan said as soon as the woman was gone and he entered the room.

Next wife? Papa recollected her face, only so briefly offered to him to view—the long nose and thin lips. It had been an all too brief glance, and the quickness of the re-veiling and withdrawal were as annoying as they were intriguing. But the impression the woman's face had left was profound—a strong beauty that seemed designed to tease. Within the candlelight of the living room, the woman had appeared as something mystifying even in the long dress that covered her features but suggested reserved sensuousness, especially when she walked past Papa as she was leaving the room, the buds pushing against the dress in the chest region and the sway of hips that the dress hugged tightly. She begged to be discovered and Papa was already eager to discover.

"What do you think?" Anan asked.

"I...I..."

"I have picked the perfect wife for you. She's from a good home, perfect reputation. It's a fertile home too, plenty of babies."

"She... she...."

"I don't want to put too much pressure on you. But you've seen what you've seen. If you're interested, the rest is easy."

"I hardly know her."

"If you want to know her, I will facilitate that."

"I want to know her, but ... the dress... the veil... she's a Moslem?"

"That she is. Why, is that a problem?"

"Of course, Anan. I am a Christian. How can I marry a Moslem?"

"Oh, Pascal," Anan said, "That has nothing to do with anything."

"But how can we live as one when we worship different Gods?"

"You don't worship different Gods; you just worship Him differently."

"But my faith teaches me that mine is the only way."

"It is the heart that matters. She is willing to get to know you and she's the best I could find for you out there. If she is willing, why wouldn't you give her the chance?"

18

Papa's trust in Anan, the glimmer of what he suspected was a deep sensual well from which he could drink.... "I'm not sure, but I am willing to give it a try."

"Good. We have to work quickly. She comes from the Yenza region and is here only briefly visiting a distant relative. You need to win her before she leaves; otherwise, it will be difficult to court her."

Papa, still unsure, would meet the woman again, at least to sate the curiosity that she'd released into him.

Anan arranged the meeting three days later, during which Papa's curiosity had morphed into awe as he recollected the moment, now glaring under the focus of his imagination, when he walked into the room to see her seated and then the slight movement of her sheathed arm as it lifted the veil while the room's weak lights partially illuminated parts of her face as much as it half-dimmed others. Had she smiled? Papa questioned his memory. Or was it a frown? This question dominated his thoughts until he wasn't sure what she had tried to signal to him. So dominated, Papa approached their next meeting with caution, if eagerness, when Anan left them alone in the dimmed lights of his living room. Closer to her now, Papa could feel the heat of her body, its unfamiliar perfume. As before, she unveiled her face before Papa could speak, but left it unveiled this time. She looked at Papa for a quick second and then averted her gaze and for a half-minute after that, neither spoke. Papa observed the shy eyes that seemed almost closed, and the prominent nose that gave her face purpose, modified its gentleness with strength and beauty.

"Anan tells me you're a good woman," Papa said

"And he tells me you're a good man," she said.

"He is a kind man," he said, "for speaking the truth."

Mama looked at him closely, the traces of a smile in her eyes. "The truth about which of us, you or me?"

"Shall we say about both of us?"

"I agree."

And now they had begun to mold the space between them, bend it toward affection and the higher feeling that none can describe adequately enough. He would learn that her name was Hadidja, that her parents had passed, that she was raised by an ailing uncle (and an aunt who had also passed), that she was restless to find newness and escape from all those

19

relational deaths that trailed her, and that she was twenty years old, about five years Papa's junior. Raised in the madrassas in Swahili, she'd still managed to pick up Kinyarwanda. He would reciprocate with a story about himself, about his parents, who had also passed (which they each declared was a remarkable detail of no mere coincidence, but a sign that their stars were well aligned). Not just her face, its striking charm, but her mellow voice, her measured speech that indicated humility and thoughtfulness, all begun to knit something deep inside him that he found irresistible. When Anan returned, Papa wanted to beg him to give them more time alone, entreat her to stay a while longer, but he suppressed these yearnings that would seem desperate and perhaps inconsiderate.

They would meet under similar circumstances two more times before Hadidja returned home, although with what each had stirred in the other continuing to expand, they urged Anan to arrange additional rendezvous. They would therefore meet two more times: once under the cover of night in her hometown after Anan had managed to steal her away for a few minutes so that Papa could declare to her how much she'd touched him; and once, when she managed a brief trip to Butare. Realizing that the long-distance courtship could work against him, and now convinced of his total need, Papa announced to Hadidja (Mama) that he wanted to marry her. She confessed that she would love to marry him, but asked, "Are you not worried that I am a Moslem woman?"

"Why, does it worry you that I am Christian?"

"Yes, to be frank."

Papa had still not completely overcome the disturbing hindrance of their different faiths, but he feared that life would be miserable if he allowed this woman to slip from him. After Mama Ange, he had gone searching for another woman solely for the purpose of reproduction. But even that now seemed (temporarily) irrelevant on account of his new found love, which seized him beyond his comprehension and convinced him that he would be happy, no matter what, if he married Hadidja. "Do you believe I am a good man?" he asked her.

"Yes," said she.

"And I believe you are a good woman. And I will tell you one thing, Hadidja. I love you like I've never loved before. I can speak of my love only in so many words, but I know you know that I love you deeply.

I will ask you one question. I think I know the answer, but I need to hear it from your mouth and I want you to be honest. Do you have any affection for me? If we got married, would it for you be out of affection or convenience?"

Mama would later tell Papa that she was puzzled by the way he'd phrased the question. Why not simply ask, do you love me? Why "any affection for me?" And Papa would explain that he didn't want to risk a negative response. If he was assured Mama had some affection for him, then he could be certain that he could marry her—any feeling approximating love would do, for he could, even if little by little, turn that into full blown love.

But he needn't have worried. "I love you," Mama said. "With all my heart."

Even if he considered this declaration too bold from her, he was still delighted to hear it. "I have never said this to anyone," Mama said, "But this is so unusual for me that I even don't care about decorum."

"So long as we're prepared to stand by each other, we have nothing to fear," Papa said.

"Are you sure of this?"

"I have no doubt."

Without a ring, but acting in the manner of Westerners, Papa got on one knee and asked, "Hadidja, will you marry me?"

And, in addition to her own elevated emotions, she was too touched by this gesture to say no. "Yes, I will marry you," she said. And he hugged her and between them they were already married and all that was left was for them to convince their families and then solemnize the agreement. But they discovered that the love they deemed to be burning bright inside them was of little consequence to their families, distant members at that. Mama's uncle was adamant that his niece marry one of like religion, as were Papa's aunts and uncles. Shama, Papa's only sister/sibling, argued in favor of the marriage. "He should marry whomever he chooses," she said. When Papa thanked her sister for the support, she winked and said, "Just remember to name a child after me."

"I will and that is a promise I will keep if Hadidja and I have children," Papa said.

But the rest of the family wouldn't budge. Papa began to shrink in size as he refused to eat, claiming that he could not summon his appetite when his love was away from him, claiming that his hunger for food was of no consequence until his hunger for her was met. His uncles and aunts met several times, worried that their nephew was headed for a premature demise. On one of their meetings, Papa had Anan attend to assure them that marrying Hadidja would be best for their nephew. Afraid for the health of Papa and given Anan's respectable stature as a young man of enterprise and bright future, the family acquiesced and sent a delegation, including Anan, to see Mama's uncle. Given this overture, and the gift of money Anan took with him, the ailing man gave his begrudging consent. They performed the traditional phase of the wedding as the families gathered in tents opposite each other as a prelude to their mutual familiarization, a little mock haggling and agreement on the bride price, which consisted mainly of a cow, the presentation by Mama's family of gourds of milk to Papa's family, and then feasting and dancing. They skipped the church ceremony given their varying religious tenets, and held another grand reception in Butare financed by Anan.

This was a new beginning befitting of Papa's full attention and devotion and he gave it his focused energies, becoming such a doting husband that Mama was held out for envy among the neighborhood, and respect for turning Papa's potentially wayward ways around, especially in focusing his attention on the tea plantation he co-owned with Anan. Theirs was an arrangement of mutual respect so that Papa never intervened when Mama devoted time to her five prayers a day or the times during Ramadan when she withheld intimacy from him on religious grounds. But if he accommodated these brief periods of abstinence, Papa had become singularly bent on producing offspring now that he had secured his love, and that became his paramount concern. He wanted a son, he told Mama; she'd like a son, but she wanted a daughter also, she replied. Despite this accord, two years after their marriage, Papa and Mama didn't have any children. Nor was it for lack of effort. Papa ate various nuts and drank concoctions designated for potency and so equipped was at it at the least opportunity.

Meantime, Papa found out that his first wife Mama Ange had remarried and borne twins, as though doubly to tease him. He concluded when Mama Ange's twins arrived that he was the one who'd failed to fertilize her obviously agile eggs. This discovery was so emasculating that Papa cursed God and the gods in equal measure and considered suicide to negate the sorry creation that he then believed he'd become. He even ceased attending church, despite pleas from Rev. Murenzi. What were others saying when his back was turned? What use is a man if he can't implant fertile seeds in his wife?

Papa descended into deep despondency. He turned unusually quiet, refusing to talk to anyone, his eyes always bloodshot, head bowed. At night he would wake up several times, sometimes saunter about absentmindedly and occasionally sit outside, exposing himself to the elements and risking illness. Awake most nights, he would sleep all day, usually neglecting the tea plantation that only recently was thriving under his refocused energies, although Anan's indulgence of Papa's attitude and attention to the plantation kept it from collapse.

In the few hours when Papa slept at night his snoring was so loud it was as if he was protesting sleep, not to mention the dreadful smell of his suddenly earsplitting farts that drew Mama's protests. He hardly ate. Mama heard him once or twice sobbing during the quiet night hours when he went and sat outside in the abysses of the night. She pleaded and cajoled and threatened, Papa was too deep in his dejection for her to reach him. He could tell she began to worry that he would lose his love and she too approached despondency, as though his condition had infected her.

It was Anan who rescued Papa from this seemingly hopeless brink. After all, as Papa had explained, they'd grown up as brothers since childhood, fostering a relationship that seemed so well balanced. Above all, Anan had served as the liaison to Mama. So it was natural that after failing to pull Papa out of his funk, Mama would go to Anan, fearful that Papa would do something foolish in his depression. Although he'd registered his concern before, with this plea from Mama, Anan rushed to see his wasting friend immediately.

At first, Papa was afraid to admit to Anan the cause of his condition. How does a man admit, even to his closest friend, a failing he deems so spiritually dispiriting, so shameful, that he considered it a total

23

failure of his core function as a man? "Leave me alone, please," Papa said. Anan didn't push the first time, but he sat by Papa for hours, talking about his travels even when for long periods Papa was silent or responded laconically. Anan was back the next day, again to provide company and unrequited talk while Papa resumed his silent brooding after a short outburst of energy when Anan provided some banana beer. These long visits continued in similar fashion for about a week. The men would sometimes sit outside, one quiet, the other jabbering, which prompted some observers to remark that one of the men had put a spell on the other, only it was not clear which had put the spell on whom. On the eighth day, Anan asked again, "What is the problem, my brother?" But now the distance that Papa had tried to insert into the relationship had weakened under Anan's patient prodding, and like the elements with their eroding powers Anan's onslaught of concern and attention erased Papa's resistance. Still, it would take another week of such prodding before Papa managed to emerge out of his sense of hopelessness.

Fifteen days after Anan's first visit on a mission to rescue Papa, the latter smiled. This smile, however, had more purpose to it than mere relief, coming as it were on the buoyancy of a solution. Papa knew exactly what he had to do at that moment when he smiled at his friend. And now that the solution had come to him, he wondered why he'd so stupidly ignored it when it was so close. He looked anew at his friend. And in a manner of speaking it was for the first time. Anan was a strong, handsome, virile young man, and he wasn't married. Women swooned and men warmed up to him. He had confessed to Papa how he'd impregnated a few women in Kigali and had the fetuses aborted. He was fertile. He must be able to help Papa.

That night, Papa held Mama with a new sense of purpose. The kiss, the caress, the embrace, all embodied the vigor of his new mission, the boldness of his solution. And in the serenity of the night, his suppressed depression lifting, his exposure to the elements avoided in favor of his wife, Papa broached *the matter* to Mama, bracing himself for a major fight, the first one in their marriage. And that was what he got.

The matter. How could a man who loved his wife even contemplate such a monstrosity of blasphemous proportions, such a taboo, such sacrilegious nonsense? "No!" Mama exclaimed, her body shaking with rage, breathing heavily, voice barely available, lost in the suffocating noose of the request. "I am shocked," she said, "totally shocked that you of all people, Pascal, would ask me to do this. I've been mindful of all your needs and endeavored to be a true wife, willing out of her love for you to satisfy your every need, anticipate them even as best as I could, nurse your whims and accommodate your desires." Her radar of affection, physical and spiritual, was focused on him and him alone, to whom she'd pledged her body and love. How was she so arbitrarily to retool that radar for another man? She had already withdrawn from his embrace and was pacing the room by the time she said these words, her body shaking harder, her visage contorted, transformed into a flesh of flashing rage that appeared about to lose control. This was the first time in their marriage Mama seemed close to calling her husband an idiot, and a callous one at that, to be willing to insult her with this lewd proposal. Had he lost his mind? Had he become possessed by some diabolical spirit bent on causing irreparable impairment to their marriage?

Papa had expected some resistance, as he had to if he believed his wife loved him, but he hadn't expected this level of fervent rejection, which sent Mama into her own state of brooding. If she had been on the verge out of concern for her husband, she now plunged into that well of melancholy. And so now, just as Anan had waited by his side in constancy, Papa's turn had come to erode his wife's resistance with patience—not an easy task given that he had never seen this aspect of his wife's character and had assumed that it didn't exist. Because he had come to believe that she was incapable of such deep anger, he struggled to face it in its naked wounds. In a way, their roles changed, as Papa was the one who now waited on Mama, servicing her needs, those emotional vacuums wreaked over a short time by Papa's suggestion. It would take companionship and singular attention to her.

In the early hours of the day, Papa was sure to express his unequivocal love, holding and caressing his wife, even when she turned her back to him. In the afternoons, he would hasten from the resumed backbreaking work at his plantation and come visit Mama at the marketplace where she sold beans, rice and the tea harvested from his farm, and he would sit with her a while before returning to work. In the evenings he serenaded her with love songs he'd learned in his childhood days and she would pretend she didn't like them when he knew she did. He unleashed his caressing at night with as much gentleness as he could summon and on rare occasions he managed to have her smile at him in the darkness. Mama knew that this wasn't selfless service, nor a newfound tenderness expressed without expectation. But despite its selfish motives, she must have loved it and because she must have loved it she wanted to reward him for it. If he had opened a trapdoor, she could no longer resist walking through it. The monstrous brush with which she'd painted him began to lose its garish varnish on account of his charming service. Plus her conscience began to haunt her, Mama confessed. If she withheld her consent on matters of such utmost importance to him, then perhaps she was the one being selfish? On such an important matter, was it not time for sacrifice? She renewed her perspective, she told him. It had taken courage and humility for him to confess his infertility to her, his face so somber she thought he could pass as a saint on a sacred mission.

Two months after he first mentioned the matter, Mama gave him hope when she asked, "Are you sure this is the right thing to do?"

"With every part of my being, I am sure."

"You will still love me?"

"Always."

"You will love the child as your own?"

"The child will be my child. How can I not love it?"

"We will still have sexual relations while he comes to me?"

"We will."

"If that is your wish, I will do it."

Papa leaped from her side before she could change her mind and rushed to see Anan. He seemed stunned when Papa broached the matter, but he didn't express any outrage. Papa thought he could detect a glitter of joy as Anan looked at him and he wondered who wouldn't if given such free passage to his Hadidja. "Are you sure you want this, Pascal?" Anan asked.

"Why is everyone asking me this? I am absolutely sure. I have thought this through very carefully and I know it's the right thing to do. And I wouldn't ask just anyone to do this, you know."

"And Hadidja, what does she say?"

"She's in complete agreement."

"Very well, then, Pascal. I will be glad to do it for you. But you must understand that I must first speak with her, to be sure, if you know what I mean."

So Papa arranged for Anan to meet alone with Mama, as though he had become the liaison just as Anan had been to bring them together. Minutes later, Anan confirmed to Papa that he was convinced Mama was in spiritual accord with the arrangement.

The first meeting was a little awkward for all, perhaps except Anan, who came charging into the home, whistling. Now that the actual action was about to proceed, Papa almost retreated, nearly swallowed by dread and loathing, although he wasn't sure if the loathing was directed at Anan or himself. But he suppressed the simmering jealousy in favor of the anticipation of what it could sow, especially the overcoming of the jeers behind his back at his fatherless state. Additionally, because his trust in Anan was complete, the concern loosened somewhat. Mama didn't say anything, her eyes downcast as if ashamed, heart clearly pumping hard, sweat beads over her face. "I will leave you two alone now," Papa said.

He roamed the town hoping for distraction, refusing to imagine Anan and his wife together as Anan performed the function that Papa had previously presumed to be exclusively his. But finding himself now an outsider in the brief moments of *their* union, which brevity was lost on him, given its stresses, for some seconds, thoughts of suicide and then murder intruded into his mind, an urge to end the underlining misery of it all. Oh, the contradictions. But he cast them away, finding security in the fact that this was his brother for all practical purposes. If they had started out as water, they had now found common blood so that he could imagine that blood commingling in this enterprise in a way that would benefit him.

An hour and a half later when he returned home, it was, on the surface, as if nothing had happened. Mama was fully dressed, and looked herself, just a little quiet. Papa didn't want to ask any questions about the intimacy, afraid of what he might hear, even though an annoying curiosity tugged at him. At least, he would have liked to know how he measured up against Anan—a man's greatest sexual insecurity. Mama served Papa dinner and the two ate in uneasy silence, punctuated by some occasional idle talk—Can I get some more water?/There's some oil on your lips, please wipe it away/It looks like we might get some rain tomorrow....

It wasn't until later after Mama had taken her bath and was preparing for bed that a tear rolled down from her left eye. In strained empathy, Papa rubbed the tear and hugged his wife, but the attempt to restore conditions before the preceding events was weak, both of them fully aware that they'd crossed a forbidden path and that something precious had been sacrificed, pawned; and that they could never gather enough strength of spirit to recover it. It was therefore the beginning of an end, a long end that wouldn't destroy them but would forever taint their relationship, and as much as they would each deny it, reduce the respect they had for each other. Papa was now more willing to dismiss Mama's needs and requests and Mama was more likely to talk back to Papa when she disagreed with him, traits they'd both suppressed out of love and respect. They would restate their love to each other that night because they knew they were on very dangerous ground, and it was love truthfully professed. Acting as if Anan hadn't just been with Mama, they would even make love that night (and during the course of Anan's visitations). But was that enough?

The path stepped on, though, any damage that could have been done now done (except for the risk of causing additional damage beyond repair), they had to follow where the path led; otherwise, they would have sacrificed so much for nothing, they assured themselves. Anan would visit the household many more times until Mama conceived. The pregnancy assured, Anan's visits to sire a child ended. He still continued to visit, but as a family friend, and although the visits were at first suffused with embarrassment, with time they all adjusted to the embarrassment such that it seemed normal.

Papa now walked with shoulders raised higher, taking Mama wherever he went, proudly announcing her pregnancy to whomever would listen, dotting on Mama, struggling to meet her needs during the early stages of the pregnancy when she developed a large appetite, turned averse to certain smells and became cranky. As Papa suffered through this, he noticed—or thought he did—a new respect from those whom he'd heard whisper about his impotency and doubtful manhood. He attended church more regularly and in church Rev. Murenzi said a loud prayer before the congregation for the blessing upon Papa. Now he believed he'd rediscovered that manhood in public and, as much as he touted this, he privately bemoaned the loss of that manhood in his mind.

# Four

When Placide was born, Papa found that he loved the child without condition. True, he saw Anan's reflection in Placide but he also saw Mama's reflection in him and perceived the presence of his (Papa's) spirit in the child. Even if he merely saw what he wanted to see, it worked for him nonetheless. This, then, was a child of multiple parents. Papa reasoned that he and Mama were joined together as one in marriage. If therefore this child was a part of her, then by virtue of their oneness in marriage the child was a part of him as well. He knew it was a crude way of saying it, be he did say to himself on many occasions that because he loved his wife he loved his child (or her child).

Papa had his wish; Mama didn't have hers. A year after Placide's birth, Mama went to Papa, carrying the child. "I need a favor," she said.

The sacrifice she'd made evidenced in her hand, the presence of their child strengthening him with pride, Papa announced, "Anything you want."

Uh oh—the equivalent of a Harold-Salome promise?

Not as gruesome a request, but a hard one nonetheless. Papa should have paid more attention to the sweat on Mama's face in order to be forewarned this wasn't going to be an ordinary favor: "I want a daughter," Mama said with a wavering voice.

"Don't you love our son? Is he not good enough for you?"

"I love him, but I need a girl also."

He didn't need to be told what that meant, but he remembered that she'd stated her preference for children of both genders when he'd first proposed Anan as a potential progenitor. Papa cringed at the thought of further fathering visits by Anan. Still, how could Pascal Rugwe deny his wife? After all, he'd initiated this. He was more worried this time, though. Yes, he knew Mama had wanted a daughter, but now he considered whether this particular request was truly to fulfill that need or her way of getting Anan back into their bed. Had she enjoyed those moments so much that she wanted them to continue?

"What if it's another boy?" Papa asked.

"At least we'd know we tried."

30

Every emotional impulse urged him to fight this request, but every practical inclination pointed to his own compromised hands. "Just this one more time and no more?"

"Yes, just this one more time."

With reluctance, his step heavier than usual, Papa walked over to see Anan. His friend didn't ask any questions this time, his enthusiasm palpable: that smile, that glow in the eyes. Had he also enjoyed it so much that he was this enthused to reprise it? Anan put a hand over Papa's shoulder and said, "I am honored, Pascal." And despite that under-chorus of jealousy ringing in his ears, Anan's ease of demeanor and friendship were reassuring.

And so it happened again that Anan came over to the household until I was conceived.

When Papa ended his monologue, I was so disturbed I couldn't think. How could he? I kept asking him. And how could Mama participate in this outrage? I was a result of their actions, Papa said, and I was not an outrage. If the result was not outrageous, then the process that bore it could not be outrageous. False logic, I said. He loved me, Papa kept saying. And I could see his eyes moist with tears. This was the man I had called my father all along, and here he was saying he wasn't. Well, not quite. He was not saying that at all and he had performed all his fatherly duties, sometimes with distinction; but still I felt betrayed, utterly cheated.

I was in that state that I approached Mama the next day, accusing her. "How could you, Mama? How could you?"

"Your Papa told me last night he'd told you," she said. "I think he did the right thing, Shama. It's time we told you."

"How could you?"

"You wouldn't have been born otherwise, Shama."

"And the marriage vows didn't mean anything to you?"

"It would be easy for me to say that I did this for your father," Mama said, "but the truth is that I did it for myself also. Yes, he started it, but I completed it. Shama, sit down and listen. I too have something to tell you."

31

I would rather not listen to her if it was a continuation of this bizarre version of my conception. But if I had given Papa audience, I ought to give Mama hers. Plus, a certain part of me hungered with curiosity for more of this unusualness and her agreement to be a part of it. Why?

I sat with Mama and she told her story. What I recount next concerning my birth is what she told me and what I have gathered myself over the years.

How could she allow, no request, another man's presence in her bed when she was married to Papa? She had never expected that Papa would make the first request of her. But that was not to say that she didn't want children, and she was distressed when it became clear that her husband was devastated because they hadn't had any a few years into their marriage. But she loved him and was prepared to bear the burden of her childlessness. This was God's fate for her and she had to accept it, even if she lamented it. And then came Papa's solution, which, because it offended every cultural and spiritual instinct in her, she impulsively rejected at the beginning. But the man had released a side of himself that, despite his show of tenderness from the beginning, bared a new vulnerability, if selfishness, that eventually eroded her resistance.

Yet the decision had come slowly. If there was going to be any victim in the scheme, it would be her. She was the one who would have to endure the physical act. Not to deny that Anan was physically desirable. He was, in fact, more physically attractive than Papa. Tall, energetic, muscular. But that was only part of the issue. Could her spirit endure this act of intimacy without some negative effect? To do it, she would have to convince herself that it wouldn't. She had to believe that she could separate the physical from the emotional.

The graphic nature of what Mama said next, surprised me; but, like Papa, I believe she too was less concerned about such matters now as death loomed everywhere and she was prepared to release everything in a manner she otherwise wouldn't have.

In Anan's hands, it was as if she was a tool he could tune as he pleased, unleashing physical pleasures she'd never experienced or expected. It was as though the man had undergone special training in the art and science of sexual pleasures, and that's what he made it seem—an art with his patient caresses as well as a science with his trained hands that touched the right parts at the appropriate times. Each act was like a potent drug meant to kill her spirit, because she knew the spirit of love and devotion to Papa despised this; but, at the same time, because it was laced with such pleasure, she could hardly resist its force. At the end of it all, she was torn, loving it and hating it. She looked forward to his visits as much as she resented them, looked forward to moments she made love with her husband as much as she hated it because at some times she wasn't sure to whom she belonged as a wife.

Around this time, Anan gifted the family with a female dog, one of those Belgian shepherds. Was it a reward for the pleasures he'd derived from the Rugwe bed? But both Mama and Papa were so preoccupied with their thoughts, said Mama, that they took little notice of it and it roamed the town most of the day, returning home from time to time to rest in the backyard or to eat crumbs wherever they could be found. Papa named the dog Anan after his friend.

And then Mama conceived and Anan's visits to sire a child ended.

Now sated by this briefly warm, if sinister, liaison that worked a kind of magical effect on her physical sensations and sharpened them, Mama's thoughts kept returning again and again to those coital moments. How was she expected to make the sacrifice her husband had demanded without seeking her own price? Mama confessed that when she told Papa she wanted a daughter, she had lied—half-lied, that is. She had wanted a male and a female in the beginning, but after the first child was born, she no longer cared if the second was a daughter or a boy. But what better way to convince her husband of nobler intentions than to assert her right to have a female when it was largely a scheme to lay claim again the pleasure of those brief moments with Anan? And although she didn't want to accept it then, with hindsight she had come to believe that it was also her way of punishing her husband. For all he'd done, turning her body into a vessel for childbearing in such an unorthodox arrangement, he deserved the punishment. After all, with her intuitive antennas, she'd realized that no matter how proud Papa was of Placide, there were times when he wished he was the progenitor. Not that she didn't consider that by taking this step she was conceding any higher moral ground that she may have held, that it would morally bring her at par to him. But she was burning with desire and vengeance, and she had sated both.

With the second set of sessions, Mama cultivated her imagination more than before, knowing that these would be the last and that to survive on them for the rest of her days, she had to register indelibly every moment even if, as tabooing as they were, they remained closed in the catacombs of her shame, where they would have remained (to be used as a proxy when her husband held her) had not her husband's guilt and conscience compelled him to divulge their secrets and had not her daughter come asking her about those hidden matters. With pumping heart she spread all that was precious in her physical being for him and tried hard to suppress the guilt but the guilt was resilient, pervading her even long after the act was over. She could never look at her husband the same way again, she would not love him the same way again, even if she continued to love him strongly. Burrowing into memory, she would often imagine Anan when her husband made love to her as a way of reprising the past pleasures. And she would realize that she had crossed a line that she feared she should never have crossed—that she would never love Anan the way she loved her Pascal, but that Anan had taken away from her a portion of her love for Papa. Anan didn't love her, she knew; he had performed a chore, even if he'd enjoyed the performance. And that part of her—call it love or some other emotion—that he'd taken was merely dispensed into resounding echoes of diminished trust and respect, not for Anan but for her husband. It hurt her, but it was a price to pay for what she had derived from the experience

She was soon preoccupied with other things. They all were. To start with the pregnancy: a minor protrusion of the belly at first that ballooned disproportionately in the second trimester, enlarging to twice the size of her belly compared to its size the same period during the pregnancy with Placide. This became such a strain on Mama that she could barely move about, her back and hips in continuous pain. Still, she bore proudly this ballooning manifestation of the scheme hatched in darkness, one level happier because despite the pain it was she who now harbored the child; it was she whose chromosomes were part of the child, not Papa's. Papa tried hard to demonstrate the same level of enthusiasm for this pregnancy as he had the first, but it was clear to Mama that something had changed. Papa's laugh had diminished, his attention ebbed. Or perhaps it was she who had changed? Perhaps it was she who could no longer gauge the depths of his laughter.

Despite her upbeat approach to carrying the child, Mama was also infused with partum feelings that pulled her in opposite directions—an enhancing stratospheric buoyancy as well as a primitive urge to kill the growing life in her. There was no reconciling these two opposites. It wasn't any easier that these were feelings she felt she couldn't divulge to anyone, ashamed as she was to have them in what she had come to consider her mangled conscience. These found vent in her frequent yells, requests for sweets, and for Papa to buy her meals at odd times of the day so that he sometimes had to beg neighbors for food when the regular selling spots were closed.

What afflicted her in the second trimester multiplied in the third, and what comforted her increased likewise and this perverse equilibrium remained, only more intense, until, bedridden with the strain on her back, she became almost intolerable in her moodiness and demands for special treats; and Papa seemed less and less inclined to accommodate them.

Mama and Papa yelled at each other with little or no provocation.

"You are not the woman I married," Papa would say.

"And you call yourself a man for what you have allowed to happen in your household?"

But as matters seemed headed for a climactic battle of changed personalities, the gestation ended and a child was born to turn heads. That child was me, of course.

# Five

Mama labored from early pangs in the morning's wee hours until my birth in the evening. I was delivered into the midwife's weary hands and welcomed with Mama's hoarse voice and the tired drips of her sweat as I was placed on her bosom. The thrill of the birth silenced at first the enormity of my size as the weariness of mother and midwife hang over the room momentarily until within tired seconds my size told them a story that explained much: the quantum size of Mama's belly during the gestation and its impact, the physically devastated Mama who lay exhausted on the edge of death, her legs still open as if she was afraid to close them, close the pain that ravaged her under parts.

"You have a baby girl," said the midwife after a while stalled, as it were, in her jubilation. She then added, needlessly when Mama recollected what she could of the moment, "What a bouncy baby."

That was an understatement. The midwife would say that I was the most sizeable baby she'd delivered in over twenty years of experience, twice the size of normal. What else was she to say? How could such a fat baby come through the vaginal walls of its mother? That the size of the baby was approaching something monstrous? This was after all a time for celebration and she had found the most celebratory word she could find at that moment. And not just that, if I was about twice the size of the biggest baby she had ever delivered, the midwife must have decided that the celebration had to be twice the normal. She therefore began to holler hard and loud beyond her tired lung capacity: "A girl! A girl!" A now barely conscious Mama only saw the baby through the mist of her drained vision. My cry was more meaningful to her in her fading consciousness, more indicative of life, than my physical form or the bellows of the midwife. Having heard the voice of her new child, Mama slipped into unconsciousness.

In the next six days Mama would live in that dangerous state of uncertainty between death and life, marked by brief periods of consciousness and long ones of unconsciousness when it wasn't clear if she would survive birth of the life force that she'd brought into existence, as if having labored to gift the world this new being, she herself was ready to retreat. My father sweated day and night as the midwife stayed to help

36

raise me and they both wondered if Mama was capable of reconnecting with life again after this massive life force had been taken from her. But she was capable, rising gingerly from bed on the seventh day and immediately asking for her baby. She registered no expression when I was handed to her and she saw me for the first time without the mustiness that her pain had erected on the day of my birth.

She held me close to her bosom and rocked me slowly, which took considerable effort, given my abnormal size. Mama then asked to be left alone with me. Bonding, she said, required this. Alone with her baby, Mama examined me, her mind and what she had seen so far forewarning her that there was something outside the ordinary about me. And so she was not totally shocked when she noticed an abnormal mass—more like an extra piece of belly—attached to my body. She was in fact drawn to this extra body mass, as if it was reason for extra joy, and she brought her lips close and kissed it ever so gingerly.

It was Papa who would soil this state of bliss when he walked into the bedroom to pronounce his belief that God had brought curses on him and his family for what he'd done, the contrived means of conception. Both parents certainly knew what he was talking about, but Mama's desire to find enthusiasm in the situation wouldn't be so easily tossed. "Where is the curse?" she asked, and Papa pointed to the mass on me. Mama reckoned that to dwell on this would cause both of them much pain, an imperfection that could be attributed to other causes but would, under their circumstances, be attributed to one cause that would ever trigger guilt. *Oh, that accursed means of conception.* She would frown hard and change the topic immediately and by so doing signal that she wanted this to be the last time Papa raised it.

"What shall we name her?" Mama asked.

While they had discussed a few names earlier, they had not agreed on any. "I have decided she will be Shama," Papa said, intending to fulfill the promise he'd made to his sister.

"Are you sure?"

"Yes, you know how much this will mean to her."

Mama knew my aunt Shama had left for Kigali in her teens to trade and had become quite successful at it, but to date she had not found a husband, let alone carry a child. And at forty it appeared her chances of

37

settling down and bearing a child had narrowed significantly. Playfully, she'd sent word to remind Papa that she would like to have them name their first child after her. But as Placide had come a boy this wasn't possible. Now that they had a girl, Papa was granting his sister's request. For her part, Mama noted to Papa that she liked his sister, perhaps even admired and loved her, especially since she'd stood with Papa when the rest of the family initially opposed his marriage to Mama. My aunt Shama had been resourceful enough to leave Butare for Kigali and succeed. She was so generous that she'd frequently been sending them gifts, including money. These were qualities that Mama admired, but she didn't have the familiarity of everyday observance and interaction. This troubled her. Nor did it please Mama that Shama was childless. Still, whatever caution ringed in her ears, Mama decided her sister-in-law had showed adequate qualities. "I like the name. Shama it shall be." And so Shama I became. And there was a flicker of joy.

But my body condition seemed to hamper me. It appeared the mass on my belly controlled my every move, led me if I wanted to move and on account of that rendered me immobile. Even when Mama would feed me, I would drink only briefly and then with my feeble hands appear to move Mama's nipple toward the mass on my belly. It took a while for Mama to recognize this, given the uncoordinated and jerky movements of my hands, but with close attention Mama determined the gestures' meaning. At first Mama didn't know what to do with this message and all she could think to do was worry that I ate little and she often tried to feed me by forcing my mouth open and squeezing drops of breast milk into my mouth. I regurgitated some of this but Mama found hope that at least some of it was ingested. This made most of my feeding sessions periods of intense coaxing and protests that drained both mother and child but seemed to deplete the mother more. Despite this ostensible lack of nutritional fortification, my girth continued to widen and both Mama and Papa marveled at the fattened and fattening baby who ate little.

After a while, Mama discovered an antidote of sorts. Once when I signaled in my uncoordinated manner for Mama to move her nipples lower to the body mass on my belly, she noticed a few drops of her breast milk spill over that mass. For the first time since she'd started breastfeeding me, Mama noticed me giggle. Stalled for a brief while as this seemingly meaningless development stunned her, she immediately replayed it in her mind. Mama squeezed some more milk on the body mass on my belly. Again, I giggled. Mama did it again and again. Again and again I giggled. If she'd tried to suppress in her mind any sense that I was abnormal, she was now confronting frontally the possibility that her child possessed something unusual within that mass. But what was it?

Was Papa right that this was some form of a curse? His conclusion, after all, stood rooted in potent logic—some spiritual dysfunction that produces its tactile equivalent in physical deformity. This concern began to form a gloom that enveloped Mama, although she couldn't fathom a solution to the abnormality and continued to squeeze milk unto the body mass whenever she fed me, which facilitated the feeding process and ended my previous protests.

Mama's worry would take a different turn after my aunt Shama came to visit, a visit hastened when she heard I had actually been named after her.

Aunt Shama arrived in Butare full of gifts for Papa, Mama, Placide and me. But rumors circulating about her namesake reached her before she entered her intended destination. When she was seen arriving from the outskirts, the rumor mongers informed the proud aunt that her little niece, the one whom she wanted to consider her budding soul mate on account of the shared name, was carrying a curious appendage on her belly that was neither belly nor breast. "She's an abnormal one, that child," Auntie Shama was told. How was this little secret leaked? No one could tell, but for weeks it had spread beyond our household. This, when few visitors were allowed into the household, this when I was always clothed when in the presence of visitors (even close friends), this when no one but Papa and Mama was allowed to hold me.

Papa had been furious when he heard the gossipers mention this in the marketplace and had immediately accosted the midwife, who swore on her grandparents' grave and invoked a pox on her household if she was lying or if she was the source of the leak. As Papa asserted his child's normality whenever he heard the rumor, the more the rumor spread.

So when Auntie Shama was made privy to this and announced it when Papa met her at the door of our home, he wasn't surprised, just disappointed that he'd not been the one to tell her. "Come and see for yourself," he said, ushering his sister into the inner chambers of the household, the bedroom where mother was feeding child.

Papa opened this most inner sanctuary and beckoned Shama the Elder to behold the "Feeding of the baby," announcing this with solemnity as though of some biblical revelation. Mama, seated on the bed in the bedroom, with her back against a wall, raised an eyebrow at this intrusion and acknowledged Auntie Shama's presence with a slight nod, but otherwise remained unperturbed in her feeding of me.

Papa and Auntie Shama watched, both fascinated, Papa for the umpteenth time, his sister for the first time. They watched as Mama squeezed her breast and I drank, and then Mama eased her nipple out of my lips and brought her breast closer to the body mass in my abdominal region and squeezed her breast and little droplets of milk eased onto the mass and ran down its sides. I giggled. Mama returned her breast to my mouth but I refused it, my lips closed tight. Mama returned her breast to the body mass and fed it more droplets of milk as I giggled. For the second time, I refused Mama's nipple when she gave it to me. Mama spread more breast milk on the body mass, the level of white liquid running over it into the bed sheet. It was only after this third breast milk showering that I accepted my mother's nipple and fed on its milk for a while.

After this showing, Auntie Shama was de-energized, struggling to fathom the significance of the ritual. But she also felt privileged in that she'd been let into a great family secret and when she later took me in her hands for the first time, my weight almost bringing her hands down, she declared that it was this sense of privilege that bound her most to the namesake—love at first embrace built on a sense of special access. "What a beautiful child," Aunt Shama said, and no one doubted her sincerity. And Aunt Shama announced she was proud to be the aunt, even if it was evident she was bothered by that mass that was attached to me like a part of me and still appeared not to be a part of me.

Aunt Shama observed in a short week how my insistence on feeding my body mass drained Mama, who seemed to partake of the process like a zombie going through a preordained ritual of deep significance. And Auntie Shama noticed how Papa, her own brother, appeared awed by what was happening, hardly uttering a word. She complained that she sensed a level of alienation within him, as if he'd encountered a hurdle so high that it kept him from getting closer to his wife and child. She hoped her concerns were unfounded, she said, but that her older brother seemed completely outside the female circle drawn by mother and daughter was palpable to her. But at least Papa had the privilege of observing the breastfeeding sessions. Not so Placide. When I retell these events, I can surely conclude that he was the most lonesome one among the lot. Papa had little interest in spending time with his son, as his attention seemed diverted toward nothing in particular. So Placide formed a friendship with another little boy in the neighborhood: Jean Pierre. Later, Auntie Shama would tell me that she came to believe that something was critically awry, but she couldn't be sure whether it was the newborn causing it or something else she couldn't yet trace.

My aunt's discomfort was worsened on the evening Anan came to visit for the first time after she'd arrived. "What do you think of the baby?" Anan asked.

"I love her," said Auntie Shama. "She's my namesake after all. I feel we have some spiritual connection. And you, what do you think?"

"Oh, I love her. But not just her. I love her body mass also. It's beautiful the way her mother feeds them both."

This disturbed Aunt Shama—the revelation that Anan had been let into the family secret. And also disconcerting were the words *them both*. Aunt Shama immediately believed that Anan had said this purposefully to show her that he was privy to as much as she, removing any sense that she had special privileges that were denied him. These were not feelings she meant to have, nor did she intend to embrace the jealousy. She knew that Anan was a close family friend. She'd observed how Papa and Anan had stayed close in their formative years—a relationship Aunt Shama had viewed with some suspicion and even jealousy in those days when she lost her brother to the outsider. But with time she thought she'd overcome that pettiness. Was this merely an unwarranted resurrection of those feelings? She knew it was through Anan that Papa met Mama and although she expected closeness, she hadn't expected—on closer observation—how reverential Mama and Papa were toward him. This went beyond mere fraternity.  But these were thoughts she didn't tell anyone until events led me to her much later.

And with this unease tormenting her, Auntie Shama was more troubled whenever she remembered Anan's words—*them both*.  As much as she couldn't understand exactly why, she began to link the foundation of all her current suspicion and unease to the body mass on my belly, especially the strange way Mama *fed* it.  Something was wrong with it and she worried that it was unhealthy and that some action had to be taken about it.  My aunt began to plan.

Aunt Shama was supposed to stay three weeks and return to Kigali.  But five weeks later, she was still in Butare, plotting and bidding her time and continuing to study the situation to be sure she was right.  In addition, she was nervous about what she was planning to do, given that it could cause much rift in the family.

A couple of nights, when everyone was asleep, she seized her chance, stole to my crib and with candlelight studied me as I slept and by so doing fallen deeper in love with me, her little niece.  On one such night, she also studied the body mass that lay on my belly like a pillow of flesh, felt it under her fingers, soft and hard in places, and affirmed her belief that the mass was an unnatural appendage that had to be tackled.  It was not a part of the body, or it shouldn't, she concluded.  It lay on the belly like something independent that had chosen a parasitic modus operandi.  No wonder Anan had referred to *them both*.  Her resolve became rooted that night in the desire to rid her namesake of the *thing* on my belly.  She would do definitely something about it.  She began to reach out to her contacts in Kigali.

Not many nights later, my aunt whisked me out into the night on a pre-arranged trip to Kigali.  She'd made arrangements for her close friend, a doctor, to arrive that night, car loaded with baby food, feeding bottles and bibs.  Holding the baby with the pretext of giving the drained parents some rest, no one thought anything of it when she stepped outside with me.  But she hurried into the awaiting car.  It was a trip full of wailing and protests from my infant body.  For long periods no cajoling or comforting could end the wailing and then suddenly I'd stop and go quiet, and then the wailing would start again. It was as if they were dealing with two personalities, my aunt would later say.

In Kigali, Aunt Shama temporarily moved into her doctor friend's home, afraid that the trail from Butare would lead to her house. Posing as my mother, she arranged immediately with her friend's help to get me examined by the best doctors available. After x-rays, tests, and examinations, the doctors diagnosed me with an unusual case of *fetus in fetu*. "What kind of disease is that?" She asked.

"In everyday language," one doctor said, "It's when a twin is formed completely while the other is only partially formed."

"Why are you saying, doctor? You mean Shama is a twin?"

Said the diagnosing doctor, "She is a twin, yes, but the partially formed twin actually resides in her body, not outside of it."

"Doctor, please explain."

"I can understand your surprise, madam. It's a highly unusual condition. What happens is that the other twin, what we call the parasitic twin's embryo, stops developing in the womb and develops instead at the non-parasitic twin's expense. The parasitic twin becomes installed in the body of the other twin and it's in the body of its other twin that it grows. So what we have here is an incompletely developed fetus in the belly of your daughter, which explains the mass in her abdominal region."

Confusion overwhelmed Auntie Shama as she grappled with the information and she tried to speak but could only gasp.

"Who is the child's father?" the doctor asked.

"He's dead," said Auntie Shama. "He died in an accident shortly before my child was born."

"Sorry to hear that. But don't be so perturbed, madam. It's not the end of the world."

"Can you do anything about it, doctor?"

"The only thing I can think of is a surgical excision."

"You mean cut out the… the…"

"Yes, cut out the underdeveloped twin. Now, you need to think very hard about this as it involves great risk, including death. But if you want it done, now would be the best time. Most doctors will not do the surgery, given the level of difficulty and attendant risks, but we have a visiting doctor from abroad who has done this surgery before. He leaves in a few weeks, so if you want this done, we don't have much time."

Although she now knew it, this had been a part of her thoughts, if only in its margins, that the body mass would need some form of elimination. But Auntie Shama had hoped that it wouldn't require such a radical measure. Nor had she expected that it would require such immediate action. Couldn't they do this with some form of medication that worked gradually to eliminate the mass? To face it—a body in a body—and to end one in its current form for the benefit of the other. Who was she to decide whether the incompletely formed part was not a life form of its own that deserved its parasitic existence? Who was she to determine that the fully formed one should exist separate and apart from its stunted twin? No to mention the risk of death to her niece, her little soul mate. Why had she been so foolish to bring her niece to Kigali without the parents' consent?

She would send word to Butare immediately that she had me. No, she would take me back and apologize to Mama and Papa. Settled on this, my aunt Shama was relieved as much as she was concerned over the reception she would receive in Butare. But as she prepared to leave for Butare, she couldn't shake the pestering sense that to redeliver me to my parents would be to betray me. Her doctor friend told her, "Your niece deserves a normal life, not an indolent, lethargic existence as a non-functioning human who might forgo a normal life and die young as that parasitic mass drains it. That's what is likely to happen to her if you don't take action." Auntie Shama went back and forth in indecision, now assured of what she ought to do, now completely unsure, sometimes bold in her ability to decide but now and then completely afraid of reaching the wrong conclusion. She made her decision in an early morning as I began to cry and she recalled her friend's warning that her niece might die young. Childless herself and desperately seeking a daughter, how could she let the closest thing to it slip away? Running her fingers over the mass and hearing me cry, Auntie Shama decided to interpret it as my call for help.

But even on the day of the surgery, she continued to hold an uncertainty that hammered at her. Weak in the knees and faint with a heart in tremor, teeth gritting, even gnashing, during the entire nine hour surgery, she could barely wait to hear the result.

My aunt celebrated with a prayer when it was confirmed to her—on the third month anniversary of my birth—that the operation to remove my parasitic twin, quite grown with hair, tiny limbs and a miniscule head but without much of a brain, had been successful.

Returning to her house, Aunt Shama rejoiced as much as she worried that she may have gone too far in this unilateral act. After several sleepless nights and days she finally sent word to Mama and Papa that she had me. The suspicion that the aunt had taken the baby because both of them had disappeared at the same time was now confirmed. Papa, Mama, Placide and Anan found Aunt Shama in her house in Kigali. First expressed was Anan's fury. "Kidnapping," he kept saying, which Aunt Shama rebutted with her own refrain of "taking." Was it her child to take? Anan questioned. Was she not a family member? Aunt Shama countered.

"If you were she not my sister, I would report you to the police for what you've done," Papa said with rage, which Mama seconded.

But even more enraging than the *kidnapping* was the surgical procedure Aunt Shama had sanctioned without the parents' consent. This was criminal, Anan said and called for a drastic response. But as enraged as he was Papa, couldn't so easily exscind his familial connection to his sister, nor could Mama completely shed her admiration for her sister-in-law. Still, some action was necessary, if merely to assert himself as head of the family who should never be taken for granted. "I don't want to see your face again," Papa said. My aunt knelt before her younger brother in supplication and, in tears, begged for forgiveness. Papa rebuffed her. Brother and sister would never see each other again.

# Six

Back in Butare with me, Papa started earnestly to cultivate goodwill in the neighborhood, as if to erase the odium that had begun to attend his household with its secrets, steadfastly attending church to Rev. Murenzi's pleasure and praise and continuing to hold on to Anan's friendship. On Sundays, he would walk to church in his white suit and black shoes, Bible in one hand, Placide's little hand in the other. (I would only join them years later). On weekdays, he would accompany Anan as they went visiting friends, acknowledging the greetings of acquaintances along the way. Church-going, raising two children, relatively successful with his tea plantation, continually upped in stature by Anan's continuing friendship, Papa was now considered a respectable part of the society in many portions of Butare. On occasion, Papa would receive invitations to dine from Paul Kajangwe. He attended the same church and was considered one of the most important leaders of Butare, being also a successful businessman with connections to key political figures in the country. To be acknowledged so visibly by him was considered a status promotion. Most times, after church, with his Bible in hand, Paul Kajangwe would shake Papa's hand and say with a smile, "God bless you, my friend." Later when I started going to church with Papa and Placide, Paul Kajangwe would often pull my cheeks gently and tell Papa what a beautiful daughter he had. "She has your bright eyes and her mother's prominent nose. Those high cheek bones, though, I'm not sure how she got them." And indeed, as I got older, I could see my bright, almond shaped eyes in Papa; in my mother I saw myself in her prominent nose and in her curvy, heart-shaped, full lips. And in both of them I inherited my slimness. The only one close to us with high cheek bones was Anan.

But I may be getting ahead of myself. Returning to the days after I returned to Butare from Kigali, I became even more inactive. "See what your sister has done to my child," Mama would say, while also frequently wondering aloud whether I wasn't better off without that "unsightly mass." Many times, she would suggest to Papa that he change my name from Shama; and many other times she would counter herself by acknowledging that my aunt may have done them a favor by having the

46

mass removed. Confused by these contradictions, Papa did nothing about my name. If there was any miracle in all of this as far as my parents could determine, it was that my wounds healed quickly, leaving only a barely noticeable scar, a broad map the color of charcoal, as if my body wished to rid itself of any evidence of the surgery, to leave little trace that another being had resided in or with it.

For a long time, I, as reconstituted, did nothing. I wouldn't walk or talk. I just fed and got even fatter than before. And this growth in size worried Papa and Mama, concerned that my aunt's actions had indeed caused irreparable damage to me, and it took Papa considerable strength to convince Anan not to take some form of retaliatory action against Auntie Shama. And all this while, my brother Placide had no idea how to interact with me. I barely seemed to notice his presence, showed no reaction to the songs he sang me or the funny faces he made for me. And he would complain to Papa and Mama that he wished he didn't have a sister because then he wouldn't feel this rejected—a case of none of the loaf being better than half of it?

For over three years, the family dealt with this situation that frustrated all of them. And matters got even worse when in my fourth year I developed sleeping beauty sickness: sleeping almost non-stop, waking up for brief periods to eat—actually, Mama or Papa would force me awake to perform this function, sometimes to no avail. Of course, I myself do not remember this and so I've relied on what my parents told me. On one occasion, I slept for three days—no amount of shaking or noise would wake me. Even the physician that Papa invited to examine me was flummoxed. "I can't find anything wrong with her," he told my parents.

"Is my daughter dying?" Ma asked, but the doctor could only say that they ought to hope for the best, which they interpreted as though it was a death sentence. Mama cried, Papa brooded, and Placide felt more alienated and a period of mourning set on the Rugwe household like a bleak cloud. There was no redemption; there was only a sure march toward death—this was the conclusion they drew about my future. But if I died in this process, then I resurrected, as I awoke from this condition of sleep just as inexplicably as I had fallen into it almost a year after it started. When my parents realized I was awake and would not return to the baffling condition, they had a family feast of chicken and rice, with Papa consuming large amounts of banana wine, despite Mama's complaint that he was overdrinking. Anan was the only non-resident in our household who was invited to this feast.

For my part, when I retell this part of my life, the one thing that comes to mind—and it's a wonder that this remains vivid even after all these years—is a faceless, even shapeless person, not clear whether male or female, appearing and crooning in the night, teardrops from this being falling on the floor with the force of a rainstorm and a voice speaking but seeming to sing a velvety tune, urging me to stay awake, to live for the future. When I look back, I begin to think that I imagined this being at the time, but I can't be sure.

I became a wandering, wondering ghost the night I died, the being said. *But what manner of ghost? Was it a fearsome banshee or one of those benign spirits portrayed in fairy tales?* It continued to speak. No minute of silence was devoted to me, no mass mourning, no flags flying at half-mast in my honor as they do when important people die. I wondered if my passing deserved such quietness. Need I have become this wandering, wondering ghost the night I died? Had I escaped the prison of my physical frame but not its burdens? And if I had escaped the physical, escaped it into what? I would have died, if I were not already dead, for a drop of rain, a ray of sun, a strain of mind, a shadow of darkness, a thrust of pain, a petal of roses, a bolt of dread, a bead of a tear, a drip of saliva, a toot of an alarm, a bolt of joy. All in the physical sense, of course. But here I was; or rather, here I wasn't. The surgeon's knife may have forestalled the burden of stale friendships, the dying sympathies of family, the ageing, senile memory of lost love, the imagined sneers of the youthful. But the alternative is that I am now an unframed soul, moving on in the infinite vastness. And yet you and I remain as one because I was and remain a part of you, at least in your imagination. In the infinite vastness, my voice reaches out like vapor. I am neither flying nor walking. If this is a prologue to purgatory (or hell) it is an eloquent one. I stare at myself with a benign medley of empathy and disappointment. I will make you a gift. The being gave me the gift. The gift looked like a box, but it wasn't a box because it had no contours. *What shall I do with this?* That's up to you. Do as you wish with it. Go on, look into the gift. Use it. I grabbed the gift. For a long time I stared into this open-ended-box-like gift, which offered its contents in all of its myriad contents like a kaleidoscope. *Who are you?*

Call me Amash if you will.

*Very well, what now?*

That's entirely up to you.    How you choose to use the gift you have is up to you.

*But I am too frightened by it.*

Dare a little. Amash. Ahtilatiumic. Wake up.

I did. But it was not until my sixth year that I began to crawl. I wouldn't walk until I was seven, and it was only shortly afterward that I uttered my first word. Mama, Papa and Placide had struggled to entice me to say their names with funny sounds and faces. Even Anan the dog joined in by barking at me repeatedly. But I rejected all these entreaties…

I spoke my own name first. Papa, Mama, Placide and Anan had gathered in front of the house to pass the night. I was sitting on Papa's lap. As I understand it, my first word wasn't a careless blurt, as babies seem prone to do, but sounded carefully rehearsed and released at the appropriate moment, perfectly pronounced. *Shama.* The audience fell silent for a short while in awe and admiration. And then Mama moved forward to gather me in her arms, as if claiming me from Papa, proudly indicating her joy at the development. And Papa proclaimed relief that the baby had said her own name rather than any of the others' and thereby averted jealousy from the adults. And he was so impressed by this virtuoso performance that he began to ovate. "This is the joy of my heart," he said.

After that night, as if spurred by this applause, I began to display an impressive vocabulary that transcended my age and experience. "Gifted child," Papa said, theorizing to Mama, Anan and Placide that I had been mentally drinking the conversations around me, parsing words and distilling meanings in preparation for the opportune moment to showcase my prowess. And as if I was now noticing more things I asked Mama about the scar in my belly region. "It's a birthmark," she said.

Despite this exhibition of brilliance, however, I hardly spoke to those outside the circle of Papa, Mama, Placide, and Anan. On the few occasions when I did, it seemed others shunned me, staring at me in silence or speaking in whispers not meant for me to hear. The more they did this, the less I was inclined to engage the outside world.

"Why do people not like me?" I once asked Placide.

Before Placide could answer this question, his friend Jean Pierre responded, "You are abnormal, that's why."

"Never say such a thing again," Placide said to Jean Pierre with a clenched fist. "Apologize to her!"

"Sorry," Jean Pierre said.

"Promise me you'll never say that again."

"Why?"

"Promise," Placide said, his fist raised to strike.

"Okay, Okay…I promise."

I was so proud of my brother at that time, even as he and Jean Pierre left me alone with Anan the dog, scampering off to play football. I had been aware of Jean Pierre as my brother's friend, but until he made that remark, I'd not really seen him as a person but more like part of the landscape, if you will—there and noticed but not particularly observed. But I began to watch him after his remark.

# Seven

Not long afterward, Papa said he'd enroll me in school. I told him I didn't want to go. "You are too gifted to stay at home," he said. "You have to go. Don't worry, Shama, you will do well."

I didn't believe him. Based on what I'd heard my family say, I knew I was talented, but I had not measured this against the world outside my family. I wasn't sure how I would measure up. But papa made it clear that this was not negotiable. He had to pry me from Mama the first morning I went to school.

The other children pointed at me and whispered words such as "dumb," "refuse" and "retard" within my hearing range. During break, none of them wanted to play with me. Placide was too busy with Jean Pierre and their other friends to notice me sitting in the corner of the play yard by myself. On the few occasions when he did, my brother seemed almost oblivious to my plight. "Go on and play," he would say. With whom? I would have liked to ask, but I waved him off and found another corner to hide and watch others at play. I would often saunter to the *gacaca* behind the school building, used sometimes for games, and walk around it for a while just to pass the time.

But the classroom was mine. I found that I easily mastered the subjects and could answer questions with ease. Over the course of several weeks, I managed to leverage this budding intellectual prowess into a modicum of popularity, if a thin one. Even at that early age, my academic brilliance was evident and although I started school late, I gained ground so quickly that I was soon promoted a couple of classes ahead. It was then that I became classmates with Delphine. She called me her "friend who knows everything." I started helping her with her homework and explaining concepts that were simple to grasp to me but seemed complex for others. Soon, she was broadcasting me to others so that they also came calling on me for help. Shama, can you help me with this; Shama, can you help me with that. If I had been unpopular and remained an awkward companion in the play yard, I gained in stature and fame in the halls of the classrooms.

51

Over time, my initial reluctance to go to school eased so that with my newfound "popularity" I sometimes looked forward to days in school where at least feigned affection provided some peer company.

In adult company, though, I cherished most the times when Anan helped us on the little tomato garden that he and Papa had started in the backyard. (By the way, it was around this time that I also learned that Anan was an acronym for Alphonse Napoleon Alexandre Nsengiyumva). I knew that one of Anan's passions was farming, and when he wasn't busy working on the tea plantation he co-owned with Papa, he would come calling and ask if the family wanted to do some work on the tomato garden. I had never seen anyone demonstrate such unbridled pride in gardening tomatoes. Anan would often stay for supper and keep Placide and me laughing with funny faces and jokes. It was seldom that he visited without some form of gift for my brother and me, a toffee here or an exotic toy there. Placide and I *loved* him. Whenever I was saddened and Papa and Mama said something I deemed offensive, I found solace in the company or words of Anan. As I got older, turning nine, I became even fonder of Anan and wanted to believe that he was a blood relative, not just a close friend of Papa's. I even said to Placide, "I can't believe Papa and Anan are not blood brothers."

"I know," Placide said. "They act as if they were brothers."

"And he acts as a real uncle, even a father."

"And I love him so much."

"Me too."

But if I loved Anan, who was not a blood relative, I craved to know about the relation by blood—Auntie Shama. I wanted to raise the subject of my aunt, the one who'd been banished. All I'd heard at that time was that the aunt whose name I bore had once stolen me to the city because she couldn't have a child of her own. At the time, I couldn't fathom why this transgression was so egregious as to warrant permanent banishment, and I was especially grieved when I once found a letter from her in Papa's documents. Papa had asked me to get one of the books Anan gave him from a cabinet he kept in his bedroom. As I picked up the book, a piece of paper fell on the floor. I'm not sure if Papa had forgotten to remove it from the book. I picked up the letter and read it even though I

52

knew I wasn't supposed to read things belonging to grownups. I recall in particular the portion that read:

> Placide, I know that I have done you and Hadidja wrong, but please believe that I only had Shama's best interests at heart. I fell in love with the child when I came to visit and I was trying to give her a normal life. I hope you will find it within yourself to forgive me and I am prepared to pay any price to earn this forgiveness…

I put it in Papa's cabinet of books and papers, but I could not get the handwritten letter out of my mind, stealing again and again into Papa's papers to read and reread it, holding it to my face as if the ink would come alive and hold me, even memorizing its contents, from the address to the salutation to the signature of the name that was also mine.

I'd asked Papa about my namesake and received the following response: "She's a very bad woman. Forget about her." Still, I wasn't fully convinced, enamored as I was with the idea that an aunt of the same name existed somewhere.

When I asked Mama, she told me never to mention that name again. "But it's my name, too" I protested, to which she had no response.

I next went to Anan, expecting a favorable resolution of the matter. "Left to me alone, your parents wouldn't have named you after her, that witch." There was such an uncharacteristic vehemence behind Anan's words that I cringed. Within me, I still couldn't believe that my namesake was as diabolic as the adults claimed. Perhaps it was that letter and her confession that she loved me or its tone of contrition or perhaps it was that we shared the same name. With my desire to know my aunt unsatisfied, I felt an unfathomable closeness to my namesake that was being made increasingly distant by the adults, which in turn fostered a sense of incompleteness within me. This would be worsened when I got into a minor altercation at school and at age ten received as an insult that I was lucky I still didn't have my dead twin inside me. At ten, I was beginning to get a strong sense that people were keeping many secrets from me and revealing some at times when they were not supposed to.

It was only when I confronted Mama about this revelation of a twin that Mama, with Papa's consent, told me the truth about my aunt's actions. And I realized that the dark map in my belly region was a scar, not a birthmark as Mama had earlier told me.

It was also around this time that I heard rumors about my second birth. When I strain my memory I can only recollect Placide saying to me after I threw away a banana peel over which he slipped, "Be careful with the trash. After all, we are children of the refuse." When I asked him about this, he said, "Don't you know?"

"What don't I know, Placide?"

"Don't you know we are of trash?"

"Are you not well? What are you talking about?"

"No one wants to tell you because they don't want to hurt your feelings, but the truth is that we were discovered in the trash."

"So you want to hurt my feelings?"

"You are my sister. I need to tell you before someone else does. I don't want you to be unprepared."

"You are lying. I'm not from trash."

"I'm not lying. Listen, Shama, this is what I have heard."

"I don't believe whatever you're about to say."

Placide said it anyway. "Mama had gone out one day to the market. When she was returning at dusk, she heard a baby crying by the rubbish heap close by. When she went to check, she saw an abandoned child, which she took home and kept when no one claimed the baby."

"So that baby is me?"

"No, that baby is me, but she found you the same way two years later."

Placide narrated the identical discovery of a female child—me. I didn't believe him. I thought he'd said it to unnerve me, as I believe he was angry he'd bumped his head when he fell over the banana peel. It wasn't until I heard the term "child of the refuse" used against me one day in school that I began to wonder whether Placide had been truthful. "My mother says you're a child of the refuse," someone said, as if to seek my opinion on the matter.

"Stupid lies," Delphine had retorted.

54

When I asked Mama about it she said it was "nonsense." "Don't believe such trash." Papa was equally dismissive. But over the years I heard gossips and those willing to tell me what they knew in order to formulate a cohesive account of this alternative version of my birth.

As it is told, many suspected someone entered Butare in an unmarked car and deposited two babies, one newly born the other a little older, by a heap of trash next to the marketplace. No one had actually seen this happen, but it was rumored that a sedan was seen speeding into town and then out minutes later. When they heard that two children had been abandoned near the rubbish and no one claimed them after Mama discovered them, they pieced together the conclusion that the car had come to deposit the children. I asked those who cared to converse about this whether they truly believed it. Someone said not to believe in such a "fantastic creation myth" while another swore that it was as true as my very existence.

And just when I was dealing with these revelations, Anan died unexpectedly from cholera. I was made to understand that it happened while he was on a trip to Kigali and that he was buried there to avoid contamination. We were all in shock. He had told us he was going on a business trip and then this news. We kept expecting that he would be knocking on our door at any moment and we would sit down and he would share a joke or that we would go to work on the tomato garden and he would sing us a song or tell us about his many travels.

I never saw this with my own eyes, but I heard people swear that Anan was capable of shape-shifting (now tall, the next moment short), weight-shifting (thin one day and fat the next), and even height-shifting (tall in an instant and short in another). However incredulous this sounded, there were those who insisted on it, claiming that he effected these chameleonic alterations in accordance with where he found himself, so that to the tall, he was tall and to the short he was short, and so on. I was hoping that this was true and he would acquire one of his rumored bodily forms and reappear as a young girl.

Papa in particular opened the door several times calling Anan's name—when the wind hurled at it and moved it or when it was silent and Papa claimed someone had knocked. But our expectations were in vain.

And with his death a novel rancor overtook the family. Papa became easily irritated and often yelled at Mama and at us. And this disease of irritability also infected Mama. Where she would have been quiet before, she now yelled back, even sometimes threatening Papa with bodily harm (and he would sulk about how much respect he'd lost from her). Placide and I recoiled into a tunnel of sadness. It was clear we all needed Anan.

When Anan died, I began to dream about a boy, looking exactly as me (except he was a boy). As much as Placide and I looked alike, I knew it wasn't Placide, although I felt this oneiric boy and I shared some form of kinship. In the dream, his face was in a grotesque grimace of pain as knives began to cut into his skull and he begged me to help him. I stood by, however, immobilized while the knives cut into his skull, spurting blood into my eyes. I would always wake up at this point in sweat and a voice that sounded like mine ringing in my ears, saying *Amash, Ahtilatiumic.*

And then Anan the dog gave birth one morning, but when we woke up, much to everyone's surprise, he had eaten the puppies—not actually eaten them, but crushed all six puppies with her teeth. "I didn't know that dogs eat their own," Mama said.

"Under certain conditions, I guess it happens," Papa said. "We haven't been good to this dog. We have neglected it all along."

Papa and Mama promised to take better care of the dog. But they didn't have the opportunity as shortly after Anan died, Anan the dog disappeared, never to be seen again.

In a loneliness that engulfed my parents after Anan died, they engaged in long periods of love-making, as if to find in physical intimacy all they had surrendered. And a year after Anan's death, Mama conceived. "How is this possible?" Papa asked "I am infertile." If he didn't know his wife better, he would have accused her of cheating. Papa knew that wasn't possible. Had he then prematurely and hastily misdiagnosed himself as fertile? The child, however, died only a day after his birth.

56

# Eight

Papa noticed the emptiness encircling his family—the nocturnal cries of his daughter, the sadness of his son, the gloomy outlook of his wife (most likely on the loss of her third child), the loss of the dog Anan that no one had noticed until its death suddenly seemed to have created a vacuum. Papa decided to take action. But he struggled a long time to find a solution, as he was himself deep in the depths of the sorrow of Anan's death, and he couldn't shake it, let alone comfort his family. After attending church one day and hearing a message from Rev. Didier Murenzi about finding strength in all things, he hardened his resolve to stem the abiding sadness. But all day, intention and deeds traveling parallel paths, he fought with Mama and yelled at Placide and me. That evening, Mama, Placide and I remained indoors. Papa escaped this triumvirate that he said was suddenly closed to him, which years of the long album of intimacy as father and husband couldn't decode.

Papa stood outside, hopelessly. Anan was dead. His sister Shama the Elder was banished. Where could he find comfort?

And then, as Papa told it, in the faded evening, a shadowy profile stood tall as a tree near his doorstep, like a gift from nothingness, like an upstart come to usurp the pervasive melancholy. Papa peered at him in the waning discomfort of the moment, hoping for a sign, any sign to register familiarity. For moments they stood facing each other, words muted by dawning recognition. There was no tension, just some uncertainty.

"How are you?" Papa ventured into the unbroken silence.

"I'm well," the man replied in bass.

"May I be of help?"

"I'm selling tomatoes," he said. "I thought perhaps you'd be interested in buying this basket full."

It was only then that Papa noticed the basket in the man's hands, as though suddenly illuminated by the offer, precariously but evenly balanced in both hands like a treasure. Papa looked harder as the man seemed to come clearer under the dusky opaqueness of moonrise. His recessing eyes were piercing in their gaze. Papa noticed the man's hair was a lush brush of unspotted white (as if a thousand years had woven webs of whiteness on his head). Methuselah's hair couldn't have been

57

whiter. His upper body was wrapped in a thick woolen tailcoat, one of which Papa had not seen in these parts in a long time, if ever. His chin, wet with sweat, rested on a scarf thrown carelessly around his neck and tucked into the opening of his coat in the front. A boutonniere protruded from a lapel. His trousers were of bright purple. Even though they were partly covered with garden dirt, the red shoes adorning his feet glistened in the night's darkness. By the man's side, was a dog, its eyes dark-pale as the night.

After Papa recovered from this impressive appearance of dog and man, he managed to say, "Thanks, but I have my own tomato garden," alluding to the tomato garden that he had cultivated with Mama, Placide, and me (and Anan, before his death) and recalling the joyous, if strenuous, effort we'd put into it.

Papa made to return to his family, but the man hastened a response. Papa was glad he did, as he didn't want to leave yet, sensing an incompleteness with the encounter, a process yet to reach its end, if there was even one. "These are special tomatoes," the man said.

"Special tomatoes? How so?"

Papa's famished curiosity must have been palpable, for the man fed it well. "They are redder and richer and sweeter. You've never had any like these. I guarantee you that. Why don't you try one?"

The claim sounded false on its face, even outrageous. Tomatoes are tomatoes. How different could one be from the other? But how could Papa think that? He checked himself, recollecting Anan's exceptional pride and effort in gardening tomatoes. Given such pride and effort, it had to stand to reason that exceptional effort could produce special tomatoes. Teased by this false logic, Papa had to believe the man as he found himself craving the tomatoes, which suddenly attained special status, served in the power of Papa's recollections. Nor was it simply what the man said and the recollections that prompted pause. It was also the manner he said it, the confidence he put into his words that were so daunting, and the way he held himself within the dawning night. Holding a tomato in a hand pushed toward Papa—a gesture of physical proximity that mined Papa's common humanity—the man said, "Here, try one."

Could they truly be sweeter? There was only one sure way to tell. Papa grabbed the tomato held out to him and took a bite. As Papa chewed

58

on it, the man's face lit with the recognition of *I told you so*. At first, Papa wasn't sure, especially given the raised threshold of his heightened expectation, but then after a little more chewing and reflection, the tomato tasted sweeter, perhaps a lot sweeter than any he'd ever had.

"I told you these are special tomatoes," the man said. "Won't you buy this basket full?"

"I will," Papa said. "But you, who are you?"

"I'm a trader of sorts."

"Your name?"

"Call me Nana," the man said.

"Well, Nana, you have made yourself a new customer," Papa said, even as he wondered about the man's name.

And with that Papa bought the basket of tomatoes over a handshake. He realized that the man had garden dirt on his hands, which transferred to Papa's after they shook.

Papa brought the tomatoes to Mama, Placide and me, announcing their uniqueness. Mama looked them over, rolled her eyes and stifled what I suspected was a strained laughter laced with mockery. This angered Papa. "Try some for yourself and you'll see," Papa challenged Mama. "You too, Placide and Shama." Mama refused, but we complied.

"Well?" Papa asked.

Placide said, "I've never tasted tomatoes this good."

"And you, Shama, what do you think?"

"They taste as sweet as sugar, Papa," I said.

"Nonsense!" Papa responded. "How can tomatoes taste like sugar?" If Papa suspected I had said that to irritate him, he was right, for how sweet could tomatoes really get that he would worry us with these ones? And irritated Papa was as he went and sat outside.

The next day Papa summoned the entire family to go to the tomato garden to harvest our tomatoes. He had woken up barely before dawn broke, itching to show his family how inferior our tomatoes were to Nana's. But there were no tomatoes to be harvested when we went outside. "How could this have happened?" Papa queried.

"Someone has stolen our tomatoes," I said.

Papa was angry with me. Need I state the obvious? But now Papa saw an opportunity to turn this misfortune to his advantage. "You see how much foresight I have?" Papa said. "If I hadn't bought those tomatoes yesterday, we'd have no tomatoes to eat today."

"I could have gone to the market to buy some," said Mama.

Papa didn't reply to this, but it was obvious from the flare of his nostrils that rage was building within him. All he murmured at the time was, "Anan's gifts." Time to begin anew, Mama announced. And the family returned to growing more tomatoes. And Papa said how he wished Anan was there to help us.

Working on the garden seemed to help. Even under the sun's spanking, we would each recall something about Anan—the way he held himself over the soil, how he wiped sweat from his eyes, his face-wide grin, his high cheek bones, which I thought needless in a man, more accentuated as the sun lit it—all observed when he'd joined the family to work the little garden of tomatoes.

As it were, Anan's tomatoes served the family well for a while and the rest of us partook of them without dissent. And it seemed the family had found some peace after the gloom. Most days we gathered near the garden and recollected Anan. Had Papa restored the status quo?

# Nine

Perhaps he had, at least in so far as the lifting of the immediate funk that had descended on the family after Anan's death. This liberated us from the tethers that had bound us from continuing with our lives the way we lived it when Anan lived. So the new life unleashed post-Anan found its crevices and places of comfort, freeing Placide to return fully to Jean Pierre's friendship, reengaging his friend at a time when they were beginning to study women—or rather, girls. The initial distaste of all things feminine, excepting family and close acquaintants, had lifted with the entry into pre-adolescence. Started, as it did, with their appreciation of the female face, a crude visceral appreciation that asked for nothing more than the overall pleasantness without regard to its curves or proportions. But they would soon progress from this rudimentary appreciation to the full female form, the bosoms, bust, backside, legs, the contours and variations. They would glance and discuss which one of their subjects had the best shape, the most attractive walk that accentuated that shape, and of course the attraction of the face. With this sophisticated appreciation came curiosity and with this curiosity came anxiety and how long they would have to wait to get close to one of those who were at the time anatomical curiosities to them. The friends agonized over this for a long time, discussed strategies for pursuing some of the girls in their class, but refrained out of a sense of shame, a feeling that this simmering curiosity was wrong, even deviant. So they settled on the easiest solution they could conjure from this miasma of admiration, appreciation, longing, curiosity, and bugging shame. They would trade sisters. "I will give you mine in exchange for yours," Jean Pierre said.

Placide was baffled that anyone would have the slightest interest in me. But if that was what Jean Pierre wanted, if that would help him befriend a girl and gain even better understanding of females, then so be it. And, thinking of it, seeing Jean Pierre's sister through his upgraded lenses, she was not bad looking. They agreed to facilitate a meeting of boy and girl and girl and boy. So it was that Placide invited me to accompany him to Jean Pierre's household at a time when his parents were both at work. I followed my brother.

Jean Pierre and his sister were in the living room when we arrived. Placide had seen Jean Pierre's sister, older by three years, several times before that day and had not ever until then anticipated that he would have an opportunity to woo her. And now with the pressure of the anticipated wooing, Placide felt awkward and incapable of initiating the first move towards his potential paramour. Jean Pierre played the more suave role, inviting his sister to the backyard. He returned to the living room alone and whispered into Placide's ears: "She's waiting for you out there."

Seizing the moment as soon as it was offered, Jean Pierre declared to me: "You look very nice today." He said it as though it would erase any prior insult. I remembered that he had called me abnormal in the past. "You know I've been watching you," he continued. "You have become so very beautiful."

I said nothing, stunned by this baffling declaration of interest. "What do you want?" I asked.

Jean Pierre narrowed the distance between us and reached for my hand. I refused him. "I am trying to tell you how much I like you, how much I want you to be my friend," he said.

Still baffled, I didn't respond. And perhaps the young man took that as his time to make his boldest overture, turn his sparse words into daring action. Jean Pierre closed the distance between us even more. He pushed his head forward and put his mouth over mine the way he must have seen it done in movies and tried to thrust his tongue into my firmly closed mouth. With all the force I could gather, I pushed him back. He stumbled a little, his mouth opened as if in shock, but before he could articulate anything of import at this unanticipated rejection, his sister walked into the living room, clearly propelled by anger, her fists clenched.

Placide, following her into the room, immediately commanded "Shama, come, let's go!"

I hesitated a second, but my brother grabbed my arm and forced me                                                                outside.

"Why are you behaving like that?" I asked. "What happened?"

"Just be quiet," said Placide.

"Did you also try to kiss her?" I asked. "Is that why she's so upset?"

"How can you ask me that question? Have you no shame?"

"Shame? Am I the one who tried to kiss someone?"

"Why told you I tried to kiss her?"

"Why would she be so upset?"

"Did Jean Pierre try to kiss you?"

"Yes."

"And you are not upset?"

"A little, but not as she is. She looks really infuriated."

"I didn't try to kiss her. It was something else."

"What?"

"I can't tell you. It's embarrassing."

"I told you what happened. Why won't you tell me yours?"

"I told you, it's too embarrassing."

"But you are my brother. I am your sister. There is no shame between us."

It was only three days later, after Placide had refused to divulge what had transpired over my protestations and had considered and reconsidered my declaration of no shame between siblings as though it was of fact, that Placide succumbed. As he weighed those words that sought a closer relationship within him that transcended friendship, something must have broken inside my brother. It closed years of alienation when he had merely seen me as another life form with which he coexisted out of necessity than choice. After all, he'd had little to do with me in those early years that were full of clouds and murkiness when Mama monopolized me and hardly let him close to me. Those were the years when he thought he should be granted the opportunity to play with his little sister, his only sibling. But it had looked to him like a closed circle headed by Mama and Papa and the fat infant who didn't respond to him anyway. And then I'd disappeared and he had wept at nights in longing for the sister he hadn't known. And then there were the years of my indolence, sleep and muteness, another era of impenetrable circles, this time seemingly belonging to me alone. And Placide had learned, although perhaps more by instinct than design, to contain his affection in the knowledge that to continue to love freely was to open himself to the continuous pain of rejection.

But now I'd burnished anew the little seed inside him with my declaration, perhaps a plea to him that I wanted to grow our relationship.

And to think of it, I hadn't even complained that Placide had led me to Jean Pierre for that crass, if noble, attempt to seduce me. And Placide wanted to love his sister, he said, without qualification and he knew that to do so he could start by being truthful, no matter the embarrassment it might cause. So he sought me out and confessed what had happened, all the time unable to look me in the face.

They'd gone to the backyard and Placide realized how unprepared he was for this moment of seduction. He couldn't think of what to say. "Jean Pierre said you wanted to talk to me?" Jean Pierre's sister Celine said. He could tell she was beginning to get impatient.

"I have something to show you." Placide had said. "I'll show you mine if you show me yours."

"And what do you want to show me?"

Placide took this as sufficient cue, permission to proceed. He started to unbuckle his shorts…. "Are you mad?" Celine said, now aware of where this was headed. "Are you stupid or something?" She walked away, leaving Placide to wrestle with the oppressing sense of defeat and shame.

"You won't tell anyone, will you?" Placide asked me.

"Oh, Placide, how can you even ask me that? Am I not your sister?"

And he realized that I meant it and from that moment Placide vowed aloud to make me his soul mate of sorts. I promised him the same. We spoke our words to each other and to the wind, binding ourselves and asking the world to bear witness—let the wind carry this stated bond between brother and sister. Perhaps this was all bound to happen, for Placide and I were almost carbon copies. We both had those wide eyes of Papa, prominent nose of Mama, and high cheek bones. I saw my visage imprinted on my brother's face. I wasn't so fond of his outstanding cheek bones, which I thought gave him a feminine quality. When I asked Mama why Placide looked so much like me, she chuckled and said, "He is the older one. You're the one who looks like him."

"But why do we have to look so much alike?"

"We are all versions of one another," she said.

In any case, in the days following our avowals, Placide and I would walk to school and back together, except on seldom occasions when one of us had to make some detour out of necessity. If any such detour occurred, it was often because Placide had to attend to some social calling, he still being the more popular of the two of us, although I was also gaining in fame (more than popularity) on account of my increasing intellectual prowess in school. On the occasions when I missed Placide, and Papa was unable to read to me, I helped Mama in the kitchen and tried to learn her cooking techniques, although I never became the master that she was, and Placide in particular liked to mock me for being a bad cook. Whenever Mama heard him comment on my cooking skills, she would say, "A woman's place is no longer in the kitchen. Shama is too bright; she is going to make something out of herself, you'll see."

At first Jean Pierre left Placide and me distance to devour our newfound relationship, and he watched jealously in the foreground, in respect and, I presumed, out of shame due his botched attempt to seduce me. But within weeks he was back in the circle, ostensibly intending to woo me in earnest. Knowing that the boys had planned that ill-fated rendezvous as a trade of siblings, I dismissed Jean Pierre's advances at the onset. But his patience and tenacity, his continuous words of affection and coquettish smiles, convinced me that he had moved beyond that experimental phase and became the argument for me to pay him serious attention. I did. He waited for me in the corridors of school, eyed me in the playgrounds, even ogled me in the hall rooms.

"Why do you keep bugging me?" I asked him.

"I am looking for my future wife," he said.

"That's funny. You are already thinking of marriage?"

"We're still so young, I know, but to me you are my future."

I rolled my eyes and walked away. He didn't relent.

"Good morning," he greeted me every day. "Is your day going well?" he asked during breaks. "Do you need me to do anything for you?" he queried from time to time.

Even his sister Celine told me that Jean Pierre was "crazy" about me, bugging her all the time about my looks. I asked her what she thought of my brother. "He is a prankster" she said. "I don't think he is interested in me. He is just curious about girls."

"And how do you know this?"

65

"He hasn't said anything to me since that stupid thing he did the other day."

"Are you angry with him?"

"I was, but not anymore. I realize he was being curious. He meant no harm."

"Perhaps he hasn't showed interest because he's shy?"

"Do you see your brother as the shy type?"

"I don't think so."

"That is my point. But you, you have Jean Pierre's undivided attention."

I had to admit that Jean Pierre was beginning to win my interest, but I was still unsure, mostly because I cherished the relationship I was building with Placide and did not want it tarnished with someone else's involvement. "He's a good guy," Placide had assured me and although that endorsement strengthened my infant affection for Jean Pierre, I still continued to keep him at considerable bay. In fact, at that time I wasn't so sure about boys. I had outgrown the stage of disinterest in the male species, but I didn't know enough about them as romantic interests to seek their attention actively. With Jean Pierre's interest, that was gradually beginning to change.

With this simmering affection, I was obliged to support Jean Pierre when he and Placide invited me to a wrestling match after school.

"Jean Pierre is fighting Thierry," Placide explained.

"But why?"

"Jean Pierre called him a worthless Hutu after they got into a fight over a dispute in a football match."

"But why would they fight over that? If Thierry doesn't consider himself worthless, why would it matter what Jean Pierre calls him?"

"He feels insulted, Shama. He says he'll teach Jean Pierre which is the worthless of the two—Tutsi or Hutu."

"So they have to settle this with a fight? Can't they find a better way?"

"What better way, Shama? A fight has victors and losers. It's the best way, I think."

"No, it isn't. They can talk about it."

"Thierry has challenged Jean Pierre. He has to show up or Thierry will think him a coward."

"Who cares?"

"Thierry has framed this as a contest between Hutu and Tutsi. Jean Pierre has to stand up for Tutsis."

"He's not standing up for me."

"There is no turning back now, Shama. He needs our support. You will be there to support him, won't you?"

"Why should I?"

"I thought you liked him."

"That's the more reason why I shouldn't support him in something so foolish."

But I couldn't stay away from the event, a wrestling match hastily arranged to settle a verbal insult, although even at that age, I realized it had more epic significance than that, aware of the lurking tension of histories and relationships between Hutus and Tutsis. Were these about to be enacted between Jean Pierre and Placide? I became doubly troubled when in the few days preceding the fight each camp increased the verbal jousting, boasting that its side was the superior and that the fight would demonstrate this. On the basis of physique, I thought the fight ought to be pre-called in favor of Jean Pierre, the tall and muscular and better proportioned of the two, Thierry being pudgy in the midsection and inches shorter. And when I considered this, I began to accept how physically attractive Jean Pierre was—embodied as he was in that muscular frame of a body—and I wondered when this admiration of the male physique had taken root.

In any case, I wished to shun this show, demonstrate to Placide and Jean Pierre that their manner of settling the dispute was unacceptable to me, but I felt indebted to them: my love for my brother and the strong wish not to disappoint him, as well as the growing affection for Jean Pierre. These were the boys now most dear to me, my closest male acquaintances. How was I then to stay true to an ideal that couldn't grant me friendship but which could instead unhinge the relationship he was building? I would show up for the fight, I decided, but I wanted additional support to assure me that I was not completely wrong to attend. I turned to my closest female friend Delphine. She was the only one at that time who, besides relying on me for intellectual support at school, took time to chat with me outside the classroom without the perfunctory, distilled talk that failed to mask the apathy of most of my colleagues toward me.

I asked Delphine if she'd heard of the fight. "Yes," she answered. "Everyone has heard of it."

"Are you going?"

"I won't miss it," Delphine said, "it's the fight of the century."

"Whose side are you on?"

"Thierry, of course."

"Why?"

"Because he's Hutu."

"Why should that matter?"

"Why shouldn't it?"

As I was Tutsi, would this mean that the fight would pit Delphine against me in a way? I didn't want to so alienate my best female friend. I wanted her to be Tutsi like me, or conversely for me to be Hutu like her.

"Papa," I asked my father later that evening, "Are you sure we're Tutsi?"

"You know we're Tutsi. Why are you asking?"

"How about Mama? Is she Tutsi as well?"

"She's Moslem, but before her grandparents converted to Islam, she was Tutsi."

"I don't understand. What does her religion have to do with her ethnicity?"

"Well, it's just that Moslems are just considered Moslem. They're not really thought of as Hutu or Tutsi. It's as if they've acquired a new identity."

"Why should all this matter, Papa, whether we're this or that?"

"You're right, Shama, it shouldn't matter. But everyone is this or that, one thing or the other. It's the way of the world. Yes, I think it's all silly sometimes. But I don't make the rules, I just live with them. You know what's interesting is that my grandmother was Hutu. But what does it matter now? Now I'm Tutsi and that's all there is to it."

I was a reluctant spectator when I walked with Delphine to the scene of the fight, the *gacaca* behind the school building. The event had been planned for evening, when school was out and the adults had left the building and we could escape from home for a brief period. There was already a sizeable crowd there when we arrived, no less than thirty, forming a thick human circle around the combatants. I was on time to hear my brother announce the rules. "No hitting below the waist," Placide said. Why such polite rules? I wondered. Perhaps my brother was just intent on putting some order within the madness about to unfold, inject it with some sense of fairness. Or perhaps he wanted to do all he could to protect Jean Pierre, in case Thierry turned out to be the better fighter. "You win if you put your opponents back on the ground three times," my bother explained. Clearly, both sides had enough faith in Placide to pick him to umpire the fight, even though he was Jean Pierre's best friend. This must either signal stupidity on Thierry's part or his high confidence in Placide, and I preferred to think that it was the latter. A number of supporters from both camps protested these rules, some insisting that the combatants should be made to fight until one was completely defeated to the point when he could no longer continue the fight or otherwise begged for mercy. But Placide wouldn't budge, and unfazed by the catcalls, he was able to instill begrudging acceptance of the rules as he had outlined, especially when he announced that "This are the rules both Jean Pierre and Thierry have agreed to."

"I want to be like my brother," I said to Delphine, who just shrugged and said nothing.

As Placide moved back from the center of the arena of imminent battle to yield the space to the combatants, silence enveloped the crowd, buzzards and kites flying past, as the moment of reckoning reminded us, the spectators, that victory or shame awaited. But that silence was brief, as not wishing to be the one that lived with shame, each side began to chant its combatant's name, I suppose hoping that the oral encouragements would provide some form of spiritual fuel to the preferred fighter. I stayed silent until I noticed Delphine chanting in Thierry's favor. I hesitated a moment, but found that I was alone in my silence. Whose side was I on? I felt that, even if I didn't wish to, this was a fight and in a fight I had to pick a side. I was Jean Pierre's friend. I was Tutsi. I turned around to see Celine bellowing in her brother's favor. I too began to chant with the part of the crowd in favor of Jean Pierre, an act that distressed in as much as it energized me and because I wanted to overcome the distress and to feel like I legitimately belonged to the camp I'd chosen, I chanted louder and louder, to out-chant the others, even those in my camp. In less than a minute of doing this, I felt as though I was being elevated by the strength of the cheers from my mouth, as if my cheers had joined with those of the others to offer some blanket of comfort so that within that warmth I was part of a group whose cause, whether right or wrong, would protect me from my doubts. And for brief moments, I had a thought that I not only wanted Jean Pierre to win, but that I needed him to cause serious harm to Thierry in a way that would justify the sacrifice of myself that I was making to the cause.

Now that it was past sun-peak, the earlier heat had declined, with a converse drop in temperature. The fading glow of twilight vaguely lit the bodies of the combatants such that they appeared more like effigies in profile than full-fledged bodies with contours. It seemed a moment for sustained lethargy, not the evocation of energy required for the occasion. And as I observed the two so profiled, the encroaching darkness shading their features, I momentarily was able to see them as abstractions rather than bone-and-flesh humans, a weird approximation of humans and not their real selves, and this made it easier for me to put distance between them, distinguish between pulsating chest of combatant and pulsating chest of myself as observer.

Bared chests, especially Jean Pierre's, displayed the promise of burgeoning youth, angular muscles waiting to over-bulge under exercise. The young bodies moved closer to each other and then apart, each apparently weighing options and trying to forecast the other's next move in what had become a lethargic dance, languid in pace if quickened in anxiety. But this was a deceiving posture, being full of malice and therefore potential menace. The supporters were beyond anxious, yelling for action, urging, urging, urging….

It was Jean Pierre who made the first move, a feline lunge for Thierry's neck that was well anticipated and dodged, sending the attacking body falling to the naked part of the ground where the grass was worn out, and where Jean Pierre breathed dirt. Thierry's quick reaction surprised me, now silent, my attention fully focused on the fighters as the abstract distance I had created vanished out of worry for Jean Pierre.

Thierry swiftly seized his advantage to sit astride Jean Pierre's back and keep him pinned to the ground. So disadvantaged, Jean Pierre attempted to throw Thierry off his back with a muscle straining lifting of the torso, but this only provided additional advantage to Thierry, who made use of this lapse to grab Jean Pierre in the midsection and turn him around, making Jean Pierre land on his back. This was done with such force that it was clear Jean Pierre had underestimated the strength of Thierry (as had I and probably most of the crowd).

Placide quickly moved to the center of the arena to ask the fighters to separate and announce, "One point for Thierry," as the supporters of the leader thus far cheered. Others might not have noticed, but I could detect the quiver in my brother's voice as he made the announcement. Was he as shaken as I by this lead registered against Jean Pierre?

Jean Pierre's body shook with rage at this insult and he made a frustrated charge at Thierry, another full charge without tactical forethought. Thierry sidestepped the charging body, tripped Jean Pierre's legs and pushed the falling body such that it landed on its side. Before Jean Pierre could recover, a hard push from Thierry put Jean Pierre's back to the ground. "Two points for Thierry," an even more shaken Placide announced, and it must have been obvious to all at that time that he was suffering from developments so far. In a rare show of open bias to his friend, Placide said to Jean Pierre, "Use your head." This generated protests from the Thierry camp, but they were so overjoyed by the lead that they didn't follow the protests with further action.

My worry was weightier than I had imagined possible. The Thierry camp was in a chanting frenzy, but the Jean Pierre camp had been shocked into silence. No, we couldn't concede this way when the battle was unfinished. It was I who now led them to start a new chant on behalf of Jean Pierre in an effort to steer the morale advantage in favor of their fighter, in an effort to restore the sense of solidarity we had earlier established with our chanting before the fight began, in an effort to lift Jean Pierre's spirits. My enthusiasm infected the quieted ones and Jean Pierre's name was raised high among his supporters once again, even higher than the one who was at the point of victory.

Jean Pierre's rage still intact, he was also now evidently imbued with fear, fully aware that one more false move and he would lose the

71

fight without having even scored one point. His friend was right, he must have realized, and he needed to fight like a thinker and not merely with the brawn that had failed him so far. And thus began another dance. But for the knowledge that this was a real combat, the circling, clinching, leg locking and unlocking, chock holding, kicking, and screaming that followed, while strenuous, were too cautious and would seem choreographed for entertainment than to secure victory. If it were seen as a dance, then what a graceful dance it was with sweat-wet bodies straining in athletic movements and acrobatic flexibilities but finding no advantage in a well balanced action, until Jean Pierre's knee seemed to stray from his body and found Thierry's groin, bending his opponent's body nearly double. Thierry wobbled on his feet and Jean Pierre moved swiftly to trip and push him to the ground. This illegal move brought immediate protests from Thierry's supporters, some of whom moved threateningly toward Jean Pierre. Placide moved quickly to restore order by announcing, "This will not count. It wasn't a legal move."

This concession satisfied the Thierry camp, and the irked Jean Pierre camp couldn't protest, knowing it was the right call and also that Placide was one of us.

But...

"No!" Thierry said. "Give him the point," he ordered from his position on the ground. "He won it."

I was torn, put in a new place I'd not anticipated. First, the illegal move by Jean Pierre diminished his moral value for me, if only temporarily. I'd expected him to fight fair, show more gallantry, which I had been made to bestow grudgingly on Thierry when he called for the point to be given to Jean Pierre. More painful was Jean Pierre's acceptance of this, his conceding of the higher moral ground. Had the risk of defeat made him so willing to accept such cheap points? I wanted to support Thierry for this bravery, even if I suspected that he had made a shrewd political move to gain favor (even from Jean Pierre's supporters), confident that he, after judging his opponent's fighting tactics and strengths, was assured of victory. But, second, and opposing this grudging admiration for Thierry, was what I felt (or its increase), for Jean Pierre. And it was at that point when he looked on the point of defeat, so vulnerable and desperate, that I felt that crawling sensation churn within me like I had never experienced. I couldn't explain it and why it became so manifest at that particular point when I was disappointed in him. But perhaps it's because it's so defiant of logic and so unexplainable that it's love. Could I really suppress it on principle at that moment because he had fallen, both literally and figuratively? I realized that I couldn't, that despite the shame I felt for Jean Pierre, there was something stronger within. I knew that to publicly withdraw my support of Jean Pierre at that moment could permanently damage my relationship with him.

Both sets of supporters watched nervously, Jean Pierre's more so, as the combatants started another long dance, more of the same of the old, with no clear advantage to either, although Thierry's movements appeared more languid. The contestant's bodies, as in the profiles that they had become, came together in a mutual hold of no clear advantage, an equilibrium of seemingly mutual checkmate, when, despite the differences in body, it was almost impossible to tell who was whom. But then, in one quick movement, Jean Pierre disentangled his body from this entanglement of no certain victor, and delivered a hefty knuckled blow to Thierry's face, drawing thin blood. This blow sent Thierry staggering steps backward, which apparently increased Jean Pierre's appetite as he lunged forward for the final kill. The mistake—a repetition of the first. Although Thierry wobbled on his feet, he had retained enough strength and composure to sidestep Jean Pierre. With identical movements as before, only this time a little slower, Thierry sent Jean Pierre tumbling to the ground, at first frontally; but a quick shove sent the latter lying on his back.

As his supporters rushed to the arena of victory, Placide belatedly proclaimed Thierry the winner of the bout. I saw Celine fleeing from the arena of defeat. Thierry fell to his knees, the thin blood that Jean Pierre had drawn increasing into a more noticeable stream. His supporters carried him shoulder high, singing his praises.

I was still uncertain, knowing that the victory deservedly belonged to Thierry, until I saw the vanquished, deserted by all as his fans left in shame and silence. Only Placide stood by his friend's side. Where I'd initially hoped for bravado and even seen it at the onset, I now saw surrender and shame; and this disappointment must have been fully registered in my face, for one look at me and a tear dropped from Jean

Pierre's eye. Jean Pierre started to walk in my direction and then stopped, turned around and walked away. I wanted to walk after him to assure him that I was still his friend (although I wished I could also say I was proud of him). I even wished I could lie and express pride in him, but I couldn't bring myself to do so, not even for the sake of his ego. I would wait until the next week to assure him that he was a hero of sorts to me—and although I wasn't able to tell him at the time, I now had no doubt that I was falling in love with Jean Pierre against my understanding and for that, a heroic feat of his, I had to acknowledge that despite his errors I was willing to make him a hero within a sacred part of me.

After the fight when Thierry's supporters had carried him high, the crowd had immediately drawn the attention of a number of adults who were horrified to see the object of triumph: a bruised, even bloodied, teenager. Upon learning of the events just unfolded, these adults had immediately carried the matter and the boy to his father. Seeing the blood on his son's face, the aggrieved father immediately sought out Jean Pierre's family to complain, which resulted in a battle of words that almost created a fistfight but for the timely intervention of concerned neighbors. While the war of words raged, some men in the neighborhood came to Papa to beg him to intercede, afraid it might escalate into something fatal. Papa then went to see Paul Kajangwe.

Papa and Paul Kajangwe begged the parents of the combatants for calm, which took them a considerable amount of time, as anger and a stream of self-justifying words from both sides greeted them. It was only a reservoir of goodwill they commanded among both camps that enabled Papa and Paul Kajangwe to hold some sway. "This is not the best way to settle a dispute," Papa urged. "Let's call together some elders to help us settle this, I beg of you." Reluctantly, but out of respect for Papa and Paul Kajangwe, the feuding men agreed.

On a Saturday, a large section of the neighborhood gathered for justice on the *gacaca* where the fight had occurred. A group of ten recognized elders, including Papa and Paul Kajangwe, sat to arbitrate the dispute. First, Thierry's father presented his case—the brutality of the act of violence by Jean Pierre on his son was an act of barbarity deserving of severe punishment. Jean Pierre's father countered that it was an

74

unfortunate result of children's foolishness. Instead of coming to him as an adult, Thierry's father had approached with insults.

After this presentation, one by one each elder rendered his opinion. Invariably they agreed that this should be viewed as a children's squabble gone awry, with neither parent to blame. While they could appreciate the anger of Thierry's father on seeing his son's condition, they urged him to show more restraint in the future. They urged the men to consider the importance of their friendship, the peace of the neighborhood, the example they wish to set for their children. After this, Jean Pierre and Thierry were called before the entire gathering and admonished. The parents were then asked to share a gourd of banana beer, after which they had a long conversation, and it was as if no fracas had occurred.

After this, Paul Kajangwe came to our house and dined with us, telling Papa how proud he was that they had managed to resolve the issue. "We should not let such matters get out of hand, Pascal," he said. "No one wanted to admit the truth, but I can't believe that these children fought over such ethnic matters. God save us if we don't stamp out such divisions."

"I couldn't agree with you more," Papa replied.

"I'm glad you and I are serving as good role models to our children."

I was so proud of the two men when I heard them speak this way.

But my friendship with Delphine suffered after the incident. We barely spoke. I'm not sure if I was the one who turned cold and she merely responded to that or if it was the other way around or if it was spontaneous.

# Ten

Papa came home late one night, a little full of banana wine and lamented the loss of commonsense and decency in the land, although he didn't elaborate on that. And then he wailed over the loss of Anan. "I wish he were here," Papa said, which was unexpected because he hadn't mentioned his dead friend in a long time, reading some of the books Anan had given him instead. Papa even seemed to have entered a new stage, prouder than ever on account of Placide's entry into the National University in Butare (as had Jean Pierre). And I was expected to follow soon. Not only that, it was now clear that Papa had become the envy of many. Placide's success was sufficient to draw envy, but my academic brilliance surpassed Placide's—in fact, I towered over my classmates, invariably topping them in all subject areas, especially in English. Not only that—I suppose I'd become a kind of cynosure, as many told me that my once dormant beauty had blossomed. I now attracted flattering comments when I accompanied my mother to the market from time to time, cutting a striking figure, I was told, with my slimness, motion of lithe limbs, budded bosoms, and rounded behind, my height seemingly accentuated by the thatch I would weave into a garland of sorts on my head on which I balanced Mama's market wares. Even those that bid Mama "Assalaam alaikum" and received her friendly reply of "Wa alaikum salam" seemed to eye my bosom a bit too hard. And Mama would carry with her loose change, which she gave those she met on the way whom she deemed deprived, saying it was Allah's will for us to give alms to the poor.

I don't know if Papa suspected the compliments I received from all over, but his eyes turned sharper on me, insisting I be home by five p.m., which I fruitlessly protested was too strict.

We'd all missed Anan, but over time the throbbing had become a manageable ache and we preoccupied ourselves with other matters—Papa with his plantation, Mama with her trade in the market, Placide with the challenge of higher education and I with getting into university. Amid these preoccupations, why would Papa suddenly invoke Anan? And with this invocation, it seemed he unleashed a bad smell that had been bottled up for a while but never erased, so that this simple allusion sufficed to drag its malodor back into the household. Now came memories long buried to haunt each and to reintroduce the funk that once had enveloped the household.

All of a sudden Papa relit his interest in the family's long neglected tomato garden. At the least opportunity, murmuring "Anan's gifts," he would summon Mama, me and, when he was home on vacation, Placide, to go to the garden and work on it. This seemed to imbue Papa with renewed vigor, albeit not enough to lift him out of the depressed state into which he was beginning to sink.

And so it was that at some time, the day before harvest, when Placide was home on vacation, *the man* returned. I can find no better way to describe him. This time, he was a wobbling mass of flesh, as Papa described him, a sow approaching with leisurely pace, short and almost one with the soil as a snake. And his hair was now darker than bitumen. Despite this changed appearance, Papa knew it was Nana, recalling the time, quite a while now, that the man had visited. Again, he carried a basket of tomatoes. His voice was mellow, but he didn't have to convince Papa this time. Papa bought the basket of tomatoes and invited Nana to join the family for supper. He declined. "For our mutual good," he explained.

When Papa took the tomatoes indoors to describe the latest encounter, this time Mama refused to sheath her disappointment. "These tomatoes are the same as any," she said.

"Be quiet!" Papa stormed out of the room, utterly infuriated, murmuring, "Anan's gifts." He refused to partake in the family supper, preferring instead to feast on a couple of Nana's tomatoes, biting into them slowly and appearing to relishing every taste of their fleshy redness.

The next day, Papa summoned the family to go to the garden to harvest our tomatoes. But again, as had happened the last time Nana had brought his tomatoes, all the tomatoes in our garden were gone. "Someone has stolen our tomatoes," I said.

"Be quiet!" Papa yelled. "Now you see how wise I was buying Nana's tomatoes!"

Once more, the family relied on Nana's tomatoes for a while, as we started growing our own again. And peace was restored as before and Papa's depression lifted. As the rest of the family detested his most recent bout with it, we were glad the depression was depressed.

Amid all this, the one thing I always enjoyed was a supper Papa and Mama organized every year as a form of thanksgiving. No matter his mood, this event always sweetened Papa's attitude. After Anan died, this was the one day when, even if he was in mourning, Papa would sing all day. Papa and Mama invited friends, and even mere acquaintances to this event. Over the years, Reverend Didier Murenzi and Paul Kajangwe were the constant attendees. Everybody else was invited periodically. Papa and Mama kept the number to twelve in order to keep it manageable. I saw large quantities of food consumed, wild laughter burst forth from the dinner table, and conversation that lasted deep into the night.

With the verve that newly enveloped him after Nana's most recent visit, Papa's laser focus on me eased gradually into a new laxity so that I could stay outdoors a little longer, which was a seamless segue to what happened the next time Placide and Jean Pierre came home from holidays from the National University.

In the musky dusk of an early day, as fog lay in the air like a steamy carpet, Jean Pierre walked over to our household and knocked on the front door long before the first cockcrow. A surprised and alarmed Papa answered the knock. "Isn't it too early to come calling for Placide?" Papa asked Jean Pierre. "Is something wrong?"

A calm Jean Pierre hesitated but for brief seconds before he pulled his chin up and said calmly, "Sir, nothing is the matter. But I am not here to see Placide. I am here to see Shama."

"What did you say?"

"I'm here to see your daughter Shama."

"What business do you have with her?"

Papa's surprise must have been tampered only by his familiarity with Jean Pierre.

"I would like to take her for a walk, and I would like to have your permission to do so."

Papa's pause was long, most likely prolonged by the young man's audacity.

"Is she expecting you?"

"No, sir. The idea just came to me during the night."

Papa must have thought he was about to do one of the craziest things any father would do, but there was something so sincere and pure about the young man's approach that he came to summon me. "Jean Pierre is here to take you for a walk," Papa said, and then returned to bed.

I would have to go outside to assure myself may father wasn't joking, and when Jean Pierre echoed Papa when I stepped outside, I could barely find the voice from the enveloping surprise to ask, "What is the meaning of this?"

"I had to see you, Shama," Jean Pierre replied. "I can't do this any longer... this hiding... It's killing me. I just have to let you know how much I care for you."

I took a step back, at once flattered and flummoxed. "And you had to come to my home in these wee hours of the morning to wake my father up to say this?"

"I didn't intend to wake him up... Take a walk with me, Shama. Please."

"Are these the kinds of tricks they teach you in the university?"

"This is no trick, Shama."

A moment of hesitation stayed my response until he reached for my hand and pulled me closer. "Please," he said, his voice taking possession of the early morning quiet, cutting through all that would prolong hesitation, all that would cause suspicion. His elevated boldness inspired me to acquiesce. His derring-do grabbed my admiration. The silence of the early hour's walk was like a prelude to his further declarations, a clearance of all clatter before the refined song of his words. When the venturesome Jean Pierre led me to the town's lush fields, he told me, "You are the part of me... you have become the part of me that I was afraid of finding. The feeling that I am now complete with you is so strong I don't know that I can survive it; it's as if I will choke on it. Now I know that without you I cannot be complete. I know we've been playing at this for a while. With my going away to school and being apart from you for long periods, it has only grown more certain."

"But…"

"I know it sounds strange that I'd come to you so early in the morning, but this thing has been burning all term and I've been fighting it, but it was too much to take and I had to come to you as soon as day began to break."

"I don't understand why this sudden rush, Jean Pierre. I know we have affections for each other…"

"I know, Shama, it's strange, even to me, but perhaps that's why it's so real. Don't say anything now; Shama, let's just spend some time together, let's spend time alone, really discover each other more than we ever have."

"And if I can't provide the kind of discovery you want?"

"I will accept whatever more of yourself you can offer, even if it's only your companionship."

And so began Jean Pierre's earnest courtship of me, his sincerest effort yet to secure fully what he had come to believe without any doubt was the love of his life. If at first we didn't love each other, he would create the love that would survive time. If we were not sure, he would erase all doubt. If at first we loved each other, he wanted to ensure that we could love no other.

He would repeat his early morning calls so frequently that what once irritated my family became a source of pride—the love figure standing outside the door knocking to announce his interest in the daughter/sister. If Papa was bemused at first, he now totally admired Jean Pierre's dedication, even if he worried where this relationship might lead his young daughter. Placide mocked his friend for what he perceived as infantile courtship, even stupid in its focused dedication, but he was proud his sister solicited such attention. Mama observed in applause at what she said appeared of a spiritual quality that dared anyone to question its authenticity.

Around this time, Thierry approached me one afternoon, barely able to look me in the eye. Although I knew him, especially as Jean Pierre's vanquisher a while back, he and I hardly spoke. Unlike Placide, he'd failed to make it past high school. In fact, until he approached me, I hadn't seen him since he graduated from secondary school. Now looking at him in a faded, apparently threadbare brown tee shirt and over-worn jeans, he said as he avoided my eyes, "I see you've made a new friend." I was surprised by his question, not expecting him to be interested in whomever I kept in my company. Perhaps he realized this as he added, "I mean you and Jean Pierre are really close nowadays."

"Yes," I replied, smiling.

He must have been encouraged by the smile, for now he looked at me; but I didn't like what I saw. Unless I was blatantly misreading him, I thought he had both contempt and admiration in his now half-smile, now half-smirk expressions, shifting by the second like the changing colorations of a kaleidoscope. By what he said next, I attributed the contempt to be directed at Jean Pierre and the admiration at me. "You know I beat him in a fight."

"Yes, I know. I was there."

"I am the stronger man," he said. I looked away from him without responding. "I was hoping you'd give me a chance."

"You mean…."

"Shama," he said, "you must know I admire you." I didn't. "I just haven't been able to approach you yet. You have seemed so much out of reach, as if none of us deserved you. But then recently I have been seeing you with Jean Pierre so much I wondered…. Perhaps you will allow me to reach you."

"Thierry," I said, "Jean Pierre and I are already involved. I appreciate this, but I am already spoken for."

"But you can cancel him or allow me to cancel him."

"Thanks, Thierry, but it's too late."

"You can change your mind."

"No, I don't think so."

He left, his kaleidoscopic face a contortion. If he was deflated, even infuriated, I could understand why. I almost felt sorry for him and I turned around. If he turned around, I would soften the rejection by telling him I was sorry but perhaps we could be friends, just not romantically involved. He didn't turn around as he continued to walk away, his steps slow, his head bowed, cutting a forlorn figure as he merged with the distance.

Thierry's proposal drew me even closer to Jean Pierre, as if the mere proposal was a blemish that we had to erase with renewed intimacy. In the mornings, as fog cloaked the distant hills like a life force, through the perfume of lilies, we wove through banana trees—or sometimes when we changed location to add variety, eucalyptus trees—to find an open spot. Sometimes, Jean Pierre and I would walk, as we had on the first day of his dawn-hour calling, into fields as the fog now hang like a sheet of vapor across the land and the dew on the grass touched our skins where our feet were exposed. Jean Pierre would hug me often, which I resisted only for a short while, finding the warmth of his body comforting against the coldness of the hour. After I accepted his hugs, we would hold that embrace for long seconds and then, at his suggestion, play hide and seek, hiding futilely behind shrub or tree or grass, easy to discover because it wasn't hiding anyway, pretending to be startled when discovered and laughing at the giddiness invoked so freely in carefree childishness. As the fog lifted and the early ray of sun broke through, we would engage in an elaborate body dialogue of hand holding, leaning into each other, coy glances, cheek kissing. The world was our world and we embraced it, ate insatiably from the presence of each other. So filled but hungering for more, Jean Pierre would then walk me back home, both of us sated, even sometimes when we did rain-gifted, muddy walks home. For the first time, I began to know the challenge and joy of inhabiting another's space, thoughts and emotions

Jean Pierre also called in the afternoons sometimes. Then, too, we would walk under the lush sun, our dark skins touching in places that permitted us to continue to write our epic love tale by stream and hills and under trees and canopies wherever we could find them.

Out of respect for Papa's permissiveness, Mama's acceptance, and Placide's unstated encouragement, Jean Pierre seldom made evening calls. When he did and we were outdoors, night beckoning, he hushed me with quick, nervous kisses when I was now wont to express the outburst of love that he'd released. "Patience," he would say. "When you say you love me, I want it in pure form." I didn't understand this, but I would watch him, hungering, wanting to allow him to share of me more fully, in my most secret place, as a demonstration of the love we were both palpably experiencing, convinced that mine had grown equally to match his, convinced of its strength, a facsimile of his, but equal in purity and purpose. This love of his copied in mine was what convinced me to lead him to my secret place.

I'd considered doing it under the cover of night so that the darkness might shield it a little, but that wouldn't do. If I was to do this, he had to see it in its starkness. Only then would I be convinced he'd shared of me without reservation. I would do it in one of our afternoon rendezvouses. He'd in a way led the way by drawing a portrait of me in the sand—a depiction of me in my nudeness as best as he could imagine— as he declared inscrutably that this sandy portrait was an affirmation of the portrait of his love for me in his mind. But as soon as he said this he added that it was foolish and that he regretted doing it, and he apologized to me for being so elementary and even crass (for he had added outlines of breast and nipples).

I said he ought not worry. "But this is not all of me," I said. "Come with me and I'll show you," I said, leading him behind an empty building.

Looking directly in his eyes, I removed my tee shirt so that I was topless, except for my bra. He continued to look into my eyes, transfixed, as if afraid to look at the bare skin beneath my chin. I reached out to touch his cheek and then said, "Look down at my belly region, Jean Pierre." And slowly he let his eyes drop and stay on the faint scar that had remained where the excision had occurred years earlier.

And then Jean Pierre began to weep, a tear chasing a tear.

"Do I disgust you?" I asked. "Does this part of me disgust you?"

But I had underestimated the sophistication of what Jean Pierre felt for me. He did not respond orally to my question. Instead, he kissed me on the forehead and without my prompting, knelt in front of me and kissed my scar, gingerly at first, until I exhaled a deep moan, instinctive and unforced from somewhere that was so unexplored it seemed to exist outside of me for its sheer novelty even though it belonged to me. Jean Pierre pulled out his tongue and licked the scar, the belly map of my expired part/twin, as if he wanted to erase it with his saliva as much as take it into himself. I held on to the back of his head and he continued, an unfathomable moment when I believed we had become the same person, joined by this scar of twinning totality, that bore a part of me, a history exposed to him as a sign of utmost intimacy. To continue would be to lose control, we both must have known this. Jean Pierre stopped before we reached that point when we might not be able to return. But we were not sure we were ready yet.

"Thank you," I said.

"I am the thankful one," Jean Pierre replied.

He knew I'd just spoken to him of the fullness of my love, more than I could otherwise have said and we both were convinced our love was sealed. This was as far as we could go, except for that one occasion when I simulated sleep and I suspected he knew I was merely pretending. But it was like a game. He searched me as his hands roamed my face, from forehead to cheeks to chin. He opened my lips and gazed, smelled my mouth, searching, as if looking for pleasant odors from teeth and tongue. He took off my clothes. He explored my neck and then my chests. He stayed on the breasts longer, filling the hollows of his hands, as if measuring my chest. I could feel him touching the darkly aerolated nipples, fondling them slowly. And then the belly and the pubic region. He spread my legs and peered down the dark regions of me. He quickly examined my legs, turned me over and started from top to bottom, feeling and looking. He even opened that darkest region of me, bringing his eyes close. And then as though exhausted from unconsummated physical urgings, he put my clothes back on my body, collapsed beside me and fell into deep sleep. We were as one.

Above all this, Papa seemed to welcome Jean Pierre as a part of the family by inviting the young man to help on the tomato garden. And the older man even taught the younger one some of the songs Anan used to sing, as well as tell some of his dead friend's tales. Or perhaps it was a masterful ploy, as the times spent on the garden were times when we were not alone outside Papa's watchful eyes.

Thierry continued to pester me with his amorous interest and I continued to rebuff him, although remembering the first time and how sorry I felt for him, I was more gentle. "I will treat you better, Shama," he would say."

"I am sure, Thierry, you are sweet, but you are steps too late."

"But you know how much I adore you."

"I don't doubt you, but you also know that these things are very complicated, these matters of the heart."

"You break my heart, Shama."

"Time mends all broken hearts."

Thierry seemed more lively, more gregarious when I received him more graciously, but he began to speak with me less and less, apparently content to greet me on the roads and receive my greeting without mentioning romance. I ran into Mama Ange once. I hadn't seen her in a long time and had almost forgotten that she was once married to my father. She hugged me and said she'd heard good things about me. "Keep up the good work, my child," she said. Looking at her, I realized that she could very well be my mother, for she seemed genuinely enthused.

And then I was also admitted to the National University.

## Eleven

Time at the university was a continuation of the strengthened love between Jean Pierre and me growing stronger still. Because Jean Pierre was a couple of years my senior, he had already developed his own crowd by the time I arrived on campus, but he minimized his mingling with that crowd as much as he could in order to bring me closer. His friends complained, teased him; but on account of the beauty of our relationship, they also cooperated to facilitate our frequent rendezvousing.

My greatest challenge in spending time with Jean Pierre was the new friend I made: my roommate Chantal, from Kigali. After my friendship with Delphine froze, I'd not found anyone I deemed worthy of total friendship (except Jean Pierre, of course). Chantal and I recognized something familiar in each other: a lonesomeness that only we seemed to understand of each other. Despite my closeness to and love for Jean Pierre, I had come to realize that we were not one of the same kind, that the foundation of our mutual feelings had guaranteed our closeness. Remove the love and we might not spend much time together. Jean Pierre was more gregarious and more interested in sports, mostly football, while I considered myself more of an introvert, preferred to read and had no interest in sports—two major differences that could have set us wide apart. With Chantal, it was different. Quiet and studious, seemingly incapable of finding friends, Chantal had turned talkative with me when she met me in class and we'd immediately created, without speaking it, a zone for ourselves, full of comfort and non-judgment. Chantal also spoke English very well, preferring, as I did, to converse in it as a way to speak the language better. We were both very fond of our English teacher, Mrs. Murekezi, although we were majoring in sociology. And she spoke highly of us in class as her best students. Despite my increasing popularity among women (for my fierce academic brilliance) and among men (for my so called beauty), I preferred the company of Chantal above all, excepting Jean Pierre. When I wasn't with Jean Pierre, Chantal and I ate meals, studied and spent many leisure hours together. By the time the first term was over, I was certain of two things: I would one day marry Jean Pierre and we would live close to Chantal.

Speaking of Jean Pierre, his initial suspicion, even jealousy, of the growing bond between Chantal and me gradually thawed when she repeatedly showed her loyalty to us: by buying us gifts, excusing herself from my presence when Jean Pierre showed up, and never once giving him any cause to dislike her. And then, during vacation, Chantal visited me in Butare and I reciprocated the visit in Kigali. In Kigali, I remembered that my aunt Shama lived there and I thought I should try and find her, but I was worried of what Papa and Mama might say if they found out. Perhaps another time, I decided.

Placide then confessed to me his interest in Chantal. "You better be sure of this before you make any move," I warned him. "I don't want you to spoil my friendship with her."

But was Placide sure? He said he wasn't, and because of this uncertainty he decided to tarry a while. Still, he began spending more time with Chantal when we returned to school the next term. They adamantly denied any mutual love, preferring to use the proxy "friends," even though all others deemed them romantically intertwined. I observed in silence, if anxiety, pleased of the gradual buildup and convinced that such slow simmering would guarantee a perfect result.

This pattern of events continued for a long while, term in and term out, vacation in and vacation out—an inertia of sorts, but one that was desirable because it was tranquil. And then Jean Pierre and Placide graduated and suddenly Chantal and I were without our best male friends. But the new graduates would come to visit often, usually carrying gifts and treating us to special meals. Both men had now found employment in Kigali working as math teachers. Jean Pierre and I started discussing marriage, where we would live (Kigali to be close to Placide), how many children we might have (three, which just seemed a good number). Other students, seeing the possibility of a romance with me now that Jean Pierre wasn't resident on campus, redoubled their efforts to woo me, some telling me that I was "ever enchanting," that my "public reticence and reserve added" to "my appeal.' But their words and efforts, numerous and overly flattering as they were, failed to dent my commitment to Jean Pierre. Still, all such attention augmented my fame, even popularity, on campus. As much as I tried to maintain a level headedness about this, I found myself buoyed.

And Although I thought he'd surrendered the pursuit to reality, I realized that Thierry hadn't. He renewed his propositioning and I rebuffed him as gently as I could. I came to realize that, having failed to gain admission to university, he had become a car mechanic of sorts, and now hang around with a few of his friends on the streets, often caterwauling. Sometimes, I saw Delphine in their midst, although she was often quiet. She was developing a reputation as something of a minx. I ignored them as best as I could.

But coming slowly and growing in its polluting force was the tension in school, at first unspoken, although everyone was aware it existed. We began to hear of tensions in Kigali, of Hutus and Tutsis in clashes and imminent clashes. A certain unquantifiable chill seemed to have come over the school in the form of whispers and stares. Perhaps it was always there and I had just become more aware of it on account of my awakened senses, given what was unfolding in our capital city. Mrs. Murekezi whom I had greatly admired on my account of my love for English, which she taught in my first year, one day saw Chantal and I together across campus and then said to Chantal, "What are you doing with a cockroach?" This was not the first time either one of us heard the use of that word, but we hadn't expected it to come from that otherwise genteel teacher, nor had I heard it so blatantly and frontally said to me.

"I'm sorry," Chantal said later.

"Why?" I replied. "You were not the one who said it."

Nor could Chantal imagine saying it, as she explained to me. That would mean calling herself a cockroach. Her mother, after all, was Tutsi. But, as was soon evident, in a creeping madness, in which ethnicity had become a badge and would soon be a talisman for survival, the call for choices to be made was becoming a necessity, a means of survival. And so Chantal, caught in this mad but tenacious wind beginning to sweep over the land, stood at the crossroads, unwilling, though officially classified a Hutu, to discard with the other half of her, or for that matter the young man she might marry some day.

Around this time new haunts started to attack me. I couldn't quite call them dreams because they were too vivid to be classified as part of some stream of events that occurred in the dormancy of my sleep. These were more vivid than that, and I felt as if I actively and consciously lived them. In fact, I sometimes thought they were real, when I encountered this half formed body, at times with a head the size of a coin, at times with a head the size of a football. His body was half physical, half nothing—full of emptiness where nothing gathered and where I felt I could deposit something. Looking for a word to describe it, I settled on "entity." The entity came to me with lips turned upside down, arms (or what I conceived as her arms) stretched out and in a sound that echoed like a voice (for it never seemed to come from the entity), produced five letters: "AMAHS?"

A question. A puzzle. An enigma. I recalled the same name a while back when I was in a long period of sleep. I tried hard to decipher the identity of the entity that asked it. Many times when the entity visited, I tried to ask the question, *Who are you?* But even though I thought to ask it, I never did, for I believed I knew the answer. I believed hard that I knew the entity, that somewhere we were very familiar. But that was all I could surmise. At the same time, I felt I didn't know the entity at all. This pendulous thinking hurt and puzzled me. I was torn into two: believing I could trust it, be comfortable in its presence, at the same time as I felt I had to keep a distance because the entity was full of spite and at any instance could wreak destruction. So I hoped for as well as despised the visitations. In the middle of the night, my schoolmates asleep, I would occasionally utter the word *help*—a solo sound in the quiet of the deep night that only Chantal could hear, or rather, she was the only one who would wake up. Chantal would console me for long hours in the night

With this phenomenon shadowing me, I left after graduating top of my class with deep uncertainty and the hope that time among family and friends, especially Jean Pierre, would serve the antidote. "Love, deliver me," I said loudly the next time I saw Jean Pierre, as we began to make plans for me to find a job in Kigali so we could be closer more often. In the meantime Jean Pierre and Placide visited Butare often, almost every weekend. He informed me his sister Celine had moved to Kigali to work as a seamstress. His closeness was good comfort, but not comfort enough, which made me question for the first time whether he was man enough to sate all my needs, be they physical or spiritual. But even then I knew this was unfair, for what I was confronted with was beyond anything any man could be expected to contend with and triumph. And I was swept into a state of doubt and worry, even as Papa summoned me to help on the tomato garden, which had become some sort of perennial part of our lives. Much as it provided a brief distraction, especially on occasions when Placide and Jean Pierre joined us when they came to visit, I couldn't escape the lingering presence of the entity's visitations. This continued until the next time when Nana came to visit.

It was the night before harvest. Papa was waiting as though he expected him. It was as if a bond borne of the spirit had developed between them. This time he was of medium height, his head bald like a calabash, and he wore a goatee.

"Nana," Papa said before he could speak. "I have missed you. Here, give me those tomatoes."

He smiled and asked, "I will be seeing you?"

And then he was gone, faster than the darkening horizon that swallowed him. Papa wanted to chase after him, beg him to help him. How could he face the family solo, when Nana's visitations could become a poison that polluted the mood everywhere? How could Papa close the abiding chasm that had begun after Anan's death and continued in spats afterward?

The family greeted Papa with silence when he brought the tomatoes indoors. But because no one voiced disappointment, it was clear Papa had to bury the abuse he'd practiced in his head in case anyone said anything unkind about Nana's tomatoes. I think he supposed we'd either seen the wisdom of his ways or surrendered to his will.

The next morning, the family faced an empty tomato garden. Again. History seemed to continue to replay its unending tune. "You see," Papa said to Mama, "Once again, I've saved us from tomato drought."

Slowly, ever so slowly, Mama turned to Papa and said, "My dear, have you wondered how every time Nana brings his tomatoes we come to an empty tomato garden?"

90

"What are you saying?" Papa asked.

Mama didn't respond.

But that night, there was too much tension in the house, too much left unspoken. Had Papa worsened matters with Nana's tomatoes? The cloud that lay thick over the household threatened to derail whatever goodwill had been built recently. Papa must have felt a little alienated on account of his failure to convince the rest of the family of the efficacy of the tomatoes he brought from time to time, although they always seemed to restore some semblance of normalcy. This time, though, Papa was at such a loss at the pervading unease in the household that he pretended to excuse himself from home, telling us he was off to visit a friend.

After some idle talk, Mama asked, "What do you think of these tomatoes?"

"Has anyone ever seen this Nana that Papa says has been selling him tomatoes?" I asked.

"No, have you?" Placide said.

"No."

"None of you has seen him?" asked Mama. "How come?"

"Remember we are always indoors whenever he comes," said Placide. "Papa goes outside for a while and comes back with a basket of tomatoes."

"Have you noticed that whenever Papa brings the tomatoes he seems to be out of breath and his feet are dirty?" I asked.

"Where does that leave us?" Placide asked.

"I have heard it said," remarked Mama, "that it is the fool whose own tomatoes are sold to him. But I don't believe your Papa is a fool."

Or, was he?

## Twelve

So for the first time, given the challenge from Mama and the behind-the-scenes wonderings of the family and perhaps his own reconsiderations concerning Nana, the visit and tomatoes failed to lift Papa's spirits and by extension bring peace to the rest of the family. Papa sulked most of the time. Short of temper and accusatory, he often left home early and returned late, aware that he was deepening the funk that had once again seized the family. We attended church and prayed (that is, Papa and me and Placide when he was in town) but nothing changed. I particularly liked going to church, the songs and the company. It kept me from thinking of the threat of destruction emerging in the country. I enjoyed Rev. Didier Murenzi's sermons, the messages concerning hope and salvation. He delivered his sermons with his constantly motional body seeming to generate solar heat that could burn naysayers, his voice rumbling, his arms gesticulating as if chopping away at any invisible resistance in the air, his hooded eyes unwaveringly focused on the congregation. Oftentimes, he would end his sermons with an exhortation to remember that we are more than conquerors, that the earth is the Lord's and the fullness thereof. He would posit that since we are children of God, we should know that the land belonged to our Father and by extension to us, not to any particular person. "Wherever you go, remember to be fruitful, filling the earth and subduing it. It belongs to your Father. "

To me, Rev. Didier Murenzi liked to say, "Talitha cumi; you have great potential."

I would often stand outside after service was over and admire the beautiful lawn and its well-trimmed green grass as well as the bougainvillea lining the lawn. Paul Kajangwe, who used to pull on my cheeks when I was younger and shake my hands firmly when I got older, stopped coming to church, rumored to have gone to Kigali on some form of business. As I recall these matters, I realize that he had stopped inviting Papa to dine with him for a while and he had not been to visit us in a long time.

I also note that Mama never once attended church. With time, her prayer sessions had become routine, almost invariably performed five times a day, the first beginning before dawn and the last at night, with midday, noon, afternoon, and sunset prayers in between. After her ablutions of washing her hands, mouth, nose, arms, face, hair, ears, and feet, she would engage in repetitions of standings, bowings, prostrations, and sittings. With the hideous news hovering around us, perhaps it was just in my mind, but Mama's prayers seemed louder, her movements more brisk.

And as I think Papa and Mama had decided to accommodate each other on the matter of their faiths, only on occasion did I hear Papa say, "Hadidja, why don't you convert and follow Christ, the only way to God?"

And Mama would reply in one form or another, "You have taken my children away from Islam and now you want me to follow also? Never, Pascal, never."

Papa didn't respond to this retort. Sometimes, as we left for church, Papa would shake his head when Mama refused to come with us.

I once asked Papa, "Why don't you make Mama come with us?"

"She doesn't want to, Shama," he said.

"But you can make her come along," I replied. "I thought you were the head of the family."

"That I am, but remember, Shama, that it's about persuasion, not imposition. If I impose this on her, I will have a false convert—a convert for a season, a rebellious convert, even an apostate; if I persuade her, I will have a true convert—a convert for life. In fact, a false convert is no convert at all."

The only time when Papa seemed embittered was during Ramadan, when Mama fasted from sunrise to sunset.

I think I better understood Papa's frustration as I got older and, in an inadvertent eavesdrop, I heard him complain to Mama, "You can practice your fasting, but does that mean that I have to be denied conjugal rights?"

It's only for a month," Mama countered. "We have gone for longer periods without it."

And matters were worsening as the events hovering over the entire country gathered more ominous-ness. To turn on the radio was to invite the venom corrupting the airwaves through the Radio-Television Libre des Mille Collines (RTLMC), continually chorusing voices calling for the need to exterminate the *cockroaches*. I shuddered and feared, but kept hope in the likes of Chantal, who had come from Kigali to visit a number of times since graduation. In Chantal, I held hope that the hate would wane, ebb under the necessity for mutual co-existence. There was just too much at stake to risk in a bloodbath.

Although Jean Pierre had still not formally approached my parents to request marriage, our slow march toward marriage was now deemed inevitable. Both he and Placide assured me that Kigali was safe, but I didn't believe them, not when the airwaves bore such poison. I asked Placide to look up Auntie Shama and he said he would, but he said it had to be at the appropriate time so as not to vex Papa and Mama.

Meantime, with Papa's mood often fouling mine, I found as much refuge as I could in the company of Jean Pierre (on his frequent visits to Butare), who was now beginning to hint that he was on the verge of asking my parents for my hand. He wanted to save enough so we could afford a place of our own, he explained. I had decided to take some time off before seeking a job. I wasn't certain what I would do with my sociology degree, but I would do my best to save also, so that Jean Pierre's decision would be hastened. This prospect and the company of Jean Pierre lit my mood, dimmed still, though at night when I lay alone and the silence of the hour allowed my thoughts to travel through my disturbed mind and I worried over the future of the country.

But now the entity that visited me from time to time suddenly became a source of comfort. The returns in phantasmagoric flashes had begun to lose their horror of expression, ease their sternness— after all, familiarity, usually breeds comfort. Rather than echo enigmatic questions, the entity would come echoing hushabies that soothed me, calling out: "*Amash, Ahtilatiumic.*" Now that I no longer feared the entity, I tried hard to gauge its existential stratum—ghost or human? Dream-world or reality-world (or a combination of the two)? Issue not resolvable, I decided.

I became even more worried about the country when I heard more accounts of Tutsis under siege and then the fatal shooting down near the Kigali airport of President Habyarimana's plane. This unleashed more violence against Tutsis and Chantal made a desperate trip to Butare to

94

warn the family to flee, at a time when Jean Pierre, Celine and Placide had come home to visit. Her own mother was under threat, but her father had managed to protect her so far, Chantal said; she couldn't tell how long he could do that without risking the entire family. She told how her father was even considering leaving the country. She begged Papa and Mama to leave with Placide and me. It was only a matter of time before the violence against Tutsis intensified and spread across the country. She warned that what lurked within the constraints of order and fear of retribution in civil society had come unleashed and become incontinent and would only end when it ran its course and became spent. Placide assured her with seeming insouciance that the madness would soon pass. He was seconded by Papa and Mama and, against my better judgment, me. Chantal left Butare almost in tears, crestfallen.

After Chantal's visit, Mama got more worried, especially when soon afterwards both Placide (now more concerned) and Jean Pierre and Celine went to Kigali and then returned to Butare, claiming that Kigali was no longer safe for Tutsis, recounting the growing butchering of Tutsis.

News of the massacres of Tutsis, especially in Kigali continued to mount. I worried about Auntie Shama, but felt helpless. For the first time, I heard Papa voice concern about his sister's safety. The hope that the United Nations forces would take action to contain the violence was rendered void when on April 21, 1994 the UN reduced its forces from about 2,500 to 250 following the killing of Belgian soldiers who were supposed to protect the prime minister. In Butare, we heard of the intensification of the massacre of Tutsis in Kigali, of marauding fowlers seeking their next prey.

"The young woman spoke the truth," Mama now said to Papa, recalling Chantal's warning. "We need to leave this place before we all get killed."

"Leave and go where?" Papa said, as it seemed his funk had frozen him into inaction (although he was hardly alone in this, as is neighbors all stayed). Jean Pierre and I discussed the matter and concluded that the carnage would soon enough be stopped by the outside world before it reached Butare—there was no way the world would stand by and watch such brutality continue. Looking back, perhaps we were just hoping against reality, as the withdrawal of most of the UN's forces must have warned us that we would be left unaided.

Mama and Papa debated whether to hold their annual supper. "Things just don't seem right, Placide," Mama said. What do you think? Should we cancel the supper this year?"

Papa nodded, but did not reply immediately. A few days later, he told Mama, "Hadidja, I think this year calls for circumspection; but I don't want us to grant the perpetrators of the evil around us any victory. Let us have our supper."

If Mama disagreed with this conclusion, she didn't say so. And with that we began our preparations. Papa and Mama sent word inviting a range of people, including Rev. Murenzi and Paul Kajangwe. The latter declined, citing previous commitments. In his stead, Papa invited Christophe Shimirwa, who attended our church on occasion. A few days before the event, Papa suddenly said, scratching his chin, "I just thought of something. You remember that boy who got into a fight with Jean Pierre a while back?"

"Yes," Mama said, "You had to help mediate the matter."

"I want to invite him."

"Why, Papa?"I asked. "Why him?"

"I think it's a good gesture."

"After so many years, Placide?" Mama asked.

"In this year in particular, I think we should."

"I'm not sure Jean Pierre would appreciate that," I said.

"Tell him we are doing this in our own small way to demonstrate the need for tolerance and love."

"We already have twelve guests," Mama said. "That would make him the thirteenth guest."

"This is an unusual time," Papa replied. "Let him be the thirteenth guest."

Jean Pierre wasn't pleased with the idea, but he said he could understand Papa's position.

The event itself was a bit more subdued. Amid an array of food—including chips, rice and chicken, beef, fried pork, banana and peanut sauce—the laughter sounded a bit too forced; the conversation, contrived. No one mentioned the massacres. It was as if we were at least for that moment in a world of perfect peace. Our thirteenth guest, Thierry, arrived late, took a seat and hardly spoke. He looked around from time to time, seldom made eye contact with me, and was the first to leave, after thanking us for the food and good company. That night, the rain fell heavily, constantly lashing the roof.

And soon we began to hear of the murder here and there in Butare itself of some Tutsis and Tutsi sympathizers at the hands of Hutus, although these seemed to happen at night and no one as yet believed such killings to be widespread. We widely believed that so long as you were not caught outside in the night but stayed in the confines of your home, you were protected.

In church, we prayed for peace.
I ran into Delphine. "Are you still here?" she asked.
"Why are you asking me this?" I replied. "Isn't this my hometown?"
"If I were you, I would leave town."
"Why?"
She walked away, shaking her head.
I seldom saw Thierry. Once or twice when we met, he averted his eyes, said a quick hello and scurried away.
I had a feeling something bad, something very bad, was about to visit us.

July 1, 1994.
The day Papa took me outside to divulge the secrets of my conception—or his version of it. As I have said, the man must have expected what was coming and wanted to clear his conscience. When we returned home, he seemed so burdened that, in a reverse-reprisal of days gone by, I picked up a book and read to him. He closed his eyes as I read. And then he fell asleep in the living room.

July 3, 1994.

97

A day seared in history—as far as I am concerned. I had gone to see Jean Pierre that morning and returned home to cook lunch for the family in order to give Mama a rest. Placide had entered the kitchen to complain that he was hungry and to tease me about my cooking skills. "God took away your cooking skills and put it all in your brains," he said.

With steam and sweat on my face and the smell of boiling beans in my nostrils, I could barely find a witty response. But I didn't have to think, for the banter between sister and brother would soon be a miniscule matter.

We heard a scream, Mama's scream no doubt, but loud and grotesque: a sound neither of us had ever heard before from anywhere, whether human or beast—primal and guttural, speaking of awesome woe and utmost distress, a gross blend of a goat's bleat and a human-howl. It was that powerful, that bizarre. This was followed by Papa's exclamation: "My son, what have they done to you!?" Placide and I, carried by anxiety and fear, rushed outside.

I nearly collapsed when, on arriving outside, I saw Jean Pierre wobbling on his feet, his face blood-soaked, a huge gush in his forehead, as Mama and Papa stood open mouthed, stunned. Placide and I rushed to Jean Pierre as he uttered these words: "Hutu," "killing," and "coming from market." And then before we could reach him, Jean Pierre's body fell to the ground like a sack of steel suddenly emptied. Dogs barked, nay shrieked, in the distance. I went down with Jean Pierre with a wail that strained my body and mimicked Mama's earlier sound. I had no idea I had such sounds in me, exhaled without control. I held on to Jean Pierre's body and continued to wail. Placide checked for a pulse. "He is gone," he announced, a teardrop falling from an eye.

"No!" I exclaimed again and again as I fell completely on the fallen body. Jean Pierre couldn't be dead. I would revive him. My body, my voice, would call him back wherever he was and he would respond to the love-call, the future we were going to build. The rest of the world was going into oblivion at that moment, everything becoming a blur where life outside of the one I needed revived was inconsequential.

I heard as though from a long distance the words, "Run for your lives!" I later realized that it came from a large pack of familiar Tutsis in the neighborhood who were running by.

Placide tried to pry me off Jean Pierre's body. "We have to go now, Shama," he said. "There's a mob coming after us."

I couldn't move. "No, I won't go anywhere," I heard my voice say.

Placide slapped me. "Snap out of it." I didn't—not really, but Placide forced me up and pushed me along. I am not sure I was running as I felt so devoid of life, but I must have, for, with Papa and Mama, we followed the fleeing group of Tutsis. "Stay with me," Placide kept saying to me, as he made sure that he wasn't leaving the age-slow paced Mama and Papa, though they seemed to defy age somewhat at the relatively fast pace with which they moved.

I took cognizance of the happenings, although it seemed so unreal, as if I wasn't involved, as if everything was happening in a distance and although I was involved in it I was watching it—perhaps like a dream.

The group was racing aimlessly on, not sure where to go. "To the church," someone suggested. That seemed to inspire the group and none argued against it. Everyone, even the blood thirsty, would not dare enter a church to shed blood, many reasoned. If there were any doubts, they were suppressed by the lack of other alternatives. We could not outrun the pursuing mob for too long, especially not with the elderly, frail, and young among us.

We entered the church, where Rev. Didier Murenzi was already praying on his knees. He welcomed us and closed the doors. Rev. Murenzi urged us not to fear, entreating us to pray instead. Jean Pierre's fallen body still clear in front of my mind's eyes, I began crying. Placide and Mama consoled me by holding a hand each and squeezing gently. Mama then held me close and wiped away tears that returned. Papa entreated me to be strong; Jean Pierre would want me that way. When we turned our attention to the rest of the group, we realized that everyone in the church was on his or her knee praying, except a few awed children who stared on. Papa, Placide and I got on our knees and joined the prayer. I could hardly concentrate on my words, my mind still struggling to

99

contend with... with what had happened to Jean Pierre. Mama also knelt to begin her own prayer.

Suddenly, we heard a large yell outside of the church door. And then silence. Everyone stopped praying. Still on our knees, we turned our attention to the door in wonder and excruciatingly painful suspense. Seconds were like raining bullets, or the equivalent in emotional damage. Then we heard the sound of banging on the door, which began to shake under the force of those outside trying to reach inside the church. Instinctively, the group congregated in the farthest corner of the church as we saw the door being shoved once, twice... and then pause. The room alternated between silence and yelps of fear and of desperate despair.

Shove! Shove! Shove!

Fear growing still, families clung together, now in shrieking fearfulness, now marked by a stench that came from farting and even defecation. But this was no time to worry about such matters. I clung hard to Mama. Papa put his arm around Placide's shoulders. All were fully aware that at any moment, death could come visiting.

Shove!! Shove!! Shove!!

Hollers of despair filled the air.

Shove!!! Shove!!! Shove!!!

The door collapsed to the discord of loud shrieks from the cowering group in the church. With the fading sun in the distance, the sinister was heightened when the silhouettes of men toting rifles and *pangas* came to view. It looked like a slow motional reel from a movie as a bunch of them uncorked their guns and took aim. I closed my eyes, held on tighter to Mama and found that I'd lost the ability to say anything as paralysis seized total authority over me and my mouth turned completely dry and my body turned wet with bathing sweat and I could feel my heartbeat as it seemed to resound through my body entire, with my knees threatening to buckle at any second. This was more than fear. This was indescribable.

"No, not in the church," I heard one of the entrants say. The voice was familiar, the voice of neighborliness. "I know this man," Papa whispered to us. Not only Papa; we all knew him. "It's Paul," Papa said. "He is a good man." We all knew that. "I think we'll be safe." As we were being shoved out, Papa paused a second as he approached the ostensible leader of the group of power-intoxicants, presumably to appeal to him, but the sight of the man on close encounter was discouraging. The face of Paul Kajangwe, once pleasant, was totally transformed into a massive, grotesque grimace, no less repellent and freighting or exacting than if death itself had worn it. "Move!" he hollered before Papa could recover from the stupefying transformation. This, clearly, was an order of finality, not an invitation for any form of appeal, entreaty or negotiation. "But…" I strained courage to begin to speak, but the raising of the *panga* in the man's hands silenced me, as Papa held and moved me along with the rest of the group to the outside, where a larger group of armed men waited in the waning rays of faded sunlight.

Paul Kajangwe then moved outside and without tarrying for a second, in a voice filled with the guttural brutality of the ensuing carnage, gave the order for the massacre to commence. I thought I saw Thierry for one brief moment and then I couldn't locate him. I heard Rev. Murenzi yell for the men to stop, but his voice was immediately silenced when a *panga* cut him down. The *pangas* started falling, ubiquitous as a downpour of rain. From my position in the group, I saw the flying bodies of those falling under the onslaught. I considered attempting to flee, but refrained when I saw that those who so attempted were wasted by gunfire. The choice then for me was whether to die by *panga* or by gunfire. Now in the pandemonium of the moment, I looked for the rest of the family, but bodies trying to move helter skelter to seek some unavailing protection, caused the family to separate. And now came my greatest fear at that moment, the fear that I would die alone, die without the familiar hand of Papa on my shoulder, the comforting embrace of Mama, or the friendly grip of Placide.

A step in one direction and I saw Papa's unhinged body falling to the ground. Before I could fully exhale my sorrowful gasp, a scream brought my attention to Mama in the short distance as she fell under a rain of *pangas*, and then Placide when he attempted to rescue Mama through a fruitless attempt to shield her. As I witnessed the slaying of Papa, Mama and Placide, something left me—a spirit almost snuffed out—and I no longer cared if I lived. This was not made any better when I saw Celine's slain body on the ground, when I hadn't even realized she was with the

101

group, her lifeless body nailing into me once more the death of Jean Pierre. I stood still and lifted my head, with closed eyes, to the sky.

Pain came in the shoulder and another in the ribs.

As I fell, although much in pain, I felt I was in that state of uncertainty again when I encountered in the haze of the pain the entity that had visited me in the past. Was my imagination conjuring this vision as a dying tribute to its presence in a life too short or was this some actual occurrence, the entity's voluntary appearance in a farewell gesture before death? I felt an urging to go on and I discovered some strength I hadn't thought I could find under the circumstance to move my body—or sense my body being moved—underneath a pile of fallen bodies. Finding a little room to breathe through, I stayed there. Searing pain ate at me, became me, claiming my body. The only comfort I could eke from this was the sense that I was not alone. All around me I could hear screams and the thumps of bodies falling on the ground. But, after a while, the screams ceased and for a moment it was totally quiet, except for the echoes of screams hammering into my ears as if multiple, invisible boomerangs had been flung abroad and returned into them. And then, "Be sure they're dead," someone said. My body turned even more tense as I waited for the final cut of a sharp instrument or the searing heat of a gunshot. Neither came, but I felt someone kicking me in the leg, an exposed part of my body I'd failed to hide. I gritted my teeth and didn't otherwise react, nor was I even sure that my weakened body would have reacted anyway. After a while the voices of the group that had inflicted the massacre receded, mixed in my ears with the reechoing screams into a dissonant tune. Wishing then to disentangle myself from the harvest of corpses and find some refuge, I instead found myself slipping slowly into unconsciousness until everything turned blank.

My next recallable conscious moment came on the floor of a dank room, the consciousness returning very slowly. At first it was as if a voice was calling out to me. All that I could make of it was *Ahtilatiumic, Ahtilatiumic, Ahtilatiumic.* And then I was struggling against something that I couldn't understand, something intangible, it seemed, that didn't want me to wake up. But I was also being elevated by the other more persistent saying *Ahtilatiumic.* When I finally managed to open my eyes

102

pain consumed every part of me. Through the unfocused mind and the throbbing body, I could discern some glitter of light from the half opened window opposite me. Wincing, I tried to get up but found that I couldn't move much. It was only then that I noticed the woman next to me. She got closer and gingerly put a hand on my head. I tried to recoil. "Don't strain yourself," the woman said. "I am a nurse. Please try to take it easy."

As my mind gained more focus, I asked, "Where am I?" I knew this was my voice, although it sounded raspy and distant and strange.

"You are safe now. It's a miracle you survived. We found you outside our door a couple of weeks ago. You were almost gone. But you will be fine."

"Who are you?"

"My name is Nicole. I am here to help you. I am with the International Commission for the Red Cross. This is a French camp."

"A French camp? But the killing...."

"It's over. The RPF just captured Butare. Those who were committing the atrocities are fleeing by the thousands to Zaire. Rwanda is free."

The words strayed over me like an abandoned dream, as haunting as they were meaningless. What was I to do with this freedom? These thoughts would be suspended by the momentary relief of unconsciousness, which rescued me from the immediate strain of the pain in spirit and body, so that I wouldn't feel the full consequence of what had happened until at least a week later when, much against my wish, I had long bouts of awareness and therefore prolonged thought and consideration of my family's demise and the physical devastation that had occurred as well as my own spiritual deprivation, more devastating to me than my healing physical wounds. Sometimes the wish for death was so strong that I envied those who had perished. What was I to do with a life without Papa, Mama, Placide, and Jean Pierre?

I also wondered how I had managed to make my way from the church to the camp, a camp I didn't know existed. When I thought hard I could recall strong arms around me and the smell of stale sweat and alcohol, but I couldn't quite determine what part these images had played. I searched my mind for more contexts to these fleeting images, but to no avail.

I would battle these thoughts in the four weeks it took me to recover sufficiently in body. My nurses told me how lucky I was. Nicole said, "The wounds to your shoulder and rib are a bit severe, but the wounds in your back are very superficial. It's as if those who inflicted them were careful not to cut too deep, as if they were sending a message rather than intending to kill." This revelation perplexed me beyond my own comprehension, but the more I contemplated it the more confused I became. Around me, there were other survivors of the massacres. In this, I was fortunate in that many of the others had severed body parts, the one next to me in particular—her name was Valentina—had both legs severed. She was in constant pain and her wailing chorused in my ears almost all day and night.

My nurses now urged me to go outside. "Vileness has stained beauty" Nicole said. "But now you need to restore that beauty. You will choke to death if you stay indoors all the time. You need to get some fresh air." In fact, she and the other nurses insisted on this. I looked at Nicole in particular, so young, even pretty. She couldn't be more than thirty. And here she was expending a part of her life so that I might have life. But I wanted to yell back at Nicole and the other nurses that I would rather die than step out of the camp's protection, that they ought to understand what the outside held for me, the horror it contained, which would render it more claustrophobic than the tight confines of the camp. Pain over the demise of Papa, Mama, Placide and Jean Pierre seemed now to hover over me, but I preferred to brood in these confines, where I felt that I could lay claim to them somehow, than outside where they had been claimed from me. Nor had the entity that visited me abandoned me, appearing now like me and another time in grotesque appearance, except now it shared space with the rest and, having encountered my family's ghosts (if in dreams), I had no fear whatsoever of the entity, grotesque appearance or no. And it was the entity that whispered the name Shama to me. "Shama, Shama, Shama." And I knew it was not my own name being invoked, that it was in fact the elder one, who had become non-existent in my life.

Shama. My aunt. Suddenly this gave me some hope. I knew I had to go to my aunt. But this hope was immediately besieged by the fear that my aunt might be dead. This was a real probability, considering the Tutsis that had died in Kigali and elsewhere. But once my aunt entered my head, I couldn't evict her from it. The name would ring in my ears in my conscious hours and sound in my mind in my dreams during my sleeping hours. I had to find Auntie Shama, or at least determine if she was dead or alive. As I reached this decision, Valentina died in the night. As they carried her body outside and all I could recall of her was her voice bellowing in pain, I resolved that to stay in the camp was the equivalent of death, but to venture outside at least in search of my aunt was an offering of life.

It was this resolve that urged me from my bed and outside where, apart from the temporarily blinding sunlight, a sense of agoraphobia suddenly set upon me like some suffocating steam. But I had a mission to fund Auntie Shama, which must begin soon, so I took a step and another, as tentative as the uncertainty that shackled me. I was taking steps, one cautious move after another, even though my heart beat uncomfortably hard and I perspired profusely. I seized all the remnants of courage I could and walked on. In a few minutes I saw the church building, its broken doors left opened, as if inviting me to the past, the bougainvillea in front not as vibrant, as if sharing my gloom. And my nest of emotions hatched vivid images in what I considered extreme grotesqueries: Papa's severed head was flying through the air, blood spilling in all directions, Mama's slain body tumbling down, as was Placide's and Celine's, the spreading of my limbs, the brutality, the indescribable stress to spirit and the vile rampage of my body. And I was under constant siege to all the influences and ravages that time wields and yields.

This would happen again and again each time I walked past the church. It would follow me like a shadow even when I left the vicinity of the church. I wanted to go home, see what had become of it, but I feared that I would not be able to face the memories it would invoke, the resurrections of Mama, Papa, and Placide that was sure to come, and the slaying of Jean Pierre at its doorsteps. But I also wanted to go just so I could confront those fears and, as I had heard it said, perhaps by confronting those fears I could conquer them. But I could not lie much to myself about this: when I considered that visiting the church had not helped me conquer anything, going home might be worse. In all this, my resolve to go in search of my aunt hardened. Butare had nothing left for me.

I told my nurses what I intended. Some, particularly Nicole, attempted to dissuade me on the basis that I needed more rest before I made the journey, but I believed they were only trying to tell me kindly that my aunt was dead. Nicole, her face haggard with stress, eyed me for long moments—and as I looked at her, I knew that the part of her life she had shed for those like me would be futile unless I left and tired to rebuild myself and that by so doing I would indirectly be giving her that diminished life back. Insisting that I had to go, I managed to solicit some funds from them. Nicole gave me their donation, hugged me and wished me well. Starved by the circumstances into pencil-thinness, I boarded a bus for Kigali, a journey fraught with the mental—heavy memories of my slain family and friends becoming bonemeal for grass—and the visual (the roadsides dotted with gardens of rotting flesh and bones, as if the earth had decided to vomit exhibits of the grand, diabolical opus of its children).

# Thirteen

I was relying on memory battered by time and the poisoned fruits of mistrust sowed by my parents, mistrust that had thawed under the necessities of recent events. It was a memory gained from the letter I'd once found among Papa's belongings. I recalled that the letter itself was very brief, begging Papa for forgiveness. I remembered how I had felt drawn to my aunt, knowing my aunt was *persona non grata* in our household. But as if I knew I would need it one day, I had memorized the letter's contents, including the address. And although it had been a long time and the memory was faint, I relied on it. It was the only thing I had to try and find her. My determination was strong and my mental map came clearer and clearer under my resolve so that my compass took me to the vicinity of my aunt's house, which I was able to locate after minimal inquiry.

It wasn't what I was expecting, although when I thought about it I realized I shouldn't have expected better. Where the gate must have once stood, there was nothing: a gap between the two front walls. I could see a bungalow and its front compound, strewn with debris, as though it had just been used as some sort of marketplace. The paint of the building was a faded white, browned in places by dirt.

I hesitated several seconds before gathering the courage to step into the compound, all the while wondering if this seeming remnant from a battered time past still housed any living being. I now feared most that my aunt had indeed died, leaving the house in its desolate state. My knees were weak all of a sudden, and I was unsure whether to go any further, but further I went still. "Hello!" I hollered when I got to the front door, which I found locked. For a few seconds I received no response but my courage was strengthened because of the locked door, which I took as a sign that the house was inhabited even if locking it could mean the outside world was not welcome. Whether inhabited by beast, human or human-beast, friend or foe, I would find out. As seconds turned into a minute, I thought the inhabitant may have left the house at that moment but feared that the locked door may indicate that the house was abandoned—until I thought I heard some movement from inside. I yelled again.

And then came the response, "Who is there?"

Hope and joy blended like air and wind, rose together as an invisible buoy inside me—call it a sweet emotional fragrance. "It's me," I said. "It's me Shama."

Immediately, the door was flung open, wide as hope itself, unrestrained as joy. And a woman stepped out of it, her loose clothes more noticeable than the emaciated body that inhabited them. No one needed to tell either one of us that she was looking at the other Shama. Each knowing that the mirror before her was reflecting the namesake, we embraced for the span of three minutes, dotted by brief moments of disengagement by one to observe the other. "You look so much like your mother," Auntie Shama said, "that prominent nose; but you have your father's bold eyes."

My aunt ushered me inside, holding my hand, eager to offer me water, over-eager to apologize for the shabbiness of her house. "It was never like this before the madness," she said as she handed me a cup of water. The water drank, as we simmered from the excitement of our first encounter as adults, we entered a phase of recollections and truths. But like any loaded thing, these matters had to be unsheathed slowly lest they harm the hearers beyond repair. But Auntie Shama couldn't hold her anxiety over Papa, Mama and Placide. On hearing of their demise, my aunt buried her face in her palms, body shuddering with clear grief. I joined her in this. Auntie Shama said, "We have each other. We will keep each other."

That was the beginning. There were a lot more stories to tell, but we allowed the first night to pass with a guise of normalcy, pretending we each needed to sleep. I slept (or rather went to bed) in the guest bedroom with much relief at the rediscovery of (or the opportunity to rediscover) my aunt. Still, the silences of the night were only external, for I shuddered several times from memories that came haunting for prey. Strange, I thought at first, that even with my aunt so close, I couldn't completely foreclose the image of my family's slain bodies. Still, with her so close, I soldiered on in the night in the solidifying belief that things would turn out well. Had my aunt not promised that we would keep each other?

Three days in a row, we kept close to each other, told stories before the massacre and what had happened during the long span when Auntie Shama was banished from the family home. I leaned how successful my aunt had been running her business. She told me of the trades she had made, buying assorted goods and selling them at a profit, the money she accumulated and the enhanced lifestyle she led. But she stopped when it came to the period of the massacres. I knew it had to contain something extremely unpleasant, just like mine, which I also had refused so far to share in its completeness. We were taking care of each other, eating breakfasts that Auntie Shama made and served, performing chores together and, under my prodding, cleaning the compound. But we couldn't continue this way. How long, really, could we keep at bay the period each of us knew had inevitably affected the other in extremely wounding ways? Oh, but the fear that to touch it would uncover too much. And we might have prolonged this convenient, if unpleasant, dance had not the fourth night brought out to the open like pent-up vomit, a major character in my aunt's life.

We'd said our goodnights after a long day cleaning the house and sharing supper together. I had gone to bed to face my torments in dreams and attempted to hush them with my will when, in the depths of night I woke up, startled by a sound that seemed novel to the repertoire of the night's sober disturbances of crickets that I'd faced so far in Kigali. But, even then, for a while I thought I was asleep and deep in some manner of dream or nightmare. After all, dream and reality in those days were meshed. And then I recognized a groan and a grunt, followed by what sounded as knocking on the walls. Repeat. Repeat. Repeat. As I heard these, I realized that another, a man, inhabited the house at that hour. Whether friend or foe, I couldn't tell as yet. I listened harder, feeling as though I was an intruder. Now a moan, and now a deeper one still, and I concluded that this was no foe. I smiled under the covers of the darkness—so Auntie Shama had a lover. Why hadn't my aunt told me? Not once, in recounting her stories over the past years, had she mentioned a lover, except for a boyfriend she claimed she'd long dumped. But as I considered this question, and as much as I felt somewhat betrayed by the withholding of this detail, I soothed myself that this was not my business.

Plus, I had myself not divulged all the details of my life to my aunt, including Jean Pierre's part in it.

After a brief silence, when my aunt and the visitor—or perhaps it was presumptuous to call him a visitor—spoke in whispers that I couldn't decipher, I struggled back into sleep, even though on the edge of sleep the resumption of another round of grunts and moans woke me up, became somewhat familiar, a sort of lullaby of the night, a balm of pleasurable sounds that balanced the painful aspects of those dark hours in as much as they reminded me of agonizing moments in front of the church in Butare.

When morning came and I walked into the living room, I expected to see a cheerful Auntie Shama, ready to present me with breakfast (as she'd done in the last three mornings) and to begin some conversation centered on how beautiful I had become, and how lucky we were to have each other. But instead of this pre-ordained opening, I saw a burly man sitting in the living room, on the couch I'd shared with my aunt, drinking tea. His face seemed permanently squeezed into a displeasing countenance. Startled, I looked at the burly, fleshy-nosed man without speaking.

"You must be Shama's niece," the man said.

"Where is she?"

"She went back to bed. I guess she needs some rest."

I detected a smirk. I stared at him. He got up from his seat and walked toward me and I almost retraced my steps back to the bedroom. The man stretched out a hand. "My name is Alexandre Napoleon Alphonse Nsengiyumva. Call me Alexandre, I am a friend of your aunt's."

Why he would mention his full name, I couldn't fathom. A second or two of hesitation preceded my strained smile, as I worked hard to be pleasing; but there was something about the man that disturbed me. Was it merely that he'd robbed me of the morning I expected to share with my aunt? Was it because he seemed so cocksure of himself, so at ease in my aunt's home and therefore threatened to displace me as my aunt's most important companion? Was it the level of intimacy he'd reached with my aunt, which wouldn't be so bad if he weren't so graceless in appearance?

"Good to meet you," I said as I processed these questions.

"Won't you join me for a cup of tea?" he asked.

"No, thanks," I said as I turned around and walked away from him, closing the bedroom door as quickly as I could, collapsing into bed and cursing the circumstance, which I knew wasn't merely on account of the brief encounter with Alexandre, but the need for the continuing purging of what still nagged me so deeply that a minor catalyst evoked so much more. Minutes later, I could tell that my aunt and Alexandre were in some form of argument. Because they were trying to keep their voices low, I could only hear a few words: "Tell... myself ... wait... what..." Moments later, it was all-silent and I knew the man was gone.

Auntie Shama knocked on the door of what was now my bedroom. Still grappling with a sense of betrayal, I was disinclined to respond. "Can I come in?" Auntie Shama asked. After seconds of silence, Auntie Shama asked, "Are you in there?" Rather than answer, I came out of the bedroom to face her. "I am sorry..." Auntie Shama started to say.

"He's Hutu, isn't he?" I asked. This had leaked out of my mouth without forethought and, to myself, I suddenly wondered if that was the source of my reaction to him.

"Yes."

"How... how could you share your bed with him after all that...."

"Listen, I owe you an explanation, but...."

"A Hutu? How could you?"

Auntie Shama bowed her head and raised it again as if nodding away the moment in shame. "Let me explain this," she said.

"I don't know what there is to say," I said.

"Shama, we can't keep pretending that the last few months didn't happen."

"Exactly. That's why you can't justify why you'd sleep with one of them. After all they've done to us?"

"Hear me out."

"What's there to hear? These are the people who killed Papa. They are the people who killed Mama and Placide." I could have thrown in Jean Pierre and Celine's name.

The outburst seemed to stun Auntie Shama, to wound her. "What do you mean?" I'm not sure she thought about this question before she asked it.

111

"Don't tell me you don't know. You very well know what they did to us. Why are you asking me this, Auntie?"

"Let's not let this come between us. At least, hear what I have to say first before you go passing judgment, please. These have been trying times, times of tough, compromised, hard choices."

A moment of thought, of deep hesitation and resistance, gripped me as I wrestled with the need to accommodate in turn the aunt who had accommodated me. I determined that I had no other choice at that moment. I was the only one who could lend her some support, but would supporting her unholy alliance with that man not fill her future, and perhaps mine, with gloom?

My hesitation offered her an opportunity, and she began immediately to fill the silence. "It was a very difficult time," she said. "I was afraid. We were all very afraid. I don't even know if fear describes it adequately. Perhaps terror is more appropriate—you know, that feeling that at any time you could face a brutal death." Auntie Shama then proceeded to paint for me the portrait of what had happened, distilled perforce because it was being narrated and not experienced. Still, it was as lucid a showing as could be expected, especially considering the terror that I also had experienced in Butare.

All over Kigali there were massacres and rumors of massacres. Neighbor had risen against neighbor, and the hunger of sharpened machetes had tasted to the death the flesh of many Tutsis and their Hutu sympathizers or even perceived sympathizers. Women had been physically brutalized and raped ... Auntie Shama had heard and seen so many accounts without being herself touched that she was beginning to cultivate a hope, perhaps merely to numb her fear, that she would escape the mayhem. But it would soon reach her, become so personal as to establish the link that was until then lacking between the personal and the rumored (as well as her own witness to killings and other brutalities).

It was nightfall. Auntie Shama was at home when she heard noises in the distance. With all that was happening, she knew at once it was an advancing army of bloodthirsty men ready to wreak pain and invoke death. Instinctively she turned off all the lights in her house and considered leaving at once to find refuge somewhere, but besides the fear that it might be too late to leave without encountering the armed men, the *somewhere* was also not clear. Where could she hide? As she panicked with indecision and the numbness of fear, she could hear the noises getting closer: yells and then pleadings and cries from proximate neighborhoods. The indecision replayed itself: there was no way she could leave home without detection, but to stay at home was to be trapped, to wait for death. Sweat soaking her body and clothes, still de-energized by fear, she found the ability to think rationally fleeing her.

Auntie Shama heard banging on her gate. It was a weak gate to begin with, erected more for appearance than actual protection. Prayer upon quick prayer prayed, on her knees she begged for the gate to hold steady, at least bargain some time for her. But no, the gates were broken from their hinges in minutes, and through her window, she saw a throng of men advancing armed with machetes, *pangas*, and those nail studded *masus*. She readied herself for her doom, full of hard-beating heart, pounding temples, more free flowing sweat.... She didn't know exactly how, but her body somehow became a motional object that moved from the clearly visible, vulnerable position in her living room, that was but an advertisement for death to claim her, to the bathroom, where, lying fetus-like in the bathtub, she closed her eyes.

The men were soon in the building, calling for her to come out. "Cockroach!" they hollered. We will find you, they assured her, and if she made them search hard for her, they would make it hard for her, prolong the agony of her death. She could hear their voices so loudly it was as if they were in the bathroom, in fact, standing over her and yelling. She could hear them possessing her apartment, dispossessing her of what she deemed private, even inviolable, objects carefully arranged over many years that they had acquired not just sentimental significance but spiritual importance as well. But this was inconsequential when compared to the dread that filled her when she realized, as she must have known would happen if she'd thought rationally ahead, that someone was in the bathroom. Whoever it was didn't give her much time in her state of elevated dread as in one quick moment he covered her mouth with one hand before she could scream, his other machete-toting hand raised as though he was ready to bring it down into her body. Instead, the man— whom he realized as Alexandre Nsengiyumva from down the road—

dropped the machete beside him and put a finger over his own lips, signaling that she stay silent. He brought his head closer to her and in a liquor-laden breath whispered to her, "Stay here. I will protect you. Don't come out until I return for you. I promise you I will return." Much as she feared who he was at that moment, she found his words reassuring. They'd met on several occasions and chatted as friendly neighbors are wont to do. She knew he was in the army, that his wife and children had left him and that he was in his fifties. Under certain circumstances, she'd call him a casual friend. But given the current circumstances and despite his reassurance she had a strong linger of doubt. He walked out of the bedroom. "No luck," she heard him say loudly to his cohorts. "She must have left before we got here. Who knows, perhaps she's escaped to her neighbors. Let's check the rest of the neighborhood." Clearly the man carried much credibility or authority or both, for none questioned him.

The miracle had happened. Death had come creeping close and then clawed back at the last moment. Alone in the dark house, she contemplated leaving the bathroom and taking her chances outside. She was fully aware that would be suicidal, however, and she could think of no option at that time but to wait until daybreak when she might be able to elude attackers or, if sooner, until Alexandre Nsengiyumva returned to rescue her or cause damage.

He returned within two hours, pulling up in an army jeep to find Auntie Shama still in the bathtub, her limbs gone to sleep. In the darkness, he carried her to the bedroom and without turning on the lights helped bring back life into her limbs by first encouraging her to move them and then by massaging them. It looked innocent enough when he began, but it soon became evident to Auntie Shama where he was headed so that she wasn't surprised when he pulled off her sweat and urine sodden underwear and mounted her. She did not protest, as she deemed it the price she was paying for the rescue. It seemed more like an act, a performance intended to send a message. Although he wasn't rough, it was done without passion, even with seeming tenderness. When it was over, he said, "I will protect you, but you have to trust me completely." Auntie Shama didn't reply. Alexandre Nsengiyumva continued, "You can't stay here. They will find you and kill you. Can you imagine what they'd have done to you if I hadn't found you first? Instant death would have been welcome. I know what they are capable of. With me, you will be safe. No one will come to my place looking for a Tutsi. I am a champion of their cause. I am above suspicion. But if this will work, I need you to promise me one thing right now. I am risking my life to save you. You must be discreet once I take you home. If they find you, they will kill us both. Do you promise to stay inside, not bring any attention, never leave home?"

"I promise," Auntie Shama said, lying side-by-side Alexandre Nsengiyumva, the bravado of his presumptuousness stunning her. But could she make a case when she'd waited for him exactly as he'd asked (or was ordered?). Was it why he would later refer to the act he'd inflicted on her as "the night we first made love?"

With the promise secured, Auntie Shama thinking how foolish he was by assuming that a promise obtained under the circumstance held any substance, he carried her to the jeep, looked around, and put her in her in the back. "Lie low," he said as he drove off. Given that he lived so close, the drive took less than a minute, during which Auntie Shama considered yelling to draw attention and feeling ashamed that she wanted so much to live that she was willing to compromise so much.

He pulled into his garage and invited her inside. For a man's home, she thought it well kept. The first thing she noticed was the huge photo on the wall of the living room of his wife and four children.

"We are home," he said. "Feel free to use anything here as if it belongs to you. But never open the door. Never come out of the house. Stay inside and be quiet always. Never cook anything when I'm not home. If I expect company, I will let you know so you can hide in the bedroom. Never open the door for anyone, not even for me."

He would be gone most of the time and would come home at night reeking of liquor and disrobe her and engage in carnal intercourse. She never protested; he never asked for her approval. At first he was eager to begin and end with no foreplay, but he was always gentle. In a while the gentleness became more tender and prolonged to incorporate caressing and stroking. At first he hardly spoke, but in a while he began to talk to her, seeking details of what she did in the past, her family background. Only once did she ask him what he did all this time when he wasn't at home. She'd noticed how thorough he was with cleaning himself when he came home, the long baths. The night she asked him about his activities, she'd noticed blood on his hands when he came home and before he could engage in the nocturnal ritualistic cleansing. "Where have your hands been?" she asked.

She saw a cloud of anger becloud his face like she'd never seen before. "Do you think I enjoy doing this?" he asked. "I do it because I have to. It's a matter of survival. If I don't kill I become an object of suspicion. I am doing what I have to do to live. I am doing it for us." She said nothing and she noticed the anger leave him abruptly, as if he regretted the outburst. He came close to her and for a minute she feared he would touch her with the blood stained hand, but he didn't do so then, withdrawing the hand before it made contact. "Look, Shama, this will soon pass. This madness can't last forever. And when it's all over you and I can live together."

She was still quiet. A life together? If you anticipate an end to this, she wanted to ask him, why soil your hands so? She looked at him and his anger seemed to thaw even further and this time he came a little close and actually touched her, soiled her too with his bloodied hand, as if to assure her that she was too deeply involved with him, that she too was soiled. She lost control and wept—a pierced tear-fountain of suppressed pride, sour ironies, pain flimsily held in abeyance. She wept into his chest and he held her closer and, without prior cleansing, he disrobed her. And, at that moment, she decided. She'd been fighting internally for too long and she was breaking, her spiritual innards tearing apart. She decided to surrender to the circumstance, not finding any relief in fighting it, she would now love it, or try, and in loving it or trying she would live more fully, as fully as she could under the blighted circumstance. The question she had for herself was whether she was capable of loving that which she hated. Could she create a tunnel strong enough that she could render oblivious the blood, rape and mutilation that had so badly smeared the land, smeared him, and now smeared her?

Within the unknown terrain of this new ground, in that period of total surrender, she found herself inexplicably, unbelievably, levitated in spirits, and she held on to him for the first time, for a while imagining him to be a lover she'd had a long while back; but she jettisoned this approach, for it didn't sate her, and she searched instead for that faint pulse within her that was capable of loving the hated. She kissed him fully for the first time and then gave of herself what she could. In those moments, she knew they were forming something new, something neither of them had dared envisage, but which was now offered to them because she had gone contrary to reason and surrendered and in this surrender she felt she could gain control. And feeling this surrender, he told her he no longer had any suspicion that she would betray him, believed that she would not condemn him. He told her that he had loved her for a long time and was moved to so tell her earlier but for his estranged family and the lack of guts.

From that moment, Aunt Shama affirmed her decision—that she would *love* him. She redefined love, rejecting the notion that love happened in the heart, affirming that perhaps love brewed in the heart is just one version of it, that the malleable one made in the mind is just as valid. She would love with her mind and perhaps the heart would follow. With this decision, she welcomed him home with warmth, spoke to him (not just tolerated his questions) and continued to offer him of her as best as she could.

When the RFP took over and the massacres ended, Auntie Shama returned to her desolate home, and Alexandre would come to visit her from time to time, often spending the night.

"I'm sorry I didn't tell you, that you found out this way, but I was going to tell you. I was just looking for the right time, and I wasn't expecting him that night. He had told me he was going to be away for a while and so I thought I had more time. And then when he showed up that night, I decided I would introduce him to you in the morning, but he woke up before I did. I'm sorry, Shama, but I am sure you will like him if you get to know him."

"Auntie, I don't want to know him."

"Shama, please try and understand..."

"He raped you."

"I..."

"He killed your people."

"Shama, please..."

"I'm sorry. This is none of my business anyway. Whatever you want to do with him, that's up to you, Auntie. But please don't tell me to like him. I won't. I can't."

The elder Shama seemed to accept this in order not to jeopardize her relationship with me, I supposed. I imagined she understood how incomprehensible I might judge her actions, given how ridiculous they seemed to me. So we tried hard to quarantine this part of her life from our otherwise glowing relationship. Whenever Alexandre appeared in the house, sometimes reeking of alcohol, if it was daytime, I left the house; if it was nighttime, I buried my head under a pillow in fruitless attempt to escape the poisoned noises of their unwholesome alliance, in my view a rape reenacted with the victim facilitating the act. Worse for me, this sparked memories of my own ordeal in front of the church in Butare, those atrocities that are wont to mutate the soul, and I would toss around in bed in helpless anger, at times tempted to walk into my aunt's bedroom and strangle the beast. But I had to accommodate this because of the love I had developed for my aunt (which made it even harder to bear the unfathomable compromise she had reached, rationalized on some inexcusable grounds that escaped my threshold of tolerance). It affected our relationship, however, reduced the freedom with which we'd interacted without destroying it.

## Fourteen

But it was the lethargy that began to afflict me that affected my relationship with Auntie Shama the most. Suddenly, I was always tired, usually puking in the mornings and often falling asleep, unable to spend much time with her. "You seem to be getting bigger," my aunt teased. "I am feeding you well." I worried about this, but dismissed my concerns as unwarranted. Soon, however, Auntie Shama paused to observe me more carefully. Her conclusion at once filled her with joy and worry. "You will bless me with a grandchild,' she said to me, but I could detect the strain in her frown.

"What?"

"Don't tell me you don't know what's happening to you, Shama, what's going on inside of you."

"What are you saying? Nothing is going on inside of me."

"You are pregnant, Shama, and you know it."

"I am not pregnant."

I immediately left the living room where these tabooing words had been uttered and went to my bedroom. I'd protested, first to the voice inside my head and now to my aunt, but how long could I protest when my body made it clear to me that a sad seed had been implanted in me and was growing, whether I protested or not, whether I liked it or didn't. It was an inalienable part of me; despite the protest, it was feeding on my vitamins, sharing of me. This was a miracle I ought to celebrate. Still, how could I abide this thing that would always, always remind me of that night in front of the church that I didn't even want to think about—the hate?! I couldn't live with it and now that what I'd harbored in secret had been voiced by my aunt, I would ask for her help.

"I need a favor," I said.

"Anything for you," Auntie Shama replied.

"I have been trying to deny this, but you have noticed it. You said it, Auntie, I am pregnant."

"Oh, yes." Auntie Shama was grinning. "I told you so."

Had this old woman lost her mind that she would grin at the situation?

"That's where I need your help."

119

"I will be here for you, Shama. Always. You know that."

"Are you sure?"

"Without a doubt."

Drawing closer to my aunt, I said, "I need to abort it."

The older woman drew away. "What? Don't speak such an abomination."

"Abomination? The abomination would be carrying this abomination to full term, this product of rape."

"You never told me you were raped."

"You never told me you slept with your rapist."

"Please, don't bring that into this. We are talking of a human life here."

"It's the seed of rape. It must die."

"It's a child of God, no matter how conceived. You can't kill a child of God, a blessing. Do you know how some women labor to conceive without success? Look at me."

"To bear the fruit of rape?"

"To bear fruit. Don't ever think such thoughts." Auntie Shama drew closer to me, but I moved away.

"You killed my twin once," I said, "so why are you reluctant to help me get rid of this?"

"Your twin? Is that what you call it?"

"He was a part of me."

"I did it to save you, to save your life."

"So do this for me. Save my life again. I will die if I have to carry this thing to term."

"You won't die. I will take care of it for you. If you don't want it, then do it for me. I know you are young. I know your life is ahead of you. You don't have to worry about that. I will raise the child."

"I just can't carry the child."

"So you want to get rid of it? Don't you know it's against God's will? No Christian woman will do what you're thinking."

"I am no Christian woman. My mother…"

"What? Your father, God rest his soul, will weep to hear this."

"Why are you being so judgmental? What about you? Are you not sinning? Is fornication not forbidden?"

120

Auntie Shama was silent, her chests heaving, but it was not clear if in anger or shame or sadness. She turned her back on me and we remained so for a while. Then she walked away, as I realized it was not in repudiation of me but because she did not want me to see her cry, and I knew then that I had caused great pain.

The next day Auntie Shama informed me that she'd thought hard about her situation and concluded that, while she'd continue to see Alexandre, she would no longer fornicate with him. And true to her word, even when Alexandre spent nights in the house, I didn't hear the sounds of intercourse as before. Auntie Shama began to attend church, and to take Alexandre with him. She invited me several times, but I refused, afraid that I couldn't execute what I planned to do if I allowed my conscience to be challenged by humans, but more so by God.

At the moment when Auntie Shama made the vow to me, she embraced me, even kissed me on the forehead. I am sure she believed that her promise to stay chaste and her church going would show me a commitment to change that would encourage me to make my own commitment to keep the child. But I had other ideas that formed a route in my mind, which I continued to perfect in the next few days until the route's paths were clear even as I wrestled with my thoughts and worried about the enormity of my plans. They had serious consequences, no doubt, and besides the risk to body and life, my conscience was not at rest; in fact, it was under serious assault. I slept little in nights of sweat and unending worry and harassing thoughts. I questioned whether I was even capable of executing my plans. Many times, I resolved that I would carry the forming progeny to life. It was no fault of the child that was now a part of me, that contained my genes. How could I punish it with such premature expiration, deprive it of the chance to create its own path? Who knew what it might become? It deserved to live, to grow, to experience the thrills and pains of life, although I questioned, given recent events, whether it was worth bringing any new life into a world capable of such brutality. At the same time as I argued for the child's life, the hatred within me was too poignant, the recurring nightmares of my family and Jean Pierre and Celine being slain and the brutality with which the child was conceived weighed too heavily. And even without the love sounds of

Auntie Shama and Alexandre, whenever I saw the man, I was filled with hatred for the fetus, which tilted the scale against keeping it.

I walked to Alexandre's house one evening. He opened the door with the gleeful cheer of a child, expressing how happy he was to see me. "Welcome, welcome. What a joy," he said. "Please sit while I get you something to drink."

I noticed that he was nervous. Good, I thought. "I can't sit," I said. "I need something from you and I need to know if you can give it to me."

"Anything for you, my dear. Anything."

"I need a bottle of whiskey."

"Whiskey," he returned the word, his eyes opening wider. "But what for? Drinking is a bad habit."

"But you drink. If it's such a bad habit, why do you do it?"

"But you are so young, my dear. Why start such a bad thing? Let me get you something nice, eh? I'll take you shopping. I know where to take you. Clothes, whatever you want. Jewelry for a beauty as yourself."

"I don't want clothes or jewelry. I want a bottle of whiskey."

Alexandre frowned and pursed his lips. "Your aunt will not forgive me if she finds out that I've given you whiskey."

"I won't tell her. Will you?"

"But what do you need it for?"

I didn't speak back; instead, my response was a stern frown.

"Please, my dear, be reasonable."

"I won't tell my aunt you gave me whiskey, but if you don't do as I ask, I will make up and tell her things you won't want me to tell her."

"Like what?"

"Use your imagination."

"Shama, I didn't know you could be like this."

Neither did I. What was it? Desperation? Hatred? Both?

"You are wasting my time," I said.

"You really don't like me, do you?"

"Look, I'm not here to make conversation. Will you get me the bottle or not?"

"Okay, but please, not a word to your aunt." He disappeared to his bedroom and returned with a bottle of whiskey. "Remember, not a word to your aunt about this."

I took the bottle and left without thanking him, one step farther on my route, although what I'd just accomplished had been the easiest. I put the bottle under my bed and then I waited. If my aunt noticed that I was unusually nervous and moody, the older woman said nothing. In the darkened home, I waited some more, sleeping only a couple of hours. I prayed for the first time in a long time, although my prayer was not directed at the God I knew, but a god I created for myself, who would empathize with my situation and pardon me for what I was about to make happen. The night of this prayer, I knew my aunt would be gone in the morning and I needed those precious lonesome hours to effect my plans. In the morning, I waited while my aunt did her ablutions, prepared breakfast and ate while I declined to partake on the basis of not being hungry, looked on, increasingly nervous, barely able to carry on a conversation.

"Are you alright?" the older woman asked.

"Yes, just a little tired."

"Everything will be fine."

I gave my namesake the benefit of a smile.

After Auntie Shama left, I faced my freedom, but a freedom that urged me to go to a very hard place bereft of comfort. The light entering the room through the windows discomforted me and I drew the curtains to darken the room. I remembered the night, as described by my aunt, when the bloodthirsty men had entered the house and I remembered the night in front of the church in Butare, but I immediately refused to draw further comparisons. I went to my bedroom and retrieved the bottle of whiskey I had obtained from Alexandre. My hands shook badly as I opened the bottle. I took a coat hanger and went to the living room. Immediately, I concluded that this wasn't a good location for this. With my weapons in hand, I went to the bathroom and closed the door.

Auntie Shama was looking at me. I looked at her and at the unfamiliar surroundings. "Where am I?" I asked.

"You are in a hospice under the care of Dr. Gracia Marquez," Auntie Shama said. "The official story is that you had some serious stomach virus that required admission. Remember that."

Dr. Marquez came to my room often to check on me and to ensure that I was taking my pain killers.

Alexandre also came to visit me. Except twice, he came in the company of Auntie Shama. He would sit in the corner and observe quietly as though unsure what standing he had with me under the circumstances and whether he'd managed to elevate that standing. Determined to find out, he'd come visiting solo on one occasion, pulled a chair close and asked, "How are you?"

"Fine." I couldn't muster any hate at that time, and I didn't care to. "Thanks for your help," I said. "My aunt told me what you did, that you helped bring me here."

"No need. I did it for your aunt. I did it for you. It was done out of love."

I wasn't prepared to go that far and the quickness with which Alexandre invoked love vexed me. I pretended tiredness and sleep, so that we could not converse further. The next time he came alone, he brought a box of chocolates. "Thanks," I said. "But you shouldn't have bothered. You've done more than enough."

This emboldened him to reach out a hand to touch my arm as a sign of affection, but I stopped him. "Please don't," I said.

"Shama," he said, "I know you know I've done some bad things, some very bad things. I know you may never be able to forgive me. I can't blame you for that. I don't know if I can even forgive myself for those... But I want you to know that I am no worse or better a human being than most. I am not trying to excuse my misdeeds. They are inexcusable. I'm just trying to put them in some context. When you are not caught in a vortex, it's easy to stand outside and judge, but anyone in the wrong circumstance is capable of horrendous acts. Some are braver than others, some are more spiritually anchored, some have more willpower than others, and perhaps that is what makes the difference, separates good ultimately from bad..."

"Please, you don't need..."

124

"Shama, please hear me out. For the vast majority of us, we better pray that we're not caught in the wrong circumstance so we don't become a pariah in the eyes of the judging. Right now, I don't know how long I have. They've started talking about some sort of tribunal that will put some of us on trial. Who knows what will happen to me? Who knows if I'll live? For now, I want to try and live a good life. I know I can't make right what I've already made wrong. I've managed to survive because for all I did, I also helped save some lives. I won't get into that now, but perhaps someday I can tell you more about that. I know you love your aunt. I can tell. I want you to know that I too have come to love her very much, to adore her, her capacity for love. I'm hoping that you will not turn her against me. I could lose everything, but the two things I don't think I can survive losing are my children and Shama."

"I will not turn her against you. It's her prerogative to love whom she pleases."

"Thank you." Once again he reached to touch my hand, but I shook my head, and he nodded his understanding and left.

Torn, I tried to consider him anew. In my mind, I could feel arms carrying me, but I knew they were not Alexandre's. He had carried me to the hospice, my aunt told me. It was on account of his connections that I enjoyed this care, this privacy in the hospice. I owed him my life (which at some level I didn't want saved anyway). Yes, I owed him, and if my aunt could forgive him, then I ought to be able to do so also. But, then, what of the crimes he'd committed? What of his murder of the innocent? His rapacious acts? If I forgave him, what freedom I would have, freedom from the abiding hatred that could stall me at every step. But if I forgave him, then I ought to be ready to forgive those who killed Papa, killed Mama, killed Placide, killed Jean Pierre and Celine, forgive those who committed those unspeakable acts against me, my body, my spirit, and my sense of self worth. How could I, on account of one man's specific noble act, paling in comparison with his other monstrous acts, let loose such a flood of forgiveness? I couldn't do it, I realized—I could not genuinely claim that I had forgiven. And so I suffered for the days when I was bedridden and had time to weigh these matters for long uninterrupted periods.

After a little over two weeks, the day before I was set to be discharged, Dr. Marquez came to see me, wearing her signature smile. My daughterly instincts told me I would rather be with Dr. Marquez than return to the chambers at my aunt's home, which would now become a tunnel leading me into the horrendous memories of what I'd done and what had been done to me. Can I stay longer? I wanted to ask Dr. Marquez. Will you be my new mother? But these were questions I only contemplated for the teasing luxury of their comforts, not for the possibility they offered. What a blow it would be to my aunt, so loving, so well meaning, to learn that I was hesitating returning to her household.

Dr. Marquez sat next to me, asking about my condition, calling me "my child," repeatedly, which might have sounded patronizing except when Dr. Marquez said it. I in turn assured the doctor that I was well, thanked her for her help and support and assured her that I would never forget her kindness. It had been a pleasure doing it, the doctor assured. Now looking a little concerned, Dr. Marquez said, "I've been talking with your aunt." My sense of impending trouble was assuaged when she added, "She tells me you just got your bachelor's." When I acknowledged this, the doctor went on, "How wonderful. I have two daughters myself, both have finished college also, twins. One is a teacher and the other is on a trip in Europe, discovering herself I suppose. After they left home, I was beginning to get a bit bored. My practice in the US is fine, but I needed change after so many years. That's when I volunteered my services. I thought about the Peace Corps, Medicines Sans Frontier. But I had a very good friend who worked for CARE and he suggested they could use my services in Kenya." She said CARE did not usually accept such volunteers, preferring instead to use local hands, but they were in dire need of some additional medical help. "So I packed bag and luggage and went over to Kenya, to a refugee camp, actually a number of them in the dessert called Dadaab. Oh, Shama, it was the most fulfilling time of my professional life, helping so many people in such dire circumstances. I had come to Rwanda a couple of times to assist CARE with its maternal care program. It was during one such visit that I met Alexandre Nsengiyumva. We became friends, as he seemed genuinely interested in my work. We would have long talks in the evenings. But with the state of affairs after the president's death, we had to suspend CARE's activities in

126

Rwanda briefly. I went back to Kenya for a while and returned after the RFP took over."

"But how about your husband?" I asked. "Did he remain in America?"

"My husband passed a few years ago."

"I'm sorry."

"Oh, don't be silly. Anyway, the reason I tell you all this is I want you to know a little bit about me because I want to help you. I have come to really like you. You have a special quality about you. Not only are you beautiful on the outside but you have a beautiful spirit as well. As a doctor I have met so many people, and I think I've learned to judge people pretty quickly. Anyway, I want to tell you about this group I came across when I was in Kenya, the World University Service of Canada. It has a refugee program that brings student refugees from other countries to Canada. If you are interested, I will offer you up for consideration. They could place you in a university in Canada where you could get your master's or doctorate if that's what you want. Would you like that?"

Where was this suddenly coming from? I, expecting to return to my aunt's house and suffer in the blood soaked memories of my recent past, now being offered a chance to flee from the proximate spur of those memories. "Yes, I'd really like that. But will they consider me, since I am not a refugee?"

"We'll never know till we try. Besides, your aunt tells me the recent massacres have orphaned you. I think we can make a case for you."

Let the case be made then.

It was with this hope that I left for my aunt's home. But even such hope couldn't completely erase the difficulty of facing that house again. My heart sunk deep as if falling into my stomach and I felt my knees weakening the way the liquor had done to me immediately before I let flow the stream of blood, and it appeared the events of the day were being replayed—here I was, standing in the living room, bottle in hand, coat hanger in another; here I was walking into the bathroom…. I felt so faint I had to sit and drink water. My chest beating strongly, I listened to my aunt welcome me home gladly and serve me a meal of rice and beans. I drew strength from her presence as she embraced me with the talk of happiness at the return of her beloved niece. Alexandre stopped by a little later to express his gratitude to God that I was back. He gave me another box of chocolates and told me to rest so I could regain my full strength. Perhaps realizing that the women would want to be alone, perhaps sensing my reluctance to embrace him fully, he didn't stay long.

I went to bed afraid of what the night would offer me (and I had tried to stay up with Auntie Shama as deeply into the night as the older woman would last). But at last, facing the moment of dread, I lay in bed and closed my eyes reluctantly. And dreadful it was, starting with Jean Pierre, then the church as we waited, and then the slaying of Papa, Mamà, Placide, and Celine. It continued with the physical erosion of my being and the spiritual dispiriting that accompanied it. It ended with the.... I could not bring myself to label what had been done to my body or what I'd most recently done to it. And then it started again. I had drunk just a little water that night, afraid to fill my bladder. But now came another dreaded moment when, unable to hold the pressure any longer, I had to visit the bathroom to pee.

I walked very slowly, a step gingerly taken one at a time, afraid that some force unknown would walk up on me to do harm for what I'd done, afraid that something would come floating in the air to strangle me or with accusatory hands point me to the pits of doom. Be doomed. Be doomed. Be doomed. Voices rang in my ears. I stood still for a while, trying hard to still the voices, quiet them with the willpower I needed to summon to stay sane. Teeth grated, hands made into fists, I moved on, unclenched one hand, and stepped into the bathroom, turning the lights on immediately to confront the emptiness. Yet, the images I was sure I'd see were not there—just the spaces that echoed those images from yesterday. I was almost disappointed, relieved disappointment if I could label it.

I pushed my urine out as hard and quickly as I could and, still filled with fear, rushed back to the bedroom. This would continue for the rest of the time when I stayed in the house. Even in the daytime, I hurried to do what I needed done there in the bathroom in order to avoid its mentally framed possibilities. I avoided looking into the bathroom mirror.

Amid this struggle, I clung to the hope that Dr. Marquez had offered, continued to offer. I visited Dr. Marquez three times in a week and learned that CARE was consulting with World University Service to consider me. It was on the fourth visit a week after the last that my hopes were raised even higher. Dr. Marquez introduced me to an even older man: Professor Curt Bailey, a professor of sociology at Northwestern University in Evanston, Illinois. The white haired professor shook my hand and said, "Gracia speaks very highly of you. She's in love with you, you know. And now that I see you, I can understand why."

Professor Bailey and I spoke for almost an hour, an engrossing conversation in which we covered my background (and I boldly, without sentimentality or tears, told him of my educational background, my graduation at the top of my class, and the demise of my parents). We focused on my degree and what else I might be interested in pursuing. I assured him I would like to continue my education. "Will you be interested in a doctorate degree in sociology?"

I said I would be interested.

"Good" said the professor. "I have a lot more influence in the sociology department than any other."

"Am I reading you correctly, sir, that..."

"I am asking you to apply to my department, the sociology department. I'll have forms mailed to Gracia so she can get them to you. Apply as soon as you can."

"I will, sir. Thank you so much."

"No need to thank me. You've done it yourself. I have only one favor to ask of you."

"Anything, sir."

"I'm here for only a week. I don't know Kigali. Would you by my guide and show me around?"

"I don't know Kigali very well myself, sir, but I will be glad to. That is, if you don't mind getting lost every now and then."

"That will make it even more fun."

It was during those times together, when I took directions from my aunt as to places to go that I discovered Kigali just as much as Professor Bailey, that I got to learn more about the older man. Even when we visited areas, including the Avenue du Commerce, Mille Collines, Moslem Quarter, that had been decimated or dampened in spirits by recent events, our conversations kept us both energized. A married man of over twenty years, with two children, he'd grown up in Chicago, attended high school on the city's South Side and won a scholarship to Stanford University, where he completed his bachelor's and doctorate degrees. He'd then moved back to Chicago, started teaching at Northwestern University, gotten married, become tenured, had kids, and risen through the ranks. "I've always wanted to come back to the motherland," he informed me. "But time was always a problem, you know. With the wife and the kids, teaching, I never thought I would find the time to come. I've known Gracia for a long time, since our time together on the board of trustees of a not for profit organization. When she same here, I said to myself this is the time to do it. So I packed and told my wife I got to go. I came to Kenya, but I couldn't come all this way without seeing Gracia. And then when I arrived she said I just had to meet you. She said she'd treated you for some stomach infection and that you were so charming and intelligent with a compelling personal story to boot. I haven't known you long, but I am convinced she is right."

"You are very kind, sir."

"No, Shama, you have something about you that only comes from God. Safeguard it. Don't ever lose it."

How could I lose something I myself couldn't identify?

I found my brief time with the professor refreshing. I admired his gentleness, the way he seemed to take pleasure in everything, even in things as ordinary as a car horn and his comment that it could jar anyone taking a cherished siesta to the fact that life was passing by, the manner he would sip from a cup of tea as if each drop was the sweetest, most savory thing he'd ever tasted, or the horselaugh that accompanied his conversations which seemed inconsistent with his gentle nature. I wished he would stay longer, become a father to me, for I had become very fond of him and could see myself spending long periods with him, learning from him. I wanted to, but it was he who appeared hungry to learn from me, to ask my point of view on anything. *What do you think* became a refrain to his conversation, and even when he offered an alternative point of view, he did it in the most inoffensive manner, speaking as if he was apologetic. He wanted to know what I thought of Americans, about African Americans, whether blacks all over the world could realistically be expected to return to Africa someday, the conflicts marking the hotspots of the world, on international cooperation and its limitations. The topics seemed endless and I felt challenged and valued, digging deep to frame and articulate opinions I hadn't realized I had: I admired America for its power, African Americans for their tenacity, other Africans in the Diaspora for their industriousness.... I felt I was living, that there was a wider world outside of my own that needed discovering and for this I hungered to go to the US more than ever. The glow simmering within me was slightly dimmed, however, when on one of my walks with Prof. Bailey, I thought I saw in the corner of a street my old friend Chantel. We made eye contact and, for seconds, held the gaze. Then I moved toward her and, I could swear on this, like a mirage, she seemed to vanish into thin air as I got closer; although it's possible she just turned the corner. "What's wrong?" Prof. Bailey asked me. I'm sure he saw the puzzled expression on my face that bespoke worry.

"Nothing," I said.

"Are you okay?"

"Don't worry, professor; I'm fine."

He didn't push me, but I knew I'd not given him sufficient assurance, although what assurance could I have given him? I would wonder if I'd seen a ghost. As it were, I never again saw Chantal, whether in apparition or physical form. Perhaps she lived into old age or perhaps she perished in the genocide like countless others, forgotten. A memory to grow faint over time and perhaps disappear. This made me think of Delphine. What happened to her? I never found out.

I took comfort in Prof. Bailey's presence.

So it was with sadness that I bid the professor farewell when he left Kigali. When the application forms from Northwestern University arrived as Prof. Bailey had promised, I filled them as quickly as I could without sacrificing meticulousness, weighing every word, every sentence, making sure my English was grammatically perfect. I then added a letter, as advised by Prof. Bailey, asking that the admissions committee waive the graduate entrance exams on account of financial hardship and my academic excellence. Prof. Bailey sent word that he would weigh in with the admissions committee with his own recommendation.

I now could only wait, anxious in that disturbing period when, although confident that I would gain admission, still contained ample doubt filled with the *what ifs* that exhaust imagination and body and

## Fifteen

It was during this time that my aunt informed me that as much as she was proud of me, she was very worried of being alone. "Do you want me to stay?" I asked.

"Oh, no. I can't live with myself if you do that. When you are admitted, I want you to go. But I tell you that I am afraid of being alone because I am indeed. I need someone with me."

"But you have always been by yourself."

"That was before. Those were different times. I don't think I can do it again. Not after all that has happened."

"I won't go if you are so afraid."

"You will go, Shama. But what I'm trying to tell you is that Alexandre and I are getting married."

I was still opposed to the relationship. I had tried my best to forgive Alexandre, but I couldn't—not the way forgiveness ought to be given. I had in the past few weeks tried hard to move beyond the man's acts as Auntie Shama had described them to me, his involvement in the genocide, and whenever I felt I was on the verge of forgiveness, I would encounter the memories of the past and I couldn't. So I had resigned myself to accommodating him as best as I could for my aunt's sake, even though I still detested that my aunt was consorting with her rapist. I had declared my truce, eager not to fight the previous battle of omission I had embarked on against him. And in recent times I was not so hasty to leave the house when he visited, and I marveled that (at least according to my aunt and as far as I could observe myself), they still refrained from carnal knowledge of each other. Perhaps the man loved my aunt after all. If the two of them wanted to marry, who was I to stand in the way?

"Are you sure of this, Auntie?" I asked.

"I am absolutely sure."

"You are not doing it just to have someone and not be alone?"

"That is part of the reason, but I have also grown very fond of him."

"And his wife and children?"

"They are divorced. The children will continue to live with their mother. Of course, they will visit from time to time."

"Congratulations," I said to Auntie Shama, but I couldn't add that I was happy for her.

"You approve?"

"Yes," I lied. "I approve."

"You are the best thing that has happened to me, do you know that?"

"Oh, Auntie, and what would I have done if I hadn't found you?"

All they were concerned about was the proper civic registration of the marriage, without needing to worry about the consent of extended family members. Given the circumstance, they decided to forgo all the long traditions of a marriage, especially with death having claimed so many relatives in the genocide. They would marry in a manner as they designed. Still, they had a church wedding, with Auntie Shama looking glorious in a simple white wedding gown. But she was even more stunning when she changed into a *mushanan* for the reception held in the front lawn of the residence of an aunt of Alexandre's, the silky long skirt and shoulder draping sash of the golden colored *mushanan* sitting on and around Auntie Shama's skin as if in a soft embrace. Alexandre looked quite charming in his white suit, and they both projected a sense of the regal seated in their leopard print patterned tent at the reception.

There were only about fifteen attendees at the church, consisting of only close family and friends, with the reception attracting ten more, including Dr. Gracia Marquez. "I just got word from Professor Bailey," she told me when she arrived at the reception. "He tells me that you have been accepted into the doctorate program in sociology at Northwestern University."

Something surreal and beyond joy seized me. "Are you serious?"

"He says they've just sent you a letter to my attention. We should be getting it shortly. They'll be offering you a scholarship, but you will need to do some work-study to supplement that. Professor Bailey says he will arrange for you to be his research assistant...."

When had I stopped listening? The remainder of what Dr. Marquez said became a backdrop sound. The joy had become a seizing rush of scarlatorial intensity. I was hugging Dr. Marquez in one instant, dancing across the room to hug my aunt in the other instant. Filled with

134

the buoyancy of the moment, as though part of a linear progression of my state of joy, I hugged Alexandre for the first time. And I hugged him hard and long, so hard that he, in a spirit of gratitude, ordered a drink and, taking a sip of the firewater, toasted to, "My niece!" I too, in the recalcsence of my heart, toasted with orange juice to, "My aunt and my uncle." And I felt unleashed for the rest of the evening to dance with Alexandre, and others, and for the first time in a very long time, I could look forward to the future with unburdened hope and confidence.

The letter arrived a couple of weeks later. The only problem was the plane ticket. Where was I going to find the money? Alexandre, learning of the predicament, procured the ticket for me. "I am grateful, but where did he get the money?" I asked my aunt.

"He says he has connections," Auntie Shama said. She smiled at me. "I am so proud of you, Shama," she said.

I had no doubt about that. "Thanks," I said. "But, Auntie, if I may confess, as I start this new journey I sometimes wonder whether I am equipped for it. I have big flaws."

"Who doesn't, Shama? But I believe in you. I believe you are meant to achieve great things. You have that quality about you. A great person without flaws is like an ocean without fish—empty, even if it is vast. It is not having flaws that makes or unmakes greatness; it is how those flaws are managed that determines it. Be sure to remember that."

So came the time for me to leave for the United States of America, at a time when I'd regained all the weight I lost in Butare. America was known for innovation and renovation. The past was the past, I would like to believe. I would leave it in Rwanda. Even if it continued to try to follow me, I would fight it on neutral land. I told myself that I had to find a way to channel the anger left in me because it would otherwise be soundless bombastic fury, dead as a voice without echo.

# One

What she would be like and whether I could find favor with her occupied my mind so much that I could barely sleep. Not that Fiona had given me reason to be so (dis)inclined, but it was jarring to receive, without expecting it, the phone call from the woman who could become my future mother-in-law, whose son had been reluctant to reveal details about her, except to assert that she was a brilliant person at all levels, including as a lawyer. That's what I found most worrisome—the lawyer part—which usually conjured images of a litigant in court battle cross-examining a hostile witness. I'd cringed at the adversarial tone of lawyers on TV shows and movies and, unfairly I knew, developed a mild distaste for litigation lawyers (at least as I'd seen them through the distilled images of motion pictures). When I'd mentioned this to Juju, he'd laughed and said, "Uh, oh, brace yourself for Mom. She's a combatant alright."

The closest person in his family Juju said had knowledge of our relationship was his sister. He'd given me her phone number and made me promise to call if I needed anything. "She's really cool," Juju had said. I'd thought about calling her in several lonely moments, craving for another form of connection to Juju as a way of knowing him more, gleaning as much as I could about him. But I worried that I'd say the wrong thing to her, perhaps even antagonize her. I'd worried that she might not like my accent. I'd worried and not called. I'd put the piece of paper aside, that numerical equivalent of Juju's invitation to friendship with his sister. And it remained a mere assurance residing in the back of my mind that Juju's sister was within easy reach and that someday soon I would make the connection. And six months had already elapsed since Juju left. And now, instead of the cool sister, I had to contend with the obscure, litigant-mother.

Trying to unburden my mind of this smothering worry, I pulled out a family photograph that Juju had given me before he left, together with three notebooks of material that he claimed was written by his father, Jojo, a diary or memoir of sorts. I preferred to call them his notebook-diary. Juju had said it would help me understand his father better and perhaps also help me understand him better. Parts of it were noticeably torn out. I had tried to read it, but each time I opened it and saw the handwriting of

Juju's father on the pages, I felt as if I was intruding into something that wasn't meant for me. And the best I could do was hold the notebook from time to time without reading it, except for one time when I had breached this stalemate and read its opening pages in search of some form of assurance I couldn't quite explain. And the first few pages had such a poignant motif of death and a rather negative reference to Fiona that I cringed. The photograph seemed friendlier.

So instead of returning to the notebook, I reexamined the family photograph, trying to remember the exact words Juju had used to describe each one of them, which in my recollection mixed with my own impressions so that I wasn't even sure which was Juju's and which my own: the seated Papa (Jojo Badu)—the gray in his hair palpable, his slightly excess weight showing in his slightly pudgy cheeks—was a good but distant man, perhaps timid (a word that made me wonder whether this was a genetic trait bequeathed from father to son), who had died from unclear causes that the pathologist labeled natural; the standing Mom (Fiona Harris Badu) – beautiful in her youth and still beautiful (in her later years), as slim as her son, smiling in a way that accentuated the fierceness of her stare through narrowed eyes and a face dominated by high cheek bones and deep dimples and an almost aquiline nose, hovering over the seated father as if she was ready to unseat her husband in a way that belied the hand she'd placed on his shoulder, and whom Juju had called tough; and then the cool one, the sister (Ama Badu) standing on her mother's left (with Juju on the right), as slim as her mother, but without the fierceness of expression, in fact almost inheriting her father's rotund cheeks, and fully reflecting the dimples of her mother.

Studying the photograph with Fiona's impending visit in mind, I looked harder at the elder woman of the family, searching for signs of kindness, receptivity, anything to put me at ease. I couldn't hold my disappointment unchecked when I couldn't find any such sign. I had to find an outlet, but which?

Seeking assurance in a nervousness that perplexed me, I started searching for Ama's phone number. To subdue my nervousness, I affirmed the opinion that Juju gave me his sister's number as a way to connect us, in fact, as a request for me to take the initiative to call her. I liked to think of Ama Badu for the moment as Juju's female half, even as I hoped to assume that role some day.  If Ama possessed the selflessness and kindness (or even half of it) that Juju had showed, then she too would be worth knowing, even worth befriending.

After thirty minutes of searching for the paper Juju had given me with his sister's number without success, I acquiesced to the reality that I'd have to face Fiona without the hoped for assurance I could have teased out of a phone conversation with Ama.

I next looked for relief in the conversation that had triggered such anxiety, and to think that almost a week had passed since it happened on that Sunday afternoon when my phone rang and I hesitated to answer it, not recognizing the number on the caller ID.  But bored at the time with my studies and wishing that it wasn't a crank call I'd picked it up in expectation that it would bring some relief from the tension in my head from hours of reading.

"Is this Shama?"

My first instinct was to hang up, this question betraying the fact that this wasn't someone I knew first hand, indicating that the caller was fishing rather than asserting.  For a brief while I thought it might be some salesperson hoping to market a product to me, but even those salespersons had become too sophisticated to ask such a blatant question.  Besides, the question had such self-assurance and vocal poise that I concluded it was no crank call.  After also considering that the voice was feminine, I was less inclined to dismiss it outright.  The caller must have worried that I was on the brink, given the seconds that elapsed without a response.  Even over the distance, with the relative anonymity, were responses and therefore characters being weighed or judged?

"Shama," the voice said, "are you there?"

"Yes?" I replied, hoping I had neither revealed nor confirmed my identity by responding in the form of a question, hoping to play the caller's terse game in a way that would allow me to withdraw if I got uncomfortable.  But with my name repeated and with that assured voice that had already established intimacy between *caller* and *called* in a way that left called uncomfortable considering that caller knew more about me, at least the detail of my name, than I knew of the caller, I was somewhat weighed down by the reticence of the caller, the silence, except a sigh that followed my response.  "Who are you?"  I knew immediately I asked this

139

that I'd ceded the upper hand to the caller, revealed a curiosity by the tone of my voice. I was beginning to believe that this was no ordinary caller.

"This is Fiona," came the response in due time that seemed neither too long nor too short.

Fiona. The name but not the person that had become intimate to me, memorized when Juju told me his mother's name, re-memorized when he gave me the family photo. And yet I could not make the connection, did not expect and therefore would not conclude, or even think it, that the mother would call me. And now faced with this name and the silence that followed, I was begging to succumb to the anger that was beginning to lurk in a way that would cede no more control to this caller, more so when I realized that I could not hung up. Curiosity held sway. "Fiona who?" I asked, unable to disguise my wish to show the anger that I inserted in my voice.

"Fiona. Fiona Badu."

And suddenly I made the connection that I knew I should have made at the first mention of the name Fiona. After all, I knew no other Fiona. After all, the name was now as intimate to me as Juju's. And I felt my world shimmering with worsened anxiety. My voice now shook. "Juju... Juju's mother. Juju's mother?"

"Yes, I presume he mentioned me to you."

"Yes, ma'am, he did..."

"Good." But now the caller, Fiona Badu, no longer toyed with pauses, perhaps satisfied that I was willing to speak. "How are you?"

I thought I responded I was well, but my heart beat so strongly I wasn't sure how coherently I sounded. And then I heard the words, "Great. How are things up there in Chicago?"

"Well..." I searched vainly to find a topic that might interest Juju's mother and I was immediately grateful when the older woman continued to speak.

"Listen, I know I called out of the blue and you weren't expecting it. I got your number from Ama. I hope I can take a few minutes of your time?"

"Oh, yes... yes, ma'am."

"I understand you and my son have gotten close. Or, let me put it this way, I understand that you were seeing him before he left for Ghana."

140

Was Fiona subjecting me to some form of cross-examination in the quest for damaging information or was this a friendly line of questioning? Was it the beginning of a forthcoming attack?

"Well… I was seeing him… I mean he and I were… We were…."

"Do you hear from him?"

I thought this question odd, but I could find no escape from it. "Yes, I do ma'am."

"Good," Fiona said. "Listen, I don't want to take too much of your time, but I will be in town next week. I would very much love to meet with you. Of course, that is if you have the time."

I wanted to meet Juju's mother. It would be an honor. But the request seemed so unusual, was so unexpected, I was afraid it had some hidden agendum. Was the older woman disapproving of the relationship? Did she want to break us apart? Or, even if she had no such motive, was I ready for her? Would I meet with the approval of the matriarch without Juju present to umpire the meeting?

"Uuumm…."

"I promise not to take too much of your time," Fiona said.

Did I have a choice? "I will be glad to meet you, ma'am," said I.

"Great. I have your address. Ama gave it to me. I will pick you up for dinner seven-ish next Saturday. I can't wait to meet you in person, Shama."

"I am looking forward to meeting you, ma'am."

"Call me Fiona. See you on Saturday."

*Call me Fiona.* The relief I was able to eke out of this short conversation wasn't much, considering the tension that had otherwise characterized it. Fully aware that no matter how hard my efforts, I'd have to wrestle the lion called worry until the meeting was over, my new resolution became to woo the woman who'd mothered Juju. That I would be so blessed twice in my life flooded me with brief comfort, since after Jean Pierre I'd never believed I could love another so fiercely, find someone to whom I could surrender my sacred parts, and had resigned myself to a loveless fate—until I arrived in the US and met Juju. Thinking of it now, my relationship with Juju seemed so normal, so far from where I'd been when I arrived from Rwanda. Thinking of that day seldom failed to inspire me. I reached back.

Professor Bailey himself had arrived at O'Hare to meet me, his wife Anna at his side. In one instant I was being overwhelmed by the drudgery of bureaucracy, the demeaning questioning about my business in the US as though I were some scavenger, at best a nuisance to be tolerated. I had endured the hard stares that I would take to signal my otherness when I most wanted to shed all that was different in a way that would make me belong (at the same time as I didn't want to surrender my core).

"I'm here on a valid visa," I'd say again and again to the question "What's the purpose of your visit?" This isn't a visit, I wanted to say. This is the second part of a journey, can't you see? Patience, Shama, patience, I kept telling myself from point to point until I cleared Customs and walked to the baggage claim area.

And then in the next instant I was sandwiched in the embracing arms of Prof. Bailey for a minute, at least, and then for a shorter time in the arms of Anna Bailey who was saying, "Curt has told me so much about you."

"My wife insisted we bring you these," Prof. Bailey said as he presented me with a stem of roses.

Unleashed from the placid facelessness of immigration to the glowing embrace of the Baileys, flower in hand, I nearly breached a promise I'd made to myself to remain calm under all circumstances. I managed the relief and joy by breathing in deeply, but I could scarcely dwell on the makeshift sangfroid as I was escorted through lanes of bodies, airport restaurants and shops and bookstores, and escalators, all a seemingly endless labyrinth of the mammoth O'Hare Airport. After a chorus of "welcome" from Anna Bailey (she must have said it at least ten times) and questions about my trip and whether I was comfortable, and how tired I must be, we were off on the highway, paying tolls, existing toward Dempster Street, a turn here and onto Skokie Boulevard, another turn there, past a sign saying Evanston, and then a little more of a drive and then onto a quiet drive as we finally came to a stop in front of a Victorian house. "We're home!" Prof. Bailey exclaimed.

What I noticed most when we entered the house was the photograph on the family room wall of the Baileys, including their two sons.

142

And here it was indeed. Apart from adjusting to the food and the new environs, I could barely tell I was in a different country—that is, whenever I was at home with the Baileys. As their children had left the homestead, I was free to roam the house as I wished and to do as I pleased, respectful though of the Baileys' privacy and a keen eagerness not to abuse their hospitality. In the first week or so, the story was the same: as the Baileys left home early and returned in the late afternoon. They left me breakfast and lunch and came home to eat supper with me. Prof. Bailey gave me a book on sociology "to get you started." But I barely touched it, preferring instead to watch TV and read magazines. Within that week, Prof. Bailey took me to the sociology department to register, with my remedial classes scheduled to begin in three weeks.

When I wasn't watching TV or reading, I explored the house and slept, finding that my strength was low. Jet lag, explained Anna Bailey.

My first weekend, the Baileys decided to introduce me to Chicago: a drive along Lake Shore Drive, Lake Michigan stretching long on the side with teeming numbers jogging, sun tanning, playing sports, strolling, then a right turn onto Michigan Avenue, down the Magnificent Mile, past the John Hancock building, then on to the Loop, the Art Museum on the left, Millennium Park, Gant Park also, and then down Jackson Street to see the Willis Tower with its poking antennas. They drove me back to Lake Shore Drive to see Soldier Field, and the Museum of Science and Industry. Then we stopped at Navy Pier, where we rode the Ferris Wheel that presented the city's panoramic, majestic buildings, took pictures, ate a meal of hamburgers and strolled down the Pier's length amid large numbers of mostly thinly dressed people eating an ice cream here or a lollipop there, with the lake in view, a few boats sailing slowly on it. This seemed a city that had managed to find a great equilibrium between action and leisure, a tricky combination if you ask me.

By the time we returned to Evanston, night had fallen. "You need to explore on your own as you settle in," Prof. Bailey suggested. "This is just a little intro. There is more, much more to the city."

And I would, taking the train downtown the following week to revisit at a more leisurely pace some of the places the Baileys had showed me, in particular walking down the Magnificent Mile, venturing into the many shops that flanked Michigan Avenue and staring at prices of clothes that made me gasp. But I found that walking through Grant Park afforded me relaxation and, for that reason, I spent long hours strolling the park, leaving it late and arriving home in the aged hours of evening. I did this pilgrimage to my new city many times. If the Baileys were anxious over my absences, they didn't mention it; but I found that they'd eaten already by the time I returned home. Guilt-ridden, I shortened my stays at the park, prompting Anna Bailey to remark casually in the form of the question: "Have you broken up with your new friend that you're not spending as much time with him?"

I smiled, although I very well may have admitted guilt because indeed now that I was away from Rwanda, I realized that I could learn to love this new place, but that there were aspects of it that, despite its teeming populations, remained so impersonal it could never even approximate the casual warmth of Butare that I had taken for granted—of course, before the outbreak of hostilities. Here, I realized that everyone, even those without jobs, were on some form of business that preoccupied them—if not to work, then to panhandle in a way that had a brisk, businesslike approach to it, or to stay fit through some form of exercise that often fell prey to the consumption of large quantities of food, many fatty. Still, it had its other face where amid the bustle I found beauty; and Grant Park presented me with its allure of quiet, a form of seduction that was stealing my heart—I, a participant wanting to abandon the past to the newness in whatever form that my new environs offered even as I wanted to retain that part of me that defined me as a unique person amid the whirl of the newness. How was I to be expected, or even expect myself, to get rid of that remnant of longing for what I'd left, the familiar with all its brutality and torment, which at the same time held memories of Papa, Mama, Placide, Jean Pierre, and Auntie Shama?

And I came to believe that it was for this reason that, on the day I commenced remedial classes in sociology at Prof. Bailey's suggestion to get a "head start," my dreams returned. Days spent in class and now working as Prof. Bailey's research assistant, I could hardly find time to go downtown and I returned home in the evenings exhausted, expecting a night of complete rest. Not so, however, for I would be visited by those same images that had tortured me in Butare and in Kigali, which were exacerbated by two events that happened in the next two weeks.

The first "event" came to me unsolicited and unexpectedly. I had had Prof. Bailey contact Dr. Gracia Marquez to inform Auntie Shama that I had arrived safely and would write to her soon. I'd not expected her letter, as I was hoping to write to her after I found a place of my own. (And this reminded me I had to start searching, now that I'd started working). It was a long letter, meticulously written, covering over three pages. My aunt spent many words on how she missed me, how things could never be the same in my absence. Nevertheless, they were coping and she and Alexandre were enjoying their time as a married couple. She asked me to pray for them, for talk was beginning to escalate that many more would be tried for crimes against humanity at a tribunal in Tanzania and it appeared investigations were drawing close to Alexandre. I would never pray for that man, I vowed, even if for my aunt's sake; but for her sake and for the brief glimpses of kindness that the man had showed, I would not wish for the retribution that he deserved. That to excuse Alexandre might mean I'd have to excuse all the other perpetrators worried me so much that for minutes I could not continue reading the letter. I had to recall the times spent alone with my aunt to overcome the wearing worry. Further, my aunt told of the rebuilding of the country, but noted in parenthetical terms that the physical and psychological damage was so gross that it might take a long time to do this. Although, rather than the word psychological Auntie Shama used the phrase "damage to feelings." And then in a paragraph that stunned me, my aunt noted that despite all she'd done, her marriage to the man, when on occasion she thought of what had happened, she had this sudden urge to strangle Alexandre in his sleep or poison his food. And, despite this confession, she ended by saying that she and Uncle Alexandre sent their love. If I could reconcile the internal inconsistencies in the letter, I might have felt some relief, but the contradictions created more tension within me – and I worried. The fear that my aunt might do something rash and thereby put herself in legal jeopardy worried me. The possibility that Alexandre Nsengiyumva might even suspect her intention enough to preempt her with his own homicide haunted me. These series of worries triggered memories, those nightmares, sometimes even during the day, so that it took remarkable effort for me to control my thoughts. I wrote to Auntie Shama, telling her all would be well and that I would he in more contact once I moved to my own place. My letter didn't bring any catharsis. In the daytime, I would walk outdoors to attempt to rid my mind. In the nighttime, waking up in sweat, I would go to the living room and watch TV, usually some frivolous talk show full of profanity.

This struggle drained my energies, and Anna Bailey commented on it, wondering if I was well. How easy it would be to say no. Yet with a "no," how would I explain the ailment that afflicted me? "Yes," the answer I gave, the most expedient, didn't provide any relief, not even if Anna Bailey ignored my affirmation with the sympathy or comfort of words or hug she provided. "Homesickness is such a hard thing," she said as she held me. Strong connection, this, but scarcely enough to ease the pressures of the past.

Even more, I met Nat Musegera, and it sunk me even deeper into my ailment. That was the second event, also unexpected.

It happened on a Saturday evening when Anna Bailey asked her husband to take me to a party organized by one of the members of the faculty. "I'm not feeling so well, dear," she'd said. "Why don't you take Shama instead?"

"No!" I exclaimed. I couldn't possibly go in her stead.

But she wouldn't relent. "What do you think, Curt?" she asked.

With a wry smile, Prof. Bailey said while winking at me, "It's not always that one gets to go on a date with such a beauty. Come on, young lady. Be my date."

"It will put a smile back on your pretty face," said Mrs. Bailey. "You need to go out more."

Judging by Mrs. Bailey's earlier concern, I believed it was jointly preplanned. To think of it, I'd given them more cause to worry. At least twice Prof. Bailey had come to the living room in hours past midnight and turned off the TV, woken me up and gently suggested, "Do you want to go to bed now, dear?" Even in the dimness of the living room, with most lights off at the time, I saw the older man's expression of concern, the furrowed face, the squinting eyes. He was obviously aware that recently, my days comprised of school, work and sleepless nights, with no time to go to Grant Park. Except for short periods on the outside trying to clear

146

my head, I had no social life. I'd allowed my seducer to slip away by not allowing Grant Park to slow me down and calm the heart continuing to beat hard with concern. And much against my will, I had allowed the unleashed worries overly to manifest and the Baileys had been drawn into the bleak world I harbored around me and they had caught a glimpse and decided to act to brighten it. But, could they, despite their best intentions, even remotely approximate in thought the depth of that bleakness of death and deprivation and hollowness? Still, I decided their attempt to help ease my strains, even if ineffectual, was well intentioned enough to warrant my gratitude. And given that I'd not met many on the faculty yet, this would be an opportunity to expand my acquaintances beyond the sociology department.

So when I walked over to the venue of the party, a mere twenty minute walk from the Baileys, I had become excited, a willing participant to the ploy the Baileys had orchestrated. I was proud also to accompany the man I was increasingly admiring more, even loving—his gentleness with me as he guided my inexperienced hands through the tedium of the research assignments he gave me as his assistant (which I knew he did as a favor, not from necessity); his concern for my welfare when he had seen me sleeping in the living room, and, in recent days, the extra time he took to tutor me himself. In some ways, I was beginning to consider him as a father. And why not? He'd shown he was entirely befitting of that role, not just in *loco parentis* but as the real thing. With these thoughts in mind, I slipped my hand into his bent elbow as we stepped into the party house and were welcomed at the door by a white haired, debonair man who introduced himself as Prof. Moreno, Dean of the School of Divinity.

The place already was packed, the conversation already lively, if as leisurely as a medley of hums as is prevalent among the reserved. "Come, let me introduce you around," Prof. Bailey said after Prof. Moreno mentioned how beautiful I looked as he beckoned us to a table of drinks. I endured the usual questions and comments I got when I was introduced as a foreign student—culture shock? Miss the family back home? Notice your accent, but where did you learn to speak English so well? This and many more whenever I was introduced as recently arrived from Africa. While I'd realized that many continued to consider Africa as a country rather than a continent, I was grateful when Prof. Bailey forgetfully used

147

Africa rather than Rwanda as the point of my origin. At least Africa elicited generic questions, but with Rwanda I'd come to expect certain questions, know them even before they were asked, some being of pity or sympathy and others being of broad concern or sometimes a combination of all. Not only did it irk me that I faced such questions and their associated unsolicited emotion, the follow up questions were extremely irritating, invoking on the spot memories I struggled to contain. How was the massacre? Did I suffer any of the brutalities? How about my family? How did I get out? And sometimes the statement, or a variation of it: So sorry what happened in your country. I'd developed an armor of monosyllabic responses: Okay; No; Fine; Scholarship. Perhaps Prof. Bailey had realized this, which might explain why he'd resorted to Africa rather than Rwanda. Could the man be that sensitive?

I was beginning to enjoy myself in the midst of a group of professors who were making small chatter and who seemed charmed by me, one of whom even remarked in echo to Prof. Moreno's earlier comment, how lucky Prof. Bailey was to have such a sharp lady for an assistant, although another professor who seemed to be in a hurry somewhere stopped by the group and asked Prof. Bailey, "Does Anna knows you're here with your assistant?"

"Hmm," Prof. Bailey replied, "I hope she never finds out," and then proceeded to kiss me on the cheeks. The inquirer blushed so brightly that for a moment I thought he might collapse. And then he quickly left.

Prof. Bailey took my hand and said, "Oh, let me introduce you to Jack."

Prof. Jack Lee was a strikingly young man (or rather youngish looking man), no more than thirty-five, I guessed, with a face that looked ten years younger. In a way I couldn't explain, I was drawn to him, his unassuming posture, although I was somewhat surprised by his American accent (and I mentally chastised myself not to stereotype by expecting Asians to speak with a different accent). Or perhaps I felt betrayed that a man I so inexplicably admired at first sight did not speak as I did with an accent that was *foreign*.

He asked the rare question: "Which country in Africa?"

Tempted as I was to lie about this, I couldn't. And so I answered, "Rwanda."

148

"Have you met Nat yet?" Prof. Lee asked me, just at about the time when someone had diverted Prof. Bailey's attention.

"Nat?"

"Yeah, Nat. He's also from Rwanda. Great guy. You'll like him. He's around here somewhere. Come on, let's go find him."

I hesitated. Nat who? I wanted to ask, but refrained as I did not want to soil the brewing friendship (or so I hoped) with Prof. Lee, who was already moving away, expecting me to follow. I did, despite my apprehension.

A man was chatting vociferously with a group of three when Prof. Lee walked up to him and announced, "Nat, I found a countrywoman of yours. Meet Shama."

And then I was face to face with Nat. He must have noticed, tried as I did to contain myself, that my face bore boldly that imprimatur of distress. Nat had a remarkable resemblance to Alexandre, so uncannily that in a foolish thought, I considered whether Alexandre had followed me from Rwanda. Why had Prof. Lee done this? I questioned. Did he not realize the risk involved? In one second or so, the night at the church, the fall of Mama, Papa, Placide, Jean Pierre, and Celine were relived with blinding intensity, coupled with all that Alexandre had inflicted on my aunt. But Nat must have resolved not to let the awkwardness linger. "Nat Musegera," he said, extending his hand.

My hand shook as I reluctantly extended my hand to shake his. "Shama Rugwe," I said, but without hesitation I added, "Excuse me, I need to use the bathroom." And then I walked away to find the bathroom. I felt faint with anger: anger at Prof. Lee for introducing me to him, anger at Nat Musegera for being Hutu (I was sure of this ethnicity from the little I'd seen) and anger at myself for being so weak, for allowing the prejudices of the past to continue to shadow me and so easily overcome me and haunt me. And being in the bathroom so soon after meeting Nat, I began to recollect that day in my aunt's bathroom… This recollection was like embalming myself with dread, for I felt transported so that the Moreno bathroom became transformed to the bathroom of that day and I knew I had to leave it immediately or risk losing consciousness. But to leave the bathroom meant being in possibly close proximity of Nat Musegera.

I walked out quickly to find Prof. Bailey to inform him that I wasn't feeling so well and had to return home. He insisted he'd accompany me back despite my protestations. "Is everything okay, Shama?" he asked on the way back. I said everything was. "You know you can always come to me if you want to talk about anything. Or, if you prefer, you can talk to Anna. We are here for you. Anytime."

"I know. Thank you. I appreciate all that you're doing for me, but I really am okay. It's just that I've had a hard time sleeping at times and it affects my day and sometimes I feel tired all of a sudden." I knew he didn't entirely believe my explanation, but didn't want to pry too much.

"I wasn't expecting you back so soon," Anna said when she saw us. "Is everything alright?"

"I wasn't feeling so good," Prof. Bailey said to my astonishment; and I could discern Anna's disbelief. I pondered why he'd said this. Was it to cover for me because he believed my lie would sound insultingly false to Anna?

The night was difficult, like many of the previous nights, only exacerbated by the meeting with Nat Musegera. I didn't want it so, but I couldn't rid myself of the unwelcome hatred developed so quickly for the man. Perhaps, I explained to myself, somewhere deep within me, I'd come to associate him—made him a proxy—for all that had happened to me in Rwanda. I knew I had to find a way to deal with him, but I didn't know how.

Temporary relief came, however, when the Mike Bailey, the younger of the Bailey children, came visiting. He could only spend two days. Still, it was a remarkable visit. More of a masculine version of his mother than he resembled his father, he displayed a combination of the best of them in intelligence and demeanor. Only a year out of college, he was working in an advertising agency in Boston while in his words he "figured out what to do with the rest of my life." He was a force, I thought, the first instance I saw him. I'd expected a handshake when we were introduced and extended a hand, but he opened his arms and enfolded me in an embrace devoid of reservation. "Dad has told me so much about you," he said, immediately referring to me as "sister." My guard went on the defensive when he inquired about my adjustment, my

150

classes; but he refrained from the more offensive of the stereotypical questions to which I'd become accustomed, especially those nagging ones about the Rwandan genocide. Instead, he was the one who introduced me to a pictorial history of the Baileys, searching and retrieving from the basement long forgotten photos of the family, especially when it was much younger. So he showed me his younger self, as well as those of his parents and his older brother Jason, a professor of mathematics in a Northeastern university. This way, I saw the young Mike Bailey, slightly heavier, in all poses, always seemingly at ease. And there were photos of the parents also, un-grayed and thinner, the nephews and the cousins. In the little free time I had, it was Mike who took me to the beach in Evanston, where we walked and talked for hours—and that we were so close in age made for easier communication, even if he jestingly tried to correct my accented words. He bought me lunch and dinner, and took me to see a movie.

His mind was a bonanza of jokes, able to muffle pain with humor. Whenever I recalled something he'd said, I smiled no matter my situation. For example, he had, with a serious expression, ask me, if I thought I could speak English well, to tell him the past tense of shit. As uncomfortable as I was with this topic, I told him "shat," but he insisted it was "shitted." He told me that his pet peeve was those who farted in church and he'd once told his pastor to preach against it as it made others in prayer lose their concentration. He told me that he would never engage in premarital sex. When I applauded him for his vow of chastity, he replied, "Who said anything about chastity? I will never engage in premarital sex because I'm never getting married.

Those few days were filled with activity and in hindsight I realized that even when they were doing nothing, the force of Mike Bailey's energies seemed to set things in motion, to create the illusion that he was doing something and in the process making others do something as well. As much as the days were occupied, they were also filled with seeds of refreshment, steeped as it were in his calm (if forceful) demeanor, seeds that I would harvest when he left, the harvest bountiful, for I was able to put at bay the sleeplessness and anxiety for a while. And my energy returned, sustained by frequent phone calls to Mike, whom I had also started calling *bro*.

## Two

Although they protested, I moved out of the Bailey residence when school opened. I resolved I would no longer impose. As afraid as I was of living alone, I decided that I had to begin to establish some form of independence in order to grow in my new environs without being handheld. Psychologically, I couldn't stay dwarfed by the past in the illusion that the Baileys' presence with me in one household, especially at nights, could hold at bay the strains of my past. And the first few days alone were extremely difficult for me as the nightmares threatened a full return, which I managed to hold at some distance with frequent phone calls to Mike Bailey and with as much study and work as I could. And I seemed to be attaining some balance where the garish images lurked always and sometimes burst into my imagination and dreams, but not with as much ferocity or frequency or draining impact as before.

This tolerable balance would come unhinged when I next encountered Nat Musegera. I was in the library reading when he came over and sat opposite me. I began to breathe heavier, staring, I believed, rudely; but at that moment I didn't care. We were antagonists in a long tale that I desired to be bereft of parley or civility.

"I know we met under... under forced circumstances," he was saying. "I don't know your circumstances, but perhaps we can get to know each other better, ease whatever it is about me that is troubling you."

Troubling you? How presumptive, I thought, even though I realized my reaction at the party exacted that conclusion. But even if true, it enraged me that he would on his own volition invade my space to express it.

"What do you say?" he asked. "Lunch?"

"I'm busy," I muttered, rather than said.

"Perhaps another time?"

I stared at him, not speaking further; and Nat Musegera excused himself without seeming offended. "I'll see you later."

What had been held enclosed broke loose after this encounter. Why? Why? Why? When I was doing so well for the first time in such a long time, why would this man—this Hutu—intrude so offensively and lend wind to the dormant whirlwind? And so it began again: the nights

152

full of vivid images of death and graphic brutality, the days filled with their reverberating recollections. I would sometimes feel so drained and troubled during the day that for the first time I developed a habit of drinking coffee, which gave me boosts as well as lows. I barely functioned—just going through my days' activities without full involvement. I tried to overcome the power the man wielded over my life by asserting again and again that I was stronger than this susceptible creature I had become, that Nat Musegera was irrelevant to me, that perhaps he was even a good man—as I suspected he might be, even on the first day we met when my reaction had been so viscerally negative. No use. These mental assertions could not withstand the torrent of images. It helped a little when I spoke with Bro. Mike, who kept reassuring me; but the distance, the lonesomeness in my apartment, rendered difficult my wish to reclaim the calm I'd enjoyed from his visit.

I would have to encounter Nat Musegera's solicitations three more times before he realized I wasn't amenable, even sensed my fierce animosity. Once more, he'd tried to make conversation in the library, but rebuffed him with "I have to go" and walked away.

The next time we'd met in the cafeteria. "Let me buy you lunch," he said. "You have nothing to lose."

"I'm not hungry," I said.

"But isn't that what you're here for? To eat?"

"I changed my mind."

"Over whether you're hungry?"

"Yes," I said and left the cafeteria.

The third time I was walking to class when he walked up from behind me. "You know," he said, now walking alongside me, "I don't understand the animosity here. All I am trying to do is be friendly. I don't know what I may have done that makes you behave so coldly towards me. Did I do or say something?"

"Sir," I said sternly, "Would you just leave me alone?"

He seemed stunned, even pained, by this. "Very well," he said, paused as if to collect his thoughts (or dignity), his mouth slightly opened, and then hurried away.

He never attempted to speak with me after that, except to say hello to which I seldom responded. And rather strangely to me, at the time

153

when he withdrew, my anger toward him increased to the point where I wanted to do him harm, and this anger was almost always with me, so much so that it assumed a more general character and I was wont to visit it on anyone in my sight of firing and it was very difficult for me not to express it when I interacted with Prof. Bailey. Tempt me, I wished to say to Nat Musegera, so that I may visit my fury on you in a manner that you will never forget. He didn't, making me even angrier. He had teased me, brought me to the brink and then withdrawn?

But my unrelenting anger was eased during Thanksgiving break when Mike Bailey returned to see the family. It was then that I met the older brother Jason and his wife Kamila, a sales agent for an insurance company. If Mike had inherited the parents' genes and qualities in certain variations, Jason had rejected them both. He had neither the charm nor graciousness that I associated with the Bailey's, being brusque in speech and it seemed unconcerned about me, although he did ask those dreaded questions about the Rwanda genocide that I detested. "Your brother is nothing like you," I told Mike. "Jason sings his own tune," he said. "But he is a good guy." If I were asked to pick which of the pair (Jason/Kamila) possessed the Bailey qualities and therefore goodness, I'd have chosen Kamila, who seemed to fit so easily with the family and showed as much grace toward me as any of them, even confiding on my vow of secrecy that she was pregnant,. She would tell the others in her own due time, she said. The Thanksgiving break, which I spent entirely at the Baileys, rejuvenated me. I had little time to brood anyway, being occupied, whether in helping make dinner or engaging in conversation, mostly with Mike and Kamila.

When they left and I returned to my lonesome apartment, I realized that my haunts had lingered so long and seeped too deeply that even the walls of my apartment seemed to have acquired them as a permanent (unseen) mural, filled them with visions of dead people, such that even the reservoir of calm that Mike (and Kamila) left me were insufficient. I wrestled those incorrigible haunts, but even more disturbing to me was a new pain that began to afflict me. Three nights after their departure and my return to the apartment, I woke up in the night with an agonizing pain in my belly region. At first I thought it was a belly pain and I rubbed my belly gently, but I realized that it wasn't my belly itself that harbored the pain.  Rather, the pain was coming from (or perhaps residing in) that part of my belly that had once been a part of me and belonged to me and me only until it had been severed and made a part other than of me, made all of a sudden to belong to other(s) who got rid of it so that it was no longer mine alone.  I couldn't understand this pain that emanated from me but resided outside of me, that ravaged my body without wrecking it.  I turned on the lights in my room and examined myself in the mirror.  I saw nothing out of the ordinary.  In my nudity there was no hiding of anything from my naked eyes.  And yet something seemed hidden, or rather something was there that I couldn't see, for I was convinced the pain was within a part of my body (or rather a part of my other body whose only physical remnant was the slight scar on my belly).  I took painkillers to help numb the pain, but the massive ache proved immune to numbness and remained unremitting.  I lay on my back and then on my stomach.  I showered, rubbing my belly with soap for a long time.  I massaged my belly gently and when that didn't work, I sang songs and then I cried.  With as much abruptness as the pain had appeared, it left me in the wee hours of the morning.  And I knew that I was bound to face a difficult day.

## Three

As these thoughts and recollections returned to me over the next few days after her call, I wondered hard if Fiona would come to render a Mike-effect or a Jason-effect. It helped me to categorize the potential encounter in such simple unsophisticated categories, especially under the self-comforting logic that there had to be a female equivalent of Mike that went beyond what Kamila had offered. Not that it overrode my anxiety, but it was a mind game that occupied me enough to tolerate my moments of heightened anxiety. As the days closed in, I opened the notebook-diary of Juju's father that he had given me, hoping that it would help me better understand Fiona. But again I just couldn't read on, as something close to fear seized me, warned me that I could be venturing into something dangerous, and that eavesdropping on the thoughts of the dead man was an act tantamount to sin. I put the notebook-diary down.

I wished the hours would grow longer, as those hours drew closer I wished the minutes would tick slower, and as the minutes became imminent, I wished the meeting-time would not arrive, which it didn't in a timely manner as Fiona was ten minutes.

But those excruciating minutes passed too quickly as I nervously and bootlessly fought time....

Fiona, whom I recognized immediately from the photograph Jojo had left, stopped her rented car in front of my apartment building on Maple Street, stepped outside and walked toward me as I stood by the street. I walked toward her, wearing a smile I knew was too wooden to fool her. Closer to her I noticed a few more wrinkles and gray than was evident in the photograph, but it was her presence that nearly overwhelmed me—that unquantifiable, indescribable part of the persona that imposes itself without the need for word or gesture. The introduction was more formal than I preferred, marked by a handshake that was all too brief and the words, "Shall we?" spoken after what I considered an all too perfunctory inquiry, "How are you?" So far nothing Fiona had done had eased my worry. She was no female equivalent of Mike, I concluded when I sat in the rented Jaguar. Fiona mentioned a nearby Thai restaurant and asked if I liked Thai food. I didn't read this as a question and gave the affirmative answer expected of me.

We didn't speak otherwise during the five-minute drive to the restaurant. Rather, the sounds of moving cars, honking now and then, and the drone of the car engine, served as the dialogue we withheld from each other. I was so desperate for noise to negate the absence of words that I was grateful for this mechanical intercession. After we were seated in the Thai restaurant, Fiona looked hard at me, smiled frozenly and asked if I was enjoying my course work. "Yes," I said.

"How about Evanston, do you like it."

"Yes."

"It's a charming town, isn't it?" I could fall in love with a place like this."

A lithe waitress walked to our table and asked what we planned to eat.

"Have you eaten here before, Shama?" Fiona asked. "Do you have a preference?"

It sounded strange for me to hear Fiona pronounce my name for the first time since we met in person. Despite my concerns about the meeting, this somewhat reduced the distance between us, or so I thought. "No... I..."

"Should I order for us?"

"That would be nice."

Fiona ordered panang dishes for both of us, and for the first time since she arrived (and of course the first time since I knew her), she smiled at me in a manner that reached her cheeks and caught her eyes, and immediately negated the earlier one. "You know, Shama," she said, "I was a little nervous coming here to see you. You sounded so stern on the phone I wondered if I'd made the right decision. I almost cancelled the trip, but I'm glad I didn't. Now that I've met you, I realize my concern was unfounded. I don't know you yet, not much anyway, except what Ama tells me Juju has said about you. I pride myself that I can read people. And most of the time I'm right. It's part of what I do in the courtroom—to be able to judge people right away. Anyway, what I'm trying to say is that although I don't really know you, I think I like you already."

It was difficult to believe that our reticent interactions so far could form the basis for this conclusion.

"So I understand you're studying sociology?"

"Yes, madam."

"Oh, Shama, it's Fiona, okay?"

"OK." If this was a performance for the juror, I as juror was accepting it, noticing the remarkable change in demeanor—more relaxed, as if she'd turned it on at a finger's snap, even the intonation of voice that had eased from formal to friendly.

"I usually am more subtle than this, Shama, but I'll tell you this. I came here to see you for selfish reasons. I will tell you soon what I mean, but I don't want you to be surprised and I don't want you to think I'm taking undue advantage of you."

"I don't understand."

"Patience, girl. I'll tell you soon enough." Fiona's statement cohered with a quick wink that I found endearing. She spoke much during the course of dinner, about her law practice and how she had become the first African-American managing partner of her law firm. From somewhere that must, in my estimation, come from deep within, Fiona intoned, "Don't let anyone tell you what you can and can't do. You are entitled to whatever it is in your wish to achieve. I know you might feel overwhelmed being in a different country and all, but don't let anyone or anything put you down." Fiona drew back from this as immediately as she'd ventured into it. "I didn't mean to lecture you," she said, "but I've been a personal witness to dreams battered by this system. All I wanted to say is that America belongs to us all, no matter where you were born. If you are here, you are entitled to be here."

I wanted to offer Fiona a little bit more than I'd done so far, having just seen the older woman's earnestness, and it was clear to me she was struggling to withhold herself.

"Juju tells me you went to school in Ghana?" I asked.

"Yeah, some high school and then college."

"How was it?"

"When I was younger, I hated the idea that I was growing up in a foreign country, but now that I'm older I know it was worth it. You grow as a person. I have no doubt it made me a better person."

"And your husband is from there?"

158

"Yes, he was from Ghana, although we met here. But you, I was wondering, do you have any relatives in the US?"

"No, not blood relatives, but some of the people I've met have treated me like family."

"Don't worry, we will be your family. Me and Ama. Don't hesitate to call me when you need anything or if you just want to talk."

"Seriously?"

"Certainly. If I like you, I like you."

But I wondered how much of this had to do with the self-confessed selfish reason for Fiona's visit.

It was eight o'clock by the time we ended dinner. "It's early still," Fiona said after insisting on and paying the bill. "What do you think? Get a drink?"

"I'd like to, but I don't drink?"

"Oh."

"But that's okay. You can have a drink. I'll get something soft."

"That won't be any fun. Why should I have all the fun?" Fiona smiled. "What do you do to relax? Name it and that's what we'll do."

I couldn't think of anything. Since I arrived I'd stuck with stuffy research and classes, and some TV and the earlier trips to Grant Park. None of these seemed ripe candidates for obvious reasons, except a walk—an invocation of my earlier love in Grant Park. "I don't do much, I'm sorry. I ... I like to take walks from time to time."

"Great! Let's take a walk."

We walked the streets of Evanston like new lovers, at slow pace, gaining in affection for each other over frivolous conversation. As we passed by the movie complex on Maple Street, Fiona casually asked, "Do you like movies?"

"Yes," I said, although, except for those on TV, I hadn't seen any since Mark Bailey's last visit.

"Let's see one then."

We watched a movie, which Fiona financed, about friends who faced adversities together that strengthened their bond. After the movie, we walked back to the rented car, more freely in conversation. Fiona drove back to the apartment and turned off the car's engine. She leaned back in her seat. "I need to ask..." I could sense her struggle as she

159

rubbed the top of her nose and wiped the top of her upper lip—much like the moment when a suitor is on the verge of propositioning.

"Whatever it is, it's okay," I said.

"I'm ashamed to ask this," Fiona said.

"Trust me…" I had to force myself to call her by the first name. "Trust me, Fiona," I said. "It's okay."

"It's about Juju," Fiona said.

I cringed. "Juju?"

"Yes. I know this is abrupt and it may even sound desperate, but I don't know what to do. Do you hear from him at all?"

"Yes…"

"He calls you?"

"Sometimes. We write most of the time."

"I'm glad to hear that… You know he and I have our differences, but he's not called or written me since he left. I've tried several times to get in touch with him but either I can't reach him or he won't reply to my letters. He used to be close to his sister, but even she doesn't hear from him. He's written to her only once."

"I'm so sorry to hear that."

"That's okay; it's not your fault. But, please, next time you speak or write to him tell him to get in touch with me. If he doesn't want to call, tell him to write at least. Tell him I miss him terribly. I'm going crazy…" Fiona's voice broke a little. "Tell him I need to hear from him… his mother needs to hear from him. Can you do that for me, please?"

"Yes. Absolutely."

"I appreciate that, Shama, I really do."

After Fiona left, I couldn't deny the impact she'd wrought, and with such skill she'd completely erased my reservations about her, hinted she wanted to be friends, and deposited respect and even affection. The remnants of this brief visit then were deep and seemingly unshakable as I recounted them, which, after being so close to his mother, reminded me of how much I missed Juju. And to think of it, he was very much like his mother as both created a lasting impression at first sight, even though one was outgoing and the other reserved.

Juju, the second love. But it had turned to be no less strong as the first, perhaps even stronger, for the first had been guarded in inexperience, just as much as it was grounded in certain shared knowledge and experiences of youth and its frailties that may have hampered rather than promoted our love. I'd approached the second, however, with the experience (not just from the relationship with Jean Pierre) and full import of the genocide, my own sufferings, the morphed spirit within that warned of the danger of others, especially in regards to carnal matters. But this one, even if it had carnal aspects, was farmed in unexpected and therefore more unguarded and deeper soil, which I believed gave me license to love deeply. Thinking now of Fiona, I would make more connections between her and Juju—as son loved so would mother? As mother laughed, so did son? (I would ignore the undertone of steeliness that I detected in the mother and was so glaringly lacking in the son).

When we'd first met in a chance encounter in the hallway of our apartment building, I was worried by the plagues of the night, which had come to include my phantom pain in the belly region, of which I was too ashamed to mention to anyone. How could I explain that I had a pain in the belly that was there but not a part of me? I would bear this burden alone, I vowed. It was a small price to pay for surviving the genocide when Jean Pierre, Celine and my family had perished, a small price to pay for the expulsion of that part of me that had been lying dormant in my belly, and that part of me that had been aborted at my own hands. And the moment I started making these connections, I realized that I hadn't escaped the guilt of the act in my aunt's bathroom, that it had simply assumed secondary status under the onslaught of what others had done to me (rather than what I had done to myself). But now I realized that I had come under such battering both by others and at my own hands that I wasn't even sure if I could point fingers at others without accusing myself. But even as I acknowledged this, I also realized that I wasn't ready to overcome what others had done to me, that I needed it as much as anything, that anger that allowed me to excuse myself where I might be at fault, that anger that offered me a source of release and the license to strike at others rather than myself.

Carrying these weights, I was not—or I thought I was not—amendable to notice potential love. But I couldn't ignore the man that day as we were about to walk past each other in a hallway of our apartment building. I turned when I had taken a step past him, and so did he. I saw a square face with the somewhat droopy eyes, which suggested sadness and made me want to hug him. I could detect something magnetic between us. Within me, something tugged at me, as if Jean Pierre had reappeared in spirit and assumed a different physical form. We had to introduce ourselves—more like introducing our names, for the introduction of selves would be a process, impossible as it were to be captured in this one instant.

"Hi, my name is Juju."

"My name is Shama. You're from Africa?" I wasn't fooled by his accent. There was something about him that I could sense was from the mother continent. Call it instinct, if you will. Or call it Jean Pierre's spiritual reincarnation before me.

"My father was from Africa," he said. "Ghana."

"Your father. And you, you're from where?"

"I was born here. And you, where're you from?"

"Rwanda," I said.

He frowned. Were images horrendous and wrenching racking him?

"You're studying here?" I asked.

"Yes, philosophy."

"Have you eaten?"

"Not yet."

"Should we get something to eat?"

I was even more certain there was something foreign about the man that America couldn't claim (or had not yet claimed) despite the total lack of a foreign accent when he spoke. It wasn't something I could articulate; I knew it just like the way I knew we had to get introduced when we were about to walk past each other in the hallway. I would later ponder if this was what, or a part of what, had drawn me to him. I would ponder if he too was in subconscious search for a part of himself that was African and whether I embodied the answer to that search. I would never ask him this and he would never articulate it so, but still I came to believe that was part of the ingredient of our attraction—this search for a familiar part of ourselves that we find in others.

And after the first meeting and lunch, we would meet again and again. Was this what love at first sight meant and what it wrought? It didn't take me long to realize that he was inexperienced in relationships with members of the opposite gender. He was shy, often unable to speak for long when with me, as if he was not sure what to say to me, and barely ventured any physical contact. Nor did I help him when he attempted intercourse and I rebuffed him. I'd gone through a night of nightmares and phantom pain. Desperate for relief as I usually was after such episodes, I'd knocked on his door. I'd done this with huge reluctance, but now that there was a potential for companionship I would test it. He allowed me in and I asked if I could spend the night in his company. He volunteered his bed and indicated he would sleep on the floor but I insisted he lie beside me. Even his pose next to me seemed awkward as I recalled it—the stiffness and nervousness. With him so close, I felt sheltered and was able to fall asleep. But I'd woken up to feel his hand moving over my bosom. What had emboldened him so? Not that I'd not expected a move at all. He was male after all and his attraction to and affection for me was palpable, and yet I'd come to believe, perhaps naively in hindsight, that it would take a long time to come to this and that it wasn't going to be that night. And here I was, suddenly debating what to do. I could pretend to be asleep but he precluded this when he asked me if I was awake. When I answered that I was he seemed to freeze for a few seconds before resuming, more tentatively this time. But then, encouraged perhaps that I hadn't resisted, he attempted to get to the skin underneath my clothes. But I was back in Butare in the night in front of the church as hands grabbed my limbs and I was choking suddenly and, much as I didn't want to repel him, I told him to stop. He did immediately and apologized. And then all we had was silence, all promise of what the night could have offered distilled into something of a failure and what must have been his regret for having tried.

Now it worried me that I might have completely sucked the boldness out of him and he would limp alongside me, afraid to make another attempt. So timid, my man, I noted mentally. In some place within me, I said silently that his vulnerability served me an offering to

163

avenge battered womanhood, mine and all others who had been offended in insidious ways by men. I could inflict our punishment on him. What did it matter that he might be innocent as an individual? Wasn't I also innocent when I was brutalized in front of the church in Butare? But when I attempted to conjure the cruelest punishment I could for him, say a comment that he was effete, I relented at the reminder that I loved him, that to punish him would risk injuring myself, risking the loss of his love, and the joy of his companionship. No, I would have to lead him back, assure him that my refusal was a refusal of the moment that should be restricted to that moment alone. But to do this I needed more time to calm myself. So I let the night pass in such stalemate, although I tried to assure him by putting my hand over his chest.

And then some nights later when I was more relaxed and felt in better control of myself I reached for his hardness when we were in his room and freed him from its confines with inexperienced strokes that nonetheless brought him to climax. And then some days later I went to his room in a disturbed condition, sweaty and unnerved. I'd unbuttoned my shirt for air without immediately realizing its effect on him until I noticed his eyes fixated on my bosom. He had made another attempt that I rebuffed again but compensated for this immediately as before by releasing him from the pulsations of his manhood with my hand.

We would continue to spend more time together meeting after classes to study or share a meal. And I preferred to sleep in his room than in mine. And I found that being around him helped ease my discomforts and torments. But I would stumble when not long into this relative bliss I encountered Nat Musegera. I was accompanying Juju to the Philosophy Department when we met him on the way. What had been a pleasant mood soured immediately. Juju stopped to make conversation, but I stood aside with my head bowed to avoid eye contact. If Juju realized any change of mood or questioned why I behaved that way, he did not raise it. But my distaste so boiled inside me that I was compelled to ask Juju about him. "I've known him a while. He teaches political science. Not my department, of course, but I met him through one of my profs." I cringed to think that Juju, my Juju, was so acquainted with Nat Musegera, especially considering that after that encounter with him my nightmares were beginning a sporadic return, the pain that I felt even though it

164

belonged outside of me was returning. This, even when I was in Juju's company.

"He deserves to die," I blurted to Juju once when the thought of him seeped into my mind even though I wished otherwise.

Juju could barely believe this utterance had come from me and he immediately questioned me about it. I had to find a way to avenge my family, I explained. Juju couldn't believe me—I had to be joking, he thought, but my stern expression debunked such jocundity. I continued to insist he had to suffer for being Hutu. We had our first fight over this. Juju tried to explain to me that I ought to release whatever anger was contained still within me, explained to me how he loved me and was concerned I harbored such bile. I relented in the argument only, not in the uncorked desire to inflict harm. I had, after all, come to respect Juju so that I felt some guilt for invoking his anger (or sadness) over my expressed wish to harm Nat Musegera. But couldn't he see that the man had become some sort of proxy that was now threatening to unhinge my reliance on him (Juju) for sanity?

I tried to remove Nat Musegera from my thoughts, but the harder I tried the more he filled them. And every time I thought of him I remembered the day in front of the church in Butare and I re-imagined his arm raised, ready to inflict damage, his body naked in prelude to a rape. I fought these images, but they stayed as a deep wound. And I hated him for this.

I would need to take some action, do something to satisfy my gnawing hunger to inflict damage; perhaps only then would I cease to make him this proxy for all things bad that had happened to me; or perhaps only then would I be able to suppress his influence over me. I had mentioned that he deserved to die, but I knew that this was a mere thought that I couldn't effectuate in deed, nor did I really desire his death. I just had to make believe and I had to convince myself that I actually meant it. I was sure that only in such convincing would I be able to reach a state of sated lust for revenge. In that state of mind, I sought something that would inspire me on. I couldn't talk with Juju about this, given his disapproval; in fact, I wasn't sure anyone approve. The only person that came to mind was the one man who wouldn't talk back, except in his notebook-diary. I took it in my hands, immediately enveloped in fear and the theme of death it embodied. As I considered this, however, I concluded that that perhaps that was the theme I needed at that moment. But it took considerable effort for me to open it and push away the voice warning me to leave the notebook-diary unread. As if I was about to perform a sordid deed, I closed all the windows in my room, turned off all the lights and read by candlelight as I took the leap of confidence and opened it. As I began to read, it seemed as if the man was aware that he was about to die and had started the notebook-diary imagining his own funeral. If it was morbid, it was exactly the feeling I needed as I plotted my move against Nat Musegera. Thoughts of death, find a friend.

Jojo Badu's notebook-diary read:

Things appear to ~~re~~disappear, or sometimes they simply appear disappeared. It so happened that I became a wandering, wondering ghost the day I died. I'd been seduced by prospects of existing forever without worry or pain and by hopes of becoming one with time and space. This seduction had begun at a time when my problems seemed too overwhelming and the future, as far as I could see, appeared as charred as burned ground. I wanted it all to go away, somehow to belong in a past, dismissed and forgotten. But I would soon know that the past wouldn't die ~~with death~~. Forget about the dead past burying its dead. I would soon know that in the growing continuum, what happens tomorrow derives much ~~im~~pulse from the past. I would soon know that I needed to reclaim myself. And yet, how could I do so as a wondering wanderer who seeks to discover things that had disappeared? Or perhaps they simply appeared disappeared.

Like finding and constructing a moated palace of many rooms and corridors, false exits and unobtrusive trapdoors, I reach the intended structure with a patient watering of its trenches, then build it little brick by little brick, negotiate its changing complexities painstaking by painstaking step. I had been a lawyer of relatively modest means and was therefore handicapped. A novelist with fabulist skills might fashion fantastic prologues, an artist would paint a masterpiece replete with deep but accessible metaphors, but a man as me without much of an imagination has to take his cue from ~~those who are able to make~~ dreams. I used that dream. I looked back through the long mirrors of time and space, starting with the day when *they* gathered for the burial. I too was able to live the moment, uncover their thoughts as though they were mine—each brave thought, each ignoble thought. What did I see in this past that I'd physically vacated?

Through a foggy vision, I saw the profile of a young female, a young male, and a pastor dressed in black with Bible in hand, a large crucifix around his neck, saying something about dust to dust. The pastor's words flowed listlessly, phlegm lodged in his nostrils from carelessness rather than sorrow—here was another duty to be performed as countless others before and after it. He might more aptly have cried *ashes to ashes*, for the events immediately preceding this were fiery, somehow burning each participant. There were others as well at the cemetery, but out of the twenty or so, those three seemed to demand attention and it was toward them that I turned. They were part of a ceremony steeped in the mystery none of them fully understood but seemed inescapably linked: the ludicrousness of it hidden behind the fleeting smokescreen of sadness, the conversations in undertones while birds fluttered and sang, the tears wept while cars hooted in the far distance, the religiosity of old ceremonies while trees moaned under the pressure of the wind, the forced ritualism while clouds thickened. In a way, there was a celebratory air as well, at least in the lengthy passions of memories. It seemed a fair give and take. A life had been lost. There had to be some level of celebration of a life given and lived. Its existence was enough justification for this celebration. Yet, persistent like life itself, the celebratory part was suppressed by the sadness.

The pastor made the sign of a cross and said something witty about the brevity of earthly life and the longevity of heavenly existence. But he too, whether he was sure of it or not, must have needed the sustaining belief that there was a better after-life that shed meaning on the chaotic here-life. He spoke in the rehearsed clichés he knew, so that his words, especially stifled by his blocked nostrils, didn't convey conviction, even if he might himself be convinced. I imagine he would have liked to say, "The wages of life is sin, but the gift of death is heaven, hell, or nothingness." But he refrained. Instead came the grave words, "May his soul rest in peace." Peace. What is that? But can one ask more for another's ended life beyond vague incantations of hope and grief? If now I would have any of the peace he summoned on my behalf, I would have to learn it like a new memory. At the juncture when he stopped speaking, the pastor invoked a disquieting silence whose only brethren were tampering sobs and wailings. The silence was as chilling as death itself.

The coffin was lowered into the grave—only six feet deep, but a gaping hole more complicated than its simple openness, suggesting something of abyssal infinity. At last came the final ritual as the earth hit the coffin, before the mourners turned their backs to leave to indicate the demarcation between the living and the dead. I, as they all would someday, had joined the majority-departed; they, as I had before, would continue living, perhaps a little diminished because it would be without me, but perhaps fortified because of that. The time had come for *life* to continue. The larger world would continue anyway without hiccup and now those affected by my passing had to make their choice: join me or join them. Naturally, they'd choose the latter option.

As the corpse lay deep in the earth, I revisited the center-stagers at the funeral. The pastor's part was done. He'd become inconsequential. The first count, though, is not the most accurate, even if it's the most genuine. The new focus: my daughter, my son, and ... and Fiona. Fiona. Fiona: the fourth and final count. What was she doing there? At the very point when I saw her so freely weepy, her necklace holding a crucifix, an unsympathetic instinct gripped me: a sweet-sad desire for vengeance. With that one instinct I thought to move my body out of that coffin, free it from its airless confines, if only to give Fiona a heart attack, yell at her to wipe away tear after ~~fake~~ tear. I had no capacity at that moment to ponder the thought that her remorse was genuine. I would have liked to do something, anything to hurt her, humiliate her. But my body lay there immobilized.

Not the same, my offspring. As I watched Juju and Ama turn and leave my body at the cemetery, I wished to rise from the pits of death and walk hand in hand with them. I'd have kissed both children and embraced them. Whether they also had given me heartache and pain, angst and anger, didn't matter. They were my children, my living blood who could immortalize me. ~~But what a vain thought.~~ I saw them leave the cemetery and I could about taste their grief.

So I lived on in the hidden tears of my son, the regrets of my daughter, the open wails of my wife, the confused compunctions of friends and, occasionally, the serendipitous sympathy of strangers. Because I'd been where they were and moved beyond it, we'd shared too much (especially in regard to my family) to let me pass easily forgotten. (*No, sir, Mr. Hymnist, we are not so easily forgotten as a dream that dies at the opening day*). They couldn't soon forget me like mere shadows trailing them in the busy clamor of an abbreviated past.

I considered myself as a candle that once burned, flickered in the wind, and died. But the wax remained. It had collected into a lump that couldn't be ignored. They were leaving me behind: the body, not the force or memory.  Those not in the immediate circle, but close enough, walked away solemnly: a father-in-law and mother-in-law, both weakened by age; a sister-in-law and her husband living in a bliss they'd created; a friend born and raised in America, ripped by grief; and another friend born in Nigeria, living in America, worried that I had died on *foreign* soil and afraid he was doomed to suffer the same fate.  There'd be further tears and sorrows, contrition and regrets, forgiveness asked and given or withheld.

~~I will die soon, I know.~~  I was dead.

And so my life had ended in that frame that no longer could move by itself and in my chest were held the as yet unfulfilled longings of generations before me, in my mind were the wisdoms (or remnants) given me by my forbears, my ambitions cluttered by the difficulties of a hardly sympathetic world.  Dead, the unfulfilled longings were frozen still, the untaught wisdoms were neglected, and the unmet ambitions were buried.

Dead.

Did someone say: Check?

Death.  I wish it were simple to detest or like it as a child opens his arms to his mother or closes it to a stranger.  But death is often a wonderment seamlessly deceptive and amoebic as the night, for it is a chameleon.  Would that an answer could break open its closed doors and let slip a secret.  But, despite its mystery, this much I know—death is not just an end.  It is also a beginning, an opportunity that offers the living a life and all its lessons for those who care to look.  Life.  Like a play with its moral, no one can fully assess it until it ends; otherwise, it is merely work in progress, no matter how brilliant, no matter how dull.  Life.

Check, perhaps, but not yet Checkmate.


This was the farthest I'd read of the notebook-diary.  Had Jojo Badu really written thin in anticipation of his death?  What about that remark about Fiona?  What I had read rendered me more confused, more in affinity with death, that it affirmed the will to inflict harm on Nat Musegera—yes, the motif of death would gird me, embolden me. I thought of death and I thought of the way it had claimed my loved ones in Rwanda. It infuriated me. I bided my time.

# Four

I'd gone to the cafeteria after classes and noticed Nat Musegera sitting by himself eating a sandwich. Suddenly nervous, and as much as I knew it could cause psychological stress, or even damage, I willingly reenacted Butare and my aunt and Alexandre and other events that had occurred in my aunt's house. And in this exercise I refused—absolutely refused—to include myself in the circle of blame. Here was Mama's blood spilling, its red joining those of Papa and Placide, flowing into the open mouth exhaling the last breaths of Jean Pierre; there was my body rendered an object of abuse and agony... And my anger was aroused, and as though I had no control, my eyes squinted, my brow furrowed, my lips tightened, and my severe expressions coalesced on my face into a severe contortion. I had to settle this somehow. I knew I radiated rage when I picked up the knife for my meal and approached Nat Musegera. I would not cut him, but I would cause sufficient fear in him to ensure that he forever kept his distance. I would lunge at him, but at the last instance I would lose the knife and make it seem like it had fallen inadvertently. Narrowed in my thoughts and only in hindsight did I acknowledge that I had totally ignored any potential legal jeopardy when I rushed forward and lunged at Nat Musegera. But he'd noticed me approaching before I could get close enough to effect my plan fully. He moved backward so that my knife toting hand strayed in the air. In the performance, I'd overlooked the most important detail about dropping the knife. Before I could get to him, Nat Musegera had already grabbed a chair and started to swing at me. With a couple of such swings he caught my hanging hand, causing the knife to fall to the floor. The script had suddenly been altered and I had to improvise and yet, with Nat holding a chair to ward me off, what I had hoped to make believe only had become real and the man was no longer a proxy but the real thing, a live threat. I felt any remaining ability to control my actions ooze out of me as my thoughts got lost in fear that Nat could, would, do me harm. We were back in Butare: Hutu versus Tutsi. Live or Die. Now acting more for self-defense as I believed it to be at that time, completely overwhelmed by the situation, I reached forward and grabbed the chair in Nat's hands, surprised that I could so easily pry it from his hands. Had he underestimated my strength? I quickly swung

172

the chair blindly, more intended to scare than wound him, but I caught him in the midsection, unbalancing him, felling him. Before I could take any other action, a number of students were upon me, prying the chair from my hands. Without the knife or the chair, I felt defenseless and struggled. Five or so students were upon me, except now they were no longer students but five rapists in Butare—vicious and with diabolic intent. I fought, clawed and bit, and it took them long minutes to neutralize me completely, finally managing to pin me to the ground, face down, until the campus police arrived, handcuffed me and took me away.

I would spend the next few hours answering questions from a couple of policemen and one policewoman. I gave my statement as completely as I could, without embellishment or subtraction. I'd done what I'd done, I said to myself and I would have to deal with the fallout. When I was offered the chance, I debated whether to call the Baileys or Juju. I decided on Juju. I was more prepared to face the disappointment of the lover than that of the surrogate father/mother. Love would forgive, but the parental type could be overly judgmental. Juju, alarmed over the phone, would not say much except that he would do something about it. He came to see me, but not blamed me as I'd expected. He left disappointed—that much was clear. And that evening, Nat Musegera walked to the police station and insisted that I be released immediately.

"Nat Musegera?" I had asked the police officer who informed me that he'd asked for my release. "Why?"

"If I were you, I would stop asking questions and be thankful that he doesn't want to press charges," said the policeman.

I went home, showered, and went to see Juju. It was he who told me how he'd pleaded with the professor not to press charges. I wept. And he joined me. I was empty and I could tell that he was also empty, staring at the woman he loved who had assaulted a professor and just returned from detention. What was he to say? What was he to do? What was I to do? What was I to say? Did he know me? Did I know myself? Would he have thought me capable of what I did? Would I have thought myself capable of what I did? What possessed me? Words would not suffice, not for the occasion. We were both disoriented and the only balm I could conjure was some form of intimacy that would become the dialogue of bodies that the dialogue of words couldn't achieve. I took his hand and put it on my shoulder and encouraged him to undress me. He ran his hands over the scar on my belly region and then his hands embraced my back and came into contact with the crisscrosses of scars there, the legacies of that fateful day in front of the church in Butare. He paused and turned me around. I looked behind me, confronting his face with my own concern as he seemed repulsed by the scars. But the repulsion must have been shallow, springing from the unfamiliarity of what he saw, the jugged skin. Yet, all that was required was familiarity and he ran his hands over them again and again and in his determined hands I imagined they simply became an art form of sorts (indeed an artful souvenir from the painful past). "You are beautiful," he said, "my unique angel." He kissed the scars. He had conquered the resistance. He could now reach with naked hands to the honeycomb. He reached. I confronted what I knew was about to ensue, suppressing for the moment a past that was as bold as anguish, transcending the pain of memory buried in each welt. We teased out an alchemy of gentleness, love and desire from my tragedy of roughness, hatred and repulsion. "This is my first time," he confessed. "Me, too," I said, as I discounted—in fact negated—what had happened in Butare that would otherwise have been my first time. We restated love to include its physical form, the somatic sensations, intimate desire and carnal joy, without diminishing the emotional importance of the act. But we found neither the unbearable, blissful climax common in fiction nor the disappointment borne of over-expectation; instead, we were both satisfied, a simple satisfaction that need not fill theses. It was a beginning.

The next few days, I was steeped in reflection, in the friendliness of Nat Musegera, my reaction, and his continued acts of graciousness. I would be now elated by the positive course of events and now deflated by how close to the brink I had come. This stretched and drained my emotional strengths. The fifth night after my release from the police station, I resolved to take action to escape from the clutches of the past as best as I was able. But how? I told Juju I needed a day for myself. I would not attend classes, nor would I work or see Juju. I assured him not to worry; I would emerge from my one-day seclusion stronger and better. This was a resolution of the mind and the mind alone. Hard as I knew it was going to be I would not let this quest be corrupted by any emotional dross that lent fuel to my nightmares. I owed this exercise, above all things, to myself, I concluded, and it was this sense of self-preservation that inspired me the most.

I woke up in the morning with the resolve at the center of my mind, ate breakfast and sat on the couch in my apartment, then I tried as best as I could to relax my entire body. Distractions such as thoughts about Juju and Nat and school came in sporadic doses until I was able to reach a point where I felt totally at ease. Singularly focused, I considered the loss of the mass on my body and asserted that it was a necessary act, done by a woman who loved me deeply in order to save me. I recalled also the taunts in those days when I seemed indolent and unattractive, those days in school when friendship was acquired on the basis of my intellect alone, and compared that to the latter years, especially in college, when many young men propositioned me. I thought of the times spent with my family, even with Anan, and as irreplaceable as they were, I considered the new relationships forged with a new family: the Baileys, especially Mark. Reliving my relationship with Jean Pierre was daunting in the magnitude of the loss, but I now had Juju. And then what I feared the most: the massacre in front of the church in Butare and a double rape, meted to me and to Aunt Shama. Images of death, the smell of blood and the grating sounds of dying noises in their exaggerated grotesqueries became an aural battering, assailing my memory so relentlessly that I needed a break. I told myself that after these recollections I had to keep a reservoir of strength to confront the most challenging part of the past. I turned on jazz music and opened my eyes. For long minutes I thought of nothing. Then I took a long shower, attempted a few sit ups and ate another meal.

I next lay on my bed, spread eagled, as if in symbolic surrender. But to what? I went through another period relaxing my body, every muscle and tissue as best as I could, and then I invoked my mind. I tried to re-imagine every moment of what happened, even when it made me shudder—not physically, but from a deep space within me that had to be spiritual. One by one I relived the past this way, each time asserting that some divine power intended me to survive; otherwise, there was no reason or plausible explanation that I would survive when others around me had perished. Thinking of it this way, I also realized that if my assertion were true, then I bore a special burden—I must have survived for a special purpose, I thought. This was not a burden I wished for myself as I again replayed the night of the horrific assault in Butare as carefully as I could, even as tears began to ease from my eyes.

Why had they not finished me off? My mind now intently focused, its eyes getting sharper and sharper, looking deeper and deeper into history…. And the images were getting clearer and clearer… As the image became clearer, I was beginning to realize that perhaps I had deliberately dimmed some images in order not to confront and believe what they said. But I had to take this step too if I could find full redemption from it and the freedom I sought. With a deep breath, the byproduct of concern, I confronted a particularly dimmed image until my vision shone with luciferous clarity.

They were done with their act of utmost violence. And then one man took control. It was he, as I recalled, who had held the others back and said that this woman belonged to him now to finish off as he deemed best. It was that man who had turned me over so that my backside was exposed rather than my front. It was that man who had brought down several times the weapon that caused the multiple scars on my back, but it was also that man who'd brought down the weapon lightly when it touched my back, so that it would not cause significant damage, it seemed. It was the same man who'd come back for me later, this time alone. I had not staggered my way to the French camp. No, it was that man who had taken me from the garden of death in front of the church and carried me in his arms and, under the cover of the star-lit night, deposited me in front of the camp. As hard as I had blotted this out, I now refurbished the image and the face, the foggy eyes looking at me, the hirsute nose dripping with phlegm, the rancid breath, the acrid smell of sweat from unwashed armpits, the overall doggy smell that nonetheless exuded a jungly warmth, even the coffee-colored driblets of saliva drooling down his chin…

That all came from Thierry. Yes, Thierry. Thierry, the once-rival of Jean Pierre, the wrestling combatant, the one time proponent of love for me. Thierry, who had, together with others, engaged in the massacre of many Tutsis and then returned with a gang to rape me. It was he who had stopped his gang of rapists from killing me and then returned to save me from the certain death that would have claimed me piecemeal as I lay bleeding among a pile of dead bodies.

I was crying out loudly at this point of recollections, asking for divine forgiveness for all that I had done wrong. Something broke loose. I abandoned attempts to think through the matter. With this emotional engagement at such a naked level, I found that I couldn't control any longer the flood that spewed out of me. I wept for a long time, and then I wept some more. I lay in bed, exhausted, occasionally shaken by bursts of tears and even wailing. I lay there and let the exhaustion of the moment lead me into sleep.

I called on Juju the next day. "I want to apologize to Nat. Can you come with me?"

"Are you sure this is what you want to do?" Juju asked

"I'm sure of it. Why, you don't like the idea?"

"It's not that; it's just that I don't know if you're ready for this now."

"I couldn't be more ready."

"Okay, let me talk to him first and see what he says."

"No, please don't do that. I want to surprise him."

"And what if he doesn't want to see you, Shama?"

"I'll take my chances, but I'm confident he'll see us if you go with me."

Nat Musegera appeared surprised to see us, but this surprise was only brief, or he was deft on soon masking it and inviting us to sit. I don't know if I imagined it, but I thought his face twitched, even as he offered us drinks, which Juju declined and I accepted. While he poured me a glass of orange juice, I noticed that his hands shook ever so slightly. He made no mention of my attack, asking instead about our classes that semester, pretending that the tension that pervaded the room didn't exist.

After a few minutes, I could no longer restrain myself. "Sir..." I said.

"Nat," he replied. "Call me Nat, please."

177

"Nat," I said. "I first of all want to apologize for my behavior. What I did at the cafeteria was the worst of it, but even apart from that I have behaved very badly. You have been nothing but gracious to me, but I have repaid you with one act of meanness after another. I hope you will find it within yourself to forgive me. But I can understand if you won't."

"Don't worry about it," Nat said. "We let bygones be bygones. Let's pretend none of it ever happened. Why don't we wipe the slate clean and start all over?" Nat Musegera got up and walked to me with an outstretched arm. "Hi, my name is Anatole Musegera. My friends call me Nat."

I stood up and took his hand, which he kissed. "Hi," I said. "My name is Shama Rugwe. My friends call me Shama."

We all laughed, including Juju.

"Thanks for not pressing charges," I said.

"Hey," said Nat. "You're breaking the rules. Bygones are bygones, remember?"

"Thank you."

"Thank *you*."

"I'm getting jealous of this love-fest," Juju said. "I'm sorry, professor, but she's already spoken for."

When I left Nat Musegera's residence, I was convinced that I could now love more freely, perhaps even live more freely. I couldn't deny that there was lingering doubt that I'd done this just to placate my own conscience, that I still held some remnant of hate for the man. But even if that were the case, I countered, I had taken an important first step. And if I could, whether now or eventually, cease attributing all that I'd suffered to the likes of Nat Musegera, then I would have conquered that vicious if hidden vindictiveness that had so plagued me; and without it I could offer my love to all who sought it. I could offer my love, above all, to Juju without reservation and he wouldn't have to battle hidden demons.

And I did. I now wanted to know all I could about him and his family. Who was his father? Jojo Badu. A lawyer. He'd come to the US from Ghana, obtained his bachelor's, married Fiona, gotten a law degree, had two children, worked for a law firm, and then as in-house counsel for a multinational corporation and then died of *natural causes*. Who was his

178

mother? Fiona Harris Badu, born in the US, spent time in Ghana for high school and college and then returned to the US, where she'd met and married Jojo, and now she was a managing partner of a major Boston law firm. Who was his sister? Ama Badu, the elder sibling, graduated college and now an accounting consultant. These broad strokes barely told a story.

Juju would offer some details over time, so that the sketch acquired color, a little flesh here and a little blood there. He loved to talk about his sister and father, but appeared hesitant to mention much about his mother. At first, I would not pry, hoping that after a while Juju would cease this bias. But when it continued, I asked him, "Do you not like your mother? Why is it that you don't like talking about her?"

"What do you mean? I talk about her too."

"No, you don't, Juju. Is something the matter with her?"

He was quiet for a while. "This is not something I like talking about and I haven't mentioned it to anyone outside my family. So it is between us, okay?"

"You have my word."

"I think my mother had a hand in my father's death."

"What?!"

"Now wait, don't get me wrong. She didn't kill kill him... I mean... Well, this is what happened. My mother had..." Jojo paused, on the verge of tears. I don't think I can tell you this myself. Perhaps it's better you read it for yourself."

"Read about it? Where? Was all this recorded in a newspaper or something?"

"Newspaper? No, my old man kept a diary of sorts, a very detailed account of his later life. He seemed quite meticulous about it. We found it when he died. There's some very heavy stuff in it."

Later, Juju gave me the notebook-diary. "Read this and you will know me better," he said.

"Jojo, this is too personal."

"I know, but I want you to read it. There are things I can't tell you that this diary will."

179

# Five

Fiona invited me to visit her in Boston. I'd come to like her, but it was one thing to enjoy her during the course of an evening and in subsequent phone calls and another to spend an entire weekend in her home. I demurred at first with the excuse that I was busy, but Fiona was relentless. She called me often and encouraged me to reciprocate. I called dutifully on occasion and stayed on the phone for long minutes with her. The older woman always asked about my schoolwork, if I was coping well with life in America and whether I had heard from Juju and when. The last question nearly always soured the mood, for Fiona seemed hurt that her son would contact the love but not the mother. She always tried gallantly but unconvincingly to mask her hurt by moving to other topics, her strained voice always divulging her pain.

The distance and her inability to see my tactile reaction to her questions and responses had been my buffer, but now I would have no such cushion. Nor was I sure how I would cope being in the home that had once housed Juju's father. You see, after meeting Fiona, I eventually more of the notebook-diary that Juju gave me. As much as I had avoided reading it except the beginning, after Fiona's invitation, I felt compelled to, hoping that somehow it would offer me clues on her character and how I could deal with her now that she was gradually becoming a part of my life.

In that notebook-diary, her husband told a tale of woe and in many ways made me question Fiona on many matters. But I decided I ought to withhold my judgment; after all, his viewpoint could be biased, even unfounded. But as I was about to spend time in the house where the paterfamilias had resided, I worried that the spirit of the man that haunted the pages of his notebook-diary, worse his ghost, would linger still and force me to take sides, perhaps confirm his notebook-diary accusations of Fiona in some way that would undermine my growing affection for her. Persuaded by this line of reasoning, I reread portions of Jojo Badu's notebook-diary, looking for any clues that might help me deal with Fiona:

I had been a dishwasher in college, had a brief stint
as a hay stacker after college, and then went on to work for

a law firm. Preston, Ingold, Thomas & Slaughter was the only law firm that gave me an offer after law school. The only one! My loyalties and gratitude to that firm ran deep as it was the only firm that thought me worthy of employment. So I worked hard at Preston Ingold, being at the office no later than eight (sometimes sooner) each work day and leaving no sooner than seven (and often staying past that time). Compared to my responsibilities, my pay was meager. As Fiona was still in law school, I bore the bulk of our household's financial responsibilities. I had to pay rent, ensure we had adequate groceries, and finance other needs, in addition to paying back my college and law school loans (which took about a third of my monthly salary). At the end of the month, I had nothing left. Sometimes, I had to use my credit card to supplement my income.

I devoted a huge chunk of my weekends to work, Saturday and Sunday having no special significance. I'd opted to do corporate and commercial work. Brad McConnell and I were the only ones hired in that division that year. I went to all the firm's social functions with the hope of making the human connections partners deemed so important. By the end of the first year, my review was excellent.

I became accustomed to a familiar pattern. The wakeup call of the alarm would summon me to another day of morning ablutions, coffee, a quick dash to feed—or help feed—our two kids, Ama and Juju, driving them to school, going to work and often thinking I didn't belong when little to no one looked like me, but trying hard to ~~confirm~~ conform, going through the rigmarole of work and then picking up the kids (unless on days when Fiona did), spending the evenings helping them with homework or playing a game with them; and then trying to spend some time ~~alone~~ with Fiona, which was not often and in any case was filled with exhaustion so that it wasn't very

181

meaningful. I would fall asleep hoping that the next day would be better, knowing that it wouldn't. Then the alarm would sound again and it would begin once more. On the few weekends when I didn't work, I would attend little league games, or, when we managed to find a babysitter, see a movie or play or visit with the few friends we had.

In my second year at Preston Ingold my work started drying up. Partners who'd worked with me the year before were now sending just about all their work to Brad McConnell. Sometimes, I'd show up for work and have nothing to do. I spent hours daydreaming, studying the tiles of the ceiling in my office, or staring into space. Given that I'd a yearly quota of billable hours to meet, this bothered me. I went to the only black partner at the firm. "Luther, I'm not getting enough work," I told him.

"Have you been asking?"

"Yes."

"I'd give you some work, but you know I do tax and you're not in Tax. Have you spoken with your mentor?"

"You mean Ralph?"

"Yeah, he's your mentor, isn't he?"

"Yes."

"Brother," Luther said in a whisper. "I'll tell you a secret. What you need is a sugar daddy. In a law firm that's so overwhelmingly white, a black man stands little chance. I'm not saying they want you to fail. The law firm has invested in you. It makes no sense to want to see you fail. But that's speaking of the firm as a whole. At an abstract level, the law firm may want you to succeed, but at an individual level... That's where you, I mean folk like us, run into problems. People have prejudices, misconceptions … People want to feel comfortable and they're comfortable with their own kind. That's a fact. You and me, we don't fit into this very well. It's tough to find a natural sugar daddy who'll nurture you, teach you, give you good work, see your weaknesses and mistakes and help you correct them. That's the only way you'll grow. Forget being smart. Everyone knows you're smart, Jojo, but that isn't enough. It just isn't."

"But you've made it."

"Yes. At a huge price, my brother... Listen, why don't I talk to a couple of the partners in your division, see if I can get some work to come your way."

A few days later, my workload increased. Luther had fulfilled his promise. But the work dried up not long afterwards. I was getting tired of showing up for work with little to no work, knocking on doors and pleading for work. And yet Brad McConnell would come by my office and complain that he was too busy.

"Really, I hardly have any work," I'd say.

"How come?" Good question. How come? "Let me talk to the partners to see if it's okay if I give you some of the work they've given me."

And minutes later I'd take some work from Brad. It was illuminating humiliating to get work from a fellow second year associate. But I had to make my quota of work hours for the year. And I was thinking, if only I could find my own clients I wouldn't have to rely on others to get work, to feed me the crumbs from the meal. But how does a Ghanaian who's been in Boston only about five years find the contacts to generate work? The trend continued.

I panicked in my third year at Preston Ingold. I saw little room for growth. At my slow pace, I was convinced I wouldn't make partner. Worse, I was afraid I might be asked "to seek alternative employment." I didn't meet my billable hours quota in my third year. I just wasn't getting work, although my yearly evaluations suggested my work quality was excellent. It wasn't for lack of enthusiasm. I still showed up early and left the office late, mostly hassling to get work, and working on matters (like articles for the local newspaper) that could not be billed to a client. I wasn't helping to bring money to the law firm; rather, I

183

was becoming a liability of sorts, an unnecessary appendage that could be easily severed. My promise, in my own eyes, had diminished. Once I had that conviction, I lost interest in attending firm functions. I called a headhunter. "Get me out of Preston Ingold,"

It was only after Fiona finished law school and started working at Crawford Raymond that we moved from our apartment into a new Tudor-styled house, counting on the continued income of two lawyers. But for the next five months, a new road of diminishing expectations opened before me. In my bid to leave Preston Ingold I was called for twelve interviews, out of which I got one offer, almost like the series of unfruitful interviews after law school. I thought most of the interviews went well, but I started receiving one rejection letter after another. After the seventh rejection, I spewed my frustration to Fiona. "I went to great schools. I have three years of experience under my belt. What do I need to do to get a job around here?"

She told me to show more drive and I wouldn't even have to leave the law firm. Indeed, Fiona had changed. She'd never before showed her drive to succeed in the corporate environment, seemingly content with her mid-level administrative job in a real estate agency. I had hardly noticed, but with hindsight, I should have seen it—the way she accepted law school without struggle, in fact thrived in it; her eagerness with her work when she interned at Crawford Raymond; the way she enthused over her assignments. It had been by stealthy evolution until she reached her conclusions and convictions about the corporate environment and the opportunities it offered. I ignored her indirect reprimand. After ten rejection letters, I finally received an offer from Machines and Papers, Inc. I would join it as Staff Attorney.

# Six

Long before I even read these portions, I remember asking Juju for the second time if he was sure he'd done the right thing by giving me his father's notebook-diary. "It's very intimate, Juju, are you sure about this?"

"No question. You've finished reading it then?"

"Not yet."

"Read it, Shama. I thought I knew my father until I read his diary."

"And now you think you know him?"

"More than I did when he was alive. I still don't know him enough."

"So what's missing?"

"I'm not sure."

"He came to the US from Ghana, right?" I asked.

"Yes."

"Do you think knowing Ghana better would get you closer to him?"

Juju didn't answer the question then. But he would tell me that this question had sparked an urging, at first minor, about going to Ghana to find out more about the birthplace of his father, who had made it clear enough that despite his later American citizenship, he considered Ghana his home. Juju remembered his father telling him in one moment that he felt somehow cheated that he'd not lived in the land of his birth, raised his children in the ways he was raised. At that moment, the confession bore little relevance, and Ghana where he'd visited as a child and could barely remember seemed so remote and even irrelevant and alien to him. Nor had he considered that he'd ever fall in love with me, a woman from the continent, who had stirred an urge that wouldn't die. The continent seemed to be beckoning. He became preoccupied with Africa in general and Ghana in particular, mainly because I had relit this fire of interest in the continent and connected him or given him license to connect to those roots that were so remote. He read widely about Ghana. He was often absentminded. When I would ask him about this, all he would say was that he was thinking about Ghana.

What he would tell me a few months later would surpass my expectation, cause me worry.   But as I read his father's notebook-diary later, I would understand better why:

One phase ends, closing a chapter that simply leads to another chapter bearing the long shadows of the previous.  Now that I had two growing children I needed to ensure their security—no crippling debts like I had when I left law school, no poverty in the schooling years either, none of those financial problems that had trailed me since I arrived on American soil.  I had to succeed at Machines and Papers.

The first day on my new job, as I made the rounds getting introduced to my new colleagues, I felt a part of me fleeing.  Which part, I couldn't fathom yet.  I probably never would.   But it had been drained, perhaps irretrievably.  All new faces.  Where was the familiar one?  I wished Dwayne or Ed were there.  I could even use the presence of someone like John.  I wished I could lean on Fiona for support there and then.  I prayed for the sustaining comforts of my children to lend me strength.  And in a month, as I had acclimatized to the new surroundings when I arrived in college, I pushed all the nostalgia-like thoughts away and braced myself with gritted teeth in my new assignments.  Perhaps I should've gnashed them instead.

The onslaught of work was unrelenting.  My days were busy—one meeting after another, one phone call following another.  I dispensed legal advice ~~speedily~~, sometimes unsure of it, but like the rest of my colleagues, making my best guess and hoping that sufficed.  At meetings, I spoke with careful measure, refusing a repeat of my performance at my first meeting, which had been called to discuss some legal filings with the government.  The head of the marketing group had suddenly said to me, "I can't understand what you're saying."  Suddenly I was self-conscious, just like the day at the law firm when I'd called a client who had said, "Isn't there someone who can explain this to me in clear English?" Determined as I ever than before, I even practiced speaking at home. Fiona thought I'd gone mad. But soon I was speaking at my slow and deliberate pace at work. But perhaps I sounded slow-witted as a result.

Therefore, to walk into my office was to leave a part of me behind, to craft a different *self* and wear it like clothes. Culturally disengaged, ethnically isolated, racially differentiated—alien, alienation, alienated—I had to smile at a joke I didn't like, smile at a smile that was faked for comfort. More and more I felt the isolation. And this takes skill—aiming for survival and refusing to stand out and therefore achieving a non-threatening anonymity. At the end of the day, I was emotionally exhausted. That I would survive over twenty years of this surprised me. And sometimes when I thought of the alienation, I knew it wasn't just external, but also the internal isolation from *self*, like a gradual erosion of layers of your core until some day you wake up and it's too late and you are caught in a strange realm of foreign-familiarity. Or is it familiar-foreignness?

Did someone say Check? Trapped. Un-trapped. Not yet Checkmate:

I would go home to Ama and Juju. Sometimes I was afraid that Ama would become her mother, and sometimes I was disappointed in her choices. But can a man's tender care and love cease towards the child he helped bear? No, I would insist, and, in my experience, not even forgetful be, though she is shaped by things he doesn't know or can't control, especially her choice of boyfriends. I wanted to reconnect to my roots. I wanted her to look *home*. She brought home boys who spoke in slang, dressed loudly, and seemed too slick. When a Senegalese family moved into the neighborhood with a teenage son who looked studious

187

and respectful, I tried to get them together. It was perhaps too soon to start thinking of marriage, but I wanted to reorient Ama's focus. I invited the family over to dinner, took Ama over to visit, hinting to her how much I liked Yusuf. She shrugged. "Don't you like him?" I finally asked. "He's a nice boy, you know."

"Come on, Dad."

"He'll make a good boyfriend."

"Oh, Dad! You only like him because he's African."

"And what's wrong with that?"

"I don't want to date no African. I'm American."

She seemed not to notice the cut she'd inflicted; as if she presumed I wasn't African or wasn't African anymore. I never mentioned her choice of boys again. Who was to blame if I lost her to this *strange* land? She who made me weep happily, remembering tears I felt the moment when I knew that I would die for her, when I held her helpless against me and drew all of her infantile helplessness with the hope that I could shield her from what was to come, ensconce her in a protection deeper than anyone could imagine. But then those years would change and she would become her own girl and woman, my heartbreak not stopping her from the transformation into an American whose accent was different from mine. When once I had asked her to go to Ghana with me, she said, "Ghana? But, Dad, I ain't Ghanaian."

"You are, too," I protested.

"I'm American."

Could I argue with that?

And sometimes, despite her adoration, I even felt as if she wished she had an American born father.

Once or twice I had protested a mannerism of hers, comparing it to the way she'd be expected to act in Ghana. "Ama, in Ghana you wouldn't talk to your father like that."

"But this is not Ghana."

188

...Or when once I'd stretched my hand to shake hers saying, "Let me show you how we do it in Ghana."

And she'd responded, "I want to do it like in America, not Ghana."

It seemed I was losing my daughter to something I didn't understand, something unfamiliar, even hostile. She didn't speak like me (sounding exactly like an American teenager), nor did she long for Ghana (behaving exactly like her mother). This daughter I loved so was shunning the country of my birth, the country I still loved so strongly (I know in a bit of contradiction for having abandoned it when I decided after school to stay, when I took an American wife and when I became an America citizen). She was becoming a part of the land I wanted to rescue her from as much as I wanted to make her a part of. So I wanted her to speak the way I spoke. She didn't. I wanted her to think the way I thought fondly of Ghana (which I did, although at times its political upheavals disappointed me, especially when a failed coup claimed the life of my Uncle Kusi). She didn't think that way. I wanted her to yearn to go to the place. She didn't.

Meantime, Juju also was growing. Here was a child who demanded attention. And when he didn't get it, he made his presence clear. It wasn't easy dealing with his demands, his vociferousness. But one event seemed a watershed. Juju had come home from school once, his face sullen. "Dad, what's a nigger?"

He was six years old. I hadn't grown up under the onslaught of that word or the ramifications of it. I hadn't been raised with any of its debilitating psychological effects. How could I raise my son against it, not knowing its impact first-hand as a child?

"Who told you that word, Juju?"

"Jim called me nigger in school. My teacher told him to hush. But he didn't hush. They took him to the principal. He's in trouble."

Should I have explained to my six-year old son the meaning of that word? But what would I have told him? It's a derogatory word for black people? It's bad word that darts into the hearts of African Americans like poison? It's a word dressed in such history you have to live it to know it? It's a word neutered by some black people as an internal word of endearment, as benign (depending on who was doing the saying) as it was malignant (depending on who was doing the saying)? Should I have told him it was just a word to be ignored?

"It's a bad word some people call black people," I said. *Oh, Jojo, how lame.*

"It's a bad word? Then why did Jim say it? Jim's a good boy."

Disarmed. I had no reply to that. But its profundity haunted me. *Jim is a good boy.* Why did he use the word nigger? *Son, is there ever an answer?*

Juju went away. But some weeks later, I noticed he was showing more interest in reading. It started with the newspapers. He would borrow mine and for hours bury himself in them. I had not a clue what he was trying to accomplish. Was he looking for answers where I'd failed to provide them? Soon he was reading books. Like mother, like son? I hadn't read much, not even in my adult years. But Juju was reading novels, historical texts, newspapers, journals and magazines, anything readable. And the more he immersed himself in reading the less he spoke with the rest of the family. It was a stupefying transformation—how a vociferous child becomes a quiet, withdrawn one.

Were there other signs that I hadn't realized? Why, for example, hadn't I taken more serious his lack of interest in things practical? Should I have worried more about his withdrawal from women when his friends were beginning to pose a threat to all organic things remotely female? "You can't live on books all the time," I'd told him. "You

need to get out and do stuff. Get into a little bit of trouble."
He shrugged. When I told him, "This is unhealthy, Juju,"
he looked at me with a disinterest more unnerving than if
he'd yelled and drawn a knife.

I wanted to reach him.

Yet how do you reach a child who won't speak
much about his internal teachings, emotions and all that
comes with them? How do you understand a child who
won't leave a trail of words from which you can glean
some meaning to his actions? I had lost my booming voice,
not necessarily my words; he seemed to have his voice, but
was losing his words. Did it matter? I'd started losing the
boom in my voice since I moved to the US; his words were
leaving him at a much earlier stage. I was at an impasse of
sorts and so I did nothing as I watched him grow, all the
while wishing I'd raised him in Ghana where I was certain
he would be more self-confident.

After I read this part of the notebook-diary, I could understand why
these passages would prompt Juju and why he would announce to me, "I
want to live in Ghana."

"You mean visit?" I asked.

"No," he said. "I mean actually live there."

"You want to move to Ghana?"

"Kind of. I don't want to just visit the place like some tourist. I
want to know the place, really know it."

"You're not serious, are you?"

"I'm dead serious, Shama."

"But what about us?"

"Don't worry, we'll be in touch. I will come visit often and when
you're on break you can come visit me."

"And we'll do this for how long?"

"I don't know, Shama. Could it be five, six months? Could it be
two, three years? Who knows?"

"I don't like this, Juju."

"I thought you'd want me to visit."

"Yes, visit, not move there—not now."

Juju held me. "Sweetie, this will be hard for me too. But I feel it. I feel it in my spirit that I need to do this. I love you, you know that. Nothing will come between us. Not distance or anything else."

I knew it would be selfish to tell him not to go. I had to liberate him, despite my worry that this could fatally disrupt our relationship. After much thinking I decided that if he needed to do it, I would provide my support. He would call his sister Ama and tell her. His mother, he would tell later.

While I supported him in this, he in turn helped ease me into my new frontier of forgiveness and rehabilitation. I made him accompany him at first as I paid visits to Nat Musegera. Each time, it took enormous effort to make the trip to the man's residence, but I persevered, helped by Jojo's presence. And each time Nat welcomed us heartily, even cooking for us on one occasion. After a series of such visits, I told Juju I would start visiting the professor alone in his office. "I need to be able to do this by myself," I explained. So I would go to his office in the Political Science Department whenever I had a break and sit and chat for brief periods. With each visit, I found my comfort around the man rising and my worry decreasing. Correspondingly, my nightmares reduced sharply and the phantom pain seldom attacked me. I had found a new friend in Nat Musegera, I told Juju. Not long afterwards, Juju left for Boston to see his family, from where he left for Accra, Ghana.

## Seven

On the Eve of my visit to see Fiona, I read as much of her husband's notebook-diary as I could.

Parallel to handling the joys and challenges of my children's *growth* was a work life significantly challenging but with little of the spiritual awakenings—even when they were hard earned—that my children offered me. (No need to emphasize that the sex life between Fiona and I had dwindled to near insignificance). As usual, I woke up in the mornings to prepare for work and, even after several years of doing so, hoped I'd find some fortune of miraculous funds that would guarantee me financial security without the need for another day of work. Occasionally, I even wished with shame that I'd suffer some form of disability that would preclude me from work while guaranteeing me disability benefits, but not so severe that I couldn't enjoy the rest of my years. But, alas, dragging myself out of bed, Fiona already in the shower, I'd make coffee, get in the bathroom and perform the usual morning ablutions.

Full of coffee, I'd drive to work and start the day, my nostrils privy to equally coffee-fouled mouths as mine. My days continued to be filled with attending meetings; making and taking phone calls; writing memos; negotiating, proofreading, reviewing and drafting boring contracts; reviewing and interpreting long, tedious statutes and regulations; making occasional presentations; and filing forms with government agencies. It wasn't like the extremely long hours at Preston Ingold, but it had its impact all the same. Perhaps I was losing some of my early stamina—physically or spiritually. I was exhausted, lucky if I finished the day without some form of work emergency. The Corporate Compliance Department was wont to call at the last minute and ask that a contract be finalized by that afternoon or the next day even if I had just received a first draft that day. With more coffee, I'd try to concentrate and, behind closed doors, go through page after page of the contract (some of which ran into hundreds of pages of highly technical language), contact opposing counsel and attempt a negotiation of disputed terms and sometimes get yelled at.

In the early days after I left Preston Ingold and joined Machines and Papers, I renewed my determination to succeed, perhaps even make it to the top, or close. This was a new beginning. I worked hard as an understudy of sorts of the Senior Staff Attorney responsible for the Corporate Compliance Department: Jimmy O'Neil. He was sharp, meticulous and ambitious. Because he was kind to me, I in turn wanted him to succeed, eager to do what I could do to help him. But the person I needed to impress, the one who made promotions happen was Al Ensor, the Associate General Counsel. But Al was a different creature who literally barked at me whenever I had to make a report to him. He reminded me of a bulldog ready for a fight, his face always contorted as if in erudite concentration. Everything I said, he either couldn't understand or get. "Speak English!" he yelled at me once. I bore his attitude the same way you tolerate an ache with the hope that it will soon pass. But some aches don't pass.

After five years, I wasn't getting anywhere. Apart from the yearly adjustments for inflation, I received neither a pay raise nor promotion. In the meantime, the Legal Department had hired a new attorney, Randy Fishetti. "I want you to train him," Jimmy O'Neil told me. "This is your chance to prove yourself. If you can manage him well, I think you'll be well on your way to becoming Senior Staff Attorney." I took the challenge seriously and taught Randy what I knew. I answered his questions, reviewed and revised his memos to his clients before he released them, and encouraged him to maintain his composure under

194

pressure. His writing was quite awful at first, but I saw it improve over time as I rewrote and rewrote the memos he sent me to review. Initially, he came often to my office to chat, inviting me for lunch and staying close to me at every turn. Over time, though, he started weaning himself off. Three years after he was hired, Randy was put in charge of the Licensing Department. A year later, he was named Senior Staff Attorney. I complained to Jimmy O'Neil. "I trained the guy," I said. "I have three more years of experience as a lawyer. How can he get promoted over me?"

"You've got to understand, Jojo," Jimmy said. "He's responsible for Licensing. The company sees that department as more important than Corporate Compliance."

"Should I have complained to the General Counsel? Would Dale Hoyt understand or side with his lieutenant? Would Al Ensor perceive any complaint as disloyalty? I could have quit or taken the chance, but my ego had been so deflated I wasn't sure I'd be hired anywhere—or even if I did, I dreaded the anxiety, the interview process and rejections. In fact, I even questioned my abilities. If I couldn't be promoted despite my hard work and good performance reviews, did I have what it took? Perhaps this was the extent of my abilities and I truly didn't deserve Senior Staff Attorney. Perhaps Randy was more competent, more intelligent, better.

After Randy' Fischetti's promotion, my interest in my work decreased significantly. I knew I had to work to keep my job. But what was the use of extra exertion if I wouldn't get promoted? Most of my mates from law school were either senior attorneys in corporations, partners in law firms, or professors in various law schools. Those that joined the government were making names for themselves, appearing on TV and receiving widespread press. Because of my perception of failure, I avoided class

195

reunions as mine paled when compared to their achievements. Amid such loss of hope, I cut back. I worked only as needed and made no extra effort. My reviews now stated that I lacked initiative and innovation. But it didn't matter to me so long as I wasn't fired. All I looked forward to was maintaining my job and working towards a ~~comfortable~~ retirement.

Fifteen or so years after I started working for Machines and Papers Al Ensor left to become general counsel at another company. Jimmy O'Neil was named Associate General Counsel. Randy Fishetti was named Special Assistant to the Associate General Counsel. These events opened an opportunity—it wasn't ambition, really, as much as it was a small step toward self-advancement without expecting more beyond that. I pleaded with Jimmy: "I've been out of law school for eighteen years and I'm still Staff Attorney. What do I need to do to become Senior Staff Attorney?" A month after I made that plea, I was promoted to Senior Staff Attorney.

I should have been happy, but I wasn't. It had come too late and at great cost. Even then, I knew that my loss of self-esteem was irrecoverable. The best years of my life had been spent at Machines and Papers. It had offered me enough money to stay afloat. I was financially comfortable, but compared to others, I was nowhere. Even Fiona accused me of lacking ambition.

"I was full of hope and ambition when I arrived in this country," I told her.

"So what happened?"

"America killed my ambition."

"No," she said. "You allowed America to kill your ambition."

Several years into our marriage. Much had happened. The reality is never the dream. Ama and Juju were growing. Fiona had made partner at Crawford, but having picked a course, she seemed incapable of extricating herself to find sufficient time for her growing children and ageing husband. The closeness we had before was a rare occasion for us, be it of bodies in search of pleasure or souls seeking spiritual equilibrium. I craved and pined for her on many nights when she was too tired. Schooled by such lowered expectations, I became a bit careless. I ate more, gained weight, went to work, felt under-appreciated, was underpaid and said nothing for the most part. Everything seemed so monotonous, so boring, that I even considered but rejected divorce.

# Eight

I called Mark Bailey for reassurance. My American brother was his usual gregarious self, chastising me for neglecting him—which I had indeed. He assured me that I need not worry, that I should consider it as an opportunity to see another part of the country. His spirits always soaring, Mike calmed me, except when he revealed to me that he was joining the army.

"Why?!" I was incredulous.

"I feel I need to do this," he said. "It's a calling."

Why were the most important men in my life feeling the need to respond to some sort of calling?

"Calling, bro? I don't like this," I said. "The priesthood is a calling, but the army?" I'd have added that people get killed in the army but couldn't reveal to him that this was the sordid thought that soiled my mind in reaction to his revelation.

"I don't feel fulfilled, sis. I need to do something meaningful in my life"

"But there are so many other things you could do. You could volunteer for something... go to a poor country and help in some way."

"But this is what I am doing."

"Have you told mom and dad?"

"Not yet. You are the first person I'm telling, so keep this to yourself."

I could suspect some doubt in his voice. Or perhaps it wasn't doubt but fear. Or perhaps it wasn't fear but just the need for assurance, the need to be held and comforted and assured that all would be well or that he had some support somewhere. And it was a detection that made me pledge my support for him, even when I cringed in worry over his fate. Was it some sort of premonition or just plain over-concern? After we finished talking, I asserted to myself that I needn't worry, that many made successful careers in the army and retired with good pensions and other decorations. And I told myself that it was just the anxiety over my visit to Boston that was warping my thoughts.

I went to Boston.

At the onset Fiona calmed my concern when she hugged me at the airport and took my bag. "We'll have fun," Fiona assured. The drive from Logan Airport to Cambridge in her Mercedes took less than an hour, and I was impressed by the sleek vehicle, its comfort and smoothness but even more by the impressive Cambridge mansion we entered, its spaciousness, the chandeliers in the living room, the furnishings and artwork on the walls. Still, I was confronted at once by the emptiness, the hollowness of the place that spoke of loneliness and, as Fiona showed me around, I pitied the older woman, even though I too had wrestled with my own issues, some identical in magnitude to the corrosive effects of loneliness, some much worse. Fiona seemed to sense my reaction when she said, "I've been alone here since my husband passed. And as you very well know, my children are both on their own now. I've thought about selling it and getting a smaller place, but the memories keep me here, both good and bad."

We spent the rest of the day shopping in downtown Boston, Fiona prompting me to select clothes that she paid for, even selected for me. Fiona prepared a steak dinner when we returned home and we spent the remainder of the Friday talking—mostly me telling Fiona of my past, which I painted in great detail, except I omitted my second and third births, my relationship with Jean Pierre, the growth on my belly that had been severed, the rape in Butare, and the one incident in Kigali I couldn't share with anyone yet who didn't already know about it. After I finished my story, Fiona was in tears. "You've had such a challenging background, and yet you have triumphed," she said. "I think you are destined for great things. I really do." And I wondered what she would say if she heard the whole story without the sanitation-bandage I had put over it. "Have you ever considered law school?" Fiona asked.

I laughed. "No, I have no interest in studying law."

"I think you'll be a great lawyer. You are smart, articulate and personable. Oh, need I mention how good looking you are? They won't admit it, but it helps in the courtroom, in negotiations…"

"But I'm still working on my doctorate."

"It's never too late to go to law school. Anyway, I just thought I'd mention it to you. Just think about it."

I wouldn't. Not at that moment.

We drove to Cape Cod the next day to visit a friend of Fiona's, a retired schoolteacher and her businessman husband. Then we returned to Cambridge in the early evening and went to eat at an Italian restaurant on Massachusetts Avenue. During dinner, Fiona fidgeted a long while before asking me, "So how serious are you and Juju?"

I suddenly became aware that the woman sitting opposite me was a mother whose son had inflamed me with love. Was the question, despite the mother's show of graciousness and generosity, a sign of jealousy or some other concern? I looked away, as if ashamed to admit before Fiona that I loved her son.

"Please, Shama, just be honest with me. I won't judge you or anything, and pardon me if I embarrass you. I just think… Well, I'm just curious, you know. He's my son, after all."

Do you always put his girlfriends in such awkward situations? I thought this through until I remembered that if Juju was being truthful then I was his first girlfriend. Could it be that the mother was simply inept at handling such matters? I looked up but only managed to focus my eyes on Fiona's forehead. "We are serious," I said.

"Serious as seriously in love?"

"Yes, but I shouldn't speak for Juju. I can only speak for myself."

"But you can tell, can't you? You can tell that he loves you."

I nodded without speaking. I noticed Fiona grinning. "I didn't mean to embarrass you or anything," she said. "I'm sorry, but as I told you when I was in Evanston I feel I'm losing my son. I don't fear losing him to you. What I fear is that I will lose him to Africa."

"But why? Africa is not a bad place."

"No, no… Please don't get me wrong. It's not the fact that it's Africa. It wouldn't matter if it were Europe or Asia or Australia. But, you know, my husband also left one continent for another. He thought he'd come to the US, finish his degree, work for a few years and return to Ghana. But one thing led to another, a wife, a child, another child, a career and he was stuck here. And he died here. Is my son going to get stuck in Ghana, away from his mother, his sister, and you?"

Had Fiona deliberately sown a concern in me—live and die in Ghana? The older woman hadn't said so explicitly but now I began to wonder if this was possible. I wouldn't mind living and dying in Ghana with Juju (or, for that matter, Rwanda, if I could conquer my history's disturbing soundtrack of violence), but what if Juju made another choice? What if Juju married a Ghanaian woman? At the moment I tried to recall our times together before his departure. I recalled our relationship since he arrived in Ghana.

It had taken a week after his arrival to make the first call, apologizing, but with an explanation that it took some time for him to settle down and acquire a mobile phone (since the residence of his uncle had no phone line). "You couldn't call from a friend's or…"

"I'm sorry, Shama, but you know I'm new to this place."

"I've missed you so much, I wanted to hear from you sooner."

He'd told me that he'd already been to the beach to witness dragnet fishing, been to the market in downtown Accra, Makola, where the noise of city life (car horns, human voices, fowls and other fauna) mingled with other noises of city life (bells to attract one form of another of in an effort to make a sale, calls to prayer) to form one huge cacophony that, though random, seemed to mesh well. "Shama, this place is so vibrant, yet in a human way. It's not like the hustle of big American cities. Here, the people embrace the hustle and bustle, they're not its subjects, they're not its slaves, if you know what I mean. I'm so glad I'm here, Shama. I'm going to love it. I can tell."

The *I love you* he added at the end of the conversation provided the assurance I needed at the time, but in hindsight and with the aroused suspicion sparked by Fiona, I wondered if Juju had been too eager to get off the phone. My current view of this was suddenly inconclusive. I remembered too the post card of the beach Juju sent me shortly after our first conversation, the beach with its coconut trees. At the back of the card he'd written how much he'd missed me, how much he loved me and wished I were there with him. But now I wondered if the words were scrawled too hurriedly. In memory, I retrieved the card and scrutinized the writing, comparing it to other writings of Juju and became convinced that the one on the postcard had too much of a careless quality to them. If the man had been in Ghana only about a week and he was already in a hurry to write to me, what was he in a hurry about? It couldn't be because he wanted to get the words to me quickly; he'd already wasted over seven days before he even wrote the words. So where was he hurrying to? Or, worse yet, to whom was he hurrying?

I was making something out of nothing, I strained to assert to myself in the restaurant Fiona had taken me as she looked on, anticipating an answer to her suggestion. I ought to find solace in the letter Juju had sent, his first since he'd been in Ghana. In it, he's made a strained attempt to sound poetic in a manner that amused me, but deepened my love for him for the effort. He'd written how he was enjoying the family of his father, the uncles and cousins and the aunts. And then in the penultimate paragraph of the letter, he'd written: When I lay at night and the darkness engulfs me, I think only of you. I remember the color and texture of your skin, and in its chocolate is the sweetest taste God ever made, its charcoal the smoothest touch of his masterpiece, your darkness that provides light."

I had carried that letter with me for weeks, reading and rereading it for comfort. It had become his voice, speaking to me often when in my mind I put his voice to his words. But now I wondered. If I was chocolate and I gave him light, what would happen if the chocolate turned soar and the light dimmed or even died? Was I only good as long as he saw me in those terms? How many women in Ghana had the same qualities? In the days to come, as he woke day in and day out to the proximity of Ghanaian women, would they stand between Juju and me in a way that blocked my light?

I would try to recollect as many of our subsequent conversations as I could. None stood outstanding, each of them simply mundane updates and professions of mutual love. None, except one—when I'd heard a female voice in the background calling Juju's name. He'd hung up saying he had to go. Go to whom? I had wondered then but dismissed my concern as unfounded. Was it? He had called the next day and nothing seemed amiss. But the warning hadn't died, I realized, as now it spoke more boldly.

"You seem lost in thought," Fiona said. "Have I upset you?"

"No," I said. "I was just thinking."

"About Juju?"

"Yes."

"You miss him, don't you?"

I nodded.

"That makes two of us. So the question is, what are we going to do about it?"

I looked at Fiona, frowning. We? I wondered.

"We both miss him, so why don't we visit?"

"You mean go to Ghana?"

"Yes, why not?"

"I don't know…"

"Why? Don't you want to see him? Don't you miss him?"

"I do, but…."

"Well then, let's go. It will be on me. I will take care of it."

"No, I couldn't…"

"You don't want him out of your sight too long, Shama. Trust me on this."

That was rather manipulative of her, I thought. Was she now trying to implant suspicion and fear?

"Listen, Shama, you don't have to answer me now. But promise me you will think about it."

The proposition stayed with me after I left Boston the next day. It was so tantalizing, so sweetly alluring. To return to the continent, to see my Juju again, to reinforce what was or, if he was slipping from me, to recapture it. But I worried I would be so indebted to Fiona if I let her pay that I would have to do the older woman's bidding. Plus, I wouldn't have Juju to myself. Would the mother not crowd the girlfriend out? Still, to see him in person, even if only briefly…. And Fiona's words continued to ring *You don't want him out of your sight too long*. Perhaps the older woman was drawing from experience. I took out Jojo Badu's notebook-diary and reread:

That at the first serious threat to my marriage I would begin to sink into those ~~unimaginable~~ abysses of no rescue might at first blush seem incredulous to observers. Through the magnified lenses of hindsight it almost seems absurd to me too. This is something that defies logic, revokes mathematical precision, leaving only emptiness: in this case, one minus one did not equal zero, but the

203

remnants of zero, for the space left by the absence of what had been was full of the echoes of what had been.

So how did I arrive at the diminished will to continue, to so easily reflect the self-portrait of the heartbroken? That Ama and Juju had left home made it even more difficult. Sure, my relationship with Fiona had had gone cold, but there is that cushioning compromise between spouses to live and let live until death do part—which, in itself, secures a spiritual calm so crucial for the twilight years.

Pa was dead, Ma several years before. I had lived in America for some thirty-two years or so. I had many moorings to the land, but where was the anchor, the root that holds firmly amid calm and storm alike? Where was the fixture or face that would welcome me in my period of distress, one I could claim as a birthright? Could I turn to Ama? How could I lay my aged burdens on my daughter? She'd finished college only three years before and was straining to find some grounding in the claustrophobic confines of the corporate workplace. How about the son, Juju? He was still in school. Could I even attempt to lay my thorns before him mano-a-mano in the hope that gender and blood would bridge years and distance? What of my brothers and sisters who were miles and voices across seas? How could I find sufficient sympathy from them? What of just going home? Isn't home where the ~~fatigued~~ sojourner returns after the journey becomes unbearable? Isn't home the resting pillow where the prodigal son goes to unwind and be solaced? Yes. Yes. Yes. But that presupposes that I had the courage to go in search of the arms that expectedly would be opened, the bed that perpetually stays warmed. For starters, I had no house in Ghana. Worse, I had no *home* there. Whether or not true, that was my conclusion. When I'd suggested to Fiona that we build a house in Ghana, she'd said no. "Why build a house we will *never* live in? Home is America." How could I argue with

204

that when I'd naturalized as an American citizen a few years after our marriage and lived in the country for so long?

Homeless.

With news of Fiona's affair taking control of me, I'd arranged my schedule to arrive home from work late when Fiona was asleep—designed to escape the conflagration I expected if we met face to face. Carrying a bottle of liquor, I'd go to what used to be Juju's room and drink, ending the night of booze with additional swigs until I fell asleep. Then I'd wake up with a headache and take a swig or two before struggling to go to work. I was fifty-five years old. I wasn't doing too well hangover-wise with my new intimacy with liquor, having been a social drinker until then. But the momentary uplift was more important than the physical distress. At lunchtime, I'd drive to a secluded restaurant and take a few shots of liquor before returning to work, almost numbed. I knew I couldn't continue like that. My work was suffering, my concentration diminishing, my temper shortening. I took a leave of absence from work, hoping that I'd be able to find rehabilitation. That was a mistake.

I felt alien:

…belonging to something else: foreign: from somewhere else: extraneous: repugnant….

Extraneous. Repugnant. That was me. The indicia so evident—an accent that betrays otherness; mannerisms that often testify to otherness, or even when careful practice suppressed these, the undeniable history that shadows everyone, no matter how far he or she goes.

Even when I tried to reach for the safe and expedient surrogacy of memories of home rather than the hard inconveniences of physical encounters, I found my mind an impoverished proxy in that the photos that my mind was sending were too feeble, so faded they were of little use. I tried to recall Ma and Pa and my five brothers and four sisters, but it was as if time had extended a long poisoned tongue, licked them, swallowed them into its wide-gapped-mouth and almost chewed them beyond meaning. So at the moment when I needed them the most it seemed the memories were stubbornly hidden. Was I merely like jetsam floating without foundation until death did me take?

Meantime, these accusations of self-inflicted abandonment as I tried to deal with Fiona's affair seemed to pound louder at me, pummeling and pummeling every pore. I lay in Juju's bed while I listened to Fiona prepare and leave for work. The sound of running water, flushing toilets, had replaced the sense of her body, even if in the casual touch of morning as she tossed before waking. Now her perfume floating into Juju's room was the extent of her tactile presence. The smell of toast and coffee, teased my memory with its pictures now borrowed from times past when I could observe each bolus chewed. And then I would hear her car leaving, knowing that the day was beginning in the bitterness of loss, as if the exit of the car were a symbol of what had happened in our marriage, the loss to what seemed outside my control. And, if so, wouldn't her return at night signal something positive? Ought not I have seen it in that potential, that eventual return despite the momentary loss?

But how was I to engage in such analyses, such almost metaphysical rationalization, when caught in the snare of the moment, its discomforting pulse? No way. So, still in bed, caressing the near empty bottle of gin (or sometimes whiskey or vodka) I would strive for more self-torment, which would provide the justification for my new course. I would imagine in my aching head Fiona wiping herself, an imagination mingled in the concrete memory of days when I'd take the towel from her and wipe the streaks of water off her and she would, as though in reward, bestow on me coy kisses that were an invitation to sex before work, an invitation to a few more minutes in the shower, rushed in urgency and all the more enjoyable because of that rush. As I imagined Fiona getting dressed, her body only slightly heavier with age than when we'd married, stronger memories of things done in our bedroom returned, a brief balm for the wounded atmosphere between us. It was partly refreshing to see in my mind the past, but because the past reminded me of what was absent, it lost the fullness of its refreshment in the severity of betrayal. I would take quick gulps of whatever liquor I had brought with me to Jojo's room.

Fiona's betrayal continued to eat deep. I lived under its burden. After I was sure she had left home, I began the day with a long shower, my mind suffused with thoughts of drowning. The water that otherwise soothed me, now came like death's motif as each bead beat against me like a lash of doom and of fear. It was futile when I attempted to close my mind from the pain. Because I'd embraced the habit for the first time in my advanced life, I would smoke after my miraculous escape from the assaulting threats of the shower. My new smoking habit didn't make sense, but then little made sense at the time. It didn't make sense that after so many years of marriage, my wife would suddenly have an affair with a man about twenty years her junior. *Or perhaps it made perfect sense.* It didn't make sense that my children seemed so far away and beyond reach that I felt abandoned. *Or perhaps it made perfect sense.* Nor did it make sense that I so desired to see them despite the piece of Fiona residing in them. No, it didn't make sense. It just was. But, then again, *perhaps it made perfect sense.*

I felt freer in the streets, the outdoors that seemed so vast, but equally held immeasurable openings for error. I preferred the emancipating mood of open spaces to the rebroadcast of past events that the indoors cast in my mind. I'd find something to eat at a diner close by, drive down the boluses with bottles of beer and walk aimlessly in wait until the bars opened in the evenings. When I couldn't wait, I'd go to a liquor store and buy a bottle, carry it in a brown paper bag and take occasional chugs. I walked the paths of the homeless, almost looking like them as I'd stopped shaving and combing my hair. Some of them would see me and, as if signaling solidarity, call me *brother*. One of them called me Negro, hesitated a second and changed the noun to African. But he couldn't have known how deeply I craved brotherhood at that moment, a connection to make me believe that I belonged somewhere in America, belonged to someone, belonged to a group. I wanted to be *them*. I was them because my home was no longer like a home. And I knew, or thought, how sad it was because every one of them was somebody's somebody. So, in a way, my house had become where I slept, no longer home. The streets had become like my past and my future, my liberation and my imprisonment, centrifugal and centripetal, all at once—like Fiona, a contradiction holding only opaque explanations. If I were a bolder man, I'd have stayed outside. Here, I could become the outside; perhaps here, I could lose myself and that sad self-pity, find power in their numerous stories of ache and heartbreak; perhaps here I could finally find a story weightier than mine, one to which I could surrender mine. But I wasn't bold enough for that.

Around midnight when I knew Fiona wasn't downstairs, I'd stumble home to be burned by its inferno, to be soothed by its familiarity. I'd walk to Juju's room and absorb more liquor before collapsing into sleep.

For at least a fortnight I walked this course, falsely liberated from the pressures that dragged me down in the quotidian bore—the repetitive fox trot of adult life that bores the adventurous, that stifles dreams, that wrestles with happiness day in and day out—until one Sunday, full of liquor, I had a sudden seizure of desire to see Fiona, to

208

gauge her reaction to my absence from her radar screen. I was exhausted, but hoped that within those tired hours would exist some reclaimable solace, anything worthy of anchorage. But in my circumstance that kind of hope was mired in the unshakable distress of a spouse's faithlessness—in the best moments, a bugaboo, a weakening of the will; in the worst of moments a torment, like consuming inferno, a zigzagged drive to and from thoughts of homicide.

I argued that she must be saddened by the dissipation of the remnants of our marriage. Was she wallowing in regret or… that's where my thought train ended, afraid to peek further into the other possibilities. That suspension of thought seemed to span ages as it was laden with pain, anxiety, a beating heart, dry lips, sweaty palms, nervous stomach. Langston Hughes asked what becomes of a dream deferred. I had no use for dreams; instead, I asked myself what becomes of unused love. Does it vanish as vapor in a storm or linger like air eternally renewing itself? Does it lose its place in mind and body or regain favor? Does it pay tribute to its past or obliterate it with the torch of disappointment? I had to find out from Fiona whether any hope existed, whether the unused part of our love was strong enough to resurrect it. I was compromising my pride but the desire drove me forward as if by spontaneous combustion.

Brazenly I walked into our bedroom (now hers only) and found her sleeping, peaceful in the night that had battled me, not even with a snore or toss to indicate tension. I was jealous. No, more than that, I was beyond jealous. I was irate. Why didn't she share my anguish? How could she sleep so peaceably? Why hadn't she come apologizing? I flung myself on the bed, the act of a drunk, a confused, even a desperado seeking courage under the cloak of drunkenness.

209

Fiona got up as though a thief had entered the bed (and I might as well have been a thief), and turned on the light. As the light flooded the room, I considered myself exposed as if caught amid a dastardly deed, and I stammered off the bed to the other end so that we were facing each other from opposite sides. "Jojo!" she exclaimed. "Look at you. What's wrong with you?"

"Yes!" I screamed back. "Look at me. Tell me, what do you see, *wife*?"

"You are drunk."

Even in my drunkenness and madness I could detect the horror ~~swell inside her~~. I couldn't read the signal—was it sympathy or disgust? Either way, I was suddenly diminished in the knowledge that the little I could detect was neither regret nor remorse. Fiona was not looking for me to absolve her. ~~My madness vanished.~~

The initial betrayal had already taken its effect (and still eating away, of course). Added to this was that horror, the witness to the feeling of ~~still~~ not been wanted, the finally dawned acceptance that I'd been replaced, and the confirmed knowledge that I was the lone bearer of the pain and regret. When I saw Fiona stare at me that way, something gave—a dislodged foundation in a house of dominos—and I came tumbling down, falling, breaking apart, tearing away internally, pore by pore, drop of blood by bloody drop. I lost control completely and against my will, for the first time, let loose before her the teary manifestation of my pain. And then I saw the horror intensify in her, as if she was telegraphing a deep disappointment in me to me with a piteous, "Don't cry."

I ran out of the room back to the ~~insane~~ sanctuary of Juju's room, pacing it like an aimless lunatic. Death, please become me, I prayed. I waited for minutes, hoping that Fiona would come to me, rescue me. I hated the weakness for her, the enlarged capacity of my willingness to reconcile. But all that I could hear was a loaded silence that suggested she was asleep. And then the voice of Dante rang in my ears, the phone call I'd received a little more than three weeks earlier.

*My name is Dante*, he had said. *I just screwed your wife.*

Blunt and to the point. You have to admire the man's style. At first, I'd thought it a prank and hang up. But they wouldn't go away, those five words. I strained time for recollection.

An early Sunday night. Not an unusual night for Fiona to be with her friends or even go to the bookstore. But tipped off by the relentless ring of that confident declaration, my senses reworked the evening a little. What was Fiona wearing when she left the house? I recalled the thin strapped, black dress with a hemline that ended just above her knees, the freshwater pearls around her neck, the perfume, the red-lipstick-lips, the high heeled shoes that flattered her still defined legs, especially the calves. Hindsight is a telescope, a magnifier, a teacher indeed. I tried to compare her appearance that night with her appearances on previous nights. The contrast was clear, rendered cloudless by the sudden strength of that hindsight. In the context of the revisited phone call, then, I was on infirm ground, wondering. It couldn't be. Fiona? My Fiona? No way in the world. But ... but, what if? A nagging undercurrent of doubt demanded answers. I waited for my wife like a hungry beast waiting ~~in the shadows~~ for prey.

Fiona returned a little before midnight. "Where have you been?" I asked like a disarmed lawyer impatient for the gradual trickery of cross-examination. I turned on the light in the bedroom, startling her. She hesitated and I could sense every lawyerly instinct in her rise, ready to make her defense. "The bookstore," she said. She'd learned the art much better than I in the confrontational maneuverings of human interaction under the pressure of

211

courtrooms, each expression calibrated for the question or the occasion for it.

"Fiona, why did you do it?"

"What do you mean?" Her voice was breaking – easier to question than be questioned, easier to detach *self* from client than *self* from husband. *Not doing too well, counselor. What's the matter?*

"Who is Dante?"

She covered the lower part of her face with one hand, her eyes widening as if in horror, as if stricken with panic. There she was, stripped of every skill of human manipulation, naked as Adam and Eve post-sin. There was no denying it. And then waves of heaping sobs seized her, as if she were the wronged one~~, and perhaps she was~~. "Why?" She didn't respond, except with mounting sobs. And me? A name mentioned over the phone and its audacious voice continued to consume me ~~as it seemed to consume her~~. The paramour, thus far kept, no longer rested content in the expedient fringes and took the calculated risk to determine whether he was expendable or would move to center stage. And here, the rest of the players may very well have determined a different outcome. If I'd probed Fiona more, sought the reasons behind her act, offered forgiveness there and then, I may have altered the script. If Fiona, rather than the ambiguity of tears, had offered her remorse to the vengeful lust of my injured ego, she may have altered the script. But none of that would happen, making Dante's call to me a maestro's masterstroke. I left our bedroom and went to Juju's room to begin the next phase of the rest of my life. It would be without Fiona.

## Nine

Dante and Fiona. Juju and ____? I didn't want the blank to be filled in by any other name than mine. I called Fiona and accepted her proposal.

"Great!" Fiona said. "But now we have to convince Juju."

"Leave that to me," I said as abruptly as I immediately regretted it, worried that Fiona might think I was placing myself in a superior position in regard to Juju.

But Fiona said with a relieving chuckle, "Yes, ma'am." And I imagined Fiona saluting as she said this and perhaps acknowledging that going forward she had ceded space to me, that I would be the primary emotional caretaker of Juju. I hope I wasn't merely wishful thinking.

I resorted to all powers of guile and persuasion I could muster to obtain Juju's agreement. Initially sounding elated that I wanted to visit Ghana, Juju soon rejected the idea. "You should come, Shama, but I think you should come alone. You don't need to bring mom along."

"She's paying for the trip. You know I can't afford the trip on my own."

"I wish I had some money to fly you over. I really don't like this. Not one bit."

"I'll get to see you, Juju. Think of it that way."

"We'll just have to wait, honey. I'll work hard and save some money so I can get you the ticket myself."

"When, Juju? I miss you so much. I need to see you. Why, don't you miss me? Don't you want to see me?"

"Of course I do, you know I do."

"Then let me come."

"But you'll be with my mother."

"So what, Juju?"

"Just be patient, Shama."

"*Why*? Are you having so much fun over there you don't want to see me?"

"Shama…"

"I want to see you but it seems you don't want to see me. I thought you loved me."

213

"Come on, Shama."

I allowed my voice to break, as if I was on the verge of tears.

"Are you crying?"

I sniffled. "All I want is to come and see you, Juju and here I have this perfect chance and you won't let me come."

"You don't understand. Mom is filled with guilt and she thinks she can make up for it with this."

"What are you talking about, Juju?"

He would sigh, inhale deeply and tell me that I needed to know more. "Tell me," I said. And he did.

"What do you think you'll find in Ghana?" Fiona had asked him when he told her he was going. "This is your home, Juju. This is where you belong."

"Was Dad not Ghanaian?"

"No, he naturalized, you know. There must have been a reason for that, don't you think?"

"It doesn't matter, Mom. He was always a foreigner in this country. He always felt it, anyway."

"Juju, your own grandfather left Africa for America. He returned. He couldn't stay away from home. I lived in Ghana once. I know what it's like. Don't romanticize that continent."

"I don't have any romantic ideals about the place. I just want to know it better."

"And you have to do it now? Can't you wait until you're done with school?"

"No, Mom, school can wait."

"Juju, please…"

"Mom, please…"

"Come to your sister's before you leave. I'm living with her for a while as I sort certain things. Stay with us for a little while before you leave."

"In that little apartment?"

"Juju, if you will do nothing for me, at least do this for me, please. Please come."

He knew what his mother wanted from him. But was he ready to provide the antiseptic forgiveness that would calm her conscience but that wasn't genuine?

He would try. He went to his sister's apartment as his mother had requested. The immediate tension was draining like a viral infection for which his mother tried different unavailing antidotes. She tried recollecting the best times from before, but they were few and therefore inadequate to override what he blamed her for doing to his father. Then she wanted to shift blame. It was always like him to be like that—withdrawn. He wouldn't confront but walk away. It wasn't her fault if he wouldn't let her atone. He was not moved by this reasoning. She moaned aloud that she feared he wouldn't return from Ghana, that the African continent would claim him in revenge for the way the American continent had claimed his father. Tit for tat. Had she escaped the continent with her father only to lose her own son to it? He was impassive to this fear. She knew she'd lost.

Her wish to close the circle and tighten it remained stymied by her infidelity, which still lay awake like a wedge between them, a swamp full of dangerous crocodiles ready to feed. Fiona organized dinner out for all three. But because of Ama's presence, she couldn't capture Juju's full attention, nor employ all her motherly sway or wiles. After all, Ama was also seeking her brother's friendship before he left for Ghana. What chance did Fiona stand in that three way dynamic? Fiona took Juju shopping the next day. That was a mistake, for he had little interest in the things she wanted to buy him. They went to the movies with Ama, but again the trio weakened the impact of the duo Fiona would have most likely wished. Yet she must have feared alienating Ama if she focused too much on Juju. She cooked for him, laundered his clothes, pampered him, but still he could not bring himself to reach across to her. She tried conversation that was mostly one way. Fiona didn't know what to do.

Fiona's frustration mounted to the point of desperation. "I need you to forgive me. I don't want you to say it, Juju. I want you to mean it. I want you to believe how so sorry I am."

"Nothing to forgive," he said

She was speechless, her voice seemingly lost in the confusion boiling inside her. He knew she was earnest, but he wanted so much to punish her for his father's death he walked away from the room.

Fiona walked after him and as he turned to look at her he saw her tears came one after the other. Compassion broke loose inside him, but he stood firm, not knowing he could be so stoic, cruel even. How could he reject her so blatantly? She wiped her face, went to the bathroom and locked the door. He imagined her sitting on the toilet and sobbing, her failure flooding her like the tears they expressed.

And at the airport, he had given her a perfunctory hug and walked away, without looking back, for that brief, farewell glimpse that can be so assuring.

"You see, Shama, she feels so guilty, she wants a way to atone for that."

"I understand how you feel, Juju, and your feelings are totally legitimate. But think about it. She is your mother. It is now that she is alive that you ought to reconcile with her. You don't know tomorrow and you don't want to live with any regrets. Take this from someone who has lost his mother."

"Okay, Shama, let me think about it."

I would pester him in subsequent calls, sometimes effect crying, repeat the phrase *If you love me you'd want to see me no matter what.* I knew I was being manipulative, but the awakened fear that I might lose Juju was of greater consequence to me. After weeks of prodding, an emotionally wearied Juju agreed to the trip. "You have to tell mom that

I'll pay her back every cent she spends on you." After I'd cozened his agreement, the least I could return to him was to promise as he requested. Promise made, I informed a thrilled Fiona who insisted that she couldn't accept repayment (which detail I hid from Juju). "You are amazing," Fiona said to me. "Through you I will see Juju soon."

If I worried that Fiona was using me as a bait to reel in Juju, I had become a willing bait. We began to plan the trip, agreed to meet in New York and fly to Accra, Ghana via Europe.

I received a post card from Juju reiterating his love for me and emphasizing his excitement about my impending arrival in Ghana. Unimportant as it may have looked to a neutral observer was the photo in front of the card—the Supreme Court building in Accra. Suddenly, the suggestion that Fiona had made that I consider law school was at the forefront of my thoughts, but I stifled it for the moment as the anticipation of seeing Juju soon grew more paramount.

In New York, Fiona took me to dinner the night before the trip to Ghana. She was a little more subdued than usual, and drinking quite heavily. "I'm nervous about this," she said. "You know my son hates me, Shama."

"No, she doesn't. She loves you."

Fiona shook her head. "He blames me for his father's death. And he has a point. I have never really spoken to anyone about it, Shama. It's like a heavy burden on my shoulders. You, I feel like you are part of the family now and I feel so connected to you. I know you're much younger, but you seem to have a matured soul, a spirit I can relate to. I want to share my secret with you."

"Please...."

"Please, Shama, I need to let it out. It's killing me."

I thought Fiona had had too much to drink and I didn't her to say something she might regret, but she wouldn't let me stop her and for the next few hours, between food and wine and dessert, she told her story.

It wasn't just the excitement of the matter that thrilled her, but the rediscovery of youth as well, that ever-seductive force of vigor and vitality. It was also the difference of him, the *wrongness* of it, the adventure

217

offered relatively late in life. She would sacrifice all the years of her history to him. Like a mother abandons a child to the unknown, or a father to the expediency of independence, she felt the guilt just as much as the thrill. Because of the sense of urgency, words were an unnecessary foreplay. For her in particular, it could only be a tortuous prolonging of the pressing longing. And then he, like a maestro with perfect timing, stepped out of his robe and in that instant, he became a panorama of all that was physically desirable.

Afterward, her desire sated, his work done for the moment, they had to endure the troubling epilogue of talk. The guilt that had simmered before the deed now boiled fully, moderated only by the lingering pleasure, the cherished aftertaste of a sweet act. Drenched in the sweat-bath of their act, buoyed by the ripples still surging through, she still was somewhat surprised by how he could please her body so masterfully. More than the guilt was her need for justification and the need for the act not to be just an insignificant experience in what she suspected were a series of conquests. If she could be convinced he craved her, that he held her in a different place than any other, then the justification would be easier for her to make. That wish spurred in her a sudden effort to reach into his mind, which was closed to her by his choice. She wanted to know, but the closer she stepped, the more he shifted the doorknob, leaving her to clutch at the door that wouldn't open.

"So what next?" Fiona asked.

"What do you mean?"

"You must have a string of women wrapped around your finger."

"Why do you say that?"

"A man with your looks?"

He said nothing. "I must be one out of hundreds," she said, her caution completely abandoned to curiosity. "I mean the way you did it... it seems to come so easily to you." I mean...the way it happened... I don't know..."

The way it happened. The first time...

Rewind to the earlier Saturday evening. She'd just fought with her husband about something trivial as not taking out the trash. Out of anger, she'd called him hopeless and he had reciprocated the insult. Then she'd ignored him the way she had so many times before, secure in what was taken for granted in the vast mileage of marriage. When she left the house, it was a mere excuse for her to calm her nerves. She arrived at the bookstore, browsed the shelves, picked up a novel, and sat down to read.

"Ma'am, may I sit next to you?"

Fiona didn't look up. "Suit yourself."

"Come on. A pretty lady like you shouldn't be so angry. It just doesn't suit you."

Intrigued and mildly offended, she looked up, her prepared sarcasm held at the ready. But, *What a ...* she wasn't sure what to call him: boy or man? Hard to say as he seemed trapped between the two stages of male-hood. But his appeal, his raw handsomeness, had no ambivalence to it. It commanded attention; it captured admiration; it provoked instant lust. Even the semi-boyishness of the face seemed to mesh with the matured features mannishly, particularly the pose that was so sure it added rather than detracted from his appeal. So despite the voice within to tell him to leave her be, she couldn't find the strength for that. He exploited the window of her internal debate and indecision and sat next to her.

"What're you reading?" he asked.

She showed him the book, still holding back as if she could rebuff him with stayed speech. But something was happening to her. It was internal and it was exciting. It was strong, though it made her weak. It was warm, though it made her shiver. It was comforting, though it made her vulnerable. She wanted to will it away, but it was not that weak. It was as if her will was rolling down a slippery slope, unable to find traction on the interest that was growing. For the time being, there could be no harm, could there? And in the meantime, what was his mission?

"That's a pretty good book. Read it once or twice. I like the way the author draws you in right away and doesn't let go."

*He reads*? Shared interest. "You've read this?" This interest in reading warranted an oral spoken response from Fiona. Actually, her answer wasn't that planned, springing more from the spontaneity he tapped with those three sentences.

"Yeah, I'm afraid it's one of my bad habits," he said

"Reading, you mean?"

"I'm afraid so. And you? You like to read?"

"When I have the time," Fiona said.

"And when you don't?"

"I'm practicing law."

"No way. *You*, a lawyer? You're too cute to be a lawyer."

"Are you trying to be funny?"

"I mean it. But I won't hold your profession against you if you don't hold mine against me."

"And what might that be?" Fiona asked.

"A starving artiste."

"What kind of *art*?"

"Fiction."

"Really? Have you published?"

"Not yet, but I'm working on it."

She liked him notches more, even as she wondered why some women fall for such fluffy nonsense.

For a full five minutes he engaged her in the play he wrote and performed for her sole benefit. He was so adept, such a genius at it, that when the balcony closed, she hardly noticed it.

"I tell you what."

"What?"

"Let me buy you a drink. There's a bar around the corner."

"Are you crazy?" she said as though his strategy hadn't worked. "I don't know you."

"But isn't that the whole point? Get to know each other over a glass of wine or something?"

"Look, you're a nice young man, but I'm married…"

"I just want to talk a little, that's all."

When she agreed to follow him, she thought he was taking her to a bar as he'd promised. She knew the place and was comfortable with it, its anonymity. In her mind, she was still on the large prairie. It was vast, fenceless and harmless. She could flee at any time. There was that certain *je ne sais quois-ness* about him that convinced her she was safe with him, that allure that made her want to embrace him, that earnestness that made her want to mother him. So she would have a glass of wine with him, take the adventure to that level only. When he stopped in front of the apartment before the bar, she hesitated.

"Come on," he said. "We'll share a drink. Just one and you'll be on your way home. I promise."

"But you said we were going to that bar."

"Why go there when we can make our own bar upstairs?"

She searched his finger for the first time, that search for a ring with all its meaning. He noticed. For the first time that something inside her generated thoughts that were to her dangerous; for the first time she was reaching a height that made her shudder at the potential of what it might bring. "Look," he said "I don't want you to get the wrong idea. I'm not some tramp off the street…"

221

Fiona had begun unraveling in his presence, and more so at the proximity to his beddings. What harm is there?

Another part of Fiona was raging: *Oh Fiona, how could you be so careless? Is desire that blind? Entering the apartment of someone you've just met in a bookstore? Is it safer because you met him in a literary setting? Fiona, this is fraught with risks. Every ounce of legal training, even common sense, should be telling you leave as fast as you can.*

Did someone say love is blind? No, friend, you might as well erase "love" and put "lust" in its stead. In this context it's not a blindness to looks, but a blindness to risk.

She was thinking: *I'll sit for a while and leave; there can be no harm.* Or at least she forced her thoughts in that direction. *All right, I'll go up for a while, talk a bit and go home.*

*He's so handsome. He seems like such a nice guy, too.*

He removed his jacket once they were in his apartment, revealing a tank top, showing the humped muscles of his arms. He didn't offer any wine.

*This is so wrong. I'm a married woman in a single man's apartment on a Saturday night. I've got to get out of here.*

He turned on his lazy music and ran his hands through his dreadlocks. He invited her to dance. She refused. He shed his tank top before she could protest and, at a pace too sped for reaction, he dropped to his knees in front of her, pushing on her thighs as she attempted to stand. With the near bird's eye view of his naked torso, she still wanted to believe she was in control. His hands started to roam her thighs and she wanted to yell Stop! Stop! Stop! She wasn't even sure if it was sex she desired or just male companionship, but who can control the flow of the water once it's poured from its source? The pleasure was well etched now, but, more importantly, in the dictionary of their actions, a new thing was emerging, the *something* that had begun internally, become outwardly manifest and shared with him, had now infected him too, even if he wasn't aware yet, and its definition was being written:

**It**: **1:** an intense, boundless pressure that weaves its way into the physical frame of those it inhabits until unleashed through some form of physical congress **2:** the emotional equivalent of such pressure **3:** a state of calm introduced by thoughts of the physical expression of that which induces the thought **4:** a state of intense guilt aroused either after sexual congress or emotional longing, which guilt often arises from the illicitness of the congress or longing **5:** a spiritual being believed often to ensnare paramours in an abyssal web of secrecy and having so ensnared them refuses to relinquish its hold **6:** a maddening sense to possess another **7:** an ache that resides in the body that is at once a subject and object of desire and may only be soothed by the kind words of its object; **8:** a state of heightened sensibilities easily leading to feelings of injured pride; **9:** an intense sense of being unloved; **10:** all of the above existing all at once or in varying forms at any point in time.

*It* was making its appearance unobtrusively. Fiona and Dante. What was the currency this young man had so powerfully used to acquire Fiona's time and body? His appearance? The mention of his novel in progress?

In subsequent visits, Fiona—fully physically sated by the young, energetic mass of flesh—unlocked herself.

223

Despite her guilt, she felt obliged to him even while her conscience persisted like a good, fading thought. Her intuition warned her to stay quiet, embrace the calm and unbroken salience, leave their relationship at its physical level. And yet the fear that she might lose this taboo they'd started was too strong. She didn't want to lose *It*. And so she started slowly, and like negotiating a street with no Stop signs, she went on and on about herself, and her husband: "… for all intents and purposes we might as well be divorced," she punctuated her narration with this revelation. "I mean, we rarely sleep together anymore… Sometimes you want to know that your husband still needs you. I mean… I don't know…."

The phone rang. He didn't answer. He made her some tea. "The phone rang again. "Won't you answer that?"

He picked it up. "Can't talk now, baby," he said. Fiona cringed at the word *baby*. "I'll call you later."

"Who was that?"

He didn't look at her. "My wife," he said.

The word *wife* turned the world around too quickly for her. "Your wife? Your wife? Your wife? You are married?"

Unflinchingly, he looked at her and said, "Yes."

The world turned even faster, miasmic, unhinging. "You mean all this time … You mean you have a wife?"

"I do."

"And when were you going to tell me?"

"Hey, it never came up, okay?"

"But…But…"

"Don't make a big deal of it, okay? Look, we were both married, we saw an opportunity and we took it."

"Opportunity. Is that what all this is to you? Some cheap opportunity?"

"I didn't say cheap."

"And this secret wife of yours, where's she?"

"She's home in Springfield."

Home. Cruel word. Fighting word. But Fiona remained exteriorly calm because she saw no other way and because it wasn't in her to be otherwise with this man who made *It* complete. "And now what?"

"What do you mean?"

"Do you love her?" She surprised herself with that question. This wasn't what she'd come to him for. Now she was asking about his love or lack thereof for a wife she hadn't even known existed.

"You know better than to ask me that."

Fiona panicked. Right before her she saw a slipping chance. She wanted it to slip away so she could take control, mend emotions, repair self-confidence, lift guilt. But still her panic sprung from fear, an old fear now injected with a new element, the fear she'd lose him. Having, in a manner, transposed her husband onto Dante, she was afraid of losing him. Jojo. Dante. Him. Which was which? Who was the *him*? And out of that fear, perhaps, she reached out to him. He took a step back at first, but *It* was there. *It. It. It. I hate It. I love It. Hate. Love. It.* Dante, also seduced by *It*, acted on the impulse, the beckoning of *It*, and kissed Fiona and they found *It* again.

*It* had survived. It must have blinded Dante into jealousy, despite his own marriage, to call Jojo and tell him about the affair, perhaps in the hope that he would gain Fiona's complete attention.

By the time Fiona finished her story, she must have drunk at least a bottle of wine and she was barely coherent. I had to help her out of the restaurant, help her into the taxi I commandeered and help her into her hotel room. I considered staying in her room with her, concerned she might hurt herself somehow in the condition, but she assured in slurry words that she would be fine. And I had a feeling this was not the first time she'd been in this condition and that she knew how to handle it.

# Ten

We were picked up at the Kotoka International Airport in Accra by a taxi hired by the paterfamilias of the Badu family, Juju's uncle. After he welcomed us, we shared a meal of rice and chicken stew, which I enjoyed but Fiona struggled to finish. Then Juju pulled us aside into one of the rooms in the family house and said, "The three of us are going to have to share this room."

"Why?" Fiona asked, a flash of irritation in her eyes. And I had already noticed the tension between mother and son. Even at the airport when Juju hugged his mother, he had disengaged quickly. His "Good to see you" remark was not convincing; he may very well have said it to a stranger. I'd contrasted this to the long embrace I'd received, the kiss, and the grin from Juju, even the glitter in his eyes. And perhaps this reception, compounded with the revelation of sleeping arrangements, had riled Fiona.

"There are very few rooms here, Mom. They've already sacrificed so much by giving me this room. They won't allow me to share it with anyone else. But the nephews and cousins and brothers and sisters are cramped into small rooms and I have this room all to myself. They'd offered to give you one of their rooms but I wouldn't let them. We'll have to manage this one."

"How can three adults share the same room? This tiny room? How do you expect me to share the same room with my son and his girlfriend?"

"Not just one room, Mom, but the same bed also. As you can see, only one bed fits in here."

"This is insane."

"We'll manage, Mom."

"That's fine, I will get a room in a hotel."

"No, Mom, they will feel insulted if you do that."

Fiona sighed.

I admired juju for being so considerate of his hosts' needs, even if it meant inconveniencing us. As it was, on Juju's insistence, he and I slept on the ends of the bed, with Fiona in the middle. Juju would excuse us in the mornings and nights when we wanted to get undressed. It was an uncomfortable, even embarrassing, arrangement, with me exposed for the first time to Fiona's nocturnal farts when she slept or her morning breath, just as I suspected the older woman bore mine. And I had to be careful not to reveal the scars in my back to Fiona, afraid it would repulse her and raise questions I didn't want to have to answer. We managed, however, even if it left me tired as my sleep was strained by the proximity of bodies.

I spent the next few days with Juju, seeing as much of Accra as time would allow, particularly spending copious amounts of time at the Labadi Beach, reminiscing, caressing, kissing, necking, and falling in love again and again (or rather falling in love in new ways). Fiona spent most of her days with the in-laws, who also did what they could to occupy her time. But after a few days of this, I insisted Juju spend more time with his mother. He protested until I feigned anger. "You can't ignore your mother this way. You must spend more time with her. You just must!" So he began to include Fiona in our activities, and wherever Juju and I went, there Fiona also went. It diminished our love-signaling acts, but I was pleased to see the dourness in Fiona transform to what I interpreted as joy for the first time since we arrived. At some point Fiona even kissed Juju on the cheek and he in return hugged her tightly.

As Juju had begun earning a little of a living as a fisherman, he took Fiona and me to work (as he explained that this work gave him more free time and he planned to find something else later). We realized that he was more an honorary than actual fisherman. We watched him in his effort at dragnet fishing as a sort of appendage than as a major contributor to the effort, as he seemed barely able to muster the muscular strength of the other fishermen. He told me that although he made a pittance he was able to get a share of the fish, which his Ghanaian family appreciated, and it also gave him the chance to mingle with all sorts of interesting people, from the fishermen themselves to the women who sold the fish to those, including some big shots, who came to the seashore to buy the fish. He also said that his uncle wouldn't accept any money Juju offered from his work, insisting that it was the uncle's duty to take care of his brother's son. But Fiona would inform me, on promise that I wouldn't tell Juju, that she sent monthly remittances to the uncle for the support of Juju and the rest of the extended family. "I only tell you this so that in case I'm not around you can let Juju know that he has no obligation to this family."

"I will need to find a better paying job soon," Juju later told me. "I would like to give them something when I leave, something big. They've all been so good to me."

Two weeks into our planned three week visit and I was beginning to dread returning to the US. I wanted now to spend the remaining moments alone with Juju, to store whatever we could make in our moments in the memory tank from which I would have to withdraw in the future. But now that Fiona had become a part of our entourage I had no way of accomplishing my wish. In fact, I would soon be faced with the opposite of what I wished.

I had noticed her for a while. A slim, generously bosomed woman, no more than twenty, I guessed; always well dressed, she seemed not to belong at the beach. She looked more like someone going to a party. She would be present most of the time when Fiona and I were there with Juju, in the background, talking to this person or that and just about everyone except Juju. But I noticed how she furtively studied Juju when she thought I wasn't looking. With a slight head movement, I'd once asked Juju, "Who is that woman?"

"Who?" Juju asked. I repeated the gesture, "I don't know," he said, barely looking at the woman.

I wasn't convinced. The woman just didn't belong there and her voice—I thought I could be wrong on this—sounded like the voice I'd heard when Juju called me and hang up to call later. But the voice had been so distant then that I couldn't be sure. I then undertook an experiment: even in Fiona's presence I would hold on to Juju tightly, throw an arm over his shoulder, even kiss him on the cheek, and then I would study (out of my eyes' corners) the woman's reaction. As best as I could tell the woman's face would fall and she would roll her eyes. "Are you sure you don't know that woman?" I asked again.

"Absolutely not," said Juju.

And still I didn't believe.

The day after Juju's second denial, I told him I needed to rest, encouraging him to go to work. "I think the going up and down has tired me out," I said. Juju didn't protest this much. I'd expected him to insist I accompany him or volunteer to stay at home with me. Fiona had also made other plans to see someone his husband had represented a while back in the US who had returned to Ghana and named his daughter after Fiona.

I waited a while after Juju left and took a taxi to the seashore, stopping a short distance from the intended destination. I walked stealthily and stopped when I saw Juju, except he wasn't alone; that is to say he had his arms around a woman, the woman he'd denied knowing more than once. I gasped, suddenly going faint, growing goose pimples. I considered returning home, fleeing from the scene of the crime, pretending it hadn't happened by refusing to confront it. But I couldn't seize this expedient option and I found myself moving (as though against my will) toward them. Within hearing distance, I yelled, "Juju, looks like you're busy."

Juju turned around, removed his hand from around the woman and, face-embarrassed, said, "I thought you were tired."

"You told me you didn't know her."

"Leave him alone,' said the woman.

"Stay out of this Chochoo," Juju said to the woman.

So that was her name. Chochoo made a face and crossed her arms over her bosom.

"Juju," I said, "why did you lie to me?"

"What do you mean?"

"Don't pretend you don't know what I'm talking about. Please, don't insult me."

"Listen, Shama. Can we go somewhere and talk?"

"What is there to talk about? You have your Chochoo. What is there to talk about?"

"Shama, do you want to cause a scene?"

"And what if I do?"

"Leave her," Chochoo said.

"Be quiet," Juju returned.

"Now you want to hush her? Let your girlfriend speak up."

"Shama, there's a bench around the corner. Let's go sit and talk."

"About what? That you lied to me? That behind my back you've been seeing this woman?"

"I said let's go sit and talk, just you and me."

229

"No, let's talk about it right here, right now."

"I can't do this," said Juju as he turned and walked away, with Chochoo following as my mouth gaped. I waited a few minutes for Juju to return. He didn't. I went home in tears and entered the room we shared, sat on the bed, hugged my legs and wept. I wept as afternoon turned to evening and then twilight became night. Fiona came late in the night to find me frozen in the same pose, engulfed in the darkness, my weeping now reduced to sniffles.

Fiona turned on the light. "What's the matter?" she asked. "Is something wrong, honey? And where's Juju?"

It took me over a minute to manage enough control to begin. I had considered not telling Fiona, but felt that I had to or I might breakdown completely, and I could think of no else to share my frustration with than Fiona. I knew it was dangerous involving the mother, but I needed to unburden this immediately because I was chocking on it, and she so proximate, so willing to hear, so seemingly sympathetic. And, after her confessions, I felt I could trust her with this. Through sniffling punctuations, I told Fiona what I'd seen. "I'm so sorry," she said as she opened her arms and entreated me to get in them. Rubbing my back, Fiona assured me all would be well. I remembered my mother as Fiona held me and at that moment I realized that, after my mother's death, I'd not felt as close to any female as I did then than to Fiona, except Aunt Shama. The relationship with my aunt hinged on our blood relations and its attendant love. It was not easily prone to swaying. With Fiona, I felt I'd met someone who understood me more than anyone one else, someone I could trust without fear of betrayal. Could it be the way she had shared her own burdens? I became calmer in her presence.

Later, I said to her, "You know, when you told me about you and Dante, you didn't say whether you managed to kill *It*. I'm sorry I am bringing this up now, please forgive me; but how does an affair end? How do you kill *It*?"

"That's okay, Shama," Fiona said. "You know by now you can ask me anything. But I don't know. I suppose it dies its natural death. Yes, we did kill *It*."

She told me how.

Four weeks after his funeral, Jojo's friend from law school Dwayne called Fiona and arranged to arrive in Boston from Washington DC. Dwayne told Fiona he'd received *The Law School Bulletin* in his mailbox. He rarely read it, but that day he'd left work early, feeling a bit fatigued—the onset of a flu, he thought. With a glass of orange juice beside him, he lay on his couch and started flipping through the *Bulletin*. He saw the usual news about professors and alumni, notes from the dean, a few campus events… and then he reached the obituaries. He didn't read that part at first glance. Instead, he drank down some juice and turned on the TV but nothing interested him. He picked up the *Bulletin* again and went through it a little more slowly. When again he came to the obituaries he wondered why they were there—a morbid wish to tell us that the old folks are dying off or what? But he skimmed it nonetheless. And he almost gasped as the sight of a name, to him inscribed sorely like a ghastly wound. Dwayne sat up. There it was in black and white. Jojo Badu. And a short description of his life in five sentences. Jojo Badu had migrated to the US from Africa, and after law school spent time at Preston Ingold Thomas & Slaughter, and was most recently Senior Staff Attorney at Machines and Papers, Inc. He had died of natural causes, it said.

Jojo, dead?

Dwayne was completely unarmed for this. The friendship that had been close once had dwindled to almost naught. But until now there'd been the opportunity of a tomorrow when he could rekindle the friendship. He cursed himself for the robbery. It was a two-pronged loss. One, his friend was dead. But the second prick of the prong was not having been warned of the death and therefore telling his friend what he might have wanted to tell him. But what would he have said anyway? Between them, there probably wasn't a whole lot to say. But the opportunity to hear his friend speak one last time, to share a beer perhaps, a joke, a laugh…

He called Fiona. "I'm so sorry, Fiona. I just read the news in The Law School Bulletin." The *news* was as far as he could label it, as if he wished not to open her wound by name and the mention of *death*.

"Thanks Dwayne, I appreciate your calling," she said.

"I wished I'd been at the funeral."

"It's been a while, Dwayne."

"I'm so sorry."

Silence.

"I feel responsible for the breakdown of communication between Jojo and me," he said. "Are you okay, Fiona?"

"I'm fine, Dwayne."

"Listen, Fiona, I need to come and see you,"

"That's very kind of you, but, really, that won't be necessary."

"Please Fiona. I need to do this."

"Okay, if that is what you want."

Dwayne flew to Boston and checked into a hotel. He arranged to meet with Fiona the next evening. She knew she'd sounded cold on the phone, and she wanted to somehow punish him for not attending Jojo's funeral. Miles away, no eyes to stare into, it was much easier to nourish her disappointment, her anger at him. But now that she was to face him, she relented. But even more threatening to her was the guilt that went beyond Dwayne and her. The guilt of Dante. Of *It*.

Only three hours earlier, Dante had stopped by, both of them itching to consummate *It*. She had admitted him into the home even though she'd sworn earlier it would never happen there. For her, it was a moment of both pleasure and guilt, coupled with disappointment and self-doubt. Morphing Dante's face into her husband's helped little, but as if Dwayne's presence in Boston was a new haunt, Dwayne seemed to hover around her with every gyration and moan. "No, Dwayne!" she'd yelled at the last moment of climax, expressing the memorial guilt.

"Dwayne," said Dante. "Who's Dwayne?"

"What?"

"Who's Dwayne?"

"*You* tell me."

"Tell you what?    You just yelled his name! Dwayne!"

"I did?  I must be going crazy."

But he must not have been satisfied with that response as he growled and left without much conversation afterward. Fiona didn't have a lot of time to dwell in her anxiety over his abrupt but still timely departure. She had to prepare for Dwayne. She took two shots of vodka, her first in several months. And then she waited.

Now they stood facing each other. She didn't know how much he knew. He didn't know what to expect.

"Welcome," she said.

And then they embraced, by instinct rather than calculation, by history rather than the spur of the moment. She led him into the living room and they held hands. "I'm so sorry," he said.

She shook her head. "There's nothing to be sorry about."

A tear rolled down Dwayne's cheek. "I can't believe I wasn't here for the funeral. Had we grown so far apart, Fiona?"

"I don't know, Dwayne."

"I wish you had called to tell me, Fiona."

"I guess I was too busy."

There were moving toward each other trying to cover the wide space that had come between them. But what they didn't realize was that Dante had returned. After the alien name Dwayne was yelled into his face, he

233

withdrew and left, but his suspicion must have brought him back. He pushed the front door open. Fiona and Dwayne turned to face him, one with full knowledge, the other fearful a thug had trespassed into the house.

Dante pounced forward. Before Dwayne could say, "Call the police," even before he could alert his defenses, Dante had punched him in the face. Dwayne stumbled backward, falling as Dante tripped him. Dante straddled Dwayne. Two more punches. "Stop! Dante, stop!" Fiona's request paused him, draining some of his evident rage. He left Dwayne on the floor and faced Fiona. "You had to go get yourself another man, didn't you?"

"Dante…"

"Shut up, bitch!"

In tense seconds, Fiona stayed silent, shivering at the rage raging inside Dante, frightening, utterly frightening. "You bitch! I wasn't good enough for you, was I? You had to leave your African husband for me. But no, I wasn't good enough for you. You had to get another…"

"Dante, what are you talking about? He's just a friend."

"You take me for a fool?" Dante looked down at Dwayne. "Hey, fool. What's your name?" He kicked Dwayne in the ribs. Still reeling from the earlier blows, Dwayne groaned. "I said, what's your name?"

"Dwayne."

"I didn't hear you, fool."

"Dwayne!"

"That figures." Dante turned to Fiona. "How could you?" The murderous rage had diminished, almost exhausted by the pummeling of Dwayne.

"Dante, please … listen to me…"

"Don't talk to me, you whore. You know how this hurts? You know how it makes me feel? What kind of woman are you, anyway? I was with you just this afternoon and now you've got yourself another man…"

He stopped in mid-sentence, the murderous rage returning. He kicked Dwayne again and then slapped Fiona across the face. She fell on the couch behind her. Dante knelt next to Dwayne. "Tell me, and don't you lie to me. What were you doing?"

"I didn't…"

"You didn't what?"

"I didn't … we didn't do anything."

"You take me for a fool?" Dante reached for and held Dwayne's neck. "All right, let's see what you've got. Take off your clothes."

"What?"

"You heard me. Take off your clothes!"

"Dante…" Fiona started to protest.

"Shut up, bitch!" From his pocket, Dante retrieved a switchblade. "Are you going to do it or you want me cut you first?" He brought the knife to Dwayne's throat. Slowly, Dwayne undressed. "Fat ass!" Dante said. Fiona had covered her eyes with both hands. "Alright, Juliet," Dante said to her, "You want him, here he is. All ready for you."

"Stop this," Fiona protested.

Dante took hold of Fiona and shoved her—against her protests—on top of Dwayne. "Go on," he said, "do it."

Fiona lay on top of Dwayne, sobbing, the unspoken protest convulsing her body with little spasms. Dante spat at them and walked out. That is when Fiona realized he had just killed *It*.

Fiona knew that the past never goes away as, in memory, it lingers, sometimes faintly, sometimes boldly. So it would linger with the humiliation of Fiona and Dwayne. Dwayne made no attempt to cover his nakedness or wallow in the pain inflicted on him. "I don't know about you," he said, "but the view looks kinda nice from here."

Fiona's immediate reaction was to stop crying, bringing herself to the reality of the naked Dwayne underneath her. "We need to clean you up, get the blood off your face before it dries up." She felt the heat of his breath on her face, the warmth of his body seeping through to her. And for a moment longer she wanted to hold on, to take all the heat from his body, to turn it deep inside her into something worth remembering, worth cherishing. So she stayed there a second longer—just sufficient as not to arouse his suspicion, just to lay enough claim to him. Before Fiona got up to go to the bathroom, she felt the beginnings of his erection, but when she returned with a pail of water and a towel, he was fully clothed.

She began to wash the blood from his face. "I'm so sorry, Dwayne. This shouldn't have happened."

"Not your fault."

But the tension of his silence was too heavy for her to bear. "You must think I'm shit."

"Why? What do you mean?"

"Come on, Dwayne. You just saw him. You heard what he said."

"Far be it for me to judge you, Fiona. I'm sure you have your reasons."

"I have my reasons? Don't you want to beat the living daylights out of me?

"No."

"Why not?"

"You want me to justify your guilt?"

"My guilt?"

"It's obvious, Fiona. But you don't have to justify anything to me. I'm not interested in what you do in your spare time."

"Really? Shouldn't you be? Wasn't Jojo your friend?"

"So are you."

She wanted his condemnation to enable her to seek his absolution. But he was refusing to play the game, leaving open the option for her to think he was disgusted with her but simply wouldn't voice it. She didn't want to leave him with the impression that she'd sullied her husband by turning to Dante, whether sexually or otherwise.

"Won't you ask me how long it's been going on?"

"Fiona, I don't think it's a good idea to talk about this."

She wouldn't be denied, however. She dried his face, got rid of the towel, and poured two glasses of wine. She gave Dwayne one and sat on the couch next to him. "I've been seeing Dante for quite a while now."

"Fiona ..."

"No, Dwayne, I need to. Please."

"If you must."

"I must. You are married for so long and everything seems so familiar and you take it all for granted. Suddenly you meet this young, energetic man who could be your son. He shows interest at a time when your husband seems to have lost sexual interest in you for the most part. Sometimes you blame him, sometimes you blame yourself, sometimes you blame the world, and sometimes you don't know whom to blame. But you have come too far with this older man you've known for so many years, whose children you've borne, but who seems to have become a stranger.

"This young man on the other hand reminds you of the vigor and power you once knew in your husband. You are attracted to him. You hear warning bells but you allow yourself to be led, knowing the precipice is there, but one way or the other you tell yourself everything will be okay. So you find pleasure in this new man and you tell yourself you will pull from the brink. But it's too late as you've already jumped too far. The pleasure, or the promise of pleasure, the thrill, seems to take control. It seems stronger

237

than you are. And so you find yourself going deeper and deeper. And all this time you're still saying it's going to be okay. But it doesn't get okay. This new man calls your husband and tells him he's screwing his wife.

"You have never seen a man look so defeated. But you are too defensive. You have too much confidence in yourself, believing you can work something out. But you have underestimated this man, your husband, the father of your children. You think he will acquiesce. Even as you know you're the guilty party, you are blinded by defensiveness and this strong, new desire in you for this other man. But what you don't realize is the strength of your husband, his power to allow himself to fall apart. All his life it seems he's dealt with adversity through weakness, finding the solution that will allow him to stay on the safer ground. But not this time. This time he shifts from the safe ground. He assumes the role of a drunkard. You believe it's a façade to justify to his children the actions he's planned to take. When he attempts a reconciliation, you trust it's a false attempt, especially when he comes to bed completely drank, completely repellent. He forces you to reject him.

"He's not done yet. He pushes it to the limit, losing his job, living half of the time on the streets. He allows his children to rescue him. They can't blame him completely. You've hurt him too much. He can't handle it any other way. You want him back, but you don't know how. You miss him. Despite everything, you really miss him. You now know that you still love him. You love him more than you'd ever thought. You don't know what to do. In the meantime, you continue to see this younger man, even when you know it's not right, even when you know it's breaking your daughter's heart, wreaking your son's spirits.

"When you hear your daughter has put your husband in a home or some resort for the elderly as a temporary measure, something inside you dies. You wouldn't believe he'd carry it that far, live there rather than return home. You feel rejected, dirty, almost worthless. You are at a complete loss. You want to bring him back home, but again you don't know how to do that. And there's a part of you that likes this new independence, this affair you continue to carry on. And then suddenly you hear that he's dead.

"The guilt compounds. You feel responsible for his death. In part, at least. Whatever his reasons, your infidelity is the catalyst for his actions. You fear you've lost your daughter, perhaps forever. And worse of all, you continue to sleep with this other man. In fact, on the day when your husband's friend, your friend, is coming to see you, you have this other man over. You think he's left, but he returns and sees you with your friend, your husband's friend."

She had stated her case. Guilt and innocence were beside the point. Perception, however, was crucial. The perception that neither blames nor absolves, but shapes itself into something real, something to live by, something necessary to blunt rejection, something required to share an embrace without fear. And that much, she had succeeded in doing, aided by Dante, contrary to his wish to destroy.

Close to tears, Dwayne hugged Fiona.

"Will you stay with me tonight?" She asked.

She poured extra glasses of wine as they spoke, not about Jojo or what had just happened. They spoke about work, DC, Ama and Juju. Tired, they fell under the influence of the wine and slouched in the couch. Hours later, she woke up. It was past midnight. She fetched a blanket, stretched his body over the full length of the couch, and covered him with the blanket. She kissed his forehead and went upstairs to finish her sleep.

One last hug the next day and then Dwayne was back in his rented car, waving farewell to Fiona. She closed the gate and looked at the house with new vision, as if seeing it for the first time. And in a way she was. It was free of the children and her husband. Not for the first time, but for the first time without anyone else to lay claim to it, Dante having killed *It*.

Somehow, the story of the death of *It* gave me hope.

Juju didn't come home that night. His mobile phone was shut off. We (mother and girlfriend) worried and neither one of us slept much that night, as the uncles and other family members confirmed that this hadn't happened before. I toiled under the reality that this was my first major fight with Juju and that it had happened beneath the cloud of his betrayal.

"I'm going to ask him to return to the US," Fiona said. "He's had enough time here. It's time for him to come home."

Home. What was home, I wondered. What did going home really mean?

Going home.

I suppose everybody goes home or wants to or has to.

*But where is home?* That is the question.

Going home. I could imagine Dwayne going home in his mind, having gained the victory from the visit with Fiona, the experience of being part of killing *It*. His disappointment at the knowledge of her infidelity must have been quelled when she spoke about it to him. He couldn't ignore her, flesh and blood speaking to flesh and blood. It wouldn't matter whether her actions were justified. That she wanted him to know her story must have sufficed. Plus he would have known that she was hurting. Even I could tell that in her retelling. That much was clear. Even if he failed, he was home and he was glad to be home and that's what mattered.

Going home. I suspected Fiona wasn't there yet, but she was close. The Fiona, whose love had started from the waning days of Jojo's college years, buoyed by the exuberance and near-sightedness of youth, its non-equivocating romanticism; held steady in those years afterwards under the more mature steadfastness amid tests and strains, glued together by practical considerations and the strength of the relationship's history;

and then moved into the inertia of latter years when it is expected to stay its course in the sentence (for better or for worse) of matrimony, sometimes joyous, sometimes painful— for various reasons, not to be disturbed, that sentence, no matter the circumstances. But it had, this one, been unable to ride this particular heave, a wave too hazardous for this tiny boat the marriage had become. And to find energy just to take the next step under such shredded expectations, the mind becomes an ally as well as a foe: a great companion in the recollection of those past episodes that wanes pain, even when the episodes are sad, for sadness through memory's long filter is easily transformable into a spark for humor and laughter.

For her, I suppose going home didn't mean the physical structure she'd constructed with her husband, the garden she had started cultivating in the backyard, the memories of children crying that occasionally followed her, the sounds of love-making with her husband in which she could find rest. That was just a partial telling of it. She must have been looking forward to the home she'd missed. The cuddling with her children couldn't be recreated, but they could be molded mature into that level of comfort that cedes nothing to rancor. So she was pushing toward that home and knowing that she had to reach it before she could return to the physical structure where Jojo wouldn't be for the rest of her life. Not true. He would always be a part of it, just not there as she was used to. But it was precisely because of this spiritual presence that necessitated the search for that spiritual home outside of home. She would open her arms wide for her son to help lift her there. It was not a battle to be surrendered. Not this time. She will have to make him see that in the vastness between them, there was a steadfast love they both had to acknowledge to each other. Perhaps he needed time. But he had to get there. He had to get there with her.

Going home. Or would he call it that? Juju was home? Where was that? The physical location where his father was born and his mother had spent many years, but whose spaces, cultures, family dynamics, and whatnot he was only beginning to experience firsthand? Or was it the land of his birth where at some level he thought could not complete him? Would he return to live in the belief of his American-ess with the African

241

like a ceremonial piece of clothing to wear or not wear? If worn, would it be underneath the pack of outer clothing that was American?

Going home. Where was home for me? Rwanda where I was born but where memories so strong continued to alienate a part of me, at least a part within me? Was it America, which I was barely beginning to know?"

Where was home for Fiona? America? I knew she would say yes. But was that a complete answer? Could she deny the urgings of her dead husband and now the son for Ghana? Was that also not a home of sorts?

As I thought over these matters, even if I would have wanted Juju to stay in Ghana longer, under the circumstances, and for purely selfish reasons, I agreed with Fiona that he had to return to America, although worried that no one could persuade him, now that he had his Chochoo.

But Juju returned on the third night after our confrontation at the beach, only a couple of days before Fiona and I were scheduled to return to the US. We had, together with his uncle, gone to the shore to search for him. We'd interviewed many, gone to his favorite haunts, all to no fruition. "Has my son just vanished into thin air?" Against the uncle's advice that she was wasting her time, Fiona filed a report with the police on Juju's missing status. But he reappeared in the night when the household had gone to sleep, except Fiona and I (who continued to converse in order not to dwell on our fears). He'd knocked once, interrupting our conversation.

With a voice filled expectation and deep anxiety, Fiona asked, "Who's there?"

"Juju." His voice was tentative.

We both rushed to the door, but I conceded the honor to Fiona, who opened it and embraced her son immediately. "We've been worried sick about you, son."

"I know, Mom. I'm sorry."

Juju looked past his mother to see me behind her and then he averted his eyes and made as if to say something but stayed silent. "We...come in and let's talk," Fiona said, and I was so grateful that Fiona was there to cushion the discomfort of the circumstance. Fiona led Juju to the bed and made him sit next to her. I sat at the opposite end.

"Are you okay?" Fiona asked.

242

"I'm fine."

"I wish you'd have sent some word to let us know where you were."

"I'm really sorry, Mom. I... I was just at a friend's place. I needed to clear my head a little, sort a few things out."

"Well, we're glad to see you again, Juju." She kissed his cheek and held his hand. "Everything will be okay, son. But you know I'm not the one you should be talking to right now." She rubbed his shoulders and added, "I'll be back soon." Fiona left the room.

Juju and I were left alone, sitting now on opposite sides of the bed, our heads bowed as if we were afraid to confront each other, and silence tormented the situation for seconds.

"I'm really, really sorry, Shama," Juju now said.

"Do you love her?" was all I could think to ask at that moment, a question I'd seen asked in movies after an act of infidelity, a question whose answer I dreaded. But with only a few days left before my departure from Ghana, I could ill afford to waste time—either I knew and abandoned the fight or I knew and reclaimed what belonged to me.

"No, Shama, I don't love her. It's you I love and only you."

"So what happened?"

"I don't know, Shama. Ever since I've been going to the beach, she's been hanging around. I ignored her at first but she was always there pestering me until I started talking to her. She'd cook and bring it to me. She'd invite me places. Sometimes I went and sometimes I didn't. She wanted me to sleep with her but I refused. She wouldn't give up and she kept coming around to talk. I thought I'd play around a little, so I'd neck with her at times and stuff, but I never slept with her. When you told me you were coming to Ghana I told her about you and asked her to stay away. But she wouldn't. The day you saw us, I'd told her I was angry she wouldn't listen to me when I told her not to come around, that she was making you suspicious. But she said you didn't suspect anything, that she'd been careful. I told her then that I didn't care anyway and that she should leave me alone. She said she would go away if I gave her a hug. I thought I'd try that and see, although I wasn't sure it would work. I didn't know what else to do to get her off my back without creating some sort of scene. So I gave her a hug and then she took my arm and put it around her

243

waist and said she wanted to feel me one more time and that I should just hold on to her for a short time and she would leave. That's when you saw us."

"So why did you lie to me when I asked you if you knew her?"

"I was worried what you might think. It was a bad mistake and I'm really sorry about that."

"So you were not with her these past few days?"

"No! I was at a friend's place. A male friend."

Juju walked from his side of the bed and knelt before me. "I'm sorry for the pain I've caused, for my lack of judgment and weakness. The past few days have made me realize how much I love you. Stay here with me. You can finish your degree at the University of Ghana. I'll find a better job or even finish my degree. We can start a family here. We both belong here."

An enticing, if completely unexpected proposal....

"Wow, Juju. You know I can't do that."

"Why not, Shama? This way you and I will be together."

"We don't need to be ever apart, Juju."

"So you'll stay?"

"No. Come back with me to the US, Juju. It makes more sense. You're almost done with your doctorate. Come back with me and finish it while I finish mine. If after we're done you decide we should return to Ghana, I will come back with you."

"But why can't we start afresh here?"

"Both you and I have invested so much already in the US. I'm well into my program and you're almost done. Why throw all that away?"

"We won't be throwing it all away, Shama."

"Please, Juju. I make you this promise. If you come back to the US, I will come here with you after I finish my degree, but don't ask me to do so now. Please."

I had made a promise whose fulfillment would turn on other things—a strong relationship, even marriage. But those were in the future and I worried now more about the present.

"I need to think about this."

I knew him enough to know that this meant he would agree. I caressed his cheek and he kissed my hand. There was an immediate renewal, an outburst that prompted arousal, and the release we sought, though hurried, vented all the frustration brewing over the past few days. We almost forgot Fiona was still outside.

"Let's go find your mother," I said. "At this time of the night I doubt that she's gone far."

Hand in hand we walked outside to see Fiona strolling around in the front of the house. Seeing us hand in hand, she remarked, "Oh, I love you." And at that moment, both Juju and I knew it could apply to either or both of us.

The next day, Fiona took Juju and me to visit a man he referred to as an old family acquaintance. "Jojo defended him sometime back and we have been in touch since he returned to Ghana." His mansion was located in the Cantonments residential area. The compound alone was about two acres with the main two storey building in the middle, a boys' quarters that could have served as someone's house on the side, and a large graveled driveway between them. A Mercedes Benz and Jaguar were parked in the driveway. A lithe man dressed in a white shirt and white trousers welcomed us and ushered us into the living room.

The man in the living room, looking more well-fed than his butler, hugged Fiona for a long time. "Oh, Oh..." he kept saying as if overwhelmed with emotion.

"This is Count Tutu," Fiona introduced us after the man finally released her. "And this is my son Juju and our friend Shama."

Count Tutu hugged us both, ignoring our outstretched hands. "You are my family," he said.

After we sat down and he asked us how we were faring in Ghana, he lamented, "You know, Fiona, I'm very sad that you didn't call me sooner. I had no idea that you were here or that your son had been here for so long until you called me yesterday. He should come stay with me. I have many unused rooms here..."

"We will think about it," Fiona said.

"By the way, Zoe said to apologize she couldn't be here. Her old man is sick so she had to travel to the States. But she bids you welcome." To Juju and me, he explained "Zoe is my wife. She was really looking

245

forward to meeting you. And the children are away in school. I hope you get to meet the rest of the family soon."

"How many kids?" Juju asked.

"Five—three boys, two girls."

Count Tutu asked the butler to bring us drinks—we all declined the liquor and opted for mango juice. He addressed Juju: "Your father was good to me. A long time ago, when I was in the States, I had an immigration issue which he handled for free. I had no money at the time, and had it not been for him, I would have been deported, returned to Ghana destitute and without an education. I will never forget his kind act. Because of him, I was able to stay in the US and go on to complete my master's degree after driving a taxi for a while."

As the drinks were being served, I asked him, "What made you return to Ghana?"

"Oh, that. Well, as I told you, I managed to obtain a master's. It was in sociology. But after I graduated I had a hard time finding a job. Tried as I did, I couldn't get a well paying job. My parents were poor, but they kept insisting that I return home if America wasn't offering me much. I returned out of desperation. I was just fed up with all the rejections. I figured I had nothing to lose but my dignity, but who cares about dignity when you can hardly feed yourself? It wasn't easy when I returned. I had to shack up with the old folks for a while. But I managed to get a job at the ministries and then with one of the local banks. That's when Zoe, whom I'd met while in the States, was able to come to Ghana and we got married. She is a lawyer. Not to bore you, but over the years, I managed to save a little, and with a loan from the bank I worked for I got into the construction business with some friends—you know, houses, roads…And the business has grown a lot. We have diversified into trading---imports and exports…"

"Count is not just a businessman," Fiona said. "He is also a politician. Right, Count?"

"Well, I don't consider myself a career politician, but I have dabbled a little."

"Dabbled? Count, don't be so modest. He is a former minister of interior and a potential candidate for president."

"Now that you mention it," said Juju, "I know I've heard the name. I haven't paid much attention to politics since I've been here, but I now know I've heard your name. Count Crusoe Tutu, if I am not mistaken."

"Yes, that's me, but presidential politics can be nasty, you know. For now I am trying to keep my profile a little low, but I won't deny that if the opportunity presents itself I will grab it. You know, my people have a saying: if you reject kingship, you don't even get to be a linguist."

Before we left, Count Tutu made Juju promise to visit him. "Fiona tells me she and Shama will leave for the States tomorrow, but you, Juju, must come and visit."

"I will," Juju said.

Later that day, Juju confirmed to me he would join me in the US in about a month. He had thought about our conversation, he said, and concluded that I was right. Above all things, he had decided that he ought to be close to me. He needed a little more time to put things in order in Ghana and say his farewells properly. "You are really a miracle worker," Fiona said when she heard of this.

# Eleven

The miracle worker didn't think she had miracles in her arsenal when she returned to the US without Juju. Despite his promise to return to the US in a month, I remained tormented by the recollections of his hand around Chochoo, whose beauty I couldn't deny. The only way I could help myself negotiate away the return of loneliness was to toil harder at school and work, especially whenever the phantom pain in my belly occurred. Because Prof. Bailey gave me freedom to choose my own hours, I tripled my work hours and produced results that surprised the professor, even to the point when he worried I was overwhelming myself. I also visited Anna Bailey on weekends and we cooked together and made idle talk. I called Mike often, sometimes at Anne Bailey's behest to dissuade him from joining the army. But he was undeterred. He assured me he would be enlisting in less than a month. I took a gift to Nat Musegera, a carving of a woman carrying a basket that I'd bought in the Accra suburb of Labadi. We'd spoken about my trip to Ghana, which I embellished in my recounting, omitting the sorrowful parts. The professor expressed elation on learning that Juju would be returning to school soon. "I do miss him," he said. And that was part of Juju's makeup that I couldn't fathom—how such an unassuming, even timid, man could have such an impact on people to the point where most, if not all, loved him. Wasn't it my luck then that I was the one he loved? Me, except Chochoo? No! Chochoo, as he'd explained, was just an appendage that served no purpose and had been severed. But even a severed appendage could grow back? My days had become restless under the weighty thought that was Chochoo, with possible access to Juju and, much as I posited in my mind that his love for me would overcome the expediency of his proximity to a willing and beautiful woman, I labored in the days preceding Juju's arrival, even though I soothed the labor with hard work and frequent visits to the Baileys. Fiona also called often, unable to hide her own anxiety over her son's return. Her greatest joy—to my mild irritation—was that she'd managed (or rather we'd managed) to reclaim Juju from Africa. This deepened my guilt, for I did not want to rescue anyone from Africa. I preferred to think of it as a victory for myself, not a battle of continental dimensions.

The first thing Juju wanted to do when he returned was visit his father's grave in Boston. He was restless about this. Why this urgency? "Visiting Ghana and tasting its joys tells me how much the old man sacrificed to remain here. Especially after we went to visit Count Tutu, whom I went to see a couple of times afterwards, I realized that may father could have achieved so much more in Ghana." Juju paused, held my hand and said, "By the way, you have never asked me how I came to own Dad's diary."

"I didn't think it was my place to ask."

"Shama, nothing is out of your place concerning my family."

"I know."

"Anyway, where shall I start? Some of the things I am going to tell you are very painful, so painful Ama won't or can't even talk about them. She has only told me once and she has sworn never to talk about them again: but I think they provide the needed context for you to understand the story better. And I have this urge to go see him."

I listened as he told the story.

Juju remembered the day they went for their father. They had received a call from Fiona, begging them to find their father who barely came home, the father from whom they hadn't heard in a long time. They had searched the neighborhood, asking if anyone had seen him. Eventually they found him, his breath reeking of vomit and liquor as he sat in a stupor in front of a local bar, his stench pungent. Ama was tender toward him, even as they watched this caricatured father mumbling meaninglessness into space. "Daddy," she said, "what is the meaning of this?" Last they knew, their father still had a job. He'd said something encouraging to Ama when she complained about the challenges of her work, something about how smart she was and not to let anything or anyone get her down. She'd received strength from him and expressed renewed hope. He'd encouraged Juju to better all his peers in school. But now they saw him barely coherent, un-bathed, dry vomit on his begrimed shirt, as the alcohol mixed with the saliva to strain their nostrils. They gathered him like a mother would an ill child and helped him into Ama's car. She drove him to her apartment and they took him to the bathroom. Ama and Juju stripped him to his underwear. At this time, their father was barely awake. Ama wet a towel, soaped it and cleaned him, avoiding the covered parts only. His once firm chests now sagged and were almost feminine, his chin was almost doubled, his flesh flabby and unshaped. But the daughter looked past these as she cleaned him. By the time she finished, he was beginning to gain some coherence. She insisted that he would have to live with her a while. Juju went back to school. A few days after her father began living with Ama, her friend Nadia, a worker at a nursing home of sorts, suggested that she bring him to live there. Ama was horrified by the thought. "We will take good care of him and you won't be so stressed having to balance your life and care for him."

"Who says I'm stressed?"

"Who are you kidding?"

"My daddy in a nursing home is out of the question."

"It's not just a nursing home, although we do provide those services. It's more like a resort for the elderly. It's very peaceful. You can go there and relax if you want to get away from everyday life."

Her father in a nursing home/elder's resort? Ama discarded the thought immediately. And so her father continued to live with her for three weeks. He was in near bliss; struggled at first but almost completely weaned off the liquor, regaining his drive, beginning to make plans of returning to some kind of work and planning ahead to his retirement. But soon she had to make a choice, which she deemed temporary. She had to take a business trip for a week. Curse a consultant's itinerant lifestyle. And she was in tears when she decided to take him to the nursing home for that week only. She'd seen him improve, but knew he still stole out and drank from time to time. She wasn't confident that he could be trusted for a whole week by himself. Nor could she ask him to return to his wife—it was just too soon.

"Daddy," she said, avoiding his eyes. "I have to go on a business trip for a week. I want to be sure you're well taken care of while I'm gone."

"Don't worry about me, sweetie, I'll be fine."

But she remembered the day of vomit and spittle and liquor and she was too worried to take chances after all the improvement she'd seen.

"No, Dad, I want to be sure you're well taken of. I have to take you somewhere, someplace I can count on."

"Where am I going?"

"I have this friend… she tells me they have a great place with great people and it's all quiet and peaceful. A place to relax and recharge your batteries."

"Heaven?"

She giggled. "It's a nursing home, Daddy. No… I mean it's a nursing home, but it's really a resort."

"I see," he said.

"I have a very good friend there, Daddy. She'll take good care of you, I promise. I'll be back in only a week." Ama tried as much as she could to uplift her father's spirits and he tried all he could to assure her that they needed no uplifting.

She took him to the… resort—isolated amid pine trees in the middle of nowhere. She would check on him from time to time and he seemed fine. But the day before she returned, she received a call that he was dead. She rushed back and went to the home with Juju. When they gave them his belongings, among them was the notebook-diary. "That's all he did while he was here," they were told. "He asked for notebooks and wouldn't stop writing.

251

Ama started reading it, but couldn't get past those first few pages of death. That's when Jojo took it from her and read it.

After Juju recounted these events, he blinked away tears and noted, "I think the old man asked for notebooks anticipating death, especially considering that he started with his own death, imagining his own funeral. Sometimes I think he willed his death. But he died, leaving a legacy, the legacy of his thoughts and recollections."

After this, I couldn't reject his request that we visit his father's grave.

On his insistence, we rented a car and drove almost non-stop to Boston for fourteen hours. As exhausted as we were, we parked by the cemetery and walked to Jojo Badu's grave. It was about five p.m. As we stood by the nondescript grave, with withering peach roses by its side, Juju whispered, "Dad, rest in peace and forgive us where we wronged you!"

Juju knelt down and sobbed, meshing the spaces between the living and the dead. I stood by him and turned when I heard the sound of approaching footsteps. A man wearing dreadlocks and dressed in a long overcoat approached us. I nodded as a sign of acknowledgment, or rather solidarity, that we were all there to mourn the dead. He returned the nod, but instead of walking on, he stopped by us. He wore heavy cologne, as if he was trying to mask a stench.

Juju stood up, his face tear-marked.

"Are you Jojo Badu's son?" the man asked.

"Do I know you?" Juju asked.

The man hesitated. He seemed to struggle to speak. "You only know of me," he said. "I have caused you and your family much pain and I can only hope that you will forgive me."

"And who are you?" Juju asked.

"I do not say this lightly and I would prefer to remain anonymous, but he haunts me," the main said.

"What are you talking about?"

"Please be patient as I tell you this."

The man had a deep voice when he began to speak. In a less solemn moment, I probably would have found him charming.

A blend of ills was unleashed at him at the moment when he fell asleep in the comfort of desired rest, entombed in its loud snore. The dead husband entered his sleep and led him out from the comfort of his bed to the cemetery, stifling all sound so he could hear only the quickened breath immediately before death, which entered into his ears like a deafening thunderclap. This was the sound of dying and of death echoed at him from all angles of the deserted cemetery. He was a hesitant man, fearful of the scene and sound, which reminded him of the ultimate, if not imminent. In the alleys next to the cemetery, noisy sounds pounded the ground. He turned this way and that, fearing that somebody (rather, something) sinister was coming at him. He wished to leave the scene as far and quickly as he could, but he was leashed to it by the fear and conscience within, a conscience prodding him to deal with what he felt responsible for. He tried to yell but inaudible regurgitations strained his throat. Now he was pushed forward toward the grave. The dead man rose from his grave in all his ghostly paleness: a hollow cloud without eyes, feeding every bit of the living man's imagination of the ghastliness of dead people, every lurid tale of horror about ghosts he'd heard and stored in memory. And then the dead man groaned as though in pain. His speaking was barely audible, guttural, unintelligible, inarticulate, meaningless except for the spiritual speech they could now engage in. The man saw the face of the dead. "You," the man said, making the recognition from a photo he'd seen in Fiona's purse. The dead man spoke *Dante's* words:

Through me you enter into the city of woes,
Through me you enter into eternal pain,
Through me you enter the population of loss.

He awoke, shivering. It was four in the morning, still dark outside. The man's first instinct was to turn on the lights. But the bedroom lights didn't drown his fear.

He felt as if he'd actually lived the nightmare, as if it would soon capture him back into its horrific theater. He walked into every room in his apartment and turned on every light, but even that effulgence didn't douse the fear. He was too terrified to return to sleep. He stepped outside at five in the morning. He didn't know where he was going, his thoughts void as air, except for the fear abiding. He walked to a florist's. The store was closed at that hour. He waited for three hours until the store opened, bought a couple of peach roses, came to Jojo Badu's grave, genuflected and placed the flowers on it. He wept on the dead man's grave. He had returned that evening, still unable to get the haunt of the night out of him.

"I just want you to know how sorry I am," the man said.

Jojo could barely speak. He offered the man his hand and they shook. "I never imagined this moment and if I would have imagined it, I would have considered curses and insults, but now that I see you, all I see is misery. May your conscience run its course."

"Thank you," the man said and walked away.

"Who was that?" I asked. "He's very strange."

"Couldn't you tell, Shama?" Juju said. "That was Dante."

"The Dante?" I asked.

Juju nodded.

It was hard for me to believe this. "How do you know?" I asked.

"I just feel it. And his story…Who else could it be?"

"If it was Dante, why aren't you angry at him?"

"Did you see his condition, Shama? He is paying the price. He is suffering. His conscience is tormenting him. There is nothing worse I could say or do to him."

We went back to the car and we both slept for the next ten hours. When we woke up, it was time to return to Chicago. It was only after we returned that I was able to welcome Juju back in earnest with the relief that would manifest itself in long hours with him that even I feared might be stifling him. Juju and I had become an ubiquitous pair on campus and we also took long walks in Grant Park.    He reenrolled in his doctorate program and resettled as though he'd never had the interregnum in Ghana. But he spoke often of his time there, of the people's hospitality;  he spoke proudly of visiting the places his father had visited as a child and met many of his childhood friends, who spoke of how great the father was as a child, a leader who'd demonstrated great potential evidenced by courage and intelligence.    Through Papa's friends, Juju came to see the full opportunity cost, the sacrifice he'd made to remain in America after America's trappings tethered him, where his potential was crippled; whereas in Ghana he could have risen to the top, as demonstrated by some of his lesser gifted peers who had become business leaders, ministers of state, renowned journalists and jurists... "I now see why the man was so frustrated. I used to wonder why he never resettled in Ghana.  You know why?  It's because of us.  Me, Ama and Ma.  He stayed because we were American and so he couldn't uproot us back to Ghana."  Juju told me why he could see the choice nagging malevolently at his father.  "Even in the short time I was there, I had a major psychological boost.  There, people respect me.  I'm not just a number.  There, you're not judged according to your race..."

"But you may be judged based on ethnicity," I said.  "Don't forget what happened in Rwanda.  You may even be judged for your foreignness, even though you're black."

"I know, but at a fundamental level you feel you're a part of the people.  You don't feel like you have to prove anything on account of your race."

"Perhaps, but even they have their ways of stifling the gifted, no?  If it's not race it's something else."

While Juju and I got closer, his relationship with his mother, although improved during the Ghana trip, was now at a standstill.  The mother would not let the gain made slip.  "I'm coming to visit," she said. "And this time I'm bringing Ama with me."

Given what Juju had said of Ama and my one phone conversation with her, I had no similar apprehension as when Fiona announced her first visit.  And my instincts were validated when Ama spent the weekend.  I insisted the women stay in my apartment.  Fiona had demurred that three

255

grown women couldn't fit in one apartment, but I reminded her of the sleeping arrangements when were in Ghana and offered to give up my bedroom (against Fiona's protests) and share the living room with Ama (who approved of the arrangement). Juju had also protested the idea, afraid that such proximity could breed dislike, but I reminded him also of the living arrangements on our visit to Ghana. "I feel your family is becoming mine also," I said, "even your dad, whose written words have provided me with a lot of insight."

"I told you, didn't I, that the dairy would help you understand us better? But about this visit, what about me?" Juju queried. "Don't I get to host anyone in my apartment?"

"No. You are a man. This is woman matter."

Ama, in temperament, was more gregarious than her brother, almost like Fiona, and just as sharp as the other family members. "I can see why my brother is in love," Ama told me during the course of the visit. "You are just gorgeous." And she was quick to add, "I don't know what you've done to him, but whatever it is keep on doing it. He has become more open these days."

We went through what I considered the anatomy of a visit—meals, shopping, visiting landmarks. I was sure never to let anyone of them see the scars on my back. Juju was more like an appendage, producing the background male chorus to our chatter, which sounded more like sisters who loved one another. The only blemish in this visit was the one time when Ama said, "How I wish Papa was here. I miss him." This created brief discomfort, when the siblings and their mother looked at one another with awkward glances that were quickly averted as though in embarrassment. I strained to accommodate this awkwardness, desirous of ending it, worried that the father could not be invoked in the mother's presence without occasioning such distress. It was I who would end the discomfort by announcing that it was time for a rice and beans dish I'd specially prepared for the visitors. On this the last night of the visit, we had a long dinner, long conversation and long laughs into the late hours of the night.

The ensuing days and months were filled with studying, deepening of the Shama-Juju love, my frequent calls to Mike (whenever he was available) out of concern for him as he underwent military training, and work. Prof. Bailey was considering retiring but he promised me he'd wait until I graduated. He remarked that "I'm in the sunset of my life but you are in the sunrise of yours and I know your sun is going to keep rising and it's not setting anytime soon."

"Nor is your sun setting anytime soon," I had said, but clearly the professor was ageing and I worried for him as he began to move slower and seemed more easily distracted. I would pray in my head for the keeping of the family that had allowed me to find my voice in a strange land. Yes, I had found my voice but I knew I was not yet singing.

*How shall we sing the lords song in a strange land?*

And thinking of sunsets, my aunt wrote me a letter that I found inspiring, if a little unsettling. She'd mentioned that the shadow of investigations over Alexandre was darkening and they were more afraid for him. "It's only a matter of time now before he's arrested and sent to Tanzania for trial," Auntie Shama had written. But then she'd asked me to stay focused. And whereas on one occasion Juju had compared me to the color of charcoal that exudes light, my aunt had written:

> Child, I remember the color of your skin even now and I am inspired. I remember your skin the color of dusk. You are all that is new and so your night is far from here. And even when your night comes, do not be afraid, for you are made to blend into the darkest and still stand out the brightest as a dark star to lead the blinding light. So sing loudly and freely.

I don't know if Auntie Shama had written that herself or borrowed it from someone else. It didn't sound like her, the poetry; but I basked in it.

Sunsets and sunrises, dusk and lights and nights… What was I to make of all these, except to conclude as best as I could understand—to remain focused. This I did so that when graduation came, I was proud to say that I'd not disappointed Prof. Bailey (who had waited) and my aunt

257

(who had exhorted). And it helped that Juju graduated at the same time. We donned our graduation gowns, received our diplomas, listened to long speeches both inspiring and boring by turns, attended parties and contemplated our futures. Both Fiona and Ama attended the ceremonies. I could only recollect in memory Papa, Mama and Placide (and Jean Pierre). And Jojo Badu. My guilt was stirred on two fronts to recall Jean Pierre, guilt that with what I felt for Juju, I still recalled Jean Pierre in memory with abiding affection and also because that affection had diminished; guilty that I'd relegated my first true love to such margins.

As our graduation present, Fiona provided round trip tickets, all expenses paid, to Hawaii. Juju had overcome the nagging wish to repay Fiona for my trip to Ghana and didn't hesitate to accept the Hawaii offer.

We spent two weeks in Hawaii free of the usual stresses. We'd eaten, we'd made love, we'd slept long hours, and we'd revitalized our love, which had seemed destined for a plateau of inertia. "I want to stay here forever," I said. "Tell me we don't have to return to reality."

"We will never return to reality," Juju said. "In my love, there is always paradise."

"And more."

"You will never leave me? Tell me."

"Never. I will never leave you."

"Even if I get fat and lazy and sloppy and smelly?"

"Even if you lose all your hair and all your teeth but one, still I will love you."

We returned to attend the Baileys retirement party. The president of the university gave a long endearing speech about Prof. Bailey's excellent scholarship and outstanding humanity, and Ann Bailey stood by to shake hands and receive well wishers. Later, I would organize my own dinner for them during which I profusely thanked them and said, "I asked myself, how shall I sing the Lord's song in a strange land? And I realized that in a strange land, the lord sends His angels to give us voice. We only need to open ourselves up to them, to find those angels. You, Prof. Bailey and you, Prof. Ann Bailey, have been my angels in this land and you have allowed me to begin to sing the Lord's song. What I have achieved, even though it's modest, I owe in large part to you."

Tears in his eyes, Prof. Bailey remarked, "You have such a sweet tongue. I can't imagine what you could do if you were a lawyer arguing before a jury. Thank you..."

These words would be stored in my reservoir for a while.

I contemplated what to do next. I had applied for a teaching position at the university, as well as many others in the Chicago area, as had Juju. That was all I'd seriously considered doing—teaching. But in the coming weeks, I would reconsider. Why did I want to teach anyway? It just seemed the normal course for me with a doctorate, but I could find no other reason for it, except perhaps that it was what Juju also wanted to do. But it suited Juju, his ponderousness, his patience. Did I have the temperament for it? I remembered Fiona's encouragement to me to enroll in law school, seconded by Prof. Bailey's recent remark about arguing in front of a jury. And as I cleaned my room one day, I chanced upon the postcard Juju had sent me from Ghana of the Ghana Supreme Court building. Were these signs I ought to seriously consider? But did I not need some compelling urge for justice in order to seek a law degree? Was it sufficient that I was capable? I asked Juju for his thoughts. "I think you'll make a great lawyer," he said. Yeah, yeah... but what else? Unsure still, I began to dismiss the thought, even when it would not be dismissed. In such moment of prevarication, which also made me vulnerable to external suggestion, I received a package from Fiona containing application forms for Harvard Law School. She followed this with a phone call. Fiona pleaded with me to apply.

"Just see if you get in. Seriously, Shama, you ought to think about it. I see such promise. I know what I'm talking about. I oversee many lawyers and I mentor many."

"I'm not sure it's right for me."

"I'll make you a promise. Fill out the application and send it in. Of course, you have to take the law school admission test. If you don't get into Harvard, then you're not meant to go to law school. If you get in, then perhaps it's a sign from God or something."

I agreed to those terms. At first, I decided not to study for the admissions test. I'd take it without preparation; but then Juju opined that I should only take that approach if I would not be ashamed of a poor score, even if it otherwise meant nothing to me. "Even if you decide not to go to law school, do you really want to fail this exam? I wouldn't if I were you, not for the sake of my pride."

I concurred. I bought preparation books and started studying for the test. In the meantime, Juju had received and accepted an appointment as an assistant professor at Northwestern University. "If I get into Harvard and decide to go, this means we'll be apart," I told him.

"We'll cross that bridge when we get to it," Juju said. "Don't worry."

I took the test, completed and mailed the application forms, all the while still unsure if I wanted to be a lawyer. I received offers in the meantime for assistant professorships but decided, with Juju's encouragement, not to accept any of them yet. Instead, I took a part time teaching position at Evanston High School.

The fall, while we waited for the response from Harvard, Juju rented a small house on Maine Street in Evanston. And then in October I was informed that I'd been accepted to Harvard Law School. I leaped with pride, but still, I wasn't sure. Juju told me the acceptance was a sure sign I ought to go. I called Fiona. "It's a deal. You got in. You have got to go."

When put that way, I had to agree that whether explicitly or implicitly I'd reached this bargain with Fiona, and while I wouldn't decide solely on account of that, or merely to please Fiona, given the doubts about the future, I now had to take this as an opportunity to be seized.

The greatest concern for was that once again Juju and I would be apart. I remembered Chochoo still, and recollecting what nearly happened sent me into periodic brooding. Perplexed by my sudden sour mood, Juju entreated me—it's only three years; he would visit soon and often; we will make it work; after all, we did it once when he went to Ghana. No! He shouldn't have said that. My mood, if sour before, turned worse; if the brooding was periodic before, it became more prevalent and approached melancholy. I wore this attitude as I began to prepare my trip to Cambridge. Fiona had already found me an apartment after I refused her offer to stay in her house.

Juju came to me carrying some loose sheaths of paper. "What are those?" I asked.

260

"You know," he said, "When I gave you Dad's diary, I tore some parts out. These were parts about me that I thought too shameful I didn't want anyone else to know them. I almost destroyed those pages, but for some reason I didn't. I now want you to read them."

"Are you sure, Juju?"

"Absolutely. I have something I want to ask you, but before I do that, I want you to know this. Read it, Shama. Immediately."

"Yes, sir."

I was too intrigued not to do as he had requested. I read:

Ama was knocking on the bathroom door. "I need to pee!" But Juju was in there, silent. "Get out of there, Juju! What are you doing?" He didn't respond. Several minutes later, he unlocked the door. Ama stepped into the bathroom and said, "It reeks like a pigsty in here. My God, what have you done to yourself?"

When my attention was drawn to the bathroom, I couldn't believe what I saw. There, standing in the doorway was Juju with feces smeared on his naked torso. I asked him to wash down immediately, which he did but with hesitation. I couldn't understand this shy, withdrawn child. I remembered when at age ten he started posing questions, which disheartened him. In a class preparation for a Christmas play, Juju's teacher asked for volunteers. "Who wants to play Jesus?"

Hands went up, Juju's among them. "Not you, Juju," the teacher said.

"I want to play Jesus," he protested.

"Jesus wasn't black," she said. "Why don't you play Judas?"

"Was Judas black?" Juju asked me.

"I don't think so," I told him.

Even at that age, Juju must have known something was awry when he was made to play Judas, the villain, alongside a blond, blue eyed Jesus. His perception was beginning to change, turning questionable, and becoming

261

influenced. Something internal had already begun to crumble. Now that implosion was being further validated. Of course both Fiona and I were furious when we heard of this, and we even considered taking some form of action against the school, but decided it was going to raise too much furor and draw attention to the matter in a way that might not be helpful to Juju.

When he heard the word "nigger" for the first time in school, it must have cut deeper than when Ama heard it. Of the same blood, but not the same sensitivity? Now quiet and withdrawn, when another student called him a "dumb retard," he told me he believed it as again it seemed to describe his condition; something he'd been led to by both omission and commission: the omission was our failure to prepare him for the reality that existed outside of the home. Not once had I talked to him about the American racial mosaic, its problems, its cruelties despite its beauty. How could I have let that slip? Lack of experience, I guess, even if it's a lame excuse. I myself had not had that preparation, having grown up in a nearly monochromatic country. "Dumb" and "retard" and "nigger" must have cut deep notwithstanding that he was a straight A student. When I congratulated him on his good schoolwork, he said nothing. He didn't even offer a hint of pride or acknowledge his brilliance. My son, I wanted to yell at him, *I am your father, your blood, your flesh, talk to me.* I wanted to pull him from that hole into which he'd plunged. I didn't know how.

One day I went to his room and rummaged through his things, hoping to find something that would help me understand him better. I was shocked and pained by what I saw, and I regretted having gone through his things.

On a piece of paper, my thirteen year old son had written the following:
BLACK SHEEP
BLACK COMEDY

BLACKMAIL
BLACKMARKET
BLACK HEART
BLACK EYE
BLACK MAGIC (JUJU)
BLACKLIST
BLACK BEAST
BLACK MASS
BLACKGUARD

And then he'd left a huge space, as though left empty to signify the deep thought that had gone into the next words, the hesitation and reluctance, the concern, he wrote:

BLACK MAN

From where erupts such venom?

I remember how he would shrink at the word *Black*. He couldn't help the frown that came whenever others used it. It realized it was a frown that summarized the rejection he felt for the word. It seemed that somehow he'd recorded its connotations in his mind one after the other, its associations, and then registered that record on paper and then refused to identify himself with a word so defiled. He wouldn't let himself be qualified by that adjective. He wouldn't use the word, inventing alternative expressions. For example, "unorthodox magic" replaced "black magic" and "the odd one in the family" replaced "black sheep." But those were easy. What of Black Man? What word would he find expressing himself while disassociating from the negative contexts that language seemed to impose? At first he chose *dark*. But was that any better? Dark? Didn't that imply something sinister (as in say forest) or something to escape from (as in say tunnel)? What about *colored*? But that too was unacceptable. It had no distinction other than suggesting something besides white, something opposite. But was he opposite? Did he wish to define himself in that relational way? How about African?

But he wasn't, was he? What of the qualifier *brown*? Wasn't he brown rather than black? Oh, but brown was already taken, wasn't it?

He had written:

*I am not black  I am not black I am not black  I am not black  I am not black  I am not black  I am not black  I am not black  I am not black  I am not black  I am not black*

*Yes, you are*

*No I'm not*

*Yes, you are*

*No, I'm not*

*Yes, you are*

*No, I'm not*

*Yes, you are  No I'm not   Yes, you are  No I'm not*

*Yes, you are*

And so his mind fought with itself? What torment. *How, Juju, can You even grow if You debate You this way?* And so he must have believed he was undefined: like the wind that blows odorless, unanchored, and aimless.

I nearly cried after I read this. My poor Juju. "We all have our battles, sweetie," I told him. "This is a complex world."

"And you still love me?"

"How can you ask me that? You think this would change my love for you? If you're trying to get rid of me, you have to do better than that."

"I love you, Shama, unconditionally," he said with a smile.

The night before my trip to Cambridge, Juju invited me to dinner. We went to a restaurant in the John Hancock Building, from where we could see the Chicago skyline, breathtaking with its silhouetting, undulating union of sky and architectural diversity as well as it's glittering nightlights. As occupied in my mind and worried as I was about leaving Juju in Evanston, I still realized that he was extremely nervous. Given my negative attitude over the past few weeks, I thought he may be worried about me or even about the future of our relationship. I had tried—and now at dinner tried harder—to steer clear of that foul mood. In the past, I

264

had managed glimpses of enthusiasm, and in the restaurant I tried hard to conjure that episodic mood. I smiled and held Juju's hands. He still looked uncomfortable, licking his lips frequently and drinking copious amounts of water. "All will be well," I said.

And then it happened. Recollecting the moment later—as I would do severally in the months following—it was like all motion had been slowed. I saw Juju almost fall out of his chair as he got out of it. And my heart began to pump hard. Stay calm, I tried to tell myself as I suspected what he was about to do. Juju was now genuflecting, one hand reaching into his jacket pocket. It is about to happen, I made myself think. After all these years, when I'd tried not to hope for it—even though I'd wished for it—after all the suppressed anticipation, he was about to do it. Stay calm! And then his hand brought the ring. "Shama," Juju said, "I have never loved anyone as much as I love you. I never thought this kind of love was even possible. Once in a lifetime to find someone, a soul mate you love and adore completely, someone you know you want to live with forever... That is what I have found in you.... My love, will you marry me?"

I had known, yes, the moment he started slipping to the floor, but before then, I'd still doubted a little. So my surprise was genuine, but it had already become manifest before he started proposing and had ran its course by the time he finished. So the gasp afterward was gasp designed to honor him and appease his ego as a sign of how much he had overwhelmed me with this proposal, but it was nonetheless a fitting exclamation point to my reaction. He was about to say something—please say yes, perhaps—when I responded, not willing to prolong the suspense past the fifty seconds I'd let elapse.

"Yes," I said. "I would *love* to be your wife."

He slipped the ring on my finger, got up as I did likewise and we embraced and kissed. Even after that, neither of us could stop smiling, eyes full of new adoration for each other, and for the occasion. He would start telling his friends and family, Juju said. As for the date of the marriage, he would let me choose, only he needed a little time to save up some money for the wedding. He knew his mother would offer to pay for it but he wanted to do this himself. But I shouldn't let it linger, he said. He wanted to make me his wife soon and not call me fiancée for too long.

# One

I spent the first night in Cambridge with the redoubtable Fiona. Juju had already told her of his proposal and she referred to me from time to time as "my daughter." Although Fiona had asked long ago that I call her Fiona, I had been uncomfortable calling her that. Now, Fiona asked to be called Mom. This was a better alternative for me and Mom flowed from my tongue more easily. "They're going to put you through orientation and give you all sorts of ideas. The one thing I want to tell you is this—have confidence in yourself. It's as simple and as complicated as that. Law school isn't easy but you will be great at it." Fiona's voice almost chocked when she added, "My husband was a brilliant man, but I think at some point he lost his self-confidence. Like you, he'd come to America from Africa and somehow managed to convince himself or allow others to convince him that he didn't fully belong, that he was some form of imposter. BS, I say. You belong just as much as the next person….actually, strike that. You, daughter, are smarter than most. I know you well enough to say that. So if you have an opinion in class, as I'm sure you will, voice it and don't give a damn what anyone else thinks. And when you really think about it, you've already had such experiences in life that most of your classmates will never have in a lifetime. You have stared death in the face and survived, in fact thrived. The world is yours. Law school is yours. Go conquer it."

Sage advice that I took in deeply, not to mention that Jojo Badu's notebook-diary had also given me insights into the belly of the vast beast that was an outsider's complex, that draining worry of not belonging. I was determined not to do that to myself. Mentally alert through orientation, I listened attentively. I prepared hard for my first class, meticulously reading and taking notes on the cases assigned for reading ahead of class. I sat through the first class of my law school career and listened as the professor queried students who seemed nervous and sometimes stuttered through their answers. I saw one student humiliated when he couldn't answer the professor's questions and the latter berated him for lack of preparation and "feeble minded responses." I watched as over-zealous students eager to burnish their egos or prove themselves volunteered answers, many of which I'd already answered in my mind, and some of which I also found feebly thought through. I was going to enjoy this. I didn't speak the first week—as I never volunteered and was not called on. But I had seen the arena of confrontation, its theatric displays of seeming intelligence, and it didn't scare me. But I knew that to maintain that level of confidence, I would have to work outstandingly hard—the workload, as I was beginning to see, was daunting.

I would volunteer an answer the next week in my torts class and the professor would proclaim, "Excellent." My confidence loosed, I began to volunteer more. I found out that if I volunteered when I knew the answers the chances that the professors would call on me when I didn't know the answers were minimized. I also developed a winning routine. I would wake up at five a.m., read over the material for the day, speak with Juju on the phone from six forty-five through seven, perform my morning ablutions and be in class for my eight o'clock class. After classes sometime around noon, I would eat lunch, study until about five p.m., and take a break until around seven, when I would again speak with Juju for half an hour before studying and doing assignments until about eleven-thirty or midnight when I went to bed. By weekend, I was exhausted, so I woke up later on Saturdays and Sundays, and always took a night off (mostly on Saturdays) from studying, unless when I had significantly fallen behind in my assignments. On my nights off, I sometimes went out with my colleagues, sometimes visited Fiona and sometimes did nothing. While I made occasional exceptions to this regimen, I tried hard to maintain it. Juju came to visit, sometimes twice in a month, sometimes thrice. My first fall of law school, we went to Fiona's for Thanksgiving dinner, and Ama was there as well. We spent the night talking and reminding ourselves of the time in my Evanston apartment.

When school broke for vacation after the first semester, I returned to Evanston to stay with Juju, having given up my Evanston apartment when I started law school. I could not fully enjoy the break, however, since the first semester exams were scheduled for early January. When I would rather cuddle up with Juju and watch a movie, I had to study; when I would rather go for a walk or read a novel, I had to study. Juju kept himself in the distance, giving me as much space as I chose. Even Christmas dinner was strained, as my mind was on the exams. "I'm so sorry," I kept saying as Juju assured me that he understood. I returned to

Cambridge in January, worried that I wasn't giving Juju enough attention (even if he never complained). I took my first exams, which were more difficult than I'd expected. Then I had a short two week break in which I did nothing but shop, host Juju, watch TV, and sleep. And visit Fiona. On my prodding, Fiona and I went to visit her husband's grave. She was reluctant to take me there at first, saying although she went often by herself, she wasn't sure it was fair to me to drag me with her. "I want to go," I told her. "You are not dragging me." The couple of times I went with her, we saw that someone had already left flowers on the grave: red roses, two yellow roses, and joined red and white roses. Neither Fiona nor I commented on this, but I kept looking around to see if a man wearing dreadlocks would appear as he had the one time Juju and I visited. I never saw him, but it was as if his presence—or call it his smell—permeated the place, joining the past and the present, memory and action.

The results of my first semester's exams were released a little into the second. I called Fiona immediately to inform her of the results: Torts: A; Criminal Law: A+, and Contracts: A+. I could almost see Fiona's excitement over the phone, as she yelled how proud she was, and she would send me a congratulatory card with the handwritten note: To the brightest law student in the world and the most beautiful woman ever. Juju bought me flowers and told me he was blessed to be married to me.

The second semester was as difficult as the first, but not as strenuous. I had managed to master the process of reading cases so that I didn't spend as much time on assignments. Too, having survived the first semester, I knew I would prevail in the second and beyond. I worked hard, followed my routine, saw Juju once or twice a month, spoke with him every day, visited with Fiona, excelled in answering questions and become some teachers' favorite, and prepared for my exams in May. I was exhausted after those exams and told Fiona I needed a long break, but Fiona advised me to put in some effort to complete my Law Review assignment. I knew my grades put me in an ideal position to make Law Review, but that was just one part of the process. I also had to complete an assignment of reading and writing that came in a hefty package. I would only make Law Review if I performed well on that assignment also. Given the prestige associated with being a Law Review editor, Fiona said it would put me in great stead, especially when it came to job opportunities after law school. So I collected the package and spent countless hours reading, answering, summarizing, editing, and writing. I flew to Chicago the next day after this was completed. I would spend the summer as a clerk in one of the law firms in downtown Chicago.

It was a relaxed summer for me, except for the wedding planned for late August, as I worked downtown. I lived with Juju and took the train to and from work each day and, during lunch, when I wasn't attending one of the firm's preplanned functions, I would take a walk in Grant Park. I found my assignments mildly challenging but routine, poring over cases and treatises and preparing memos answering various legal issued posed by partners and associates of the firm. The only incident of note was the interest shown in me by one of my fellow clerks. The young man kept inviting me out, and I kept denying him. So far, this hadn't been a general problem as my engagement ring deterred would be suitors, but not Glen Winfield, who kept saying he wasn't interested in my fiancé but in me and me only. Juju found this amusing when I told him. "I can't blame him for wanting a thing of beauty," he said.

"Oh, so I'm a thing now?" I asked, to which question Juju had no rebuttal but a smile.

I insisted Juju accompany me on one of our summer intern outings, which worked as I intended since Glen Winfield stopped pursuing me after he met Juju. "Some women just wear a ring for show, you know," he said to me. "Lucky bastard, your Juju."

I had to end my internship a week earlier in order to get married. In the meantime, I'd received my second semester's results: Evidence, A+; Property, A+, Civil Procedure, A+. "You're unreal," Fiona said. "I could barely get anything above a B+ in law school." Additionally, I received a notice that I had made Law Review. I knew this would make me even busier than before, but I preferred instead to focus on my upcoming marriage.

We were married in a church in Evanston, with the reception at a nearby club. Juju had chosen the church.

271

"My mom was Moslem," I said. "I wonder if she'd be concerned that I'm getting married in a church."

Juju laughed at this. "Since when did you worry about such things?"

"I thought I told you my mother was a Moslem."

"But that doesn't make you one. Wasn't your father a Christian?"

"He was, and not just him. I also am Christian. You know that."

Most of the wedding attendees were invitees of Juju and Fiona. For the first time I met Fiona's parents, George and Sissi Harris, both sporting totally gray manes, and they mentioned how highly Fiona spoke of me. I also met Fiona's younger sister Simone, some sort of art dealer, and her husband Jeff, an insurance executive of sorts, and their children Kimberly and Sherrie. If Fiona was more serious minded, Simone appeared to me to be more free-spirited. She invited Juju and I to visit them in Washington DC. Ama introduced her new boyfriend Jerome Webb. The Baileys came, all of them, including Mike, and Jason and Kamila and their one year old daughter Zoe. Fiona introduced me to John Owens. "John and my husband were in college and law school together. He's a big shot. He's a man you ought to get to know. He will be running for the senate seat from Virginia next year. Right, John?"

"We'll see," said John Owens. He seemed interested in me and held me in conversation for about ten minutes, wishing to know my plans after law school. "If ever you're in DC, please look me up. And that goes for you as well, Juju. Your dad was a great friend." I knew I'd heard the name somewhere, a name in a news article that wasn't so prominent to hold attention over the long haul, perhaps. And certainly I recalled the name John in Jojo Badu's notebook-diary.

The evening passed slowly, just as I wished it, as I wanted to savor each moment, which I would prefer to recall from the storage of my memory than from the lifeless reel of a recording device. We would spend a week in Rome for our Honeymoon, which strained Juju's budget. "But you only get married once," he said. With my student loans and summer job as my only source of income, I could barely contribute to the trip.

I had to return to law school immediately we returned, and it was worse than I anticipated. I had no free time as every minute was filled with Law Review work, classes (which I hardly had time to attend), talking to Juju once a day (as compared to twice as before), studying or completing assignments. Exhausted at day's end, I'd collapse into bed to wake up early the next morning and restart the process. I saw Fiona less frequently, as even my weekends were occupied with work and study. Juju now visited often, sometimes thrice in a month, but all he could do was be around me as I worked and he read school material that he brought with him. "I will make it up to you," I said.

"Don't worry, Shama. Things won't be like this forever. You'll soon graduate and then I can have all of you back."

As busy with Law Review as I was, I deliberately chose classes that wouldn't take too much time, taught by professors reputed for their leniency in awarding grades. With this strategy, I secured an A, A+ and A+ in the first semester of my second year and three A+s in the second. Then it was back to Chicago, another internship downtown with a law firm, a little more time with my husband, and then back to law school for my third and final year of law school. That went quickly, given that I was so busy. My grades were almost identical to the previous years' so that at the end of the third year I was not surprised to learn that I'd graduated at the top of my class. At graduation, I confessed to Fiona thus: "I'm so confused, Mom. I have a number of offers from some prestigious law firms, including the ones I clerked for in Chicago, but I've also applied for a clerkship at the Supreme Court. I'm not sure what to do. Juju sacrificed so much for me, I think it may be time for me to take a job in Chicago, and start being a good wife to him. Still, I keep wondering whether I should try and do a clerkship first."

"If I were you, I'd clerk if I got it. You may never get that opportunity again, but the law firms won't go anywhere. You can always come back to them. You're even more attractive after a clerkship, especially a clerkship at the Supreme Court. Heck, they'll be at your feet, with your law degree, your grades, and a Supreme Court clerkship to boot. They'll be begging you to come work for them. Of course, I can't tell you what to do. You ought to talk it over with Juju."

This, I did.

"You should take it," Juju said. "The Supreme Court clerkship will serve you well, if you...I mean when you get it."

"But that will mean another year or two living apart."

"We've done it for three, another year or two won't change anything."

"Are you sure of this, Juju?"

"No doubt."

But I would not believe it, asking again and again if he was serious. To prove that he wanted me to accept the offer when it came (as he believed it would come), Juju started applying for positions in colleges and universities in the DC area. "I've thought about this and I realize we should no longer be living apart. When you go, I'm coming to DC with you."

A few weeks later, I received a call from the office of Justice Patrick Sitter to come to DC for an interview. Juju accompanied me on the trip. I was nervous when I entered the Supreme Court building and was ushered into Justice Sitter's chambers. The man looked paler than he appeared on TV, a little trimmer and less imposing. He smiled, stood up to shake my hand and said, "So this is the genius of Harvard." For a man reputed to be a loner, the justice seemed at perfect ease, even somewhat gregarious as he made me talk about my background, from my time in Rwanda (I omitted the deaths of my family and my own sufferings and offered a very brief profile), my doctorate, and my law school years. I was grateful he didn't ask why I chose law school. He told me he had read the writing samples I had sent as part of my application and was impressed with my intellect, my meticulous reasoning. He told me also that he was more than impressed with my academic performance. "I don't usually hire students right out of law school," he said. "I usually expect them to clerk at a lower court first, as do most of my colleagues, but even before I met you, I had already decided. I look forward to working with you. Congratulations."

He shook my hand, though I would have preferred to hug him. "This was way too easy," I said to Juju later.

"You made it easy, honey. Who wouldn't want to hire someone with your story? That alone is compelling. But to add to that a PhD and graduating top of your law school class. Only a stupid justice wouldn't hire you."

That summer, I prepared to move to DC, but with anxiety as we waited for the results of Juju's applications. In the meantime, I worked with the law firm where I'd clerked the previous year. The managing partner, fully aware that I would be leaving for the Supreme Court, still dined me several times, telling me, "We hope after you're done that you will come back to us. You have a bright future with us; I want you to know that."

My anxieties were diminished mid-summer when Georgetown University offered Juju a position as an associate professor. I would miss Evanston as I would miss Chicago. I would miss Curt and Ann Bailey, and, yes, I would miss Nat Musegera. And as I considered those I'd miss, I realized that I'd not called Bro Mike in a long while, but when I called his number, his phone rang unanswered. I decided to call him later. But the most important consideration for me was that I would not have to live apart from Juju. For the first time since we were married.

## Two

Juju and I moved into a house in Georgetown. On the advice of Juju's aunt Simone, who'd helped us find our house, Juju and I toured DC with as much leisurely license as we could afford before work started. "From what I hear, the clerks have no life, so make use of this to enjoy and relax," Simone said. If I had survived law school and law review, I prophesied, I would survive the Supreme Court clerkship. True, perhaps, but I didn't have a husband living with me during law school. My salary as a clerk of the US Supreme Court was a pittance, so that we had to rely primarily on Juju's income. It didn't leave us much discretionary spending, although together our salaries made us fairly comfortable. But financial security soon would become the least of my concerns as the dictates of my new life took control.

If law school had consumed my time, clerkship engulfed it. My hours were filled from dawn to dusk with work, which I did seven days a week. It had begun when the Chief Justice hosted us, the new clerks, to tea. He graciously welcomed us but also swore us to secrecy about the inner workings of the court. "Is this some sort of Omerta Code?" One clerk had whispered in my ears. I surveyed the room, my fellow clerks, mostly male, mostly white, me being the only black, with another of Indian ancestry who was raised in the US.

Justice Sitter had made his own welcome. "We'll have a great time," he said as he introduced his clerks to one another. I settled into the routine—reviewing petitions (or writs of certiorari) filed with the Court, writing memos summarizing the facts and issues presented and making recommendations whether the Court should accept the petitions. I looked to the merits of the petitions to determine whether to recommend certiorari. Even in badly written petitions, I would recommend certiorari if I felt it would advance some key constitutional issue, bring uniformity to competing opinions in the various lower courts, serve justice (or correct an injustice). But I soon found that not all the clerks took this approach. One of them, for example, was notorious for not recommending acceptance of petitions filed with the Court. She'd told me, "I don't want to acquire a reputation for simply channeling cases. I want my recommendations to count." And I realized that I was acquiring a contrary reputation—as being too willing to recommend that petitions be accepted. "Your recommendations are too easily dismissed," my fellow clerk, Mustapha, had said. "Mine, because I make so few of them, are never ignored."

"But what if the case is important? What if it advances justice? Isn't that the most important touchstone?"

"My reputation is important. I don't want anything I recommend to be dismissed as improvident."

And I realized that many clerks had this fear—to make a recommendation that would be dismissed—as happened to one of my colleagues after her recommendation was dismissed as improvidently granted (or in the Court's parlance, DIGed). Maureen became inconsolable when this happened and thereafter never recommended a case to be heard for the rest of her clerkship. I tried to console her, telling her that she ought to stand on merit, principle and justice, not fear of making mistakes. And I realized how justice could turn on such happenstance, on the opinion (or perhaps even whim) of a group of recent graduates from law school, most in their twenties, who influenced which petitions the highest court of the land would hear.

Given my discomfort over this sifting, I came to dislike the process of making recommendations intensely. I enjoyed instead the opportunity to write bench memos for Justice Sitter, in which I summarized the case at hand, and provided him with possible questions to ask during oral arguments. I enjoyed even more, writing the first drafts of cases, where I combined research, writing and reasoning. Justice Sitter would provide general guidance of his decision and ask his clerks to draft the opinion. For those I had the lead in writing, I tried to be meticulous but concise, avoiding the verbose approach of some of my colleagues, especially Mustapha, whose opinions sometimes read like law review articles—long in an attempt to weigh every pro and con, with long footnotes and grandiose phrases. Aware that the opinion would be read by those within and outside academia, would influence (perhaps for generations to come), I aimed for clarity. In the clerk's lunch room, I often debated my approach with Mustapha and my fellow clerks and resisted some of them in the penchant for showboating. Justice Sitter would review the draft with me, challenge some of my dicta and the rigor of my reasoning, sometimes, but rarely, ask for changes. I realized that this was not the same with some of the other clerks, whose first drafts had to be substantially rewritten after Justice Sitter saw them.

Mustapha and I got a bit close, I presume because we both clerked for Justice Sitter and also because we were the only clerks "of color." But I think we would have drawn close to each other regardless of these factors, because he very well could identify with the immigrant's story, his parents having moved to the US from Calcutta when they were in their twenties. He had grown up in the DC area, left to attend Yale, for both college and law school, and returned for the clerkship and hoped to remain. He probed into my background, and although I found it a bit too intrusive that he asked many questions about the genocide, the man had an easy way about him that equally eased whatever irritation his questions may have aroused. When we weren't eating lunch at our desks, which was often, or at the cafeteria on occasion, he and I would walk to a bistro and eat lunch outside. Needless to say, this was rare. But it was on one such rare occasion that he invited me to visit his mosque.

"Insha Allah, you will come visit us at the mosque," he said.

"You are Moslem," I said. "I am Christian."

"Are you sure about that? I never hear you talk about church. Or is church going not part of your religion?"

"I don't need to attend church to demonstrate my Christianity, Mustapha."

"The Bible says iron sharpens iron, doesn't it? It says you must fellowship with the saints, doesn't it?"

"How does a Moslem go about referring to the Bible to make his point?"

"Well, think about it, Shama, perhaps I am more of a Christian than you."

I did think about it, remembering the days in the past when we used to attend church in Butare. I remembered Rev. Didier Murenzi's sermons. I had not attended even one church service, apart from my wedding, ever since I arrived in the US. Mustapha had planted a sense of guilt in me and I resolved to attend church soon, but I thought I was too busy to find the time. In the meantime, Mustapha kept inviting him to visit him at the mosque where he worshipped.

278

I continued to regret that I hardly saw Juju. I left home early, returned late, even on Saturdays. When I could, I worked at home on Sundays so that we would at least be in proximity. He prepared our meals and never complained, except once when he said, as though jokingly, "You are married to the Supreme Court, not me." I'd apologized, and as I said to him before, promised to "make it up to" him. He didn't ask it, but I could expect his mind asking, "When?" It was for this reason that I particularly cherished the social occasions of the Supreme Court when spouses were also invited. In particular, though I didn't ski, I insisted Juju come along on a ski trip to New Hampshire, where Justice Sitter kept a home. His entire clerk-group of four were invited and asked to bring their spouses or significant others. Mustapha came alone, saying he didn't have time to date. The group made the trip over the winter weekend to Mt. Mooselake. Juju and I rented skis and attempted in comic fashion to ski. Not just that, I hated being out for so long in the winter cold and falling repeatedly in the snow. But I felt closer to Juju by the time the weekend was over, such that on the Sunday we took our time making love. I'd insisted I didn't want to get pregnant during my clerkship, but that night I asked Juju not to wear prophylactic (a practice he'd often resisted anyway as unsatisfying). "Are you sure?" he asked, timidly. I responded with a kiss and an assumption of control over the congress of our bodies. It was the first time in about three months.

I knew the symptoms—the morning sickness, the vomiting, etc.— when I started exhibiting them, which was confirmed by a home test. "You are going to be a father," I told Juju. He hugged me, kissed me for many seconds. When I had the opportunity to look into his eyes, they were tender with tears. But it was difficult for me to balance the symptoms of my pregnancy with the rigors of my clerkship, finding that I was often absent-minded and sleepy. This embarrassed me when once, at lunch with some of the justices I called Justice Sitter "Judge." He'd glared at me and said, "By this time you should know that I am a justice." This was a mild rebuke that normally I would have dismissed. Instead, it caused me such embarrassment I could almost feel ill. Mustapha told me not to worry about such trivialities. But I cried in Juju's arms that night.

279

I miscarried the next day and was inconsolable for a while, and strained to occupy my time even more with work, while Juju encouraged me that there would be others. I hated him (for the first time) for saying this, although I quickly overcame this novel emotion toward him, as I continued to worry that if this mishap occurred once, it could happen again. And because of this concern I worked hard to make time for him (arranging dinner and movie watching), which made me more stressed, given the time demands of my job. And then came increased pressure of the phantom pain in my belly region. Juju noticed this, his discerning eyes alert over the obvious symptoms of my pressured life—the forced smiles, the reddened eyes, the uncharacteristic forgetfulness. "Honey, I am here for you," he said. "Don't force yourself to please me. I love you more than anything I can think of, and I am with you always." Oh my darling, I sang in my mind (or heart, perhaps), there is no man like you, you deserve better than this. While I didn't say these words, my smile eased his worry, as did my kiss.

And now I hoped hard for the year to end so that I could reclaim some time for myself and Juju. But it trickled by slowly one hour after the next, the day a tedious journey on account of the missing hours without Juju's presence, the night my only consolation, even though that too was compromised as I couldn't engage Juju as much as I'd like if I'd had more energy at that time. But time, as unkind as it may be, surely passes and the year-end came eventually, marked by a skit the clerk's wrote in mockery of the justices—accentuating their idiosyncrasies in a humorous manner. My main contribution was to script the skit about Justice Sitter's morbid concern about missing appointments, which was marked by his constant reference to his wrist watch and the verification of time with others, as though he feared his own time was wrong. For this, I wore two wrist watches in the skit about missing an appointment with Destiny played by Mustapha wearing a suit. I would set and reset the wrist watch, all the while asking what time it was as the Lady of Justice, played by Maureen in a long gown, looked on bored and then fell down and simulated death as a result of boredom and lack of attention. While I attended to the dead Lady of Justice, Destiny had come and gone. This skit drew laughter only because the clerks, as well as the justices, were familiar with Justice Sitter's habits. But the subject matter was weightier than most appreciated at the time and the laughter following the death of the Lady of Justice, drawn on account of the way Maureen rolled around before her mock death, elicited more from the physical comedy than any message I may have implied. However, received, I didn't care much, my jury-of-my-own-mind acquitting me in the knowledge that my clerkship was ending and I had accepted an offer from a prestigious law firm in downtown DC—Wood, Oliver, Resnick & Krezinksi—one of the largest in the country with offices in Europe, Asia, South America and South Africa. Given my options between the various departments of the firm, I picked litigation. I thought I was undeserving of the salary offered me, almost double that of Juju's, with the chance for an equally huge bonus, but after the relatively frugal lifestyle of the past years, I concluded with Juju's concurrence that we deserved to start amassing some wealth.

"No one has worked harder than you," Juju said. "No one is more deserving."

"I had always thought of doing something in the public interest, like defending the poor or going after criminals, not defending corporations."

Fiona told me, "You can do that later. See this as a necessary compromise to secure your future. Once you're more secure, you can do whatever you wish. Besides, you can always volunteer your services, do something pro bono if you prefer."

I thought Juju would bring up the promise I had made him earlier to return to Ghana after our education if that is what he preferred. But he didn't; in fact, he never brought it up. Perhaps he had changed his mind, or perhaps he was pulled by the potential of wealth.

# Three

I started working for Wood Oliver. I reread parts of Jojo Badu's notebook-diary. It worried me that I too might become trapped as he felt, but I decided to strive hard anyway. The partners were soon competing for my time to do research, draft motions and memos, and accompany them to court or negotiations. As long as I worked, including Saturdays, I found this better than my clerkship hours. I arrived in the office at eight a.m. and left around eight-thirty p.m., except I left around midnight on days when the case load was overly heavy. Once or twice, with extremely important cases, I slept in the office, working until the wee hours of the morning, sleeping for a couple of hours on a couch in my office and resuming work. There were days when I could leave the office early at about 6 p.m. to spend time with Juju. While I worked many Saturdays, I managed most Sundays off and I found that I was getting closer to Juju.

We went to church from time to time.

Mustapha was in the meantime working in another DC law firm—Lawrence, Atwood and Wright. We would meet for lunch from time to time. I asked him about his social life. "Too busy, Shama," he said.

"Too busy as a clerk, too busy as an associate in a law firm," I said. "Mustapha, when are you going to make time?"

"I know, I know," he replied. "I need to slow down a little. Insha Allah, I will."

Once or twice, he invited me to worship with him and I told him I would think about it.

In the middle of my first year, I got pregnant again, followed by joy and expectation, but also followed by a miscarriage that depressed me for months. After I recovered from this, I again reengaged with Juju physically in the hope of another pregnancy. But for the remainder of the year, this didn't happen. Nor would it happen for the next two years. We tried at optimal times to have me conceive to no avail. Juju, who had been the more stalwart over this began to worry openly. "Perhaps we should see a fertility specialist," he suggested.

"No!" I exclaimed.

"But why not?"

"I just don't want to," I said with finality, as images of the past replayed—the night in Butare in front of the church, and that haunting day in my aunt's bathroom, images I thought I'd long conquered began to hold sway again.

Meantime, in those years, I received stellar reviews of my work and was on "fast track" to achieving partnership in the law firm of Wood Oliver. The firm even assigned Bob Sneider, the managing partner, as my new mentor. I represented corporate clients, and helped reverse their legal misfortunes on a number of occasions, often avoiding potentially massive fines and penalties. Corporate clients often wanted to speak with me directly, bypassing partners. Seeing me as an invaluable asset, Wood Oliver promoted me to senior associate in my third year, an unprecedented move that generated as much praise as envy from my colleagues. I also took on indigents on a *pro bono* basis, looking for those in the most dire circumstances, helping avoid evictions and even jail time for some charged in criminal offenses, mostly possession of drugs. I also forced the law firm to increase its minority hiring by pestering Bob Sneider. He pointed to the number of minorities employed by the law firm—about ten percent of the firm's population. "We can do better," I said. He promised to work on it. After three months I raised the issue again, and again, and again, until he took it upon himself to interview and hire more minorities.

"We don't want a quota here," he said. "But I think we are now around twenty percent minority," he confirmed about a year later.

I remembered words from Jojo Badu's notebook-dairy about the need for sugar daddies. "Let's make sure they stay," I said, suggesting a minority mentoring program. "It's not enough to just hire—we need to ensure they stay as well and rise to the top; otherwise, we're wasting every one's time and the firm's resources." Bob Sneider asked me to head a minority mentoring program, which I did, making sure that the more senior attorneys, including me, took time to mentor the junior ones and to give them meaningful assignments and feedback, to help them correct their mistakes without presuming them incompetent. "We only have three minority partners," I said. "Let's get the number up."

Juju had now become an associate professor, en route to tenured status. Our combined incomes produced a comfortable living, and for the first time, we didn't have to worry about our financial future.

When Mike Bailey called to tell me he was being sent to Iraq, I wished him well but I worried for weeks about him. Why he would have joined the army in *flagrante bello* had always been to me both audacious and foolish.

Jojo and I took a trip to Paris and made another to Accra, this time with Juju carrying cash and gifts to those who'd welcomed him earlier. If I worried about a resurrection of Chochoo, I soon rested at ease, for she made no appearance during the two week stay.

I got pregnant and miscarried again. But before I could wallow in this latest setback, I was faced with the most difficult case of my career, at a time when I received the most disheartening news since my arrival in the US. This was in the sixth year of my life in a law firm, when partnership was imminent.

It was challenging enough that I received word that Alexandre Nsengiyumva's trial in Arusha by the International Court of Justice for Rwanda had begun. I worried about Auntie Shama and sent her encouraging letters, all the while wanting Alexandre punished. All would be well, I'd said when in my spirits I wanted him to suffer. But I could not gloat over this out of concern that his imprisonment would negatively impact my aunt.

And then came very disheartening news. Prof. Bailey and Ann Bailey called to inform me that my *brother* Mike had been injured in Iraq and was in critical condition. All would be well, I'd said, but like a premonition, I foresaw the death of my Bro the way I had foreseen it when he'd first told me he was joining the army. For hours I wept and could not be consoled by Juju. I couldn't concentrate at work and had to take three days off. I mourned at home in those three days, which I spent almost exclusively in bed wetting my pillow. By the time the news came that Mark had died, I was already days into my period of mourning so that it didn't shock me as it otherwise would. I'd flown to Evanston to console the Baileys. They'd shown as much strength as they could, but occasionally they'd both broken down in front of me—and I joined those episodes in unifying moments of surrender to grief. Prof. Curt Bailey confided that Ann Bailey sang death songs to her fallen solider-son in the morning's wee hours, as if pleading with death to render his soul back to her. I was in need of resuscitation when I returned to DC, but instead I was summoned into the office of the managing partner of Wood Oliver and asked to handle the case involving The Knights of the Latter Order.

When I entered the office of Bob Sneider, the managing partner had eased his bulky frame into the chair, his back to the door. He rotated away from the credenza as I walked in. He seemed eager to get through the pleasantries and preferred to sit in the couch in his office, where I had never been invited to sit in the countless times I'd been in the office. "I need a special favor from you," he said. "This will make you uncomfortable, I'm sure, but it has to be done."

"Okay, Bob, let's hear it."

"I need you to take a special case before the Supreme Court."

"Not a problem. What's so special about it? Are you worried because I've never argued before the Court?"

"That's not it. I know that won't be a problem. What it is … well, it involves The Knights of the Latter Order."

I gasped. "The racist group?"

"Well, that's a matter of opinion."

"I have a big problem with that."

"Before you say anything, I need to let you know this is a very important case for us."

"I didn't even know they were a client."

"They weren't. The case comes to us at the request of one of our most important clients. From what I know the CEO is related to the head of the Knights and has asked us to do this as a special favor."

"Hmmm."

"It's a simple case on its face. I'm not even sure why the Court wants to hear it. I don't think it will make new law or anything like that. The facts are straightforward. The Knights had petitioned to stage a rally in front of a school building in Springfield."

"Which one?"

"Illinois…From what I know, the building had been used for similar rallies by the NAACP the previous year. Well, the petition was denied, especially because they said they'd be carrying guns at the rally,

285

and the Knights sued. The lower courts ruled against them, and here we are."

"I appreciate that you'd ask me to do it, but I just can't. They stand for everything I hate. These guys would lynch me if they could. I can't represent hate, especially not when the hate is directed against people like me."

"A lawyer, Shama, must be able to separate her emotion from her job."

"Not like this. Will you defend this guy if he killed your child?"

"Listen, Shama, there comes a time when we are all tested in our professional careers. That's what separates the boys from the men or, in this case, the girls from the women. We are provided with an opportunity to uphold principle over personal feeling, to put our knowledge at the client's service even when we disagree, even when we hate them. Everyone is entitled to his day in court. Our system runs on this principle. Our job is to make sure it works in practice."

"Bill, please, don't patronize me."

"Come on, Shama. The right of everyone to legal representation. It is what girds our system. The right to free speech."

"This is not a matter of free speech. This is a matter of hate speech, unprotected hate speech."

"That's what the lower courts said. Let the Supreme Court decide."

"Fine, let someone else represent them. You've argued before the Supreme Court before. Why don't you do it?"

"I would have, but the client specifically asked for you."

"Me? Why? Let them ask for someone else. Which client is this anyway?"

"Sterling Silva."

"CEO of Sterling Company? That's huge. In fact, he's the biggest client we have, isn't he? I represented the company in a fraud case once."

"Yes, and clearly you impressed him."

"I still can't do it."

"Yes, you can." Bob Sneider stood from the couch but then sat back down, apparently perturbed, though he tried to mask it with a smile that appeared more like a smirk. "Don't do this to me, Shama," he said, slipping a hand over mine. "I promised him that you would do this. That's presumptuous, I know, and please forgive me. I should have checked with you first and I have to admit I was being selfish and trying to look good before our most important client. I have already committed, though, and I'm pleading with you."

"I'm not sure..."

"I promise you this. Take this case and win or lose, I guarantee you partnership. I can make it happen this year. It's a promise." Bob Sneider winked and reiterated, "Win or *lose*."

My chests heaved, full of unease. "Can I at least think about it?"

"Sure, that's fine. But please let me know by tomorrow. We need to get going on this. Please say yes. Remember all you need to do is take the case. My promise holds, win or *lose*."

I labored over the decision the remainder of the day. The legacy of the Knights involved cross burning in the past, even lynching, and rallies advocating white power. Lately, they seemed to eschew violence, but they still posited anti-immigration viewpoints, as well as separation of the races, with the belief that the white one was the best. I couldn't overcome my anger toward them to embrace the general principle Bob Sneider articulated, not in this case. Sure, they deserved legal representation, but why did it have to be me? I wanted to say no to the request, but I was dealing with Bob Sneider, a powerful managing partner, who had doubled as my mentor, one of the architects behind my rise in the law firm—a professional sugar daddy *a la* Jojo Badu's notebook-diary. I could not disappoint him, even if it meant disappointing myself, nor could I ignore the dangling promise of partnership, which, as much as I deserved it, came within the political climate and machinations of the law firm. Before I could change my mind, which I knew I would if I lingered, especially the backlash sure to ensue from the black community, I rushed to Bob Sneider's office and accepted the case. Despite the percolating discomfort and discontent, and despite Bob Sneider's allusion to the inconsequence of losing the case, I was fully resolved to give it my best. As a professional, that much, I couldn't compromise. But I was afraid also of the backlash.

I would meet with Rod Trammel, the Grandmaster of the Knights in our office building. The first meeting was the most awkward for me. A

287

burly man with a wispy mustache and a judoka's poise, he seemed to dwarf me with his size (about seven feet, blowsy shoulders, barrel chest, beer-belly, double chin). He stared at me for long minutes without blinking, his hazel eyes apparently lifeless, cold. I returned his look, erecting a façade of fearlessness, though he discomfited me so much that I wanted to leave the room as soon as possible. Because I had read the files repeatedly I was so familiar with the case that the meeting was a mere formality.

"Why did you take this case?" Rod Trammel asked.

""It's my job," I said. "And you, why do you want me to handle this case?"

"It's your job, ma'am. I hear you are the best."

Neither of us gave the other the opportunity to explain further, to explore motives—why I would represent a group that advocated psychological violence, in the least, against "colored" people, and why, despite the advocacy of his group, he accepted me as his advocate. We could only surmise these reasons and I felt that this was an opportunity lost, both of us entrenched in our ways and views and not willing, perhaps even unable, to share a conversation devoid of suspicion.

With the help of Bob Sneider, I prepared for the arguments before the Supreme Court. Our argument would be simple on its face, the case for free speech as enshrined in the Constitution. We worked on the logic, anticipated questions that the justices of the Court might ask, with me drawing on my clerkship days and the kind of questions I might suggest to Justice Sitter in such a case. As the day of the arguments approached, my discomfort increased as I received calls questioning my judgment in taking the case. "You want to do their dirty work for them," Mustapha told me over lunch. Fiona wondered if I knew what I was doing, but said she supported me anyway. "Your intestinal fortitude is daunting," she said. "I couldn't have done it." Only Juju assured me that I should trust my decision, without the torture of second guessing myself. Even one publication carried an article about the case with the heading: The Devil's Advocate," which included a biographical note of me and indicated that I was being insensitive, as a foreign born black woman, to the history and sensitivities of American born blacks. The airwaves were full of oral editorials excoriating me, with only a few, mostly white voices, speaking in may favor.

I wept.

I strove to articulate my client's position, without believing in it—I'd rephrase that: cerebrally I believed in the general freedom of speech, even those that cause psychological violence, but emotionally this belief had no home in this particular instance. I distilled the opposing counsel's position to two main arguments. First, the Court ought to recognize the unequal power between such groups and their minority targets, especially considering that guns would be present at the scene, which would create a fearful and hateful environment whose sole purpose was to intimidate the targets of the Knight's hate. Second, the Knight's words, especially when expressed where weapons were carried, would only incite acts of hate—the equivalent of shouting fire in a crowded theater. Personally, I agreed with him, but I argued that the First and Second Amendments to the Constitution recognized free speech, including hate speech and the right to bear arms respectively, that both were exercised at the same time and place could not nullify either or both of those rights. Second, this was far from shouting fire in a crowded theater with a captive audience. This was a mere rally in a public place. There was no captive audience and no one need even attend the rally who didn't want to.

Justice Sitter pounced: "It seems to me ridiculous that we ought to close our eyes to the deleterious consequences of such hate speech under these circumstances."

Here, I was battling against the man I adored, whom I expected to be the least questioning. I need not remind him that hate speech was protected too. Had the justice forgotten that I'd just reiterated that hate speech was protected speech, or was he signaling to me that this wasn't a worthy fight? "Justice Sitter," I responded, "precedent tells us that hate speech is protected speech."

"Even those that incite violence, counselor?"

"That is not the case here, Justice Sitter."

"That would be like saying that the mere shouting of fire in a crowded theater is protected."

"Justice, I think the circumstances are very distinguishable..."

The other justices, apparently enjoying the banter, almost asked no questions of me, so that when it was over, I was convinced I'd lost the case. This would be a blemish on my record, but the more important prize awaiting me was to be made partner in my sixth year with the law firm, which had never happened in its history. The earliest anyone had achieved that feat was at the eighth year mark. But even this minor stain was not to be as the decision that was rendered came in my favor, or rather my client's favor, by a 5-4 margin. This victory prompted numerous articles both in paper and on cyberspace. Most African American publications and pundits upended me, from calling me an "Uncle Tom's wife" to a "sellout."

I rejoiced.

And then I wept.

Shortly after the decision was released I, Shama Rugwe Badu, became a partner at the global law firm of Ward, Oliver, Resnick & Krezinski, to the praise of my mother-in-law. She organized a party for me in a hotel in downtown DC when she came on a special trip and remarked, "You're the best thing that happened to my son." I met Fiona's parents George and Sissi for the first time since my marriage.

Meantime, I had miscarried again. Forlorn, I took one week off from work to recuperate. Like the previous ones, it was as if the pain was a worm that had multiplied, sending its progeny burrowing into all parts of my emotions and body—tongue, ears, heart, veins, muscles, tissues, blood—such that my ears mistuned every voice or sound I heard into irritation, may tongue lost its ability to enjoy the tastefulness of food, and my eyes were blinded by visions of blood and waste so that the promise of an improved tomorrow became non-existent. Juju again suggested seeing a fertility doctor. I refused.

Juju gathered me in his arms several times, one time saying, "I know this is hard for you. I can't even begin to imagine. But I mean it when I say we'll get through this together."

It was only time that managed to tame this marauding worm and its children.

It was around this time that I received a letter from my aunt in Kigali. She asked that I call her as she'd acquired a phone line. It was urgent, the letter said. I called immediately. Auntie Shama noted how proud she was of me. "I just read about you. This friend of mine showed me an article in one of your magazines about you winning an important case in America's highest court. Your father would be so proud of you." And then, after some idle talk, Auntie Shama said, "Alexandre was just sentenced to life in prison. I wrote to you because I was expecting this to happen. His lawyer was so bad."

"I'm so sorry," I said.

"I need you, Shama. I need you to come here and take his case for him. I want you to fight for him, for me. You are the only one I can trust on this to do this as best as she can."

*I don't like Alexandre. He stands for so much hate.*

*But you just defended The Knights.*

*He is a rapist.*

*So is Thierry, but he carried you to your recovery.*

*If you defended the Knights, then you can defend Alexandre.*

*I defended the Knights because Bob Sneider asked me to. He needed me. The firm needed me.*

*You need to defend Alexandre because you aunt is asking you to. She needs you.*

I didn't want to do this, but I couldn't disappoint my aunt. If I defended the Knights in a bargain for promotion, how could I not defend Alexandre in promotion of my aunt's happiness?

"Let me look into how or whether I can do so. If I can defend him, I will do so."

I thought, over the line, I heard my aunt suppress a sob.

291

# Four

With a total of thirty days to file an appeal, I had little time to take action, as ten out of those thirty days had already expired since Alexandre's sentence. I had twenty days to inform my law firm that I needed a leave of absence and transition matters to others, fly to Kigali to meet my aunt and review the case, including reviewing the trial court's proceedings, before crafting an argument for Alexandre. I decided to make haste when Juju told me, "You owe it to your aunt. You're not doing this for him; you're doing it for her. You're all she's got." My times in Kigali with Auntie Shama recollected, I grew determined in my mission. Bob Sneider reluctantly granted me the leave of absence when I reminded him of the favor I'd done by taking the Knights' case.

Juju announced suddenly, "I am coming with you."

"You don't have to, honey."

"Sweetie, I want to be there for you. Besides, this will be my opportunity to meet your aunt, to see the country that gave you to me, to kiss its soil."

I worried. There were truths shaded, some hidden, that lay in Rwanda, truths I didn't want Juju to know, truths I believed would cause him more pain than was necessary. And there was the ghost of my own hands. Would Juju's presence unearth those truths or compromise my own resolve? But how could I reject his request? "You know I don't have much time to prepare the case. I'm not sure this will be the best time to show you around."

"I won't be in the way, I promise. But let me come with you."

Had I betrayed the burden of the case on me so much that he felt I needed him? Without any additional arsenal to dissuade him, we bought our tickets and were in Kigali with fifteen days left for me to file the appeal. I'd considered for a brief period not wasting time coming to Kigali. Since the Appeals Chamber sat in The Hague, I could easily have filed the appeal from DC. But after a discussion with the lawyer who had handled the trial, the theory of the case and the defense presented, I believed I had to be in Kigali to complete the strategy for appeal that had begun to coalesce in my mind—there was the missing element of witnesses I felt required my presence in Kigali.

292

We spent the first night in Kigali at my aunt's in long periods of embrace and with some tear-shedding as Auntie Shama, considerably more grayed and slower, admired my success and I regretted the loss of time since we'd last embraced, while mentally lamenting my aunt's loss of youthfulness.

But her house had changed. She had put in a new gate, the house was freshly painted, the bathroom expanded and completely redone so that it not only had a bath, but a standing shower and a Jacuzzi. The rooms had been expanded, the furniture new. And she had bought a BMW.

"Auntie, this place is as good as new," I said.

"Well, you know, Shama, I never moved fully into Alexandre's house even after we got married. I don't know, but staying there too long brought some unpleasant memories. Isn't it odd? I am married to the man but I can't stay permanently in his house. Anyway, when he was imprisoned, we rented out his house. I only go there to collect the rent. That's a good source of income, but I provide some of it for the upkeep of his children. Apart from that, business has been really good. Ever since the war ended and peace returned, things have taken off for me. You can see the results for yourself."

Juju was the outsider the first night, despite the gallant attempts of the Shamas to draw him into our circle. But the subsequent days would fulfill the promise sowed on the first night, as I pored over the transcripts of the Trial Chamber's proceedings and plotted strategy and tactic, Juju and Auntie Shama spent time together, talking or touring Kigali (although I made sure I knew where they were going before they left the house). Juju wanted Auntie Shama to take him to Butare so he could see my hometown, but I refused to let her take him, and forbade him from going solo. "I want to be there when you go," I said with finality. "We will come back some other time and go then." If Juju noticed the nervousness of his wife during our time in Rwanda, he must have attributed it to the strain of the case and he didn't comment on it. He also asked me why I insisted on knowing where my aunt was taking him in Kigali. "I just want you to see the best parts," I said. I still had difficulty in the bathroom, memories still plaguing my mind, my conscience, despite its transformation, and any time I stepped in there the place was no longer

293

this modern room that my aunt had changed it to, but a place of blood and death.

In the meantime, I mastered the facts and details of Alexandre's trial as completely as could be after the fact. I had read every paper on the trial that I could get, and thankfully my aunt had meticulously kept records. The prosecutor had presented the facts as follows.

Alexandre Nsengiyumva was a key army officer with access to the high puppeteers of the slain president's party; he had, with his position and access, helped arm the *Interahamwe*, set up roadblocks to capture fleeing Tutsis; he had participated and even ordered the killing of Tutsis. The prosecution had paraded witnesses who testified to Alexandre beating them, to killing a number of Tutsis under orders from a superior. One witness said he'd witnessed from a hiding place as Alexandre participated in the killing of a number of moderate Hutus. Based on these, the prosecutor prayed the court to find him guilty of genocide and of crimes against humanity. The defense counsel had presented no witnesses on behalf of Alexandre—because he claimed he couldn't find any sympathetic ones. The defense had made a twofold argument to the court. First, the defense posited that Alexandre was just a soldier who had no special access to the apparatus of power and who was just going about his duties as a soldier. Further, and this was their second argument, he was not involved in a genocide, but in self-defense. Even supposing that the witnesses, whose credibility the defense assailed, were correct, Alexandre had done these activities in defense of attacks from Tutsis. This was hinged on the theory that the so called genocide was not so, that it should be seen more as an unorganized, spontaneous civil war; plus, in the alternative, the defense argued that the notion that Hutus and Tutsis were of different ethnicities or races was bogus and nothing more than a theoretical construct. Indeed, said the defense, Hutus and Tutsis were the same people and, therefore, this could not amount to genocide, which under the 1948 Genocide Convention required that certain acts be perpetrated against national, ethnic, racial or religious groups. At worst, said the defense, they were acts against humanity that did not amount to genocide.

The Trial Chamber rejected the defense's arguments, finding genocide and acts against humanity in view of the overriding evidence.

The Trial Chamber didn't distinguish between genocide and acts against humanity and seemed to lump them together in passing the life sentence against Alexandre Nsengiyumva.

I was disappointed with the defense, first for making the spurious argument that there had been no genocide. I couldn't bring my training as a detached lawyer to the analysis, nor could I entertain the notion of the oneness of Hutus and Tutsis. Sure, I mentally noted, even if in theory that was correct, it wasn't a political reality and I had lived it, the reality that occasioned the massacres. Nor could I give any credence to the theory of self-defense—as I recalled it, this was a well organized massacre, not some spontaneous combustion as the defense claimed. Talk about building your case on a foundation of sand—surely no one could convince the court that there had been no genocide or that this was some sort of self-defense. If for no reason at all, it would be asking the court to deny a political reality of which the court itself was an offshoot; it would be asking the court to undermine its own legitimacy. Why, I wondered, had the defense not rejected such generalities in favor of arguing more for Alexandre's innocence or minimal involvement in the genocide? I knew that I had to jettison those general themes that the defense had decided on. I had to focus exclusively on Alexandre and what he did or didn't do, find some way to convince The Appeals Chamber that he was not guilty as charged. I would have liked to interview Alexandre, but with the time constraints, that had become impractical. Instead, I spoke with Auntie Shama in search of clues. The elder Shama couldn't provide any. "We hardly discussed that... his other life. As far as I was concerned, it was a part of his ugly life ... that he regretted and I wanted no part of. He tried to talk about it, but I wouldn't let him. I didn't want to be reminded of that part of him." I kept prodding—any friends I could talk to? After some thinking, the older woman gave me a name, another officer who had been a colleague of Alexandre's who had so far escaped prosecution.

I went to see Colonel Nimarambe immediately. A thin bespectacled man, I thought he belonged in the classroom than any army barrack. I asked if he knew of anything that could mitigate the charges against Alexandre. Rubbing his chin for several seconds, Colonel Nimarambe said, "Alexandre and I were very good friends. I've always thought of him as a good man, but who is to say why a good man would do what he's accused of doing? Of course, under pressure, the weak can buckle and no one judge another until he has been through what the other man has been through. I have, so I feel that I can judge a little. Whatever Alexandre did, he did out of self-preservation. I know for a fact the he participated in the killing of Tutsis and even some Hutus, but I know he did it out of fear. That doesn't excuse him, of course not; but I can tell you this, Alexandre was never a mastermind. He was a participant, yes, perhaps at times he even enjoyed the blood shedding and brutality, but overall he was a puppet more than he was the puppeteer. I also know that once or twice he hid some Hutus or even Tutsis so they wouldn't be killed. When everything is considered, does he deserve a life sentence or even death? I don't know; that is for the courts. I am just telling you what I know."

"I see," I said, "but what about you? If he was under pressure as you say and buckled, why didn't you?"

"I had more of an administrative function in those days and I was lucky because I was never put in a situation where I had to choose between killing or being labeled a traitor and potentially facing death myself."

A short while after this meeting, I wondered why I hadn't thought of the defense that came to mind. All along, I'd been searching for some brilliant theory when what I needed was a simple one that could sway the court. Given the facts at hand, the argument that came to mind would not absolve Alexandre, but it could mitigate his sentence.

I filed my Notice of Appeal with all the required particulars, including the grounds for the appeal. I also filed a motion to present additional evidence—affidavits from my aunt and Colonel Nimarambe—on the ground that a failure to include them would occasion a miscarriage of justice. The affidavit would attest to Alexandre's humane side, how he'd saved certain Tutsis from imminent death by hiding them; and his marriage to a Tutsi woman, who in the affidavit attested to his goodness, her love for him. I worked hard to furnish and file the Appellant's Brief, read the Respondent's Brief, and responded to it. I returned with Juju to DC to await the Appeal Chamber's decision on my motion and a date for oral arguments.

My motion to present additional evidence was denied, but the appeal was granted; so I flew to The Hague without the entire arsenal I'd have liked to present. I argued the salient points of my brief to the court. The Trial Chamber's error, I said, was in finding Alexandre guilty of the crime of genocide. Genocide, I noted, did take place in Rwanda in 1994, but Alexandre was not guilty of it, even if he'd committed other acts. To find genocide, I noted, there must be an intent to destroy in whole or in part, a national, ethnic, racial or religious group through acts such as killing, causing serious body harm, etcetera. I acknowledged that also punishable are conspiracy to commit genocide and complicity in genocide. I went through the witnesses who had been presented to the Trial Chamber. Even if the Trial Chamber believed them, none of their testimonies pointed to genocide on the part of Alexandre. Nowhere does any testimony say that Alexandre had the means or the intent to cause genocide. At worst, and I wasn't conceding this, one could make an argument of complicity in genocide, but that was not what the court had found Alexandre guilty of. Therefore, said I, the Appeals Chamber ought to reverse the Trial Chamber's error as the prosecution had failed to establish a prima facie case of Alexandre committing any act of genocide. The prosecution countered that in fact the testimony at trial showed intent (although it didn't specify exactly how) and that the trial court's decision had to stand. As I closed my argument, I wondered whether any of the five jurists, three men and two women, would understand why I, a Tutsi, was making the case for a Hutu, and so I told them in my closing statement: "I am doing this on principle. As a Tutsi I want those who committed atrocities punished, but as a lawyer I do not want any Hutu wrongly committed in the interest of vengeance, for that diminishes us, undermines our quest for justice. I would rather the guilty go free than punish the innocent. I am doing this in the interest of justice and fairness."

I could only wait now in distressful anticipation. I was wishing I'd convinced the court for my aunt's sake; still, I was hoping that Alexandre would pay for his crimes. Some months after the argument, the Appeals Chamber issued its decision. The Trial Chamber had erred in finding Alexandre guilty of genocide and imposing the maximum sentence of life in prison. The written decision was almost identical to my argument. The

Appeals Chamber asked the trial court to reconsider the case in a manner not inconsistent with the former's ruling. And so the Trial Chamber did and after additional proceedings and review, found Alexandre guilty of complicity in genocide, for which he received a ten year sentence.

"You are a genius," Fiona reiterated at a dinner party she once again organized for me. I sat next to John Owens, who had now been elected to the Senate. "I read about your performance in the Knight's case," he said. "And Fiona just gave me an article about the decision from the ITCR. What can I say, you are brilliant. Have you thought of public service?"

"Public service?"

"Yeah. You'd be great, with your pedigree, you could run for office. We need more like you in public office."

"I don't think I'm cut out for that," I said.

"Think about it," he said.

And I did. Public service, that is. I had acquired significant wealth in my seven years in private practice. With Juju's income, our combined net worth put us in the highest echelons of upper middle class America. Could I however say I was fulfilled? I'd won some significant victories in court, but none gave me much satisfaction, except for some fleeting sense of victory and the financial reward that came alongside it. My greatest satisfaction stemmed from the little victories that came from my pro bono cases, which involved no financial payment. Wouldn't I be happier doing something similar on a fulltime basis? Something in the interest of the public at large? But would I want to run for office? No, I decided.

A few weeks later, I received a call from John Owens. "I am recommending you to the president as a federal prosecutor," he said. "There's an opening here in DC. How would you like to be the US Attorney for the District of Columbia?"

"I'm not so sure I want this," I said.

"Shama, this is a great opportunity."

"I don't have any prosecutorial background. I've been defense counsel in a law firm…"

"But a brilliant one. It won't be hard to transition. Plus, you're going directly to the top of the pack. Some labor for years trying to get the top spot, but here's your chance. Now, I'm not guaranteeing it's a done deal. I've told the president, yes, and I think he's amenable, but before I go any further, I need to be sure you're on board."

"This is all so sudden. I need to think about it."

"Sure, you just let me know but make it quick. There are a lot of others interested in the job. We can't wait too long."

"But why me? Really, why did you pick me?"

"Didn't I tell you you're brilliant? Besides, your father-in-law was a friend of mine, as is your mother in law. Jojo Badu and I went way back. Of course, like I said, you make it easy for me with your unassailable credentials."

"The ghost of my husband," said Fiona when I informed her. "He is still working his magic from the grave."

"What do you think? Should I take it?"

"What do *you* think?"

"I'm not sure."

"Well, it's not often that one gets recognized this way, so you may want to pursue it if you're at all interested in public service, even perhaps a judgeship down the line."

"I will support your decision," Juju said. "Go with your gut."

"Are you not tired of the rigmarole of law firm practice?" Mustapha asked. "I would take it in a heartbeat if I were you."

I called John to express my interest. After those two major decisions in which I'd represented defendants I didn't feel deserved representing, I was thinking it was time to make amends, to be on the side that prosecutes, rather than defendants, and to stop auctioneering myself to the highest bidder. Perhaps this would bring greater satisfaction, not the alienation from my work that had been pestering my mind.

Despite this sense of non-fulfillment I was so proud that we now had twelve minority partners in the law firm, and I liked to claim some credit, at least as this was due to the firm's focus on minority hiring and the mentoring program I headed. And in my mind I also applauded Jojo Badu for what he had written in his dairy about sugar daddies.

Juju gained tenure at Georgetown University at the same time. To celebrate, I took him to an Ethiopian restaurant on 28<sup>th</sup> Street Northwest.

After chicken sambusa appetizers, as we ate the main course of shrimp marinated in lemon juice and garlic sautéed with onions, green pepper and fresh tomatoes, I said to him, "I'm so proud of you, my husband."

"I know," he replied. "I know, wife."

The way he said it immediately erased all concern I was harboring that my inadequate attention to him would jeopardize or marriage. I realized that I may never be able to pay him the attention he deserved. If it wasn't one thing wrestling for my attention, it was another—starting especially from my law school days, through my clerkship at the Supreme Court, my time at Wood, Oliver, Resnick & Krezinksi, and now a US District Attorney. Each time, I'd said to myself that I would find the time, but I never did.

The FBI investigation was cursory. In particular, they asked me about the incident with Nat Musegera. I told them it was a minor fracas. Nat confirmed this to the best of my knowledge and told them I was a good friend. I received the appointment, and was easily confirmed by the Senate, with John spearheading my cause. The senators sang my praises, impressed by my story as an immigrant who'd gone to the best schools, topped my law school class, clerked at the Supreme Court, and risen so quickly to partnership in an elite law firm. This was the classic American story, many senators said.

Mustapha bought me lunch and invited me to his mosque once again.

"Why do you keep asking me?" I queried.

"I want you to see it for yourself," he said, "Perhaps I can change your mind about Islam."

"My mother was a Moslem, Mustapha. If she didn't convert me, what makes you think you can?"

"Well, perhaps it's a sign."

"What sign?"

"That I'm here reminding you of your roots."

"I was raised a Christian, Mustapha. I am a Christian. As much as I respect you and your right to your beliefs, I am convinced Christianity is the only way."

"Hey, give Islam a try. I assure you, you won't be disappointed."

300

"I tell you what. I will come to the mosque with you if you come to church with me."

"When was the last time you went to church?"

"I admit it's been a long time, but that is beside the point. Do we have a deal?"

Mustapha pondered over this for a few seconds and said, "Deal. If that is what it takes."

"But I am just coming to visit, remember that, not to worship."

"Me likewise.

"Let's make it happen."

The day after this conversation with Mustapha, it was announced that Justice Patrick Sitter had been nominated to be Chief Justice of the United States Supreme Court. I sent him a congratulatory note immediately. He called me to thank me. The Senate confirmed him within three months after his nomination.

Now, a district attorney....

Apart from my day to day administrative functions, I took a number of cases myself. In particular, I was drawn to those involving rape and child molestation, although they exhausted me—the emotional pulls and the time commitment. Not only did I have to navigate the emotional labyrinth of the victims, but my own history that became a part of each prosecution as though I was being victimized again. Because of the empathy I think I managed to bring to them, most who would otherwise not wish to subject themselves to the public scrutiny of reliving the acts at issue trusted me to guide them through the process. In most cases, I felt I couldn't divorce my own emotions from those I represented and each defeat was a double stab to me, both professionally and personally. And my phantom pain hurt more whenever I lost a case. A year into my job and I felt spent, but I had garnered a reputation as a tough and even handed prosecutor.

I delegated cases involving routine murders, hijackings, illegal practice of medicine, and the like, to others. I took on the ones considered more poignant. But my approach had its detractors, the most visible friction coming with my assistant Danielle Leblanc. We were presented with two cases, both of which were to be tried at the same time, despite our efforts to move one to a later date. The question was where to put our best resources. The first case involved the hijacking of a nonagenarian man by three youths who robbed him, drove him in his car into the woods and beat him to death. It was a case of brutal murder, yes, and the more devastating because the victim was reputed to be kind and philanthropic, donating his time and vast wealth to charities. The other involved a case of a middle-aged man breaking into a home where ten and twelve year old sisters were watching TV, while their sixty-five year old grandmother was in the bedroom. The children screamed when the man entered the living room. Instead of leaving, he dropped his pants and began to pleasure himself in the unmentionables. The grandmother screamed at him to leave the house when she entered the living room. When she approached him to try and stop him, he punched her in the groin with a closed fist as the children continued to scream. As the grandmother keeled over in pain, he ran from the house.

To me, the latter was a heinous crime—to subject children to such psychological trauma was unpardonable, not to mention the assault and battery of the grandmother, and I approached the case with gusto. I would prosecute it myself and I called on the best lawyer I had to assist me. But Danielle Leblanc wanted re-prioritizing. "We have a murder here," she said. "This was one of the nicest men you can ever think of. Now compare that to this other case where apart from the minor attack on the old woman, no one was hurt, nothing was stolen. I think the murder deserves more attention."

"I can understand that," I said. "And if I didn't have this other case, I would agree with you. But we have children involved here, Danielle; what kind of psychological damage this man may have caused, we can't even imagine. He ought to be locked up forever so that he doesn't do this to anyone else or even worse."

"I have looked him up. He has no prior arrests, no prior convictions. I don't think we need to worry about him. But those other kids that killed Mr. Schmidt, they have a long rap sheet. We're talking robbery, drug possession… They pose a real danger to society."

"I guess we see it differently and I am making the call and my decision is final."

"Big mistake."

"I will live with it."

Danielle Leblanc did as she was instructed, but she sulked throughout the trial, such that I ended up doing the bulk of the work. I managed to get the man locked up for five years. The youths in the other case were each sentenced to a three-year term. Danielle Leblanc told me justice had been perverted. I knew she never forgave me.

But on the strength of my reputation I was nominated to the District Court, and again I went through the Senate hearings without much incident. I began hearing cases involving patents, pensions and the public taking of private property, hardly any with controversial implications.

# Five

It was around this time that Dwayne Dray, whom I had read about in my father-in-law's notebook-diary, an assistant of sorts at the White House and a former classmate of Jojo Badu, called at the suggestion of Fiona and her father George Harris, to invite me to join the Group Club. The Group Club? The name sounded curious to me, immediately sensitizing my skepticism-antenna and even more so when he said it was a semi-secret club. "Semi-secret" was a term requiring explanation and Dwayne offered it, brimming full of the enthusiasm with which he wanted me to join the club. "It's semi-secret in the sense that we don't particularly seek or attract publicity. We believe it's better to operate as anonymously as we can. Our power rests in the connections we have through our membership. And believe me, Shama, our members have connections. I want you to join the club because I want you to have access to the forces of black power in this country. It is power that can open doors you wouldn't believe existed."

"Why pick me?"

"I have strong recommendations from George and Fiona. I value their opinions very highly. Besides, I know of you. As they say, your reputation precedes you."

I found it odd that George Harris would recommend me, as I had only met him a few times, but I suppose he too must have relied on Fiona's recommendation.

"And who are the members?" I asked.

"Come over and you'll meet them. We're having a meeting next week."

"Why would I want to meet the members of a club I know nothing about?"

"What've you got to lose, my sister? If you don't like it, no strings attached." He sensed my hesitation. "Come on, if nothing at all, it will be an opportunity for us to get together. I knew your father-in-law very well and I have heard so much about you from your mother-in-law. I am dying to meet you."

How could I reject the offer?

But still something kept warning me, I wasn't sure what—something that would rather I stay away from this all too enticing proposition of a group of black leaders with extensive power. Fiona encouraged me to join. "It will be good for you. Dwayne's right, you know. You really have nothing to lose. If you don't like it, you just have to say no."

Dwayne Dray and I spoke over the phone a couple of times and then met for lunch. Some days later he met me a few minutes before the meeting of the Group Club was scheduled to start. "If all the members show up, we should have about forty. I'll introduce you and then another member will have to second my move to invite you formally to the club. They'd want to talk with you and see if you're a good fit for the club. Then they'll decide whether you're in or out. But at this stage it's all just formality."

"And if no one seconds your invitation?"

"Like I said, it's all formality. Trust me, with the groundwork we've done, there shouldn't be a problem. You have to do or say something really bad to be denied entry."

"Seriously, Dwayne, I'm still not sure this is right for me..."

"This, Shama, is right for everybody. You can't believe the kind of networking connections this will give you. We've got congressmen, judges like yourself, businessmen, lawyers, top entertainers... You'll be crazy to pass up this opportunity."

And yet there was that unease which tugged at me.

We entered the high-rise building where the club was meeting at six o'clock p.m. We took the elevator to the thirtieth floor and walked on to a huge conference room. There were no less than twenty men in the room already, all well coifed. "Let's get a drink," Dwayne suggested. "I will introduce you to the group when the meeting starts. It's against the rules to introduce you before that."

I sipped on a glass of merlot wine in the sea of men I was barred from communicating with, lest some rule be broken. It suited me fine. I got another glass of wine and another. I was generally beginning to feel the wine's warmth, but it also came with a weakness that pervaded my entire body (and mind). I tried hard to focus and continue my chat with

Dwayne, but I knew my words were approaching gibberish. Dwayne, unsuspecting, must have thought I was trying to be funny. He laughed and laughed.

And then I heard a bell ring. When I looked, I saw a massive man holding the bell as he announced, "Gentlemen, let's call the meeting to order." The conversational murmur in the room ceased immediately and all attention was targeted at the massive man. "The executive committee will be out shortly. It's my understanding that we have the introduction of a lady today?"

"Yes," Dwayne responded.

"Proceed."

"I wish to introduce for the members' consideration for membership, Shama Badu."

"Are you seconded?"

"Yes. He is on the executive committee."

"Very well."

The bell rang again and what must have comprised the executive committee walked into the room—an impressive group of eight men. And … and … to my utter surprise, among them was Fiona's father. George Harris looked directly at me and I thought I could detect a playful smile on his face. I tried to re-characterize that smile. Was he mocking me? Was he amused by the complete surprise that I didn't know he belonged to the club? And Dwayne? In hindsight, it probably was to be seen as a benign prank to surprise me a little, but at that moment, I was furious. Perhaps I was only now gathering (like a late storm) my latent opposition to joining the Group Club. I thought—if my thought process could be so dignified at that time—and quickly decided on my course of action.

Amid this internal cyclone, I could hear my father-in-law say, "I second the introduction of Ms. Shama Badu to our club."

The executive committee was now seated behind the table in the middle of the room. In the middle of the group, a slim, octogenarian-type, gray-haired man said, "Ms. Shama Badu, my name is Stokey Washington. I am chairman of this club. I hope you are as honored as we are in having the opportunity to meet with you. We will like to speak with you on a few matters and then, mutually as acceptable, determine your status."

I said nothing. I could feel the attention burrowing into me. I was beyond exhaustion and almost intoxicated, which was dangerous enough; but even worse, this was layered with my controlled anger.

"Judging from the dossier that your sponsor had prepared for us, you are a lawyer…in fact, a judge?"

"Correct."

"And you are interested in joining the Group Club?"

"No, sir."

If silence were the personification of shock, he would have been battering the distorted face of every person in the room, particularly George Harris. Shock would have stood taller than any man in the room. He would have reigned.

"I beg your pardon?"

"No, sir, sir."

"Shama," Dwayne murmured.

"I'm a bit confused, Ms. Badu," said Stokey Washington. "What's the purpose of your being here if you're not interested in joining us?"

"With all due respect, sir, it wasn't my idea."

Seconds of silence elapsed, during which it seemed I had stopped the group's very heartbeat.

"I see…"

George Harris interjected. "I'm sure there's been a slight misunderstanding. I hasten to say that Ms. Badu may be a bit overwhelmed by the circumstances. I propose a brief recess so I can have a private word with him."

"As you wish," I said. "But I am far from overwhelmed."

George and Dwayne hurried me into an adjoining room.

George Harris was struggling to maintain self-control when he asked, "Okay, can someone tell me what just happened there?"

"I'm not interested in the club. It's as simple as that."

"And you came all the way here to tell us that?"

"I just now made that decision."

"And what in the world brought this sudden change of mind?"

"I just saw the membership."

Dwayne interjected: "Shama, you're making a huge mistake."

Said George Harris, "We have staked… Dwayne and I, we have put our reputation on the line to get you before this group. Now before you say another word think about it. There are some very important people in the room. The last thing you want to do is piss any of them off."

"What? Just because I don't want to join the club?"

"Shama," Dwayne said. "What's this about?"

We went in circles as they tried to discern my purpose and I gave them none except that I'd just changed my mind. George Harris left the room in what I can only describe as obscene anger. Dwayne didn't speak further; instead, he gestured that I leave the room with him. We walked back to the meeting room and he announced that he was withdrawing my candidacy. The world seemed to close at the time against me, like a cloud that shrouded everyone from my sight. Dwayne turned away from me and George Harris refused to look in my direction. The sad thing called silence returned, but only briefly, for this time the men there were prepared to banish the silence, as they would me. Stokey Washington asked that I leave the room so he could commence the meeting of the Group Club. I obliged.

Later that night, I got a call from George Harris to come over to his house. I hesitated. What was the purpose? I feared he'd just berate me for my actions and I was in no mood to engage him in any detailed argument. Lawyer versus lawyer could be quite explosive, but I couldn't turn down his invitation either—this invitation from Juju's grandfather. That would be the ultimate affront. "You should go," Juju urged me. "He's generally very genial."

I went.

The old man looked relaxed and calm. He poured me a drink and sat next to me.

"Shama," George Harris said and paused. "I asked you here because I'm very disappointed in what happened earlier today."

"Do we have to discuss that again, sir?"

"I'm sure you have your reasons." He paused and bit his lower lip. "You know, you and I, we don't know each other. I mean you're married to my grandson, but what else is there? I'm sure Fiona's told you a bit about me. But we haven't even really sat down to talk. That's my fault.

But I am an old man now, quietly practicing law, tired most of the time. I have thought it best not to interfere in the affairs of you young people, but every now and then I see such talent that I want to do what I can to make sure she has all the opportunities possible to keep climbing. You don't know how proud I am when Fiona tells me about your brilliance or when I read an article about you. I haven't always agreed with your choices, that Knights case for example. It brought you notoriety, but really... Anyway, I'm sure you had your reasons."

George Harris had spoken without pause, and he seemed suddenly tired. He sipped from his glass of wine, inhaled noisily and said, "Let me tell you a story, Shama.

This must be important, I thought.

"You know I grew up in Hattiesburg, Mississippi. This was in the nineteen twenties and thirties. Those were days of major and minor indignities that made you question your self-worth. A white man would never call a black man mister. As if they'd die if they afforded us that little courtesy. Can you imagine hearing your father called *boy* by those much younger than he? The man you so much respect? At best, they called him Uncle, as if he had no name. Hell, you couldn't even enter their homes except through the back door." George Harris shook his head and I could even detect a tear struggling from dropping from the corner of his right eye. "Those days... Hmm... Those days were something else, you know. My father, he was a sharecropper, which meant a sad cycle of deprivation and poverty for himself and his folk, but he wanted something better for me, for my brothers and sisters. Most importantly, I think he wanted us to learn to survive. He would tell me, 'Son, you get your schooling done. No one can take that from you.' He wanted me to be a big something ... A lawyer, engineer, doctor. It was tight in those days, but he did his best, you know. He really tried. He saved whatever he could to make sure I went to school. He and my mother. My mother used to work in the home of white folks, cleaning their wastes. Growing up then wasn't easy, a black man couldn't assert that he was human. Everywhere you went, it was in your face. Couldn't play on the same playgrounds as white folk, drink from the same fountains, or access the connections of privilege. I began to understand these limitations. But what could a young black man do? There wasn't much you could do without getting into serious trouble. I was bottling my frustration inside, but it would want to come out and on occasion I challenged my father, told him he was too docile. He would look at me, his eyes defeated from looking away from the white man. To me, those eyes betrayed disappointment.

"Sometimes, he said to me, 'Don't be like your uncle Willie.' Now, I knew Uncle Willie had died young, but I had no idea what had killed him. The first time my father told me not to be like my uncle was when he saw me look at a white woman. I was staring at her absent-mindedly, not even thinking about it. My father chastised me so severely I yelled at him, about his cowardice. He continued to state the precaution 'Don't be like your Uncle Willie' so much that I told him to tell me what he meant or leave me be. He finally told me Uncle Willie's story.

"Uncle Willie was full of anger at the injustices of the system. He was always threatening to organize some sort of rebellion. He was sullen and brooding, which must have bemused, perhaps even amused, most of the white folk, but not when he winked at a white woman, the daughter of Ole' Jones, who owned a store that Uncle Willie helped clean occasionally. The old man caught him, berated him and warned him never to so much as look at his daughter again. But the anger must have been too much to hold in. Uncle Willie winked at her again, whistled at her and walked out. He was arrested that night for rape and thrown in the local jail. The next night, a mob broke into the jail and dragged him out into the streets. As he was dragged through the streets, the crowd around him swelled, jeering. Every time a whip touched his back, the mob exploded with a cheer. Ole' Jones held Uncle Willie while his teenage son cut off an ear as the crowd cheered and the young Jones declared, 'Got me a trophy.' From the crowd came another young man to claim the other ear. Uncle Willie was whipped repeatedly and as he lay half dead from the whipping and lacerations they tied a noose around his neck and hang him on a tree to die. All this time, the cheering crowd was taking photos. It was a celebration. And then came the bonfire. After he was taken down from the tree, Uncle Willie's body was thrown into the fire to burn.

"Shama, it is hard to recount the horror on my father's face when he told me that story. Of course, after I confirmed this from my aunt, I knew there was a force out there that wasn't to be toyed with. I have often asked myself if those who were capable of such heinous acts could ever be cured of that vicious hatred. Will they change or will their hatred acquire a different character, assume a subtler mask. You know, when I was in Ghana I heard a proverb that goes something like this: Even if you cure a mad man of his madness, he still retains the little that he uses to scare kids. Where and in what form resides that hatred, Shama? Think about it. Out here, some don't like those who look like us. When people don't like you, you're forced to look to yourself, to look to your own kind. Personally, I have learned to channel my anger. Let me tell you another story."

Two stories in the same night—the old man was really digging deep to reach me the best way he could.

"I remember when I was still quite young, maybe ten or twelve, my father joined the Knights of Order. It was started by a local preacher: the Reverend Pulliam. The black folks would contribute each month to the knighthood. Papa used to tell us stories of how they had to take an oath... Anyway, when one was in need, the knighthood would help out. They bought supplies for the school, started a local store where members could shop. It was prosperous organization by all accounts. Then one day the church was suddenly burned to the ground. Just like that. And with that Rev. Pulliam gave up on the knighthood. Who knows what may have happened to him. Rumors were that the KKK threatened to kill him. Without his leadership, the knighthood simply collapsed. I'd never seen such depression in a people, such defeat, such hopelessness. When I understood what had happened, I vowed that I would do everything in my power to retain what is mine. I felt a fire burning in the belly that still burns when I see black folk trying to do something for themselves and for their own kind because no one will do it for them.

George Harris took another sip of wine. "I have tried to do my best. When I graduated high school, I was about twenty. I'd started school a bit too late. That was the year I got my wife Celia pregnant. We'd been high school sweethearts, hadn't planned the pregnancy, but there was no running from it. The year was 1945, the year Fiona was born. Charles Houston was championing the NAACP... I had so much admiration for that man I decided to become a lawyer like him. That same year, I won a scholarship to Hampton College. From there, I went on to Howard. In 1952, I left Howard University with a law degree. Sadly

311

Celia died in 1954, and I was left to raise Fiona when she was still a child and I did this alone until I married Sissi when I was in Ghana. Before that, I was faced with the reality of making a living, supporting my daughter and making sure she wanted for nothing. Times were hard sometimes, but I always remembered the stories my old man told me and I fought on. I don't think I've done too badly for myself, but I have never forgotten the years in Mississippi, the need to look beyond the personal. I haven't forgotten the knighthood, the strength within the community that needs to be harnessed, the power of pulling together, the force of unity. You see, this whole business of the Group Club, it's not just for socializing or fun. It's self-help. Times have changed, but they haven't changed much. We have come some ways, from those days when you couldn't drink from the same fountains as whites, but there's still a long ways to go yet. When I was invited to join the Group Club, I was delighted. It does two things. First, the recognition is humbling and more so when it comes from your own folk. Second, it offers the opportunity to network. You can't imagine how extensive the connections are. Now, I know it's still a small organization. But it's a beginning. I know, wherever he is, Reverend Pulliam is smiling on me."

The old man didn't ask me to change my mind. After the lecture, he took me out to his patio, where we sat and listened to old tunes. Sissi Harris joined us. She asked about my work and urged me to stay focused and to keep making them proud. When it turned very late, I thanked them and left.

I nearly wept on the way back home when I recalled what George Harris had told me. I realized the wounds I had caused when he offered me membership in the Group Club and I so nonchalantly turned it down. I realized the depth of history and pain that I hadn't been privy to that made it so easy for me to dismiss efforts by people like him. I had just walked in and turned my back when before me there were echoes of pain and death and struggle. George Harris knew it. Fiona Harris knew it. Dwayne Dray knew it Juju Badu may have known it. I didn't know it because I hadn't lived it. I thought of how much pain I must have caused when I took the Knights case. Within me, perhaps a new day was dawning.

I got pregnant once again around the time of my appointment to the District Court. At my age, I feared I didn't have many other opportunities left and I hoped this one would stay. It didn't. I miscarried within a month, plunging me into another bout of sadness. In that stage of sadness Mustapha reminded me of our mutual promise to visit each other's place of worship.

We planned to go to his Mosque on a Friday. "Please dress modestly," he said, "say a skirt or dress that reaches to the ankle or pants if that is easier. And please, nothing too tight."

"Why?" Juju asked when I told him of the visit.

"This way he will come with me to church."

"Shama, you don't go to church often."

"I know and I am not proud of it. Papa would be upset with me."

"I haven't been much help, either," Juju said. "But concerning the mosque visit, if you think it will be helpful, I guess you ought to go."

I met Mustapha after work. For the first time I noticed that he was beginning to gray. As he drove me, I reminded him that he was ageing and ought to start thinking about getting married. "I have met someone," he said. "She worships at the mosque. It's just the beginning, but I think we can go far."

"I've never heard you talk this way about any woman. I think this has promise."

"She's special," Mustapha said. "She will be there today. Perhaps you will get to meet her."

In the foyer of the mosque, under an inscription on the wall reading DC MOSQUE, a bespectacled man welcomed us, "Assalaam alaikum."

"Wa alaikum salam," I responded. Mama would have been proud of me.

A lady, I presumed to be assisting the man, came towards us and greeted us in like manner.

The man and woman drew Mustapha aside. For about a minute, they seemed to be arguing in hushed tones. Then Mustapha walked over to me and said, "I'm sorry Shama, but you have to borrow a dress and put it over your suit."

"Really? But I wore these pants to cover up. Is that not good enough?"

"It's a matter of opinion, but they think it's too tight."

"Very well."

Mustapha spoke with the woman, who ushered me into a room, and gave me a gown and scarf. I put them on and returned to the foyer. In an instant, Mustapha called to an approaching woman dressed in a loose, all-body-covering dress: "Maria."

"You are the judge," Maria said before Mustapha could introduce us. "I am so honored to meet you."

I reached out to shake her hand, but she ignored it and hugged me instead. "You are my hero," she said.

"Don't believe everything Mustapha tells you," I said.

"He doesn't have to say much. I have read about you, your migration from Rwanda, your doctorate, your topping of your law school class, your appointments. You are so impressive."

"Maria, I think you're embarrassing Shama," Mustapha said.

"It's good embarrassment," Maria said, smiling. "So, so glad to meet you. Can I take a picture? Once we go inside the prayer hall, I can't take any pictures."

She retrieved a phone and took my photo. "I will cherish this," she said.

Maria led me to the entrance to the prayer hall for women. Before we entered, we removed our shoes and placed them on a rack outside the hall. I entered the prayer hall and sat in the back close to the wall, the men on one side and the women on another. As I looked at those in prayer, it was as if I was observing Mama in prayer: the standings, bowings, prostrations, and sittings.

Afterward, Mustapha, said, "Sorry if Maria embarrassed you, but she is very outgoing, which I guess fits her career choice as a public relations consultant."

"You know what this means, don't you Mustapha? Now you owe me a visit to my church."

"A deal is a deal."

I invited Mustapha to come to church with Juju and me the next week, but he said he had prior engagements. He gave me the same excuse two more times.

And then five months into my judgeship on the district court, I was nominated to the Court of Appeals for the District of Columbia Circuit, considered second in importance only to the US Supreme Court. But this time the scrutiny was harder, although even then my story as a successful immigrant who exemplified the American dream won me more accolades than detractors. And it helped that the president's party had the overwhelming majority in the senate. "You are on your way to the Supreme Court at this rate," Fiona said half teasingly. I found the questioning harsher during my confirmation hearings, but because I had little on the public record regarding my opinion on matters of political interest, I managed to answer most of the questions vaguely, most often dodging them on the basis that I would rather not answer hypothetical questions or pre-rule on issues that might appear before me. I continued to have a Senate ally in John Owens, who helped shepherd my nomination so that I was confirmed by the Senate, although this time it was not with the near unanimity of the previous confirmations. Perhaps, the first salvo had been sounded. One step from the Supreme Court, even if it did not materialize, was perhaps too close for the comfort of some. I had no idea how this would unfold later, especially given that the next time I went to the Senate, the political climate had changed and the president's party had lost its majority in that chamber.

# Six

Although Fiona had informed me without elaborating to expect an important call, the one from Dwayne Dray was utterly unexpected, especially given its purpose. "An important call is coming your way," Fiona had said. "Just keep an open mind." As much as I tried to extract details, she wouldn't expatiate on this, except to say that she had been otherwise sworn to secrecy. Then you shouldn't have mentioned it at all, I thought. Now that I'd been tipped, I would be overly anxious, I said. Fiona was not persuaded, leaving me unnerved for a week. And then, sitting in my chambers, the phone had rung, jarring me out of my concentration on the facts of a case *sub judice*.

Reminiscent of the day Fiona had first called me, the voice on the line said, "This is the White House." This time, however, I knew the voice of the caller. Surely, he wasn't calling to berate me over the Group Club issue.

"Dwayne?" I said.

"Yes, this is he. We haven't spoken since the... since the last time."

That was an amusing way to put it, but I had to return to court shortly and my patience began to wither, White House or not. "I admit I was pissed at you, Shama, but the more I think about it, the more I admire your guts," he said. I had started counting on my fingers from ten to one before telling him I had to return to work. But on the count of three, the man said, "All the more reason why I am happy to be making this call. The president has asked me to ask you whether you'd be interested in being considered for the Supreme Court to replace Justice Sitter."

A gasp. Goose pimples. Sweat in underarms. Heart thumping. Knees weak. Hands shaking. Stomach queasy.

"Are you there, Shama?"

"Did you say Supreme Court...Did..."

"Yes, Supreme Court of the United States of America. Of course, I'm only checking because if there is no interest, we wouldn't pursue this any further."

"When you say to replace Justice Sitter, are you saying..."

"Yes, Shama, you will be replacing him as Chief Justice."

316

I was at that moment replaying events of the last few months, about two months to be more exact, when Justice Sitter had announced his retirement from the Court. He was only sixty-seven and many expected him to serve at least another ten years, given that he had been Chief Justice for only a few years, and on account of his robust health, his vitality and his remarkably undimmed wit and intellect, although it had been long rumored that he was bored with the minutiae of the Court's work, that he'd never managed, given his penchant for solitude, to fit in with the other justices of the Court. And when he'd announced his retirement, there'd been little fanfare around it, except the usual commentators' analyses of his tenure on the Court, his legacy and, more cacophonously, his potential successor. It was widely rumored and even confirmed by some close to him that the president would appoint someone from outside the Court to lead it. I had read of the leading contenders and once or twice dreamed of the possibility of my own nomination. I'd dismissed such distilled longings as foolish, given that the appointee would become not just an associate justice, but Chief Justice, the lord justice among the justices. I'd read with controlled jealousy the names of the media-anointed candidates, reluctantly applauded their accomplishments, compared them to mine, and tried to turn my mind to other matters.

The media had speculated that among the five most likely candidates the one at the top of the list was Clay Winslow: aged 57: Chicago born: Yale Law School graduate; clerkship at the Supreme Court; professor of law at Harvard Law School; associate White House counsel; federal district court judge, and most recently circuit court judge; moderate in his views; and recommended by liberals and acceptable by conservatives. Many had opined that the young president would be seeking to signal bipartisan seriousness—and would not wish to stir a Senatorial fight—in order to create a conducive atmosphere for his ambitious agenda, marked by the twin landmines of an economy in recession and a couple of wars abroad. And also worth considering was that his party had just lost its senate majority in recent mid-term elections. No one would give the president the path towards bipartisanship than Clay Winslow. One magazine had called his nomination a *fait accompli*, quoting reliable, if unnamed, White House sources.

317

But even if this fail-safe choice failed for some unfathomable reason that would call the president's political judgment into question and even taint it in certain political circles, the general consensus was that he would pick the second most probable candidate (mind you, only if hell was freezing). Leah Lawrence: aged 60; born in Washington, DC; recipient of a law degree from Michigan University; private practice; congresswoman (voluntary served only two terms); assistant attorney-general in the Justice Department; and currently professor of law at Northwestern Law School. Articulate, intelligent, and vastly connected, she was the obvious default candidate, if Claw Winslow managed to offend the president beyond human capacity.

The remaining list of potential candidates, as revealed by the media, comprised another law school professor, a governor, a judge, and a former solicitor general. But they were discussed as footnotes or, where the papers and magazines were more generous, as mere parentheses. Clay Winslow was the man. The drumbeat of the commentariat had already anointed him.

I'd laughed, albeit with the nervousness rooted in the concern that Jojo had exposed my thoughts about a possible consideration for the Supreme Court, when he said, "The president ought to consider you for this job." He wouldn't, I'd told him; there were better suited candidates. Plus, at forty-one, I was too young. I'd chosen this reply carefully, preferring not to say "better qualified candidates" and he had not answered my reply. This disappointed me a little—he could at least have tried to make my case for me, if only to humor me.

"What do you say?" Dwayne was asking presently. "I am not guaranteeing that he will nominate you, but at the very least I can assure you that you will be seriously considered for the opening if you're interested."

Why, of all the people in the world, would he consider me? This was a question that infuriated me as it entered my head against my wishes.

"Can I think about it?" I knew this was an unnatural reaction, but that was all I could think to say at the time. Was I numbed by surprise?

"That's fair, but I would need to know as soon as possible. I will call back. In the meantime, please keep this to yourself."

"Absolutely."

I called Juju. I would be foolish not to say yes, he said, offering the argument I'd wanted from him earlier: I deserved it more than anyone else—I was already on a court considered next in importance to the Supreme Court and I was smart, compassionate, experienced... Despite the vow of secrecy I made to Dwayne, I called Fiona, swore her also to secrecy and divulged the contents of the conversation with Dwayne. "John had told me he was working the president to consider you, but he wasn't sure the president would listen, considering that John is in the opposition party. Both he and Dwayne called me to ask what I thought. I told them they would be making a serious mistake if they didn't consider you and that they should call you."

"What should I do, Mom?"

"I can't believe you're asking me this question, Shama. Are you sure you're okay? Here you are, at forty or so, being asked if you're interested in the Supreme Court, not as a mere justice, although even that would be great, but as Chief Justice, and you're asking me what you should do? Shama, Shama, Shama."

Yes, why shouldn't I? On its face, there was no reason. But what of that which lay like a hideous serpent under the veil, the blood that was ready to pump its redness with a mere pinprick? I knew that was all it would take for the contained redness of history to paint and possibly taint the present. I had concealed too much and escaped deep scrutiny, but now there was so much at stake. Would I be able, as I'd done with my previous nominations, to contain that past? Lucky once or twice, lucky this time also? Would the inevitable deeper probe into the past uncover the hideous? Would all the achievements that had shorn my appearance before man and woman be erased under the unabated scrutiny that would come with more brutality given this nomination to the highest judicial office, a part of the co-equal branches of government? Would I be able to bring along with me to the pinnacle of achievement (or infamy) all those from whom I'd withheld details of my story, so that the entire truth still resided only within me (even if pieces were known by others)?

I thought through all these, weighing and imagining considerations and my beginnings and triumphs over all that had threatened to derail me, especially the deep sufferings during the massacres in Butare and its aftermath. The phantom ache in my belly region pulsated and yet I asserted that if none of the past events had stopped me, even if they haunted me, I ought to continue to move on, embrace this opportunity. I must be able to springboard those who'd contributed in the effort to tether or break me in the past. That alone must suffice for me to stare down any foe. I would accept the offer to be considered for the Court. I would do what I could to advance the candidacy if it came to that.

And so decided, the call I received from Senator John Owens only buttressed my conclusion. The senator said he'd encouraged the president to nominate me, but the man was dithering, still unsure if I was the right choice. "He seems to have a very high opinion of you," John Owens said. "I think with the right prodding he very well might pick you. Sure, I'm saying this as a member of the opposition party, but it's based on my best judgment. I think the president realized that I'm being fair minded, that I am ready to work with him and those on his side of the aisle. He values my opinion and speaks with me often to gauge how my party will react to issues he wants to bring before Congress. I know what the pundits are saying about who he's going to choose, but I'm asking him to surprise the pundits, to do something bold that sends a message, both domestic and foreign. He can't pass up this opportunity, at least that's what I keep telling him. You are just so qualified for the job and for our times."

Our times: times of both increased international conflict and concert, and more international interaction and interdependence that were destroying national and intercontinental borders. Who better for this job of supreme interpreter than one who had straddled ethnicities, nations, and overcome the most intense of conflicts?

Buttressed! If I needed any more encouragement, I couldn't have asked for one as succinct as it was cogent. I didn't wait for Dwayne to call me. I called him instead to tell him I would be honored to be considered for the Supreme Court.

And in a day or so the FBI was upon me, raising questions about my background, alliances, connections, and affiliations, political and otherwise, asking for names of friends and family members, anyone who might have something to say about me. Much of it was territory they'd covered before in my previous nominations to the bench, but I retold what I had said with patience. I again gave them the outlines of my life in as general terms as they would allow me, including the part about my parents' death and my own suffering at the sharp edges of objects designed to inflict damage. I was at the point of decision-making, when I could alter my future forever and the narrative that might follow it, reveal the entire truth and face the aftermath or hide its most troubling episodes and hope that they were never replayed in public, and, if by chance they were revealed, then to face the consequences at that time. The urge to unburden everything was strong, pulsating within as though it were a heartbeat. But why, I asked myself, sing fully and surely bear the burden to follow when it was possible that I could hold the ugly part of my song and get away with it? Or, I thought, perhaps I could simply stall time and make my revelations at a future date—delayed embarrassment and even turmoil appeared a more palatable option than the immediate challenges of a full revelation. Also, this would not be the best forum to reveal the hidden. Juju would have to be the first to know.

I did not tell the FBI all.

That night, I was under the full assault of my conscience, when I saw my husband's body in bed, sound asleep with the full boom of snores, while I labored to fall asleep. I worried anew that the FBI would uncover new truths about me, and this worry was stronger than ever before. I considered again that I could lose a lot of what I had worked to build, not so much from the dreadfulness of truth but from the withholding of that truth, the labor of continuing to withhold such vital parts of myself, the uncomfortable deception. It would be heartbreaking, perhaps even permanently depressing, but somehow I knew I could manage to walk that uncertain matrix of rejection from society and even family, except I wasn't sure I could survive rejection from Jojo. Of all that had happened, hadn't he anchored me so strongly that I knew I had shelter with him no matter what else happened? So, of everything I had, I could imagine, even if with pain, a life without any possession or other human presence, excepting him. If this assurance came unanchored I would not survive. I was sure of this. Therefore, I concluded after much struggle, I would tell him the fullness of my story. All the details of what happened on the night in front of the church in Butare, all that I had hidden. Even if I lost his trust it would be better to lose it this way and commence the rebuilding, than to have the revelation come from a third party. What if, for example, one of the nurses in the French camp said something? What if they managed to find one of the perpetrators in Butare?

These concerns became like a continuous, harassing itch I couldn't will away or delay any further. I woke Juju up. Juju turned on the table lamp next to the bed. He blinked many times as concern began to spread across his face. I sighed. "There's something about me you ought to know, honey." He sighed. "I know I should have told you long ago, but… but I was afraid you'd not love me the same if you knew the whole truth."

"Whatever it is, sweetie," Juju said, "it's okay."

"It's not okay, but I hope you can forgive me."

"I will."

"You may want to hear what I have to say before you say that."

"This is you, sweetie. This is me."

I decided I would tell the story in two pieces, go over the first half first, which he knew only generally without the details. I would provide all the flesh to the skeleton so that he would live it the way I did; perhaps he would even reach the solidarity rooted in empathy. When I'd prepared him this way, I would then tell him the second part because he would have been better prepared to hear it and he would understand my subsequent actions. The first part concerned details in front of the church in Butare that I had tried hard to blot out of memory. I told him everything I had left out.

After the first attack that day in Butare, I managed to push my cut body under a pile of bodies. I lost consciousness. It was extremely dark when I regained consciousness. I forced myself to move from underneath the bodies that had served as my shield. My limbs were asleep and, considering also the continuing pain in my body, it took massive effort to return life to them. I managed to sit, my thoughts jumbled as I considered what to do. I tried to gauge the extent of my injuries and guessed that they were not significant. Perhaps I could find shelter in a friendly home, although I realized this would be rife with risks. But what other options were there? Or was it better to find a way to end my life? Wouldn't it be better for me to kill myself than allow *them*, if they were to find me, to do so?

Suddenly, my body grew tense as I heard the sound of approaching voices, which, although low, were audible, if barely, in the nocturnal quiet. Peering in the direction of the voices, I saw the profiles of a number of people approaching with flashlights. Quickly, I repositioned myself as best as I could underneath the shielding pile of dead bodies, wondering if they had seen me. I heard the voices of men speak profanities as they meticulously rummaged through the bodies as if seeking something of value from a dunghill. I soon could sense one of them standing very close to me and I smelled the malodorous stale sweat and booze as he bent closer to the pile of bodies. I could sense him moving the bodies on top and around me. My tired body went even weaker with fear, my heart knocking fiercely against my chest. I guessed he felt for pulses, moving each body aside as he reached for the next, until I felt his hand on my neck, feeling for a pulse. I remained as still as I could, almost as if I had willed all remnants of life out of my body. For a moment, I thought I'd fooled him, but then in the next moment I was being pulled up by at least two men. One of them jabbed my ribs, forcing me to gasp in pain as I tried hard not to scream.

One of the men laughed hoarsely. For me, the night deepened with diabolical suggestions.

Hands were at the next instant tearing at my clothes as my body was soon exposed to the cold air, my bra untangled, my panties ripped. I tried to fight back, but I could barely challenge the strength of the multi-limbs assailing me, holding my arms firmly to the ground, pulling my hind limbs apart. And then one of them was on top, in a brutal entry clearly intended to inflict maximum damage. My scream was so shockingly involuntary it would shame me when I later remembered it. I tried to look at the

323

bougainvilleas in front of the church, seeking comfort that didn't come. The stars still hang there in their tiny but distant brightness, but the pain within mounted at the roughness of the continuing assault, its agonal impact. The smell on top changed, not so much in kind as in intensity. Was this the second? I wasn't sure, as I forced hard to let my imagination roam away from the stripping away at my body and spirit, every shred of self-worth being under extreme assault. I was shedding tears without realizing it. I thought there had been five of them, but I couldn't be certain. In my mental roaming and the reality of the moment, I was seeing thorns and sunflowers and darkness and light, all intermingled without offering escape. The sweat dripping into my face, the ongoing thrusts choreographed to the encouraging chants of the gang continued to rip my spirits. As I alternated between states of awareness and unawareness, I wasn't sure if I was alive or, if alive, on the verge of death—and, given the spiritual violence being perpetrated on me, I wished that I would die. Eyes closed, I bore the rest of the ordeal as best as I could, although the ongoing roughness elicited gasps that became part of the encouraging soundtrack to the tormentors.

Next I knew, my body was being turned around. Why, I couldn't fathom. Then I felt the pain of a *panga* (or it might have been a *masu*) on my back, and again, and again. I slipped into unconsciousness and this time, for a long time, death hovered very close by, ready to claim me in any vulnerable moment.

But I was at that moment stronger than death. I would once more regain consciousness. I didn't have much control over my body as I rose from the pile like a zombie whose source of power resided elsewhere. I crawled a few inches and fell into another period of unconsciousness. And that was the last time I would regain consciousness among the pile of dead bodies.    I awoke again in the French nursing camp.

Juju was quiet after he heard this narrative, which he allowed me to tell without interruption, except for occasional sigh, which sometimes sounded like a gasp that came from a face blighted by furrowed brow, tightened lips, and narrowed eyes weakened wet with unshed tears.  He got up from the bed and moved toward the wall, away from me.  For a moment he held on to the wall and then he began to pound it with strong punches.  I walked up to him and put my arms around his midsection. "I'm so sorry, Juju.  Please, please, forgive me."

He turned to face me and looked into his glistening eyes, the teardrop interrupted from falling.  "I knew you were cut, your scars show that, Shama, and I had even imagined that you might have suffered rape, but I had hoped it wasn't so and I was afraid to ask, afraid it might cause too much pain.  I wish I could lay my hands on those bastards.  I will tear them apart for what they did to you."  He caressed my face.  "Sweetie, it wasn't your fault."

He hugged me.  "Did they also give you the scar on your belly?"

It had even escaped me that we hadn't discussed this.  And when he asked about it, this shocked me.  Why hadn't he asked about that either?    Juju, afraid of what pain he might pull out of me with his questions?  Not knowing all but still loving me?  What a man.  I told him. He held me even tighter, whispering sweet-somethings, how much he loved me, how proud he was that my spirit remained unbroken despite all I had suffered.

I shouldn't have been surprised by this.    It was Juju being his typical self.  But at the same time as I was relieved, I also decided he'd heard enough.  Could I tell him the whole story now when he'd received this piece with such grace?  There and then I decided.

Apart from my aunt, Alexandre and Dr. Marquez, who else could reveal it?  I would call my aunt and obtain her assurance of secrecy and ensure that she obtained the same from Alexandre.  He owed me this much.  I would ask my aunt to contact Dr. Marquez, although I wasn't sure the doctor was still in Rwanda.  In any case, even if I couldn't reach the doctor, she must be bound by professional privilege to hold the truth intact. Even if not so bound, the doctor was not the type to unveil such secrets, I believed. Therefore, I concluded, it was best to leave the second part of my untold story hidden. It would never be revealed.

# Seven

Dwayne called to invite me to meet with the president. "I think he's putting you on his short list."

"But that's not what everyone is saying."

"I know, and we'll like to keep it that way, so I'm going to have to ask you to keep this very secret. Take the afternoon off tomorrow. Make up a good excuse. You're not under the radar right now so no one is watching you. A car will pick you up from home around one and bring you to the White House. The only one you can tell about this is your husband, but if you think he can't keep it to himself, then don't tell him. I'm sorry to have to say this but the president insists on absolute secrecy. You will be home for dinner and back at work tomorrow."

I told Juju, assured I could trust him. He was almost in tears, reiterating how proud he was of me. "I may not get it," I reminded him.

"The president will fall in love with you. Everyone does. He will pick you."

As planned, I was picked up and driven to the White House in a rather nondescript car. In the Oval Office, the president sat across from me on a couch, his legs crossed. Given how much he'd aged since assuming the presidency, I felt sorry for him, even though I was overly anxious. If the president intended to calm me with his own calmness, he didn't succeed, and as my heart raced I realized that I ought not give him cause to doubt my nerves (which made me even more nervous), else he doubt my ability to withstand the jaggedness of the politics that would certainly ensue if I were named the nominee. But I could only hope that he didn't notice my nerviness. He smiled at me and such close range only revealed his deepening wrinkles. With this, I momentarily noticed there was also the increasing gray in his hair. The young man was under strain, I reckoned, even though he had an easygoing attitude about him. "I have to tell you," the president said, "That you are a very impressive woman."

"Thank you, Mr. President," I said, even managing a smile of my own.

"And I know with a person of your substance I need not grill you too much. Your resume speaks for itself. I just wanted to ask you a few questions." The president paused, his eyes focused on mine. What was he looking for? I nodded, as if giving him permission to look and to ask, "I know a lot of people like to focus on judicial philosophy. Now, I'm not gonna ask you how you will rule on specific cases, nor will I apply any form of litmus test. But I'd like to know a little bit more about that judicial philosophy. Would you consider yourself a strict constructionist or as some might put it a formalist, or do you take a more practical approach to judicial interpretation?"

Another nod from me... And then I found a confidence in my voice harvested from years in the courtroom so that I spoke as though without any doubt: "Well, sir, I see the law, say the Constitution, as a set of principles that are oftentimes abstract." This time the president was the nodding one. I continued, "I think a judge's duty is to apply these principles to specific situations. In that application, I think some degree of judgment is inevitable. As far as I'm concerned strict constructionism is a sham. But at the same time, I do not think as a judge it's my role to substitute my judgment for the lawmaker's. My role is to apply the law in its plain meaning, but with the understanding that facts and circumstances sometimes are such that some degree of flexibility is needed."

"So this flexibility, where does it come from? Is it not an application of the judge's own judgment?"

"Not so much a judgment that aims to usurp the plain meaning of legal text, but a judgment exercised to interpret the law as it applies to a set of facts."

"Let me push you on that a little, judge. Really, when you talk about interpretation, again are you not applying your own judgment, even supplanting the intent of the lawmaker?"

"Not where the issues are black and white. Those are easy, but in some cases the issues are not so clear, nor is the law clearly spelled out. So in such cases, yes, the judge is applying her best judgment."

"And making law?"

"I wouldn't put it that way. She is illuminating the law."

"Interesting choice of words," said the president. "So with perfectly identical facts, two judges could rule differently, wouldn't you say?"

"I would say so, Mr. President."

"And the difference in ruling would be based on?"

"Experience, empathy..."

"I think that's what I was looking for. Experience. Speaking of which, you have a great background, despite its challenges. Can you tell me a little bit more about yourself? I'm particularly interested in your years in Rwanda."

Fighting words rendered more permissible by circumstance and the generality in which they were presented. And I gave him the outline that sold so well—my birth in Butare to a farmer, the stellar academic performance, the graduation on top of my class, the genocide, my own near-death experience, my emigration to the US. He would interrupt me now and then for more detail....

Did I face discrimination because I was female? (Yes, but I never dwelled on that).

What did I think of Hutus? (They are like every other people, proud, dignified, but capable of succumbing to the grim side of humanity).

Was there a chance of longer-term friendship between the Hutus and the Tutsis? (Yes, the human capacity for forgiveness sometimes defied analysis).

He nodded at my answers. And then he began to speak, seemed to hesitate and then finally said, "I've been wondering about one particular case you took that stands out in your profile—your defense of The Knights of the Latter Order. Before you answer the question I'm about to ask, I want you to know that I'm looking for the truth, not a rehearsed response." I nodded. "Why did you take the case?"

I felt defeated, afraid of the truth and what it might do to my chances. But I believed he was too intelligent to believe what I'd wanted to say—that it was an act on preservation of the principle that everyone deserved competent legal representation.

"The truth," I said. "The truth, Mr. President, is that I was under pressure to take it..." And I told him the circumstances leading to my acceptance. When I was finished, the president was smiling, although I wondered if it was a smile of mockery or a disguised smirk. "We have to make some compromises sometimes," he said, "but in this case I'm glad it also served a solid judicial principle." And then he was thanking me and saying he would make his decision soon and whether or not he chose me, he would be calling me.

And now arrived the moment of waiting, that bleak darkness when I couldn't tell whether or not I'd be picked. Strange, it seemed to me, that having initially put this in the realm of a dream that wouldn't become manifest, having delayed embracing it fully out of fear of what it might unearth, I so much wished for it now that it was so close, so possible. Would I look on Canaan and be denied entry? I wouldn't want to attribute it to competitiveness, but still I couldn't deny that I'd feel I'd lost a great race if I wasn't named. I reviewed the resumes of each leading candidate, their pros and cons, and now I said to myself that I was the most qualified for the job. I re-searched my conversation with the president, seeking clues that would point me this way or that. When Dwayne had asked me after the interview with the president how it had gone, I had replied I didn't know. "I know he's really into your candidacy," Dwayne had said. "I can't say I have a whole lot of influence over his decision, but if I could make it for him, you would be the choice." Soothing words, yes, but how much of this was just to salve the rejection to come? How much of it was merely out of decorum, the diplomatic balm applied to all the others who'd been interviewed, perhaps more so to those who were on the verge of rejection?

And so I suffered and I couldn't sleep well. Nights... were... like... days... were like... nights and my eyes were often opened and my mind was full of thought and I didn't eat well and I daydreamed about myself on the Supreme Court and I had nightmarish episodes of a political fight over my nomination so vicious because of who I was and I had moments of depression stemming from my worry that I'd be rejected and I clawed at the air during the nights and I gestured into the air during the days and I wondered whether I was growing mad and I laughed without incident and I cried without clear provocation and I waited for the call.

It came a week after my interview with the president. He told me how honored he'd been to interview me, and my hopes fell, as did my heart, believing this was to prepare me for the rejection. I wasn't even

330

sure if I sounded sincere when I responded that I'd likewise been honored to be considered, as I considered the maddening past week, convinced I'd have to live through it again after the imminent rejection. But in the next instant, he was saying, "Congratulations…"

My fists were pummeling the air, I was on my feet, pacing as the president continued on to tell me that Dwayne Dray would call me with the details of the announcement, scheduled for the next day. I was calling Juju the next moment, urging him to drop all appointments as we were headed for the White House. He screamed into the phone, sounding even more excited than me. And so when I hugged him later, when I remembered his support, despite my deception, I realized how much I owed to him.

And now began the new song.…

With the White House for a backdrop, the wind for a blanket of comfort, the flowers for aesthetic inspiration, and the phalanx of journalists for discomfort, I watched the president begin his announcement. This had been a well guarded secret, so well guarded that of all the deafening speculation that had preceded it, none had mentioned my name. But here we were, the president and I ready to give our speeches in defiance of that presumptuous speculation. As I stood by the president's side, Juju behind me, my heart heaving, I looked into the little gathering of reporters in front of us. I'd been in many courtrooms, I made a mental reminder to myself, faced down many a judge, bantered with aggressive witnesses and verbally wrestled many opposing counsel. Still, this moment seemed to present a greater challenge than all those arenas of confrontation. Perhaps I ought not take this approach that invited fear, but rather rephrase my perception so that the faces watching me would become neutral, not as hostile as I feared.

The president was speaking already, mentioning my full name, Shama Rugwe Badu, before I could mentally replay my rehearsed speech. I steered my attention to his words:

"I take this special privilege extremely seriously. Once appointed, my nominee has life tenure. She will have the opportunity to shape the law on many of the great issues that confront us today and those that will confront our children and their children. I speak of issues defined in each generation in accordance with its norms, even if the general underlying principles are the same, issues including privacy, religious tolerance, inclusiveness...."

I quickly recalibrated the words: inclusiveness (affirmative action), and what I expected might present the most difficult challenge for me—privacy (abortion). I hoped the latter would not come up. After all, things about me were buried so deep it would take significant unearthing to uncover some of them. After all, I'd gone through previous FBI and Senatorial scrutiny and survived. For now, I returned my attention to the president.

"Here is a woman who came from Rwanda at the height of its turmoil, herself a victim of a brutal attack that nearly took her life. But she did not wallow in the past, in the debilitating state of victimhood. Instead, she seized the opportunity presented her by our great nation, obtaining a doctorate degree and then graduating top of her law school class after that. She went on to clerk with a Supreme Court justice before embarking on a career in private practice. But her thirst for public service would soon draw her to serve as a district attorney. Ladies and Gentlemen, it doesn't get any better than that. She has consistently distinguished herself wherever she's been, given affirmation to the American Dream. She's spoken for the downtrodden as well as stood up for law enforcement. She has demonstrated her humanity, toughness, and sheer brilliance..."

I made my mind wander once more, this time in closer study of the journalists as they listened to this glowing tribute, and in a perverse way I wished it were my epitaph (as only the crass would dare challenge a sweet song for the dead). I still could not interpret the mostly impassive faces, except for a few that exuded, at least in my perspective, nothing but hostility. Although Juju was beside me, I longed for mass approval, as a sign that the task ahead would be easy. I searched for signs of friendliness and thought I found a few, even though I couldn't affirm that they were in my favor, afraid that a friendly face might only be masking a hard heart. Don't be paranoid, I told myself. Stay calm. No one is out to hurt you.

The president concluded his remarks by asking the Senate to confirm his nominee and to do so quickly. As he left the lectern, the president invited me to speak. I monetarily worried that I couldn't, that whatever I planned to stay would emerge warped by my worry and be unconvincing, and for three seconds I didn't move— a lapse I hoped had gone unnoticed as I forced my mind to hold the percolating worry and walk to the lectern. I managed, against the enduring concern, to lift up my head and look into the gathering confronting me and to establish with one or two reporters that tricky connection made through eye-to-eye contact and keep it for uncertain seconds. I managed, despite the continuously brewing nervousness, to begin to speak, with only my determination holding my voice from shaking noticeably. I offered the obligatory salute to the president, thanking him for the honor of the nomination and then provided honorable mention to my departed parents and brother, Juju, Fiona, Auntie Shama, and the Baileys. I continued, "I would be remiss if I failed to acknowledge the opportunities this great nation of ours has provided me." I thought I saw a reporter wince at the sound of *ours*. Or was I just imagining that? "Here, I have gained invaluable education, in the classroom and the courtroom as well as in the public at large. I have been given the opportunity to walk the nation's most hallowed halls and institutions as well as participate in the gallery of its marketplace of thoughts, its byways and highways of personal and professional fulfillment. And I have fulfilled dreams even beyond my imagination."

As I paused to study the reaction to this ode to America, I could see—or was it again my increasingly active mind?—faces easing a little from that mass impassive screen that had confronted me. Perhaps, if my mind was being true to me, there was even a smile here and the beginning of another there. I would go on to sum up for the gathering my personal story, or rather a distilled version of it—the relatively modest upbringing in Butare, the genocide that prematurely thieved the lives of my family, and the triumph of my migration to the US.

"As a young woman, I was deeply disturbed by the breakdown of law during those trying times in Rwanda, the resort to hideous acts of violence. Having lived in America for the past eighteen years, I have no doubt that the American judicial system is a linchpin for the country's development and its greatness. And I am proud to be a part of it. In fact, my admiration for the commitment to justice for all as a girding principle of this nation was part of what influenced me to pursue a career in the law."

I couldn't tell if a reporter who held his hand to his eyes was blotting out tears.

"I look forward with much anticipation to serving on the Supreme Court if the Senate gives me the honor of confirming me."

As I stood back to receive the tepid applause, I fell into the president's embrace first, a quick one, and then Juju's, which he prolonged as if to send a message to me and the rest of the world. *She is mine and she ought to be yours.* It had been a long journey here, and standing in his arms for the world to see and eavesdrop on this message of *I love you*, I had to remind myself to hold back any tear of gratitude to my husband. No show of public weakness, I said in my mind.

After the announcement, as Juju and I walked out of the White House, Dwayne Dray informed me that the American Bar Association had just issued a rating of "well qualified" for me by unanimous vote of its Standing Committee, the highest ranking it could give. As we drove back home, I gave the implications of my nomination additional consideration: me, a relative anonym, now with my name being echoed and reechoed on radio and TV, etched into all manners of space in cyber form—the infinite vastness of the Internet and its intercontinental reach into the corners and sub-corners of the earth—all with the possibility of immortality. I considered that, no matter the outcome of the Senatorial hearings, my name had become a part of an ever-expanding landscape of nominees, perhaps a name to be jeered at or perhaps a name to be cheered. In nanoseconds after the announcement was made, in minutes at the maximum, TV and radio audiences and those accessing the World Wide Web would know. The deafening speculation would end. The blogosphere and other related spheres would debate the nomination, no doubt, and the reaction would range from yawn to yell (although the latter was more likely). The most important question for me was, of course, whether the name Shama Rugwe Badu would fade on dunghills or sparkle on mountaintops of immortality, tarnished with the ignominy of rejection or assume bold status glittering for generations.

Juju was named Dean of Georgetown College a few days later, an outstanding achievement that should have engendered long celebrations, but I was too busy to organize a party for him, take him out to dinner or even cook him a special meal. The man didn't complain. Was he an angel? I wondered. This must be love—kind, long-suffering, selfless, devoid of jealousy, offering unconditional support, a form of ovation that approximated oblation. My Juju, a man content in his own work and achievements who had never once compared our careers.

# Eight

Dwayne explained the process. "We will need to prepare you for the hearings," he said, "but before that, Senator John Owens will act as your chaperon in the Senate, introduce you to key senators who wield a lot of influence. I need not tell you, Shama, that your nomination is generating a lot of... backlash..."

Backlash or just lash? I would soon find out that the country's breath would stay suspended, and by the time it returned in exhalation, much would have been lost and hopefully gained and the future of the country, for some, would be considered destined for a bad turn, those who believed that I was an assault on everything they believed in, all the traditions, cultural mores, and even religious underpinnings that made America what it was and what they would like it to be. Yell, not yawn, as I had suspected. If I could provide them comfort at all, I would have told them to relax, that all things new, even bitter ones, become familiar with time, that bitter pill dissolves and joins the bloodstream to heal, eventually providing a cure at the minor expense of a diminishing bitter aftertaste. I'd already heard that some were reading the appointment as part of the president's self-fulfilling diabolical eschatological march, a part of his grander scheme to precipitate the end of the world, although I hadn't known the president to have such apocalyptical tendencies. I would have liked to tell them that if it were all to be reconstructed a hundred years later, although I hoped it wouldn't take that long, the reasons why they gasped at the announcement would be as important as an ant's bottom.

"You should avoid the political talk shows," Dwayne said. "The gadflies and crackpots will do you no good." Well stated. I knew, of course, that I couldn't say all that I'd have liked to say and even if I could, it would only infuriate the audience. After all, the president had just inserted the pill and they were still chewing on it, tasting its bitterness, reeling from its pungency. All I could do was brace myself for the aches to come. I recalibrated the factors I anticipated would raise opposition, none on its own sufficient to derail a nomination. But combined to sit on the highest judicial office?

| | |
|---|---|
| Place of Birth: | Butare, Rwanda |
| Gender: | Female |

Color:     Black

A black African woman nominated to sit on the Supreme Court of the United States as its Chief Justice. Nor was I naïve to what issues would be raised about my religious affiliation. Aware what many thought of the president himself, I expected that, given my mother's faith, sure to be discussed no matter what I said, I would be cast in some, even many, circles as a black African, Moslem woman.

I barely listened to the rest of Dwayne's outline of the process to win my confirmation as I battled these thoughts that had been in the back of my mind but suddenly seemed to assault me with greater ferocity now that the announcement had been made and reality had dawned. And there were the thoughts and even hallucinations of danger that dogged me in intimate ways like my very pulse during the meeting with Dwayne; dinner with Jojo that only served as little comfort in the widening space of my fears; phone conversation with Fiona during which she called me a genius, but a meaningless soundtrack in disharmony with the feeling that I was a masquerader whose mask was about to be removed; time in the shower under the beating fall of water beads that were like a warning of the lashes I would encounter, rather than the search for refreshment I had sought; or the sleeping hours that became episodes of startled wakefulness and an occasional yell of fear that had Juju worried and reassuring. The first day after my announcement thusly passed as if I were someone else caught in events totally uncontrollable.

I had to go to the Justice Department on the second day following the announcement and I had so far refused to read the news or listen to the radio, instead answering a ten page questionnaire from the Senate captioned *United States Senate/Committee on the Judiciary/Questionnaire for Judicial Nominees*. I had filled out a similar form for my prior nominations and was a little annoyed to be asked to fill out another one, with questions covering my birthplace, educational background, writings, public statements, and assets and liabilities.

Looking at my watch, I realized I had about a half hour to spare, a time gap which if left unfilled I knew would become a continuation of the torment of the previous hours. And lying there in the living room with tempting magnitude was a newspaper, which seemed to be calling me to pick it up. Dare I? I knew I'd inevitably see a news item about me in it

337

and, given the warnings, I knew it might be best to avoid it. But there it lay, as if with seductive voice, inviting me into all of its potential, news of the word in which I so vibrantly lived, which I'd influenced in my own small way and which I had the potential to influence in greater measure. I was in it. How could I avoid reading it? I picked up the newspaper and opened it to the front page in a quick motion designed to overcome any lingering hesitation. I held and breathed in deeply as I read the headline: BLACK COMMINUTY REACTS TO CHIEF JUSTICE PICK. I began to read:

> She is black, intelligent and young. Shama Badu stands on the cusp of becoming the Chief Justice of the Supreme Court. With her credentials, she should be able to walk on to the Court.

I skipped the catalogue of my educational and professional credentials. The article continued:

> "Shama Badu is an excellent choice for the Court," said Ben James, president of the NAACP. "She represents the choice of a part of the American story that is often ignored."

I paused to allow my grin to take full effect. I read further. A number of African-American leaders touted me and applauded the president for the choice. The only exception to this was the response of a congressional leader, a prominent member of the Congressional Black Caucus: "I don't question Ms. Badu's abilities. Clearly, she's well qualified for the job. But why, of all American born candidates, did the president have to pick a foreign born woman? Besides, she doesn't understand us, doesn't stand with us. Remember when she stood with the Knights. " Bobby Cline, that was the man's name. I had seen him a number of times pontificating on one or another issue. I'd always considered him a firebrand of sorts and to be honest with myself never really liked him. And here he was returning the favor, only vocally. But as I remembered the evening with George Harris, I decided I ought to put things in a better context. I closed the newspaper and put it aside. If I

338

couldn't get unanimous approval from the African-American leadership, where did I stand? For seconds, I wanted to call Dwayne, ask him to talk to Bobby Cline to change his voice. But I feared he'd perceive me as overreacting and also he might chastise me to stay away from the news as he'd warned earlier.

Later, at the Justice Department, I was led to a huge conference room. On the one end of the room was a chair with a table in front of it, remarkable in its solitude; on the other end were no less than fifteen chairs. For minutes, I sat alone in the solo chair, my only companion a cup of coffee and cookies on the table. I took a sip of coffee, but avoided the cookies. In a couple of minutes Dwayne walked into the room, apologized for keeping me waiting and introduced three men and three women who had walked in with him and would constitute the panel questioning me in the preparation sessions: a former senator, a former attorney general, two practicing lawyers, and two White House aides. The introductions done, Dwayne said, "We had to make sure we set up the room properly. We need to try and make this as realistic as we can." Together with the mock panelists, Dwayne retreated to the other end of the room, at least a yard of space between the questioners and me.

"Have you prepared an opening statement?"

"No," I answered.

"You need to prepare one A.S.A.P. It's key, as I'm sure you know. You want to set a positive tone from the very beginning. You want to hit on some human element, your background, for example, as a Rwandan émigré, your rise through law school, your rise to the top by dint of hard work… it's the American dream. It's what sells to the senators and the public…"

"Okay."

"When was the last time you read the Constitution?"

"Oh, I don't remember…"

"Read it. Reread it. I'm talking from beginning to end. And not only that, read the Federalist papers, memorize those parts that you can, and the more you can regurgitate the better. Read or reread all pivotal cases in US history. We have prepared a list for you."

"We will close early today, perhaps around four p.m. As soon as you get home, you gotta begin doing your homework."

"Also, remember to reread every speech you've ever given, every opinion you've issued, every one of them. We have a list of what we know. If we've missed anything, please get them and let's have them as well. You need to be comfortable with every line you've written, be ready to defend each argument you've made, no matter how trivial."

"Okay."

"We have confidence in your abilities and poise, but let's get a taste of your delivery. Let's just start with this question. Please state your full name and why you're here."

"My name is Shama Rugwe Badu. Why am I here? You want to know why I am appearing before you?"

"The details of your answer to the question are not what we're looking for at this moment, although I like that you are seeking clarification before answering. If unsure, it's better to clarify without coming across as smug, of course, than to assume what is requested of you. In any case, what we're looking for right now is your delivery."

"How did I do?"

"Hard to judge from the little we've seen."

"Remember to pause before you answer questions, although you must be careful not to overdo this. Pausing will make the senator asking the question think you're taking his answer..."

"Or her..." said one of the questioners.

"Or her answer seriously. You will also flatter him or her into thinking that the question is worthy of thought."

"In other words I will be stroking egos without being obvious about it?"

"You got it."

"Also, keep your answers brief and to the point."

"If they're doing most of the talking, you're in control."

"And lean forward into the microphone when a senator gets nasty. You need to demonstrate you're not intimidated."

"Okay. Lots of things to remember."

"That's for sure, but you need to be sure to practice these points until it's part of your DNA. The next few weeks are going to be one of the most, if not the most, demanding, exciting, tiring, and exhilarating of your life. And we're here to help ensure that it's all worth your time. So now let's begin with some basic but controversial issues. We have a lot of ground to cover, including race, gender, abortion, privacy..."

And so had elapsed that day, a day full of questioning when they had the introduction around eight-thirty a.m. and ended at five p.m., an hour later than scheduled, with a half hour break for lunch at noon, and one ten minute break to use the restroom. When I'd asked for another restroom break, the panel had asked me to try and keep such breaks to a minimum. I shouldn't allow any such weakness during the hearings and so if I needed to drink less in order reduce the urge to urinate, then I should drink fewer liquids. And so, although they had granted my request, I'd refused to take it, determined to show all, even these panelists, that my mind power reigned over my bodily needs. And I'd sat there and suppressed the urge to urinate, even when it became a little pressing. Concentrating on this as well as on the questions had put my body in discomfort, but I'd managed, resolved to drink less coffee and water the next day. I deduced the obvious: the Senate would be engaged in a game of mind-mining and my part was to ensure they didn't unearth anything but gold.

I wanted to collapse into bed when I returned home. After eating a pre-packaged Caesar salad alone, as Juju had a late conference in school, I retrieved one of my many copies of the Constitution, poured myself a glass of water, and read it. I read it through twice, before beginning to read the Federalist papers. Juju arrived close to eleven p.m. He massaged my shoulders and said he was going to bed, to leave me to continue my preparation. But his touch, so warm...I heard the sound of the shower from the bathroom upstairs. The touch... I closed the book and went upstairs. Juju was still in the shower when I joined him. I couldn't recall the last time we'd done this. Perhaps it was during our honeymoon? I'd never really liked it this way anyway, but in seeking newness, I was willing to recall that last shower-dance of love. As I approached him I became more aware of how our bodies were changing, both of us softer and heavier than before. I became more attuned to the belief that in youth we make love to the body and its attractiveness, but in later years, when the body is worn, we no longer make love to the body itself but to the

341

person-entire, so that if the *person* is unattractive, then the joy of the lovemaking diminishes. But looking at Jojo, I had no doubt that I was in love with the person, even if the body was wearing out its attractiveness, and that only my hectic life was keeping us from more such unions. And I touched him and he touched me and we embraced in a coital union that drained me of all remnants of energy left so that I collapsed into bed soon afterwards and for the first time since I was nominated as Chief Justice of the Supreme Court, I didn't wake until the morning.

The next morning was a break of sorts from the mock hearings as I was scheduled to meet with key members of the Senate. First, I was to meet Senator John Owens, who would then serve as my chaperon. He'd indicated to me earlier that we would meet first with the friendly group, the senators in the president's party and then venture into opposition territory. Not to worry, he'd assured me. Any opposition would be tampered because he was one of them and having him as my chaperon would be a positive signal to his party. With the night's physical release and its aftermath of rest, I looked forward to the day with confidence. I would embrace this attitude as my armor going forward, ready to move beyond that period of doubt and angst that had clouded previous days. Nor would I soil this heightened mood with any news—no reading of the papers, no checking of the Internet... Even the sunny weather seemed in tune with this new song I had begun to sing, which continued when I met with John Owens in his office for breakfast and he showed me the list of senators, including the majority leader, the minority leader, the chair of the Judiciary Committee and its ranking member from the opposition party, Senator Andrew Norwood. "He will probably be the most difficult of the lot," John informed me.

I'd met Senator Andrew Norwood a number of times. He had a reputation as a bit of a maverick and solitudinarian in his party, and a juggernaut when he wanted to be. I remembered reading somewhere that he was of a "polymathic mind." When I'd met him previously, we'd not engaged in any meaningful conversation, except my previous hearings when he'd asked some perfunctory questions and appeared satisfied with my equally perfunctory responses. He'd not voted for me in then, but he'd not stood in vocal opposition either. I remembered him as a well-coifed

342

elderly man. I couldn't recall his exact age but I guessed he'd be in his late sixties or early seventies. I remembered his almost full grayed hair, high cheek bones, aquiline nose, severe eyes, pointed chin, and lean physique. I'd never felt intimated by him, although I'd heard it said he could be severe and I could understand why some might find him intimidating—and now, with so much at stake, I too felt the pangs of that... what could I call it? Was it intimidation or great unease? But any unease was soon reduced when I met the Senate majority leader. He asked me about my views on abortion (I couldn't say how I'd rule, but I was highly respectful of precedent), about my judicial philosophy (I didn't believe in activism; the law had to be interpreted in accordance with its facial meaning and in ambiguous cases, legislative intent; not to say that life experiences never influenced these). The Senate leader frowned. I added, "But I also believe the law has to be applied to specific instances when it's not clear how it applies to particular facts." I had his full support, he pledged. I felt that the man had made up his mind out of party loyalty than what I'd told him, finding his questioning to lack rigor and that he didn't ask follow up questions even where I was vague. The chair of the Judiciary Committee gave me a similar reception, questioning me lightly and pledging his support. As it were, the other members of the president's party provided minor variations of this gentle questioning and pledge of support. My reservoir of strength had been relinquished even more after these meetings, as I was told to get ready for the trip to the White House, where I was scheduled to meet the vice president for lunch before the afternoon meetings with the senators in the opposition party.

When I stepped outside to get into the awaiting car, I was surprised to see the crowd that had gathered. There must have been at least eighty people-chanters. "Pay them no attention, ma'am," the chauffeur noted. But I could hear chants of "No Moslem on the Supreme Court! No Moslem Chief Justice!"

"We didn't expect this kind of reaction, especially not so soon in the process," Dwayne said as he bid me to calm down.

"Did the president consider it at all?"

"He never mentioned your religious background, but he is well aware of your mother's religion. The FBI dossier on you makes that clear."

"But given what he went through himself he ought to have known."

"Perhaps. But perhaps that's why he chose you, confident that if he could overcome it, so could you."

During lunch, the vice president helped assess the morning's meetings, to recall each conversation and its meaning. "We're doing good," he said. "Just keep it up, especially for this afternoon. With fifty-eight senators in our party, all we want is for your nomination to get out of committee and unto the Senate floor without a filibuster. We shouldn't have a problem with an up or down vote in the Senate. But you know, don't you, that with the political climate being what it is, there will be some opposition? It will have nothing to do with your qualifications for the job. Some will use ideology as the basis or the pretext. So be prepared for opposition, but in the end, what matters is getting you on the Court, even if it's with just fifty plus one votes."

I returned to the Senate around two p.m., by which time the crowd had dispersed except for one man holding a placard with the words: Moslem Go Home.

This was the ambiance, in a manner of speaking, in which the afternoon meetings commenced. After a short talk of encouragement from Senator John Owens, I was ushered into the office of one senator after another from the opposition party. Each received me cordially, but each tried to get me to confess some position on abortion, affirmative action or other judicial philosophy, that would hint at activism from the bench or a lack of commitment to principles they deemed basic to the founding of the country. These I easily deflected, but it became slightly heated when one senator asked me for my views on natural law. I was committed to the written law, I said. But the senator wouldn't relent. "There has to be situations," he said, "when you will be faced with a case of first impression, when there is no written law."

"It is not the job of the judge to make the law," I said. "If such a case ever comes before me, I will have to defer to the legislature."

"But what if they haven't acted?"

344

"Then they will have to act."

"You won't answer the question?"

"Senator, I have answered as best as I can."

He shook his head in clear signal of dissatisfaction and indicated the abrupt ending of the meeting by standing and extending his hand. If this was a little rattling, it was a perfect preparation for the next and last meeting of the day—the meeting with Senator Andy Norwood. First, although the meeting was scheduled for four p.m., I had to wait outside his office for almost an hour, so that it was close to five by the time I was let into the senator's presence. He sat behind his desk as I entered the room, and for a while I thought he would deny me the courtesy of a handshake. But after seconds elapsed, with me standing in front of him, he stood up and extended his hand, all this while staring directly into my eyes, his blinking very infrequent. He didn't smile—as all the other senators had on meeting me, even those in the opposition party. He didn't offer me a seat, but I took one of the two seats in front of his desk after he sat down following the handshake.

"You want to become a Supreme Court Chief Justice."

Whether this was statement or a question, I couldn't tell, but I decided to read it as the latter.

"Yes, sir," I said.

Senator Norwood leaned back in his seat, which I would normally interpret as an agreeable gesture but which now seemed like one meant to signal offense, a closure to me or emphasizing of the gap between us. No room for you in my space, he seemed to be saying. He caressed his chin as if he needed to reflect on my answer. In that period of silence, I noticed that the neck-skin that protruded from above his shirt collar was red-wrinkled like rotten tomato skin. Not to seem impolite by staring at this part of his body, I instead studied the items on his desk—a photo on the right side of the senator of a white haired woman I surmised was his wife. In the middle of the desk was a piece of blank paper with a pen lying diagonally across it. On the other side of the desk was a sign with the name: Andrew Nathaniel Anthony Norwood. Otherwise, the top of the desk was bare. As the senator continued to caress his chin, I played with his full name, the first time I had seen all his names and which seemed more potent in its fullness compared to the Andy or Andrew Norwood accorded him in public spaces. I put the initials together and then mentally said it backward. My heart beat harder all of a sudden and I nearly gasped. Senator Norwood moved forward, now leaning on the desk, but even then he said nothing in this new pose for at least thirty seconds. It was then that I noticed for the first time that the senator was wearing two watches. The one on his right wrist had a black leather strap and the one on the left had a brown strap.

I expected him to ask me why I wanted to sit on the Supreme Court when he began to open his mouth. Instead, he said, "Have you seen the protesters outside?"

"Yes, sir, I have."

"And what do you say?"

"It is entirely within their rights, sir."

"Have you noticed what they are saying?"

"I haven't paid them much attention."

The senators eyes narrowed as he asked, "They are calling you a Moslem."

"Yes, that I noticed."

"Are they right?"

"They are entitled to their opinion, sir?"

"I understand that, but are they right?"

I was about to answer when a voice told me to hold back. Against my instincts, I responded, "Would that matter one way or the other, sir?"

The senator hesitated to answer, as if he was surprised by the question. "Not at all," he said when he recovered. "I'm just curious, that's all. Now let me ask you. Why should I vote for you to be on the Court?"

I put what he'd learned into practice, taking my time, allowing a few seconds to elapse before saying, "Sir, I think I am highly qualified for the job. My educational background, clerkship on the Court, prosecutorial background... I think that I have the credentials and experience to do a great job on the Court. And I have fulfilled all my duties with the utmost integrity. And I consider it an honor to be nominated and an awesome responsibility, sir, that I will approach with the highest care and respect ..."

"That's all you can tell me to convince me to vote for you? Judge, you're not doing a great sales job at the moment."

"What would you like me to tell you, senator? Are there any particular areas of concern you'd like me to address?"

"I thought you were the smart one. You can't figure out what I need to know to vote for you? Am I wasting my time here?"

"No, sir, but I'm not sure what else to…"

Senator Norwood was shaking his head vigorously. "This is very disappointing, judge."

"I'm really sorry to hear that, senator, but I am prepared and will be glad to address any concerns you may have. I'm just not sure what they are."

"And that is what I don't understand. If you are smart as they say you are, I don't need to even ask you a thing. When you first walked into this office, I was quiet for a little while, waiting to see what you'd do. I wasn't being rude, judge; I was giving you the opportunity to show me what you've got, but instead of seizing the initiative, you just stood there, saying nothing…"

"But senator…"

"Wait. Let me finish. And now I am trying to get you to take the initiative and once again you've failed to do so. For the last time, why should I vote for you to sit on the highest court of the greatest land in the world? And I don't want to hear about your academic credentials or your stellar professional career. Tell me something I should know but don't know. I have read about what's in the public record. I'm not interested in that."

I was now totally flustered as I watched Senator Norwood stare at one of his watches and then the other.

"I will serve, if confirmed, with diligence and deference to…"

"Ma'am," Senator Norwood leaned forward even more, inches away from my face. I refused to retreat, breathing in the collected smells of his (late) lunch, with the garlic prominent in this assault on nostrils. "When you have something interesting to say, let's talk, but in the meantime you can consider this meeting over."

Senator Norwood pointed to the door and I hesitated. If I could say something to convince the senator, something, anything… but what?

He hadn't raised any specific areas of law, touched on phrases or judicial philosophy or otherwise. All my preparation, all my expectation, had proved inadequate for this approach by the senator. I wanted to beseech him to cover the expected terrain, at least play the game as others had played it even if at a superficial level, questions asked and answers given on that road toward sure confirmation, as fifty plus one was all I needed, after all. But now that the ballgame had changed, I found I could do nothing but stand, thank the senator for his time, and walk out of his office, feeling I had left an essential part of myself in the office that try as I may I'd never be able to recover. What he'd done, by such sparse words and how I'd been so deeply led in that direction, troubled me deeply that I called Senator John Owens immediately to debrief.

"I'm not surprised by his reaction," he said. "But don't be too worried about that. I'll talk to him. We're really not looking for his vote. We just don't want him to be a stumbling block."

I needed this assurance, but it wasn't enough to still my concerns and so I returned to that dreaded state of anxiety that had plagued me in previous days, suffered pain in my belly region, and pined under the cover of preparing for the upcoming hearings when I went home, unable to return to that night when amid all the uncertainty I managed to overcome myself and accepted the presence of my husband and all the salve he was able to wrestle out of the situation at my behest. Although I would be the first to admit that if any wrestling was involved, it was mainly because I wouldn't let him give freely, because I had managed to implant, despite his best efforts, a structure of strain between us. I reckoned that, ever since his return from Ghana, he'd barely given me cause for concern, but I had with my busy schedule, attention to career and percolating guilt, held him at bay. And what I found even sadder about this was that he didn't realize this strain existed. When I'd joined him the other night in the shower, how easy it seemed... and I knew he accepted it, just as he accepted my frequent absences from home. And sadder still, was that I wanted to remove the strain but it was as if I was incapable. Always, I realized, there was something else to handle that seemed of more immediate concern than my marriage; always I had to handle that before I could devote attention to my relationship with my husband. And now, sitting in the study, attempting or pretending to read cases in preparation for the hearings, I realized again that the marriage had to wait. But it was futile trying to read the cases with the bombardment of thoughts and emotions inside me. With Juju asleep, I left the study and went to the family room. I would see what the news had to say. Ill advised? Perhaps so, but I couldn't resist the temptation to turn on the TV in the hope that someone might have something positive to say about my nomination that would help wane my worries.

And there, on the major news network was one of the long-time members of the National Organization of Women: Phoebe Shaw. Her completely gray hair proffered an aura of dignity and I wished before I heard what she was saying that Ms. Shaw would pass positive comments on my nomination. I'd never sought female solidarity, but now I was desperate for it; I'd barely cried sexism, but now I wished that this dignified woman would use it as a weapon to stop anyone who might oppose the nomination whether or not on the basis of my gender. This, I reckoned, was fast becoming a war and in a war all weapons had to be unsheathed and used, especially if the opponent did the same—scorched earth approach, if you will. I was ashamed to think this way and was relieved that Ms. Shaw didn't take that route, even though the news anchor asked if she thought the mounting opposition to the Chief Justice candidate had anything to do with her gender. "No," Ms. Shaw said. "Well, perhaps on the fringes. But in the current political climate, even if the president nominated a saint, she would face stiff resistance from the opposition." Ms. Shaw continued by elaborating on the poisoned political climate, the opposition erected not out of genuine differences but for political gamesmanship and gain and its attendant showboating. "Let's not forget that some even continue to believe that the president is a Moslem and don't hesitate to use it against him. As to this nominee, if we stripped the debate of all the posturing, she should be a shoo-in. She's a classical American success story, although she was born in Africa. She has more than demonstrated her brilliance, excellence, fairness..."

The anchor thanked Ms. Shaw and told viewers to stay tuned for the next guest, Stuart Shuller, head of the Christian Forum. My intuition warned me that, amid the protests, the next interview would be daunting, an added voice to the drone of opposition I'd faced with the demonstrations. But I was hooked, expectant and unable to switch off the

349

TV. I breathed in and out several times as the commercials played. And then the anchor was back introducing Stuart Shuller. I had heard of him in passing, an energetic leader of an organization with the ostensible purpose of engaging in religious dialogue in the public space. And now looking at him, I found myself attracted to him—his youthful (he couldn't be more than 35) and general good looks and, like Senator Norwood, well coifed in a suit and tie. He smiled, his dimples adding to his attractiveness. The anchor raised the issue of my nomination after the brief period when the man's smile, I knew, had charmed many in their homes even before he spoke.

"The nation was founded on Christian principles," the guest was saying. "There is no need to usurp that with a Moslem on the Supreme Court as its Chief Justice, with the opportunity to shape the Court's processes and decisions. Bear in mind that this is the highest court of the land and the position is the highest on the court. Now, don't get me wrong. I am not advocating for discrimination against Islam, but it is one thing to give them access to equal rights and another to put them in control over our laws. The founding fathers must be turning in their graves right now."

"But we don't know that she's a Moslem, Mr. Shuller, do we?"

"We have this from very reliable sources."

"But we haven't heard her say so..."

"Come on... Of course we'd expect her to deny it, knowing that it could end her chances. But it's not what she says that matters; it's what she is."

"What she is? What evidence do you have?"

"As I've said, we have very reliable sources."

"Okay, let's stipulate to that. Are you saying that Moslems should be denied a right to sit on the Supreme Court if they are qualified just because of their religion? Isn't that discriminatory? Isn't that unconstitutional, even un-American?"

"We need to be realistic here. Do we really want someone on the Court who takes her orders from the Middle East, from some fundamentalist who wants to see the destruction of the United States?"

"Are you not making a great leap here, Mr. Shuller? This is after all a US citizen. We have no basis to say she'll take orders from anyone."

"Need I remind you that she was not born in the US? Do we want to take that risk?"

"Honestly, I do not see any risk here. This is as distinguished citizen of the United States. She's clearly qualified for the job. She's professional and by all accounts brilliant. Doesn't her record speak for itself?"

"Look, I'm not comparing her to the devil or anything, but even the devil can come in an attractive guise. But what you see on the outside doesn't necessarily reflect the truth or reality. All I'm saying is that we ought not put on the highest court of the land in the hands of an individual born outside of the US who may have ties to Islamic fundamentalists."

"Come on, Mr. Shuller, on what basis do you say she has ties to Islamic fundamentalists?"

"I didn't say she does; I'm just saying she may."

"But you have no basis for saying that."

"There are a lot of qualified people who can fill the position. Why take the risk? And let no one go accusing me of bigotry or whatnot. I'm just being realistic here. I have nothing personal against Ms. Badu. I'm just saying what a lot of Americans believe but are afraid to say for fear of being branded one thing or the other."

"Mr. Shuller, I'd love to continue with you, but I'm afraid that's all the time we have. Thanks for coming on our show. And to our viewers, please be sure to join us same time tomorrow when we will have as our guest Mr. Abdul Khan, president of the US Moslem Alliance."

It was almost one a.m. by the time the program ended—a repeat of an earlier show. I recalled that the earlier show was around eight p.m. I made a mental note to see the earlier version the next day when Abdul Khan would appear. I knew of him also—one who appeared frequently on TV shows whenever the stations needed someone to opine on Islamic teachings and matters related to the Moslem community. He was an elderly man, probably seventy or so, totally bald at the top of his head, but fully bearded, a beard peppered with gray. His thick glasses suggested a scholarly bent, but I had dismissed him as too opinionated when I'd heard him speak in the past. Why is it, I wondered, that the networks were parading the most stereotypical of characters? But I answered my own question as soon as I asked it, although it irked me that they would seek

351

such sensationalism and higher ratings at the expense of a more levelheaded discussion that could aid my nomination rather than poison brewing passions. Despite my misgivings about him, I was pleased at some level in the belief that I would have a highly vocal advocate in Abdul Khan. This wasn't what I wanted but this was where I had found myself.

And I worked hard at the questions presented me the next day at the mock sessions, ignoring the vociferous protests I'd encountered on the outside, with some protestors carrying placards and others an effigy of the devil (with horns and oversized breasts). Enmeshed in the questions and answers and feedback, the issues otherwise haunting me became less pressing on my mind. I was doing very well, I was told repeatedly; perhaps I ought to pause here or there, I was advised; lean in a bit more here and there, I was counseled. Occasionally, one of the panelists would offer me some substantive comments. Likewise, I ignored the demonstrators at day end as best as I could, glad that their numbers had declined when I left the Justice Department. I tried not to think about them, knowing that all disillusion is borne of someone's form of reality or perceived reality. How could I react anyway without myself degrading the public square?

I ate dinner with Juju when I got home. He tried conversation; I was not responsive. He tried romance by walking over and massaging my shoulders, but despite this invitation, I rebuffed him when he leaned down and tried to kiss me. "Sorry, honey," I said. "I have so much on my mind now." I could imagine him saying, *Let me take your burdens; let me share them, at least.* But perhaps he'd become attuned to my needs enough to know when not to attempt persuasion. My own inner voice was urging me to take advantage of the moment. It was almost seven-thirty and the show featuring Abdul Khan would be on in thirty minutes. I couldn't ease my anxiety enough to respond to my inner voice. Instead, I said, "I know I've not been much of a companion lately, but I promise I'll make it up to you." He nodded, cleared the table and went upstairs to shower. I went to the family room and turned on the TV.

The show soon started with news items that included a brief item on the protests at the Justice Department. And then the anchor announced the upcoming interview with Abdul Khan. I was glad that the man was in a suit. Look and sound like one of them, I whispered at the TV. Juju yelled from upstairs that he was getting into bed to read and then sleep. He was exhausted, he said. Okay, I said, ignoring what he said next—I didn't hear it anyway, focused now exclusively on the interview as Mr. Khan was asked to respond to the demonstrations against my nomination.

"I think it's really sad that in a country that prides itself of democracy and equal rights for all, we have certain fringe elements engaging in such intimidation."

"But can you understand their concerns?"

"Their concerns, whatever they may be, are unfounded. Clearly. What could they be? As we can tell from their signs, they are demonstrating because of Ms. Shama Badu's religious beliefs. No one would lift a finger or raise a voice if she were Christian. I thought in the US we adhere to the principle of separation of church and state."

"Last night, one of our guests raised the issue of... or rather wondered whether Ms. Badu would be influenced by fundamentalists."

"Why don't they judge her by her professional qualifications rather than this generalized fear? Do we wonder whether Christian nominees would be influenced by fundamentalists?"

"But, Mr. Khan, Christian fundamentalist do not go about chanting death to the US."

"I think her nomination and whether she can serve well on the Supreme Court has nothing to do with what somebody of any religious persuasion anywhere might want. I know some of our brethren on the Christian side are worried about certain fringe groups, but I also cringe when I see some of the comments made by Christians against Islam, including some of the things being expressed at the demonstrations against Ms. Shama's nomination. That is why we need to separate religion from the political sphere and focus on her qualifications and her qualifications alone."

"Do you know Ms. Badu personally?"

"No. What I know is what I've read in the public record. And I read the article that appeared some days ago of her in front of the mosque. But I bet you these demonstrators don't know her personally either."

*Article about me in front of a mosque?*

"So you don't know that she's a Moslem."

"I don't know that for a fact, no."

"Then why are you defending her?"

"Well, they are making it sound like that... like a war against a Moslem candidate for the Court and I have to speak against that. But it shouldn't just be me. Anyone dedicated to American principles of justice and equality should be speaking against what this is becoming without regard to their political or religious affiliations."

*Me in front of a mosque.*

"Okay, Mr. Khan, what of those who say that America was founded on Christian principles? Those who worry that having a Moslem on the Court flies in the face of the basic founding principles and American values?"

"Remember, we are a nation aspiring to the principle of separation of church and state. What or where Mrs. Badu worships should have no relevance to her political life. This is not a nation for one religion or another. There are people of many religions living in the US, law-abiding citizens who pay their taxes and contribute to the greatness of this country, and each of them deserves equal access to the public space and its institutions. It is for these reasons that we ought not infuse the public arena with such religion and even religious vitriol."

Me in front of a mosque. It became clear to me. I called Mustapha. "Did you give anyone the picture Maria took when I visited the mosque?"

"She told me she gave it to the press, but I don't think she had any other intention than to show that you're open-minded. She didn't anticipate that they would print an article with the photo and affirm that you're a Moslem as if they knew this for a fact. Everyone knows you're Christian. I'm really sorry this has caused such an uproar. I have seen footage of the demonstrations..."

"What article are you talking about, Mustapha?"

"You haven't seen it. You can check it out on the Daily Gazette's website. By the way, Maria has offered to speak to them to set the story straight."

I checked the Internet page of the Daily Gazette immediately and there it was: me in a scarf and long gown standing under the inscription on the wall: DC MOSQUE and with the caption:

## MOSLEM FOR SUPREME COURT CHIEF JUSTICE

I read in part the following: Shama Badu worships at the Temple Mosque. According to reliable sources, she frequents the mosque...

So this would explain the belief that I was Moslem. I thought of what Mustapha had said: *Everyone knows you're Christian.* But as I thought about it, on what basis would anyone who didn't know me well reach that conclusion? My church attendance had been sporadic, at best. I called Mustapha and asked him to tell Maria not to contact the Daily Gazette to try and "set the story straight."

The days following were a blur, a mass movement of actions, screaming, talking. The mock hearings continued a few more days, each meeting preceded by demonstrations whose participants seemed to be getting louder and louder by the day and more numerous. I concentrated with effort on the questions and answers and continued to earn the panelists' kudos for my responses and poise. I tried to avoid the media and to stay away from the news, occasionally slipping and tuning in to the news magazines on TV or a newscast at the top of an hour on radio and turning to one or two news magazines. It was through one such occasional slip that I learned that a group of Moslem demonstrators on my behalf had clashed with others protesting my nomination and that a couple of people on either side had sustained minor injuries, which had called for police intervention. "Why didn't anyone tell me this?" I asked Juju and then Dwayne. For your own good, they both said and they couldn't have echoed each other if they were twins. Not to worry, Dwayne added. These were fringe elements. The country at large was engaged in a more civil if heated discourse over my nomination. Why, I asked Dwayne, was this generating so much protest, even if from fringe elements? Was it my gender? No, said Dwayne. Was it my country of origin? Could be, said Dwayne, but not to this degree of vehemence. Was it that they believed I was a Moslem? Pause. It looks like it, although that could just be a catalyst and perhaps all the other factors added to bring the protest to boiling point. Assured Dwayne, it will pass. They were working on the votes and were assured of victory, even if along party lines as it seemed to be shaping up at the moment.

The opposing party was mostly citing my lack of extended judicial record as the main basis for its opposition to my nomination. Whether that was a pretext or not was anyone's guess, said Dwayne. "Relax," he said. "After the final vote, you and I will look back and laugh over it all." But I couldn't relax, continuing to rebuff Juju's attempts to ease me into the comfort of the affections he wanted to provide. Even Fiona's frequent phone calls to assure me, I suspected at Juju's urging, became annoying rather than comforting. Nor did it help when Ama and the Baileys called to offer their support and express their pride in me. What good does it do me? I asked myself. Will these assurances stop the spiritual bloodshed within me each day, the blood that flows with each protest, each insult, which seeps into the national fabric and stains it like a discoloring dye?

Despite my unease and anxiety, Juju was calm—or he appeared so—always eager to say a kind word or hold open his arms for me, no matter how often I rejected this. But even he became palpably shaken three nights before the first day of my hearings when deep into the night the phone rang. Both Juju and I woke up but didn't pick up the phone, given that neither of us recognized the number on the caller ID. But we both sat up, as if we knew of some foreboding. And then when the ringing stopped and Juju's prerecorded voice invited the caller to leave a message and the signaling beep sounded, we heard:

> If you value your pathetic life, you will withdraw from this
> thing. You know what's better than a Rwandan Moslem?
> I'll tell you. It's a dead Rwandan Moslem. This is your
> first and last warning.

Juju held me and I allowed him to do so as my tense body lay in his equally, if not more, tense body. He tried to assure me it was not of consequence, but even his voice shook. It was two a.m. when I checked the alarm clock. We considered calling the police, but it seemed neither of us desired to do so at the time and, although we pressed our bodies closer, rest did not come and neither of us slept the remainder of the night. But by morning we rethought our decision. I called the police first and then Dwayne. The police came over, listened to the recording and assigned me a security detail. I didn't leave the house that weekend. "I need to prepare for the hearing on Monday," was my stated reason, but to be truthful to myself, the fear abided and I felt safer being in the house as the police watched over it. I forbade Juju from leaving the house that weekend. He didn't protest much.

We spent the weekend in a constant state of alert. A sound, however benign, made my heart jump; a call and I shuddered. I tried to reread cases, but my concentration was completely gone. Even the leftover meals we ate, which we'd enjoyed earlier, now tasted too saccharine or too salty. I wanted to try making love to Juju but neither of us could disentangle himself/herself from the tension to reach the requisite point of arousal and we abandoned the project after a few tepid kisses. After this botched effort, I knew of nothing else I could do but watch TV. "Do not turn that thing on," Juju warned, but I replied I'd go insane without a peek. Just a peek. I turned it on and searched the channels for news items about me. "Seeking trouble," Juju labeled this. "Confronting the enemy," I relabeled it. He kept quiet after I said this.

The news items were a mishmash of wild opposition, rare stated support and occasional outright venom. An organization dedicated to the advancement of African-Americans saw me as antithetical to its values, calling me a "self-loathing black woman," while another group with similar purpose saw me as "a great holder of the torch." A women's organization called my nomination unwarranted, as I'd not demonstrated my commitment to issues of concern to women. Another prominent female writer disagreed, hailing my nomination as a positive step for female empowerment. A preacher man called it the worst nomination to the Supreme Court and an assault on American values. Yet another preacher man saw it as a demonstration of separation of church and state and a fulfillment of God's love for all His children, a sign of a maturing country. Someone said I would impose African values in diminution of American culture. And the vast majority of commentators on the air opposed my nomination, mostly on the grounds that they didn't trust me to uphold the US constitution. Another channel reported of demonstrations and protests in various parts of the country, mostly in downtown areas and places of public gatherings. Moving pictures on the air showed many of the demonstrators, as usual bearing placards bearing my photo in the mosque and lamenting the nomination of a Moslem or at times a foreigner, to the country's highest court, and some blasting the president for being a closet Moslem or an outright one or of kowtowing to Islamic fundamentalists by giving them one of their own, if a polished version. Station after station where my nomination was under discussion carried variations of these themes, including also reports of calls flooding the senators' offices in opposition to my nomination.

"Do you really want to continue watching this?" Juju asked, apparently in distress for me.

"One more station," I said as I changed channels, expecting that at least one would bear overwhelming indications of support. Instead, the next one carried a news report of another demonstration. I was about to turn off the TV when I noticed that this was a demonstration by The Knights, with Rod Trammel, its leader, speaking through a bullhorn: "We reject this nomination, this assault on our values, and we ask the president to withdraw it immediately."

"I defended this guy," I said.

"What an ingrate," Juju replied.

I turned off the TV then and called Bob Sneider. "You owe me a favor," I said. "Call off that attack dog. I just saw Trammel on TV protesting my nomination."

"I have no control over the guy, Shama, you know that. Even if I did, what good would it do? He's just one of many."

"It doesn't matter. I defended him once. How do you think this looks? Tell him to stop."

"I will try, but like I told you I don't control him. I can't guarantee you any results. And don't get so worked up about him. He's crazy. If I were you, I'd concentrate on those whose opinions matter."

These events relived in my thoughts, even as I lay down to sleep later. Even with the police outside, I feared that in my sleep someone would sneak past them to do harm to Juju and me. For that reason and for all I'd heard on TV, I couldn't sleep. I even expected to receive another call at two a.m. threatening me with death. Perversely disappointed when my expectation passed unmet, I left the bedroom and walked downstairs to the study. Its space was extremely dark and for the first time ever, I was afraid of entering the room, my imagination conjuring images of sinister creatures, monsters red-toothed and glare-eyed, awaiting to pounce on me from their hiding places in the study's dark corners. But, most graphic in my imagination was the image of a faceless fetus, dripping blood. For seconds I stood on the edge, unable to take the step into the four walls of the study, the night's soundtrack of silence—disconcerting. But then I considered the fight to come. If I couldn't overcome the test of the bleak corners of my imagination, how could I expect to confront the flesh—if coifed and outwardly benign—of senators and their voices of challenge the coming Monday? But, then again, perhaps it was a more difficult to overcome this monstrous flight of imagination (which, after all, was a projection of what my mind had absorbed and reformulated without garnish) than the independent bodies and voices of senators. I took the step, which I realized when I entered the room, was all that was important, for the imaginations eased in their threats as soon as I was inside the study and even more so when I turned on the lights. I sat and turned on the computer and typed in my name. There had to be a flattering report on the Internet I could embrace. Tempted as I was to click on the first item that came up when I entered my name, I instead scrolled down the computer page and randomly picked an article entitled *Searching for Shama Badu*.

The article took a neutral viewpoint on my nomination, praising me for my clearly demonstrated intellectual brilliance, my optimizing of the American Dream at a time when the sustainability of the dream was in question. But it lamented my relative lack of judicial experience and opinions, speeches or articles from which my potential views on the Court could be gleaned. It concluded that the Senate had to be sure to extract as much from me as it could so the American people could get a sense of the kind of justice I might be, if confirmed. I found this article generally pleasing, if not entirely endorsing. But if this provided the anodyne embrace I could cling to, then I ought not have scrolled down to the portion where readers had posted comments about me. Teased in, however, by the generally positive tone of the article, I read on:

Sly:          Stupid nomination. She's Moslem for crying out loud. Folks, prepare for Sharia law. They stone you to death for stealing and cut off your hands for whatever. Hey, Mrs Shama, what are you doing in my country?

359

|  |  |
|---|---|
|  | Don't you have a country of your own? Go back to your country. |
| T man: | she a middle east spy she not even american |
| Flipped: | I wanna do that black bitch. She's hot. Who cares if she's an Islam. Give me that sperm receptacle any day. |
| Sly: | She's a lesbian. |
| T man: | i won't touch that thing with a ten foot pole. not if you paid me. ugly bitch in and out |
| Hee Haa: | What her looks got to do with anything? |
| Marsha: | this nominee gonna put america back in the dark ages. We don't want any islamacists on the courts. Kick her ass back to Africa. |
| Sly: | She swings on trees and now she wants to be Chief Justice. |
| Balls: | Folks, folks, calm it. She's smart and experienced. Isn't that what matters? And last I checked America was no theocracy. |
| T man: | all they good for is sports anyway now they want take over the suprem court |
| Hee Haa: | Last I checked she was first in her law school class. |
| Sly: | Who cares? I agree with Tman. She's got to be making the bedroom and cooking. |
| T man: | wrote a poem<br>the bitch is African<br>she aint even American<br>where this country headed man<br>damn foreigners taking over if they can |
| Marsha: | she and her arab terrorist islamicists friends are planning to make jihad on america. Send her back to ethiopia. |
| Flipped: | Man, I still wanna do her though. Like a horse. That's how they like it. |

360

| | |
|---|---|
| He Haa: | She's American. And she was born in Rwanda, not Ethiopia. Flipped, are you for real? |
| Flipped: | Like apple pie baby. |
| T man: | if she get on supreme court I'm leaving america |
| He Haa: | Good riddance. Be my guest. |
| Sly: | Wake up and smell the coffee guys. These foreigners are taking over America. The Mexicans have come in droves and are breeding like flies. Now the Africans are taking over the only important jobs left. I want my country back. |
| Balls: | Go back to Europe or wherever you came from and don't ever come back. This country belongs to no one. |
| T man: | hey im native American where will i go |
| Balls: | I was talking to Sly. OK, Tman, you can stay. Everyone else, kiss my ass and go back to Europe. |
| T man: | ha ha i lied im no native american |
| Flipped: | You go back to Africa balls or whatever your name is. You call yourself balls but clearly you got none. The only balls you got are the ones you need to shove down your throat. |
| Atta Girl: | If she's so smart why isn't she in Africa where they need her? We don't need her in America for sure. Lawyers come a dime a dozen and some smart ones too. |
| Hee Haa: | You're all crazy. This is America, land of liberty and immigrants. Everyone deserves a fair shot. |
| Sly: | The Moslems don't give everyone a fair shot. Why should we? All they want to do is bomb America and now you want to put |

|            |                                                        |
|------------|--------------------------------------------------------|
|            | them on the Supreme Court? What is wrong with you?     |
| Flipped:   | Still want to do it doggie style.                      |
| Masha:     | she's got a smelly butt and a smelly mouth to boot. And she don't shower. Them Africans smell. |
| Atta Girl: | And she's a Moslem.                                    |
| Hee Haa:   | Who told you she's Moslem anyway?                      |

I turned off the computer. Tears had welled up in my eyes in a way I couldn't understand. Had I survived Butare and Kigali, the challenges that had come at me like hellfire sometimes, so easily to surrender my tears to the insults from the anonymity of cyberspace? But, perhaps, that was what hurt more? That I had been so casually turned into an object of mockery from such a distance and I could not respond.... What was worse? Those who would lambaste me because they knew me or those who did so because of a resume, characteristics gleaned or even merely suspected based on a certain profile? I closed my eyes for a minute until I was sure I'd stayed the tears. With such buried tears I resolved that if this was the caricature they were going to turn me into—and I feared the cyberspace discussion was merely a crude version of the polished opposition—then I must do all I could to get on the Court. My detractors should not be allowed to prevail.

I closed my eyes again, trying to reach as deep within me as I could for strength, that reservoir of the inner woman that sometimes springs with refreshment in times of strain. But instead of drawing from its well, I found my mind refocusing, as if drawing deep inside itself—and in my mind I could hear a whisper: *Amash Ahtilatiumic.* I had rejected those words as gibberish in the past, undecipherable. But why did it come to mind at that time? Did it have any meaning? And then my mind went even deeper still into time, recalling Butare, Papa and Mama and Placide and Jean Pierre. And also, at first like an intrusion into this familial reunion of the mind, Rev. Didier Murenzi. I was in Butare again, seated in a pew with Papa and Placide, recapturing history. As I stayed focused on Rev. Didier Murenzi, I recalled his sermons, his words, in particular the words he liked to say to me *Talitha cumi. Talitha cumi. Talitha cumi.* It was no longer a distant echo, but a loud clarion call. And then all of a sudden the mists were clearing. I was not Amash. I was Shama. Thank you Amash, your work is done. Let Shama move on. I would not live in the sorrows of that which reversed me, put an albatross of the past around my neck. And once I made this assertion, this discovery, I began to parse *Ahtilatiumic*. If I was not Amash but would live solely as Shama, then likewise, I reversed *Ahtilatiumic*. And when I put it all together: Shama, Talitha cumi. Oh, what a revelation. I replayed the words of Balls in my mind over and again until I felt it becoming a part of me: *This country belongs to no one.* It hadn't been so hours before, but the phrase was mine now. And my mind had become Rev. Murenzi's trumpet: *Remember to be fruitful, filling the earth and subduing it. It belongs to your Father.* Whether I came on the Mayflower or in an airplane, I was here and I was a citizen. I would arise. Not ever before that moment had I felt so strong a sense of entitlement to the position on the Supreme Court. No longer would I view it as a privilege (even if I would continue to say so publicly), but as an entitlement. If people could leave their countries and go conquer other lands, colonize them and change their values and mores, then I too could leave the land of my birth and seek the highest judicial office available in another land. I climbed back upstairs. For the first time since my nomination I had no fear of any sort. None whatsoever. And I mounted Juju after stirring him, firm in the belief that something fundamental about my future had changed.

# Nine

Juju and I went to the arena the following Monday. And so the game began as a group of carefully selected senators presented me to the Judiciary Committee—the chair of the Committee and two members of the president's party and notably, Senator John Owens, the only senator from the opposition party to speak on my behalf. But the calm with which the proceedings began belied the vociferous protests outside. As they had done before, the protestors gathered in the morning outside the Russell Senate Office Building where the hearings were being held to continue the oral and gesticulating opposition and to lament the end of America if I were confirmed. If any of these protests shook the members of the Committee, they didn't show it. Or perhaps they took courage in the equally loud group of supporters who had also gathered outside the building. Steeled by my newfound determination, I ignored, or rather reduced, the loudness of the faceless friends and foes and their otherwise echoing chants and listened as the chosen senators presented me to the rest of the Committee.

They were a parrot of each others' words as they (once again) lauded my personal story of triumph, my optimization of the American Dream, and my stellar legal record, both as student and practitioner, discounting as unfounded claims that I didn't have the requisite judicial experience, extolling as a virtue my freedom from the tunnel of the so called judicial monastery acquired from a long stewardship as a judge. Needless to note, Senator John Owens' presentation provided the most dramatic and cogent version of those speeches. "Here I am, a member of the opposition, heartily endorsing this pick for our highest court." He too fell into the expediency of extolling my virtues, but added, "I have known Ms. Badu personally for a number of years now and I have observed with great admiration her intellect, personal disposition, and keen curiosity. She, to me, is an embodiment of the ideals of America: brave, smart, strongly rooted, not just by words but also by deeds, in the principle that all deserve justice regardless of social status, race or creed. I have no doubt that if the Founding Fathers could speak to us now, they would tell us that Shama Badu is the kind of person they would want interpreting our

364

great Constitution." I could detect, or probably it was only in my mind, a frown on Senator Norwood's face.

I was then invited to make my opening remarks to the Committee. I had stayed up late preparing a speech, which paralleled what most of the introducing senators had already said, only it would come from my own mouth. But now, viewing the senators and the audience, my husband sitting behind me, I decided not to take that approach. Instead, I would speak extemporaneously. And I first thanked the president and the senators, those that supported me and those who stood in opposition. And then:

"Last night I sat for hours preparing a speech that I thought was well organized, hitting on points that I believed would resonate with you and the rest of the American people. The speech is right here in front of me, but just at this moment it occurred to me that speeches are limiting when it comes to events such as this one. There is nothing I can say here that you do not already know. It's all a matter of public record. And that is all I ask that you judge me on—my public record, my service to our country and to humankind. Anything else is extraneous and irrelevant to the job for which I have been nominated, even poisonous to the exchange of ideas and ideals in the public marketplace of debate, the healthy give and take so important for the growth of our democracy. I know some might say they do not know me, but honestly how much can you know me in the next few days? I hope that even as we begin these hearings, you will put everything in the context of my public service, which I trust you will find stands without blemish."

It was difficult to assess the impact of this part of my speech, although the senators sat in sure attention while I spoke. Then the question and answer session began and, as often happens, some senators seemed more interested in expressing their opinions than in hearing mine, spending most of their allotted time either praising my qualities (and covering the now over-familiar terrain of my brilliant mind, embodiment of the American Dream, and tenacity of purpose) or my lack of judicial experience or paucity of expressed opinion on key issues of the day. So for a while I basked in this relatively mild affair of easy questions from senators from the president's party, mostly asking me to expand on my brilliant legal career. A memorable question from that side of the political spectrum came from the chair of the Committee. "It seems to me that you are a very high minded attorney. While you were in private practice you represented The Knights of the Latter Order. I know many have scratched their heads over this, but I think it goes to show your fair mindedness. I don't know that I would have done it, but to all who are wondering, can you tell us why you did it?"

Not again. Much as a loathed this question, here was an opportunity. "Well Senator Mendez," I began, "one of the reasons I went to law school is the firm belief that everyone deserves access to the courts. By everyone I mean everyone. I believe that is the only way to guarantee trust in the judicial system, to demonstrate that everyone has equal access to it, even those that we strongly disagree with. It is up to the members of the legal system to uphold this principle, without which the courts will lose their credibility as a linchpin of American democracy. That would by itself undermine the foundations of our democracy. When I decided to represent The Knights of the Latter Order, that is what I was doing—playing my part without regard to my own personal beliefs. Of course, for obvious reasons, I strongly disagree with them and what they represent and advocate. But I have to put personal feeling aside as a practitioner before our courts and avail myself to it with my knowledge and skills."

The senator nodded. "And I think that demonstrates to all who wonder whether you are going to be blinded by ideology or personal feeling, that you will, as you have demonstrated, put aside all personal feeling in interpreting the law. And we all know and I think I can mention it as a matter of public knowledge that you defended a man accused of genocide, despite your own suffering in the genocide, the loss of your family. What an admirable quality."

But a more memorable period ensued when a senator from the opposition asked me, "It baffles me that you'd go to such lengths to defend such organizations and people. And I'm not sure I buy your reason. Anyone deserves a defense? Would you defend the devil if he were put before a court of law?"

"Senator," I answered, "I think the question is, would you deny the devil his day in court under our democratic system if he were brought before a court of law? If the answer is that he deserves his day in court, then I think he is entitled to legal representation; he is entitled to a defense."

"And you'd be willing to defend him?"

"Well, Senator, if he asked me to defend him, I would have to assess the merits of his case solely in connection with the particular accusation brought against him. My decision will depend on the merits of the case at hand."

"You *will* defend Satan."

I leaned forward. "I didn't say that, Senator. A defense only is about the particular law at issue. And just so we're clear, the point is that everyone deserves a lawyer and that a lawyer's responsibility is to provide the best defense he or she can put up in court; it has nothing to do with defending the person's beliefs."

The chair interjected to say that the senator's time was up, but this was soon followed by an opposing senator's line of questioning on judicial philosophy. "Do you consider yourself an originalist or constructionalist?" she asked.

"I don't believe in such pigeon-holing or labeling, senator," I responded. "I believe in applying the law equally to all in the interest of justice and fairness."

"So at any point in time the law rules. So if the law is that you can own slaves, would you apply it?"

"The law does not so state, Senator."

"What if it did?"

"I would rather not answer hypothetical questions."

"You just answered one regarding the defense of Satan. And this is not a hypothetical. Need I remind you that at some point it was legal to own slaves? Would you uphold such laws at the time?"

I didn't answer immediately, letting lapse several seconds. I leaned forward. "I would let the dead past bury its dead. I prefer to live in the present, and in the present, senator, this is a hypothetical question."

"Let me put it this way. The question is whether you would uphold a law even if it is clear that it's an unjust law."

"Again, senator, that is too abstract for me to answer. I need a concrete law in order to answer that question."

367

"You just won't answer the question, I can see, and I have to say that your responses do not leave me with much confidence."

The first day's hearings ended with routine questions about my opinions on gay rights and the right to die, both of which I dodged as being too hypothetical. But the fireworks ignited outside of the room. The headlines emblazoned in many Internet news items and in the newspapers the following day were variations of one theme:

CHIEF JUSTICE NOMINEE PREPARED TO DEFEND SATAN

The view of many, though not all, radio commentators was that I had made a fatal faux pas by admitting sympathies for Satan. On the TV news also, this theme kept receiving fuel with one pundit after another decrying my stance, its loathsomeness, some calling for the president to withdraw my nomination and others predicting that it was only a matter of hours before the president realized his error and did so. Only a handful of commentators debunked this negative outburst, agreeing that under the American system of justice, everyone, no matter how despicable, deserved legal representation. After a few hours of watching the news, I was too emotionally exhausted to continue. I went to bed early, but I barely slept as I replayed the day's events, wondering why I had not labeled the question on defending the devil as abstract and not answered it. The pain in my belly region was intense, but I also felt something like a wash of warmth within my belly, something I'd never experienced before and for reasons that defied my understanding I found it reassuring.

The way to the hearings the next day were dotted with protests holding various signs:

LUCIFER'S DAUGHTER
DEFENDER OF SATAN
SATANIC JUSTICE
JUSTICE SATAN
MADAM LUCIFER

And some had played on an earlier theme by drawing me in caricature with two horns and a goatee on the chin, the breasts grossly exaggerated. "Pay no attention to this, Shama," Juju said. It was only my resolve that I had to become a justice of the Court, that I belonged just as

368

much as anyone else, the echo of Talitha cumi, that kept me from phoning Dwayne to inform him that I would withdraw my nomination. I don't deserve this, I'd mentally noted—a mental note that registered strongly on my emotional scale. No one deserves this.

The second day produced much of the same, with perfunctory questions and equally moderated answers that revealed nothing. And then the issue turned to abortion as an opposing senator asked, "What is your view of the legal status of the unborn?"

"Outside of the context of an actual case, the question is too abstract for me to answer."

"I will rephrase the question. Do you believe life begins at conception?"

"Again, senator, I think that's too much of an abstraction."

"I think it's a simple question deserving of a simple answer. Do you, Shama Badu, believe that life begins at conception? Yes or no? Tell me what Shama Badu the person believes."

"Senator," I said, pausing, leaning forward. "In the course of my public duty as a judge, my personal views are irrelevant. What matters is the law of the land."

"Okay, so applying the law of the land today, what is the legal status of the fetus?"

"Sir, again, I must not answer such questions in abstraction."

"I'm getting tired of the word abstract. My God, can't you answer a simple question for once? I'm sure if I were to give you a scenario, you would respond that you can't answer a hypothetical."

"Senator," I leaned forward again, "I can understand your frustration, but as a judge, I walk within a narrow range in which I must apply the law to specific facts before me. It would be irresponsible for me to answer hypothetical questions or questions in the abstract and potentially prejudge issues that may come before me."

"Are there no settled laws in this land?"

"There are."

"What is the settled law on abortion?"

"Senator, again, I hate to say this, but I can't..."

"Answer an abstraction. Let me complete it for you." The senator threw his arms in the air, leaned back in his chair for seconds and then leaned forward and asked, "Let me be clear. You do believe in precedent and deference to settled law?"

"Yes, sir. The principle of stare decisis is critical to the administration of justice. Cases are not to be overturned lightly. It is adherence to that principle that builds confidence in the law and in the belief of the citizenry's ability to rely on the law from day to day in their private and business affairs. Without it, the uncertainty will undermine confidence in the law and the law will become an impediment rather than an important part of progress."

"Is that to say that settled law can never be overturned?"

"No, senator, what I'm saying is that there has to be a compelling, very convincing basis, to overturn precedent. But in no case is it to be based on the judge's personal views."

"Like what? What circumstances could cause you to overturn precedent?"

"A change in the statute on which a case was previously decided is an example."

"But could there be other basis for doing so?"

"Yes, sir."

"Such as?"

"Well, if the initial decision was based on faulty suppositions, for example, say it was decided on wrong facts…"

"Is that not to suggest that the judge's point of view determines outcomes? If the law has otherwise not changed but the judge's perception of assumptions has changed…"

"Never the judge's subjective perception, but on say objectively falsified assumptions…"

"That sounds like judicial constructionism to me."

"No, senator, I'm just answering your specific question. It has nothing to do with so called judicial philosophy or a judge's opinion, but on facts assumed and then proved false."

And with that, another day of hearings ended and I wasn't sure of my performance—wishing to say more but handicapped by the need to stay within the box that would confirm me so that I could gain the freedom to express myself on the Court. Juju faithfully cheered me, dutiful in his presence with me during the hearings and at home, but keeping his distance to provide me with the space I needed to keep my sanity, but just enough for me to know I wasn't alone. And then the phone calls I received from Fiona to laud me or from the Baileys to express their pride or from Ama to assure her support...they were the chorus, the cheer that didn't bring the sense of doom that lurked. Even Dwayne and Senator John Owens assured me I was performing well under the circumstances, Dwayne reminding me of the fifty plus one goal to nomination. All I needed was not to alienate the senators whose votes were assured as of the moment.

It was with this assurance that I attended the third and final day of hearings, the echoing words of Dwayne my balm: "We have the votes. Just stay the course and we will be fine." And so amid the ongoing demonstrations equating me with Lucifer, I would stay the course. Amid the assault of occasional self-doubt notwithstanding my resolve, I would stay the course. One more day and it would be over.


It was not a day of particular note as it seemed the senators who wanted to ask me further questions had resigned themselves to the reality that I wasn't going to provide specifics, and were aware that, absent some form of catastrophe, I was on course for nomination. They simply continued to lament my lack of specific answers and their frustration at my reticence. If there was anything of particular interest on the third day, they were the questions posed by Senator Norwood, who had been quiet throughout the hearings.

"Judge Badu," the senator began, "I couldn't help but notice the demonstrations on my way here today. I'm sure you've noticed them?"

"Yes, sir, Senator, I have."

"They are saying some nasty things about you."

I nodded.

"What do you say to them?"

"They have a right to express their opinions, including their protest."

"Would you say that they have reason to worry?"

"None, senator."

"In other words, their protests are baseless?"

"They believe they have a legitimate basis to complain, I'm sure. But if they examine my record, they'll realize there's no reason to worry."

"Well, I think a lot of it, the protests I mean, turn on the matter of religion. The First Amendment provides that Congress shall make no law respecting an establishment of religion, or prohibiting the free exercise thereof. Now these are words, I know, that are subject to various interpretations. But people take it seriously. Very seriously. And so, now comes the question, or the concern, taken so seriously by many to the extent that they seek to protest your nomination to the highest court of the land. They worry that your religion will cloud your opinion on the Court."

Pause or respond immediately? To pause would mean I had to think of my response to this crucial mater. I didn't allow a pause to infect opinions. "Not at all, Senator," I said. I wanted to ask him, what religion are we talking about here? Instead, I said, "I have more than demonstrated my ability to separate personal feeling and inclinations from my legal responsibilities. I have been able to put personal feeling aside in defending The Knights of the Latter Order and in defending a man accused of genocide, when I myself was a victim of that genocide. Let me add that in the true spirit of American ideals and consistent with the First Amendment that you so kindly quoted, I should be free to practice my religion without fear of public opprobrium or even rebuke. My religion should not be an impediment to any office of the land. To hold otherwise would fly in the face of the very Constitution that we have all sworn to uphold."

After the hearings, the first words from Juju to me were, "Why didn't you just tell them that you 're not a Moslem?"

"That would be expedient, I know, but I am standing up for a principle here."

"Shama, sometimes I wonder how you can be so high minded. It doesn't hurt to just say the truth. That's what you would be doing here. Now you have the whole country thinking you're a Moslem."

"Standing up for principles is important, Juju."

"This is about your nomination as Chief Justice, Shama. You will have all the time on the Court to uphold your principles."

I shook my head and said, "Come on, Juju, I don't need this at this time, please." He spoke no more about that matter.

Dwayne called to congratulate me. "I couldn't make it to the hearings, but I was watching on TV. You did great with that response. It's only a matter of course now, Justice Badu."

"And the demonstrators?"

"Those will die by the weekend."

I had to hope so.

Mustapha called me next. "I watched you today, Shama. You are something else, you know. You could very easily have told them you are a Christian woman, but you didn't. You know, Shama, I know I have been stalling about your invitation to come to church with you. I have never felt comfortable visiting a church. But after watching you, I think I very well want to come."

"Let's set a specific date, then."

"Name the date and I will be there."

"I am trying to lie low a bit now. How about the first Sunday after the Senate votes on my nomination?"

"Name the place and I will be there."

With the police detail outside our house, Juju and I watched the witnesses testify before the Judiciary Committee the next day. The witnesses against me included lawyers who opined that I lacked the requisite experience to sit on the Supreme Court, let alone be its Chief Justice, and professors of law who lamented my lack of written scholarship against which I could be assessed. "You will be rolling the dice if you confirm her," said one bespectacled professor of constitutional law. "We don't know where she stands on the important questions of the day. Nor was she forthcoming in her answers before you. There are other equally or even more brilliant lawyers and judges whose opinions are in the public domain against which you can assess their approach to judging and their opinions on critical matters. I would have hoped the president would nominate one such." And then there were some of my former colleagues at the US Attorney's office, including Danielle Leblanc, who opined that I was too biased, even overzealous, in my prosecution of men accused of spousal and child abuse at the expense of the facts. This, they feared, clouded my judgment and signaled the kind of biased justice she would be if confirmed.

Witnesses arguing for my confirmation included police officers who testified that I was a strong, fair minded ally in law enforcement, a mayor who indicated likewise, several US Attorneys who praised my brilliance and lack of bias, and even Justice Sitter, who extolled my virtues as a brilliant legal mind, one that would add great value to the Court. I knew that the game had to be played, for none of the witnesses would really change any minds, except with the thin possibility of the testimony of Rod Trammel of The Knights. Bob Sneider had called to tell me that, despite his public pronouncements, he would be willing to testify on my behalf. At first, Dwayne had rejected this. We can't trust the man and what he'll say, but I had insisted. "I think I can read him. I have a good sense about this. Let him testify." After interviewing him, Dwayne acquiesced. And true to my expectation, the man exuded confidence as he told the senators that when he needed help the law firm of Ward, Oliver, Reznick & Krezinski had provided him with what they called one of their best legal minds. "Do you think it was because of her race? That it would look good to have her represent you?"

"I don't know about that, but I do know that she was fair to me, open minded. And she did a great job."

"Sir," another senator said, "I will defend your right to free speech, but if your organization had its way, Shama Badu would be returned to Africa."

"That's right senator, but that's not what this is about. I'm just telling you what I know."

"Is this a quid pro quo? She defends you before the Supreme Court and your conscience pricks you to stand up for her to get on the Court."

"You can call it what you want, senator, but that is not so. I really didn't want to do this, but I thought I ought to stand up for the truth."

Later, I called Bob Sneider to get Rod Trammel's phone number. I called him later in the night. "Thank you for speaking up for me," I said.

"You're welcome, ma'am. You helped me once. I thought I'd pay back the favor."

"Oh, so the senator was right? You're just paying back a favor?"

"I will be honest with you, ma'am. Do I think you're qualified to sit on the court? Absolutely. I have seen your work firsthand. And that's all I testified to. But do I think you ought to be in this country? No and if I had my way you would be on the first plane back to Africa."

"That is such a contradiction."

"Perhaps, but I too have my principles."

"I see," I said. "Well, thanks."

I wasn't going to try and psychoanalyze the man's logic, although when I reconsidered it, could a neutral observer not have reached a similar conclusion about my decision to represent The Knights?

I sighed after this call. It had been a difficult four days, and also an emotionally challenging period since the nomination. But I had to believe that the protests would die down, I would be once again be able to move freely without a police escort and I'd be confirmed and serve my time successfully as a Supreme Court Chief Justice. Juju grinned at me. "What?" I asked.

"For the first time in a long time, you are smiling."

I wasn't even conscious of the smile.


The next day, I learned that the Judiciary Committee had sent my nomination to the full Senate without a clear recommendation. The vote had split seven-seven. "What happened?" I asked Dwayne.

"I'm baffled, Shama. We were expecting a nine-five vote with all our members plus Senator Owens in favor and all the opposition senators against it. But at the very end, we lost two of our own. We didn't find out until the very last minute when they informed us they were changing their votes."

"Why?"

"They are in some tough states. They're watching their seats, you know. They're afraid voting for you would hurt them."

"I'm in trouble, am I not?"

"Don't worry. We can't let this happen again. The president is furious, as you can imagine, and he is now more heavily involved, working the phones like crazy to make sure we get the needed votes."

"What about a filibuster?"

"No one has threatened it yet."

"Will they?"

"They could, but we'll have to cross that bridge if we ever get to it. But you can rest assured that we're working very hard on this."

"I thought confirmation was guaranteed."

"That's what we all thought, but in politics, things can change at any time."

And, once again, I envisaged a difficult battle ahead. The pain in my belly region intensified, but so did the counterbalancing warmth within.

# Ten

After the split vote referral to the Senate, I'd bided my time, chasing after Dwayne for assurances, and he gave me plenty. My chances were looking better each day, and with the full Senate debate set to begin in a few weeks, Dwayne assured me that I had sixty senators in my favor. "It is now more than ever a matter of formality," he said. "The president has really worked the Senate."

Senator John Owens also called to encourage me. "I'm sorry I've been unable to bring more members of my party along, but this is politics, and sometimes that prevails over reason. But from what I can tell, you're on well on your way to the Court."

So I was assured of confirmation once again, although I remembered Dwayne's words that in politics anything could happen. A pity that such an august institution of law would be subject to whimsical political currents. But if ever I could have optimism, this was the time.

But exactly three days before the full Senate hearings were to begin, unearthed revelations put everything in imminent collapse. I'd been feeling noxious for a while, so I'd woken up that morning and taken a self-administered pregnancy test. It was positive. I smiled, buoyant, but I'd tell Juju later, once I had a doctor confirm it. I didn't want to disappoint him with false hope. I was dancing heartily when I went downstairs to get breakfast, but I puked on the morning newspaper, which I cleaned up and read anyway.

I panicked.

Not knowing what I'd say to Juju, I hid the newspaper before Juju came downstairs. He ate quickly and left. I was glad he left home early that day because the phone began to ring non-stop. I didn't pick any of them. The only one I picked was the call from the White House.

"I'm sorry about this," Dwayne said "It appears to have been an FBI leak."

I could barely speak. "So you knew about this? The president knew all along and he still nominated me?"

"Yes. As far as he's concerned, this is irrelevant. It could have happened to anybody. And this was so many years ago, Shama."

"I am ruined."

"No, you're not."

"I am withdrawing my nomination. I can't put the president through this."

"Calm down, Shama. Take a deep breath. We will get through this."

The president called minutes later. "Mr. President," I said, "I am so sorry for this. I'm not sure this is the best way to do this, but please… I think it's time to withdraw my nomination?"

"Shama," he said, "if you are willing to fight on, so am I. I know this isn't pleasant for you, but one of the reasons why I admire you, one of the reasons why I chose you is that you are such a fighter. Your life history attests to this. Withdrawing will be at odds with the woman I admire. Why don't you think through this and we'll speak later? If you still want to withdraw, I will understand, but I want you to promise to give it serious thought. Can you promise me that?"

"Yes, sir." I was barely audible.

"Good. Stay strong."

What assumptions had the president made? Did he not know that I'd kept this secret even from my own husband? How had the FBI found out? I picked up the newspaper and once more read the headlines:

BADU ACCUSED OF ILLEGAL ABORTION

The way they'd phrased it, it was as if I'd performed abortion on someone else. I paced the family room, thinking, concerned, confused. And then I heard Juju pull up into the driveway. Why was he back home so soon? Not now. It was not even noon. Did he know? He must.

Juju opened the door and walked up to me. His brow was furrowed, his lips tightened, his eyes glaring. I wanted to walk closer and hug him. What was he thinking? "So your husband has to find out, after twelve years of marriage… he has to find out from a reporter that you once committed abortion?" He'd spoken calmly, as was his style, but his anger was so readable, or perhaps it was disappointment or perhaps it was defeat or perhaps it was all three.

Tears fell down his cheeks.

Tears fell down my cheeks.

"I'm so sorry," I said.

"So it's true."

I nodded.

"And you couldn't tell me this? You couldn't tell me something so important?"

"I'm sorry, Juju. Please forgive me. I know I should have told you, but I was afraid."

"Afraid of what?" He raised his voice.

"I was afraid you wouldn't want me...I was so ashamed.'

"Now it all makes sense. Our... your inability to carry a child to full term. I have been a fool."

Juju turned and walked away. He climbed up the stairs and went to our bedroom. I had no energy. I collapsed into the couch. But I reckoned I had to pull myself up in order to address the harm evidently wreaked on Juju. I couldn't afford to let linger this hurt so palpable. With as much energy as I could muster, I climbed up the stairs and went to the bedroom. He'd put a suitcase on the bed and packed a few clothes and other toiletry necessities.

"Honey, what are you doing?" I asked.

"I can't stay here."

"Juju, please. We'll work through this. Please don't leave. Please. I need you."

"I'm out of here."

"No, please." I went to him and held him, my arms encircling his bosom. "I'm sorry. I'm so sorry. Please forgive me."

"Your mouth stinks," he said and removed my arms as he picked up the suitcase and walked out.

I fell on the bed, the tempo of my weeping increasing as I heard Juju drive away. It was as though my world was coming to an end, and if I would surrender to death without guilt, I would have gladly done so. What pain had I caused Juju? What had I brought upon myself? I lay on the bed for hours; now quiet, now sobbing. I wasn't a drinker and the only liquor we kept in the house was for entertaining guests and the occasional wine we had with a meal or on special occasions. But I felt an urge to consume as much of the liquor available in the house. I went downstairs to the liquor cabinet and retrieved a bottle of whiskey. But at the moment when I was about to take a swig, I remembered Jojo Badu's alcoholism after Fiona's infidelity and the disastrous aftermath, and I remembered the that day of the abortion that was making the news, and I couldn't put the bottle to my mouth. Instead, I sat back in the couch. I felt pain, not just emotionally, but the beginning of what felt like a stomachache. I touched my belly region and my fingers felt the scar (now greatly diminished) of my surgery to remove the protrusion on my belly many years back.

At the same time, the president called. "I know I asked you to think about this, but this thing is going viral. We need to fight back hard. I am ready to do this battle, but before I do so, I need to know that you're in it. I won't force you to do so, but you must decide, Shama."

"I'm not so sure, Mr. President."

"Come on, Shama, more than ever, this is the time to arise. I know you are a fighter."

Arise. Fighter. Talitha cumi.

I didn't feel like a fighter, but even at that moment of despair, I was keenly aware that feeling belied my history. I wasn't sure it was the right decision, but with the president on the phone, waiting for me, extolling my fighting spirit, I had to fight on. He had risked so much already and he was willing to even risk more. "Thank you, Mr. President," I said. "I am in it to the finish." I wasn't even sure I was the one who said those words. From where had they come?

"Great! We win or lose together, but we will fight hard. We will be in touch."

I wasn't sure how the president intended to fight but the man had spoken with such confidence that I could draw hope from him. Still reeling from Juju's departure, I began to return earlier phone calls selectively. Fiona told me to stand strong. Could I ever do any wrong in the eyes of my mother-in-law? Fiona blasted Juju when I told her he'd left. "He's foolish to leave you at such a critical time. I wish I could get a hold of him so I could talk some sense into him. Mother knows best. He'll be back." The Baileys expressed regret that this was all being blown out of proportion. George and Fiona Harris echoed the president. I had to fight on. When I told Ama her brother had left the house, she said she had a few days off from work and was flying to DC. "You need support, Shama and we can't give up now," she said. "They win if we do." All these assurances without Juju's voice. I was a little more hopeful, but still apprehensive.

And as she had promised, Ama arrived that night. "I don't care what you've done, my brother shouldn't be leaving you at this time."

"You know, Ama, the one thing I had hoped for was to make sure that he was always happy, but I have failed miserably and in a way I can't blame him."

"He will return, wherever he is. He is family. Every family goes through stuff. In the end, it makes the family stronger. I remember we had to go through some serious reconciliation, especially after Dad died. I have never shared this with you, Shama, but perhaps it will put things in better perspective for you, this bond of the family and why we can't leave you alone at this particular time."

Ama recounted what had happened—why family stayed together:

First, Juju called Ama on a Saturday afternoon that was chillingly quiet as a cemetery.

"It's been a while," Ama said.

"I know. Been busy, but I'm doing fine. You? Taking care of yourself?"

"Sure. I've been busy, too…"

"Ama, I need to tell you something…"

"Sure, Juju, what's up?"

"I'm quitting school."

"What? Why?"

"I want to go to Africa."

"Juju, what are you talking about? You don't need to quit school to go to Africa."

"Ama, I want this to be real, not just a quick touristy type thing. I'm talking about living and working among the people."

"Have you really thought this through, Juju? We haven't been back there in ages, not since we were very little and Dad took us. We don't really know the place."

"But that's what I'm talking about. Isn't it a shame we don't know squat about an important part of ourselves? I've got to do this."

"If that's what you want to do, Juju."

"It is. But do me a favor, will you? Don't tell Mom. I'll tell her at the right time."

"You got it."

Ama was ambivalent about the decision. Going to Africa sounded romantic, but it wasn't a choice she'd make. Had not Grandpa George lived there and returned to America? Had not Grandma Sissi left to follow Grandpa George to America? But Juju was his own man. He'd always been different in his own weird sort of way. If only she knew Juju's journey, perhaps, she'd appreciate it better? There was meaning in that name Juju: magic, something supernatural. She remembered her father saying it had been her mother's suggestion that they name him Juju, a Ghanaian word she had fallen in love with, just the sound of it, the power of it. It had stayed in her mind, working its supernatural tricks in her memory. Then she got pregnant for the second time. It wasn't an easy pregnancy. Compared to Ama's, this one was torture. She was sick most of the time, became lethargic, vomited many times, and was in constant pain. Her husband had said as a joke, "We should get you some juju." And that confirmed the sanctity of her memory: Juju.

"If I don't die before this baby is born, we will name him Juju."

"You're not going to die. But Juju?" Jojo asked. "You're not serious."

"I'm dead serious."

"Juju isn't a person's name. It's a description of something sinister, supernatural. It's black magic."

"Black magic? I suppose that's bad because it's black? Would it be better if it was white magic?"

Her husband had hoped then that she'd change her mind, but she insisted on Juju, so Juju it became. Juju Badu.

Ama worried about Juju's last request: *Don't tell Mom.* He must have his reasons and whatever they were she couldn't quarrel with them. She was still miffed at her mother anyway for her affair.

And then the phone rang again. "Hi Ama, its Mom."

She said nothing for seconds, sorting her thoughts.

"How are you, Mom?"

The level of conversation was distilled to the point of sounding like a first encounter between strangers. Fiona sighed heavily, signaling the significance of the proposition she was about to put before her daughter. "Ama," she said, "I need to ask you a favor."

Favor? First Juju, now her mother.

"Yes, Mom."

"Ama, I know you and I have had our problems. I know things haven't been as smooth as they should be. I know I've done things that have hurt you, and I'm really sorry ... So much has happened. I ... I want us to be family again, you and me and Juju. I want us to be like we were before."

"I'm listening, Mom."

"I want you to move in with me," Fiona said. "Come back home. Please."

"I can't do that, Mom."

"Oh, Ama, think about it. I know you're a big girl now. You'll have all the freedom you want. It's a big house. I won't interfere in your affairs. I just miss you so much and I'm so alone these days. Listen, if it doesn't work out, you can leave as you wish."

"I just can't do it, Mom."

"Please, Ama."

"If it's that important to you, why don't you move in with me?"

"But it's much bigger here. Your place is so small."

"Yes, but it's my place, Mom."

For long seconds Fiona said nothing. Ama could imagine her thinking hard. And then Fiona asked, "Are you sure it will be okay for me to move in with you?"

Ama was stunned that Fiona would seriously consider the offer. But it had been made. She couldn't retreat from it now. "Yes," she said. "Sure."

"I'm sorry, Ama. I don't mean to impose. Forget it. It was a bad idea."

But Ama was afraid. Her father was gone and the guilt of putting him in a nursing home still lingered. Could she afford to live with another loss if she shut her home from her mother? "Mom," she said, "It's a great idea. I'd love for you to move in with me?"

"Are you sure, Ama?"

"Absolutely."

"I really appreciate this, honey."

"When are you coming?"

For the first time since her father's death, Ama smiled for her mother.

But these fast paced events, where were they leading? Juju going to Africa, her mother coming to stay with her.

The experiment seemed to have worked. It hadn't started so smoothly. Her mother had become used to big spaces, roomier rooms, an independence not tampered even by the supposed mutual dependence of marriage. But moving in with her grown daughter on those famous figurative bended knees, she was suddenly faced with a one-bedroom apartment, a small living room, one bath and a small kitchen. It had been too long since she'd had to accommodate such meager accommodations. The claustrophobia partly nourished her discomfort, and she told Ama only half jokingly that she had thoughts of grabbing her and fleeing back to the mansion she'd temporarily abandoned in order to bury her ghosts. But then she thought aloud that the way to bury a ghost (Juju) was to reconnect with his living legacies; the way to bury the living ghost (Dante) was to disconnect from its long shadows. Hence, the only way to bury her husband's ghost was to avoid the echoes of a home filled with its heavy memories and live proximate to his progeny; the only way to bury Dante was to avoid him. Ama didn't appreciate that her father was being referred to a ghost and mentioned in the same breath as Dante. She had to fight her urges to rebuke her mother, afraid that she was too vulnerable and that the wrong word could send her down the brink, widen the chasm with her mother. She managed it with silence and thought.

It would be a gradual effort, a matter of time. All she could do was create the milieu for her mother to grow out of her shell. As though she knew the claustrophobia (both figurative and literal) Fiona felt, Ama did it by giving her mother as much space as she could, but with companionship. There was the paradox! But who would be so base as to dwell on contradictions in such delicate moments of rebirth between mother and daughter, moments when trust competed for love against the robust currents of pain and betrayal, moments when the seed that had to grow lay under the siege of what had already happened? It was too delicate to ponder such esoteric weaknesses.

Ama would make sure she had breakfast made ready for Fiona before they each left for work, but it was a silent time, untainted by the stress of conversation. Ama was holding the hand, which she wished Fiona would see just as much as she wished Fiona wouldn't. Ama would rush home early to prepare dinner, again eaten in near silence. And then she'd rent a movie and they'd sit and watch it together.

Even the sightless must notice this foundation so firmly laid, waiting for the script of reunion, after the chasm caused by Fiona's infidelity, to be written and staged on its pillars without fear of failure.

Slowly this two-pronged approach fructified—the silence enabling Fiona to enjoy Ama's presence without erecting defenses, without guarded speech, until the comfort in her daughter's presence became complete. Soon Fiona decided to take the initiative, rushing home early from work and preparing the evening meal before Ama got home, song singing when her daughter got home. As they ate, Ama could discern Fiona eyeing her nervously as though in a remote area for a tryst with a paramour.

One day, when Ama returned home, the meal was made, the candles lit, the table set, the wine readied.

"Wow, Mom," Ama said, "I had no idea you were waiting for a date."

"You are my date tonight, honey." Fiona kissed Ama on the forehead and if Ama could blush, she would have blossomed red. "How was your day?"

"So so." Ama was still struggling with the script being written, so bold yet so tender.

"Well, have a seat. Feed your hunger, sweetie."

Fiona pulled the chair for Ama.

"Mom, this is delicious."

"How do you think I won your father over?" Fiona said. This must have slipped out without thought. The allusion chilled the air, for the implications were still too thorny and they hadn't yet cleared that field completely. But that was merely a brief setback. Fiona went on, "What do you say we go out this weekend, you and me? Catch a movie, go shopping, anything."

"I'd like that."

"More wine?"

Ama nodded. Fiona poured her another glass. The courtship was deliberate, but it was devoid of guile, which made it admirable and more potent. Ama was falling in love with her mother again. It's been asked whether a woman's tender love can cease towards the child she bore. Equally germane is whether a woman's tender love can cease towards the mother who bore her, even if she may momentarily forgetful be. So perhaps it had been a mere temporary suspension of a love that was now being fully restored, the rust simply being polished off.

Ama watched the wrinkles around her mother's eyes deepen as she laughed when Ama joked about getting used to such dinners. Ama watched her mother sip wine and look over the glass at her, the way she wiped the corner of her mouth with a napkin, the way she reached over to pour more wine and the way she seemed to love doing it. Whoever would be sitting there in Ama's chair would also be in love. Utterly. Perhaps *seductress is an inapt word*, for that seems to conjure something untoward. But this was righteous seduction.

And then Ama reached out her hands—like a lover toward a lover—and took her mother's hands in hers. "Thanks, Mom," she said. "That was really sweet of you, but Mom you can't do this again…"

"Why, honey? Don't you like it?"

"Like it? I love it. But you should let me take care of you now, okay?"

"Ama…"

"Mom, you live in my place now and you have to do as I say."

"Yes, Ma'am." Fiona did a salute.

They laughed. The script was done and it was powerful. From then on, all that was needed were minor revisions to mold it into perfection. After dinner, they retired to the couch. "What do you want to do?" Ama asked.

"Come here, baby," Fiona said, "Let's just talk."

After she finished telling the story, Ama said, "I have no doubt that those few days with Mom were important to help stabilize her. She needed me and I was glad I was there for her. Who knows what would have happened if I had turned her down?"

Ama Badu hugged me many times. Cooked for me and reassured me that all would be well. When she left the following day, she had left a part of her spirit with me. I would live on it like a scavenger dwells on leftovers. But I could tell she had told me the story as a way of reassuring me that Juju would return and perhaps, more importantly, to provide another glimpse into the Badu family—the solidarity between the women—and that no matter what happened she and her mother would support me, even if there were temporary hiccups. You have a family for life, she seemed to be saying to me, demonstrated with the sacrifice she'd made by flying from Boston to visit with me.

# Eleven

What would happen next? Dwayne called to tell me that the president was back lobbying senators to stand with him. I turned on the TV. If the president was lobbying, perhaps he wasn't doing so hard enough. Already, two senators who'd previously announced they'd vote for me had withdrawn their vote for feeling, in their words, "deceived." Another senator said he'd wait and see until he got all the facts before deciding whether to change his vote. Senator John Owens called me. I apologized to him.

"You have my support," he said. "I will speak with the president. We just need to tell your side of the story."

Indeed we had to tell a story and this time I could ill afford to disguise the truth. I would let it out and frontally face the blast of the steam.

And in the subsequent two days or so the media became a loud marketplace, as though haggling over my nomination and the shift in fortunes, with senators defending me (this was inconsequential and happened so long ago), and senators blasting me (if nothing at all, I had hidden a critical detail of my past and I couldn't be trusted, especially on issues of abortion). The president insisted publicly that I was still his candidate and that he stood by me, which his press secretary echoed continually as the press pestered him with questions: Did the president know before he made the nomination? When did he know it if not before the nomination? Why didn't he tell the public? All irrelevant, said the press secretary. "What is important is the person Shama Badu is at the moment. All these other matters are a needless distraction from her worth."

The chair of the Judiciary Committee then announced that the Committee would reopen the hearings to offer "Shama Badu an opportunity to present her side of the story. That's the fairest thing to do."

Through Dwayne, the White House informed me of a date for the reopened hearings, which was to be the next Tuesday. I had four days to prepare. On the point of emotional exhaustion, I clung on to Ama's words of encouragement, replaced her with me and Fiona with Juju in the telling of reconciliation she had shared with me. Whenever I found my mind

389

drifting, I played that story again and again and this time Juju was re-seducing me and I was embracing him and something warm spread within me. This way, I managed to endure a four-hour mock session that The White House put me through. I answered the questions they anticipated would be asked at the hearings and listened to suggestions from a quickly assembled panel and I resolutely refused to store any answers or suggestions in memory. This will be done my way. If I failed, I failed.

I called all the mutual friends, family and acquaintances I had with Juju. They all claimed they didn't know of his whereabouts. At night, I refused to turn on any light in the house as I sat on the couch in the family room and stared at the turned-off TV. I wondered what the police detail outside was thinking. Then I thought of nothing, except I grieved over Juju's absence and found more comfort in the retelling of Ama Badu's version of her mother's seduction. Talitha cumi—I let these words hover in my mind. Besides these, I would not allow any alien thoughts to corrupt the story I was going to expose from memory. I left my vigil on the couch only to eat cold meals, visit the bathroom or sleep. And occasionally I would walk briefly around the house to stretch. I didn't shower, and I knew my body odor was turning soar.

On the Monday, the day before I was scheduled to reappear before it, the Judiciary Committee opened its floor to a new witness whose testimony was timed to precede mine. I watched on TV as the cameras focused on Dr. Gracia Marquez's face. She had aged considerably, a little leaner, now completely gray, and much wrinkled. She presented a grandmotherly figure, worthy of respect, full of credibility. I wasn't sure exactly what she would say but, given her credentials and demeanor, I already knew all would accept her testimony as sacrosanct. Besides, why would she lie? It would be impossible to impugn her integrity. Of all those who could have come forward, I'd never expected Dr. Marquez to be the one. Prof. Bailey had called me to assure me he was as surprised as I was. "I feel betrayed," he said. "We kinda lost touch over the years. This is the first time I'm hearing of her in over ten years."

I now focused on the face that had looked at me once with such kindness and, as her lips began to move, I was transported with Dr.

Marquez to the past.  First, the doctor thanked the senators for the opportunity, as she put it, to "clear her conscience."

"Was it your intention to testify against Shama Badu?" one senator asked.

"No, Senator, it wasn't.  The FBI contacted me a while back.  They were doing a background check on Ms. Badu.  I think she was being considered at the time for a US Attorney position or something.  They asked me a few questions about her, if I had once treated her for abdominal pains.  I told them the truth, that it wasn't for abdominal pains."

"What did you treat her for?"

"Abortion, Senator."

"You performed the abortion?"

I turned off the TV.

Now I had no fear.  Now I had fear...

On the morning of my scheduled testimony, I woke up early and showered for almost an hour.  I dressed carefully, picking a conservative black skirt suit.  I was determined, but I also needed some reassurance.  I painfully wished for Juju but took more comfort in Ama's encouragement.  After I retold what she'd told me one more time, I remembered that I still had Jojo Badu's notebook-diary.  I picked it up one more time, acknowledging the lessons the dead paterfamilias had imparted from the grave.  I flipped through it, settling on the end, which I had ignored for the most part.  But as I held it one more time in my hand, it was if he was speaking to me, asking me to read the end, and as I began to reread it, as I put things I had learned together I could see why he had started his notebook-diary with his own anticipated demise and ended it with *his* beginning, which must have been as retold to him or as he'd imagined it.  I focused on his words:

> There they are like the smoke of night.  Clouds hover clear without the threat of a downpour, a piercing contrast to the bleakness of the larger space profiling them.  They don't seem to move or waver, appearing to be anchored by glitters in the darkness.  Then there's the moon, also resplendent.  My mother enjoys the heavenly

canopy as she looks farther down to a neem tree. In the moonlight she sees a big circle carved in its bark. Little notches punctuate the circle. She tries to tell which was the first notch and which the last, but in the circular frame, she can't. She seems unable to resolve what is becoming a riddle, but she never wishes the notches lay in a linear line. That would be too simple, too boring. It's been a long night for Mama.

She ought to be happy. It is very quiet, except for the occasional sound of a passing car in the distance, the rush of waters in gutters nearby, the occasional cough from a sleepy throat in one of the adjoining buildings. She runs her hand over her full belly: a child, her child is to be born.

A neighbor walks by, coming from a late job. He looks in Mama's direction, intrigued by the lonesome woman standing in front of her home looking up. He greets her. She responds in kind. And then he moves on. Mama looks at him again. He is an opposite, the opposite personified. He is an old man, almost bent double, his hairs gone completely gray. Yet he is not at rest, still burdened by work. She's visited by a fear that he will die soon; die without relief from the toll of work. But such is his life. She hopes better for her children.

When Mama goes back to the bedroom, Papa is snoring. This, she thinks, is the most remarkable difference between them. She bears what she knows is about to become lively. She feels that which resides in her. She is just about one with it, its fetal machinations. And yet her husband is removed from it all, so peaceably asleep, so uninvolved, even if he's fooled himself into believing he is just as much involved. How could he? This is the superiority of her species at its most profound, she concludes. This is the beginning of her power, this attachment she'd forged with the fetus, an attachment that cannot be severed easily even after the birth.

Now lying down, facing her husband, she sees his face illumined by the lantern she dares not allow to burn too brightly. Mama traces him with her mind's hand. She traces his face and its various contours. Under the sheets, she traces his arms and chests, his now flabby belly. He is a handsome man in many respects. And what she has inside her is a part of him as well. How can she not be joyous? How can she not be hopeful? In her mind, what is to come is the two of them bettered.

Suddenly a pain jars Mama. She refocuses the lens of her thoughts. She knows she can't hide the concern. Despite all the hopes, she fears for what is to come out of her—the pain, the illnesses, the deceits, the heartbreaks; yes, that pain that lines the terrain until the end. She has lived it. She is worried. How can she protect this innocence about to be? Once she gives birth, how can she take all the pain inside her so that the innocence would be protected? To Mama, that worry underscores the absurdity of the parental condition. Mama's worry keeps her awake for a long time, but the memory of the old man returns, soothing her. And Mama knows she has to be careful of the memories she creates, believing that even when memories become irretrievable, they never go away but merely become a part of us. She needs the best memories for her baby's sake.

Morning comes too quickly. It starts with the usual cocks' crows, the waking sounds in the household, the sweeping of the compound (from which she is temporarily exempted), the sound of water splashing over bodies in the bathroom, the smell of boiling porridges and frying dough: collectively, the waking of the household and by extension the town; voices in undertones, throats being cleared of nocturnal phlegm. The sun rises early and very brightly.

The morning has come and gone almost uneventfully that Friday. The clouds are now deeply clear; beyond them is a deep blue. The sunrays seem to fall

393

heavily and lick all shadows off the ground. Even the gutters that run wet shimmer brightly under this onslaught. Papa has taken the day off because he isn't well. He is lying in bed next to his wife when she goes into labor. She calls out to him, although she knows he knows. It is pain that seeks an audience. He panics a little as he goes next door to beg the neighbor to drive Mama to the clinic. The neighbor obliges and drives them to the clinic.

Mama's mind is on the labor unfolding; Papa's is tuned to the dangers. He nearly suffocates at the sight of his wife in such pain. Papa prays and waits as Mama continues to labor and to moan and groan. If he could share her pain, he would have volunteered. He can only wait. It takes two hours. After much pushing, the fetus is no longer a fetus as its head protrudes from between the laboring woman's thighs. It now has no sustenance as when it was shielded within the parasitism of the womb, the interconnectedness that is so dependent on the mother. Now it is unveiled into a world where it will be weaned into its own. The baby emerges in full, its cry breaking the tension in the room. New life. Hope.

The beginning is a beginning. I have just been born. Mate...

Checkmate.

# Twelve

*The beginning is a beginning.*

The senators, even those who had announced that they still supported my nomination, were all grim-faced. I saw no smile. I tried to diffuse this before the hearings commenced but as much as I struggled, I couldn't even effect a smile for the sake of expedience. The chair of the Committee took a sip of water. If I was reading him correctly, he was nervous. He cleared his throat and appeared ready to speak but hesitated for seconds. He checked his wristwatch as if not sure it was time to begin. Then he looked at me and attempted what might have been a smile, even if shorn of deceit it appeared more like a frown. When he finally started speaking, his voice was mellow, unconvincing. "We have heard from you and many others," he addressed me. "So we need not beat an already beaten path. But since we had our hearings, certain allegations have been leveled against you. We all have our opinions, but before the full Senate gets to vote on your nomination, we think the fair thing to do is have you tell your side of the story."

*Your side of the story*—Did they not have a better phrase to describe what I was about to unveil?

"Before I say anything, Mr. Chairman, or submit myself to questions, may I make a brief statement?"

"Go ahead, please."

"Thank you. Mr. Chairman, members of the Committee, first, I have to admit that I would rather not be here today. At least, not like this. But I do appreciate the opportunity you have given me. I cannot begin to say how much of an honor it was for me to be nominated for this position. As you all know, I come from a humble background, although others might disagree with that. In any case, never in my dreams did I ever think I would be given this opportunity. If my beginnings were humble, one thing I have no doubt about is that my background is also dignified. I will not batter my dignity for personal gain nor cower in the face of injustice. Now, in my life, I have made some decisions that I regret, some forced on me, some of my own doing. None of us can claim otherwise. We all make mistakes. I am at peace with my God. On that score, I would hope

395

that you judge me not based on some superhuman standard of perfection, but as a human being, susceptible to error, flawed in many respects even as I try to improve myself, to reach for a better place. I would urge you also to consider what I have done with my life and what I have made of the opportunities given me. Judge me, Senators, as you would like to be judged. I ask for nothing more than that, nor do I ask for anything else. As to the matter for which I am here today, I deeply regret that the Committee was unaware of it before. It is not something that I'm proud of and I have to admit that I have not been forthcoming about it, even if I haven't lied about it. I have not told it to those who did not know when it happened, not even my own husband. And as I speak before you today, that is my deepest regret. You may choose to vote for or against me. As much as I want to be on the Supreme Court and as honored I am to have this opportunity, I can live with your decision, whatever it may be. What I can't live with is the loss of my life partner over this. In other words, Senators, whatever you decide pales in comparison to the judgment of the most important man in my life. Thank you for listening and for your patience."

Silence.

More silence.

Even more silence.

"Thank you, Judge Badu," the chair managed to say. "Now you know what has been said about you that has prompted us to call you back before this Committee. What I would like you to do is address the allegation. In your own words."

I leaned forward and took a sip of water. I closed my eyes and opened them. The world was waiting. If ever I needed to do this, now was the most opportune time. And so slowly but assuredly, I took the Committee into the hitherto unspoken depths of my history.

In my aunt's bathroom, a coat hanger in one hand, I took a swig from the bottle of whiskey I had taken from my aunt's boyfriend, Alexandre Nsengiyumva. It was my first taste of liquor. It burned my mouth and I spat out what I'd attempted to ingest, disgusted by the taste, the burning. I

396

had to be strong for this, though, and so I braced myself to endure. With the next attempt I took my time, taking a sip at a time, my hands shaking so badly I spilled some of the liquor on my dress. Then I continued to take sips, forcing myself to swallow even as the liquid burned my insides. Soon, I was experiencing the effect, feeling as if I had moved to a higher plane of being, where I was losing full control over my faculties, gaining in bravery. My heart, which had beat hard and fast, now seemed more at ease. I put the coat hanger and the bottle of whiskey on the bathroom floor.

I removed my dress and looked into the foggy mirror. In my intoxicated condition, I saw my upper torso's fullness, the enlarged breasts, the darkened nipples and the tears on my face I hadn't realized I'd shed. I studied myself for a few more seconds, hoping to remember this condition as a point of change, change toward what I wasn't sure, but I wanted it to be a change from the organic manifestation of the brutality that had robbed my spirits of so much, the sexual assault by five or so men on the grass in front of my church in Butare.

I removed my underwear. Now in a total state of undress, I took deep breaths before wobblingly getting on my knees, my legs spread as far apart as I could. I took hold of the coat hanger and pulled it tightly together. I brought its tip close to my opened orifice and hesitated. I almost went into a spasm of fear, my body nearly convulsing. I took hold of the bottle of whiskey and took more sips. Whether actually emboldened by the increased inebriation or the perception of it, I felt more ready as I brought the coat hanger closer and as carefully as I could let my shaking hands be, inserted it into my lower parts and gasped, but determined to rid my body of the product of hatred, I pushed farther, winced, but pushed farther still, flinched, prodded back and forth and around, cried aloud, but continued; and then I saw blood oozing from me. And

397

a sharp pain that drew a scream and then a throbbing pain in the unmentionables and beyond. And then I felt the world slipping away from me, acquiring a dizzying quality, darkening. My body fell forward as the blankness that could be death's harbinger engulfed me. And somewhere in the remote parts of the portion of my mind that still functioned, I began to wish I would die....

When I regained consciousness my aunt Shama was looking at me. The world I had returned to was still not fully in my grasp and I wasn't sure if I was in a dream. But within the haziness I could clearly hear my aunt say as she reached to touch me, "You had us so worried."

"Where am I?"

"Somewhere safe."

"Where?"

"Hush, you are tired. You must rest."

I moved my eyes to take in the rest of the room as I began to gain better mastery of myself. My eyes came to rest on Alexandre, my aunt's boyfriend, sitting in the corner of the room. From what I could tell, I was in some infirmary of sorts, but how had I gotten there? I tried to move but found that I was in too much pain to do so. I heard my aunt repeat that I needed to rest as best as I could as I slipped again into unconsciousness. I fell back and forth from brief periods of consciousness and long ones of unconsciousness for the next few days. It was only on the fourth day that I was able to feel strengthened enough to sit up and talk over an extended period. My aunt was reluctant to talk to me about what had happened since I collapsed in the bathroom, but I sulked so much that she felt compelled to tell me.

Auntie Shama had returned home that afternoon, expecting to see me in the living room reading as I was wont to do lately. Not finding me there, she thought I'd be in my bedroom. But she soon realized when she peeked into the bedroom, which had its door wide opened, that I wasn't in there. She reckoned I had gone out. She went to her bedroom to take a nap, but soon felt the need to urinate. She'd gone to the bathroom and opened the door. That's when she'd seen me sprawled on the floor face down, naked with a strange object protruding from my groin region, blood spread underneath me, a bottle of half empty whiskey next to my body. Yelling, she'd rushed ran to see Alexandre. It being a Saturday, Alexandre was at home. He had rushed back with her in a jeep and carried my body into the jeep and slalomed to a hospice managed by CARE.

The doctor, Gracia Marquez, who'd befriended Alexandre a while back, had immediately turned her attention to me. The doctor had to perform an abortion, a dilation and suction, removing the now damaged fetus. I had lost a lot of blood and Dr. Marquez had worked hard to stabilize my blood pressure and control the bleeding. She'd put me on antibiotics. "Alexandre was a great help," my aunt told me. "I don't know what we'd have done without him, if he didn't know Dr. Marquez, this CARE hospice."

Dr. Gracia Marquez, the middle aged doctor who had volunteered her services for CARE temporarily, assured me that I would be well. She would check on me from time to time, smile at me and even hold my hand tenderly and tell me not to strain myself. Her motherly tenderness, her smile, the strands of gray in her hair, all spoke a tale of assuredness and trust to me, a tale that I believed. And I would long for the times when Dr. Marquez came to visit.

## Thirteen

The Committee, once again, sent my nomination to the full Senate, split 7-7 as before. This was a good sign, said Dwayne. We'd not lost any ground, and if this held in the full Senate, I would be confirmed. And so commenced the debate in the Senate. And it was fierce. My supporters focused on my strengths as a lawyer and public servant, while my opponents focused on my short judicial experience and what they described as my heinous murder of a human being, even if one unborn. Some stated that I couldn't be trusted to judge objectively on matters of fetal abortion and others claimed that confirming me would be the beginning of the infusion of Sharia law into US Constitutional law. After days of debate, it wasn't clear to me if there were enough votes for my confirmation. Even some members of the Senate who had stood with my side earlier now rose to oppose my nomination.

"It's all now very confusing," Dwayne said. "Despite the president's best efforts, we're losing more support than we're gaining."

My concern at the time had evolved. I wanted to win because I didn't want "the other side to win." But as I looked back on recent events, again and again I affirmed what I had told the Committee. I would trade the nomination for Juju's return. What I couldn't cope with was the loss of both the nomination and Juju.

Within a couple of days, most of the senators had spoken. There were only three yet to speak, including Senator Norwood. And when he rose to address the chamber, everyone expected a scathing attack on my candidacy for the highest court. He adjusted one watch and the other and then he looked up, poised as if ready to catch lightning and deliver it to the senators in his palms. At home the screen focused on his wizened face. For a moment, I was inclined to turn off the TV. Could I stand another attack? But he had hardly spoken during the proceedings and I was curious to hear how he would couch his opposition.

He began, "The truth of the matter is that I have agonized a great deal over this nomination, more than any nomination that has come before this chamber in my over thirty years on the Senate." He paused, pursed his lips and then continued, "I must confess I haven't always approached nominees without some political calculation. A question that often comes to mind as I consider such matters is: What would my constituents think? In the past, this has often affected my calculation and the way I have voted on a range of matters before the Senate. But now that I am not running for reelection..." There was murmuring in the Senate as this must have come as a shock.

Senator Norwood continued as the murmuring continued, "Yes, I know this is news, but I have been thinking about it for a long time and at seventy nine, I think it's time to retire. I wasn't sure of this until last night when my wife and I decided it is time. But that is a story for another occasion." The murmuring had barely died down when he went on, "Yes, now that I am sure I won't be running for reelection, I have had a lot more license to think, a lot more freedom to reach my decision. How others will react has become less of a factor. Not that I don't care what my constituents think. I do. But in the final analysis, at this stage of my political career, if I can't vote my conscience, then when will I be able to do so? In the twilight of my political life, I have to leave this august body able to live with myself and to sleep soundly at night. I hope that even if I vote contrary to the wishes of my constituents, they will forgive me for doing what I believe to be the right thing.

"Which now brings me to the nominee before the Senate at this moment: Shama Badu. My initial reaction when I learned of the nomination was not entirely positive. In fact, it was very negative, to be frank. This is not the first time this nominee has come before us, but in the past our decision was of less importance as her nomination was to lesser courts. But now we are talking about the Supreme Court, the most important court in the United States. This is now the biggest league. And she will be its Chief Justice, if confirmed. We can't afford to make mistakes. In the past, I have voted against her with an eye on what my voters would think. But as I said before, I am no longer willing to take that expedient route. I want to consider her anew. That is not to say I will vote in her favor. That is just to say that I am not afraid to speak freely.

"So I have restudied the nominee's qualifications. After careful scrutiny, there is no doubt left in my mind that she is a brilliant mind, an exceptional lawyer. No one, in all honesty, can refute that. Just look at her record in school and after, her meteoric rise. There can be no doubt about that. Nor can we refute the fact that she is diligent and dedicated to the cause of justice. Even where we may disagree with some of her choices or decisions, her record speaks for itself. Here is a lady who took on extremely unpopular cases, at the risk of being labeled a traitor to her race. Far from being such, I think it demonstrates her courage and objectivity."

I smiled at the senator's praise, but I held my joy, afraid that he was leading me like a fatling to the slaughter. The man was so smooth, deadly in this effort to appear objective. I repaid attention to his speech.

"Some have pointed to her lack of judicial experience as the basis to deny her a seat on the Court. And we could mention other marginal factors such as her age, but to me, these are not important. I don't think any of us need to be reminded that Justice Story was thirty-two when he was appointed to the Court. Let us also remember that numerous justices such as William Rehnquist had no judicial experience when they were appointed.

Nor, even if it's not mentioned, can we deny her a seat because she is foreign born. That would be un-American. We have nominated a number of foreign born justices to the Court, among them Felix Frankfurter. In fact, a linchpin of America's greatness is in offering a system that enables all citizens, whether or not born here, to contribute their talents to our national development. It is irrelevant what country or continent she comes from."

I smiled.

"All that said, however, the one issue that worries me is that I do not know where the nominee stands on major issues. And, like many of her predecessors, she has, sometimes cunningly and sometimes not so artfully, refused to answer the questions that my colleagues have posed to her on burning issues of day. That is worrisome, and I will return to this later."

So now would pour the negatives and the reasons why I should be rejected. I continued to listen to this masterful performance.

"Now, I do not wish to accuse anyone here of religious bigotry. But how many of us, really can say that we are not afraid of her suspected religious affiliation? I do not know if it's true or not, but we are all aware that she has been called a Moslem. If indeed she is a Moslem, then the question, and this is the most difficult for me, is whether as a Christian I can vote for a Moslem to sit on the highest court of the land. Oh, yes, I too

402

have worried that she will seek to bend our laws toward Islamic principles, that she may even take her orders from some fundamentalists who wish our great nation harm. Yes, I have worried. But standing firm in Christian principles, I remember the greatest commandment is to love God and the second greatest to love my neighbor as myself. It is with such love that I approach this nomination. I want to treat her as I would like to be treated."

Okay, Senator Norwood, what is your point? Where do you stand?

"I also remind myself of the First Amendment. If I am to live up to its principles, can I really bring this religious yardstick into the public sphere? If I, as a Christian, were before a majority of Moslems, would I want them measuring my ability to serve in a secular office based on such religious considerations? No; of course, not. I would hope that they would measure my ability to serve solely on my abilities, mostly based on my record or through other publicly demonstrated means of my ability to serve impartially.

"And so it is to the public record that I would direct them. This country, after all, is not a theocracy. Sure, on a personal level I would welcome the opportunity to persuade Judge Badu, if indeed she is Moslem, of my beliefs, but once I pick up the mantle as US Senator, I can no longer wield that touchstone. That is not to say that religion does not belong in the public discourse. It is my firm belief that it does. However, it is one thing to engage each other in the marketplace of ideas on religious matters and beliefs and an entirely different matter to use our religious beliefs to exclude other citizens from participating in public service."

The senator was making more points in my favor than I expected.

"And so, as I have said, the only criterion we ought to use is her public record, her publicly demonstrated ability to serve. And, as Judge Badu, has reminded us, that is where we ought to go. And her public record is brilliant. It clearly demonstrates that she is qualified for the job. As to recent allegations, which among us would like to be judged on things we did so many years ago, especially when a distinguished public record demonstrates unsullied integrity?"

But?

"However, I now return to the question of the lack of her opinions on important matters of the day. Are we rolling the dice if we nominate her? To an extent, yes, we are. But can we truly ever be sure of how a

403

nominee will rule until he or she is on the court? History teaches us that opinion before taking a seat on the Court does not necessarily indicate how a justice will rule on cases once on the Court.

"Which brings me back again to the basic question: whether the nominee is qualified as demonstrated by the record. I have found no basis to conclude otherwise, and it is for this reason that I take the liberating stand of voting my conscience and voting yes for the confirmation of Judge Shama Rugwe Badu as Chief Justice of the Supreme Court of the United States of America."

What? WhAT? WHAT?
Silence.
More silence.
Even more silence.

And then one senator stood to applaud. And another. And another, until soon over half the senators were on their feet applauding. As I watched this on TV, I managed a smile for the second time. Dwayne called to tell me that this was the political cover they were hoping for—if Senator Norwood could support me, then those who feared for their political futures would be more inclined to support my nomination. "It will be tight still, but I think we could win this one," Dwayne concluded.

And then I heard the front door opening. Startled and afraid for my safety, I yelled: "Who is there?" There was no response, just footsteps on the hardwood floor. Even before I saw him, my fear had subsided, and I knew it was Juju. I stood up to welcome him in concern, my worry now being that he would make me account for what I did. He stood before me, his suitcase beside him. And then he took a step forward and then another. I opened my mouth, about to express my regret, beg for forgiveness, but he lifted an arm, and for a moment I thought he was about to strike me. He moved the arm forward and gently and hushed me with a finger over my lips. We knew each other too well, and so by the instinct etched through years of marriage, we were kissing before we would hold ourselves back. "I love you," Juju said in an interlude to our kissing. "I just needed a few days away to convince myself that no matter what you've done, it would be better for me to be with you than without you, for my own sake. I love you, Shama Rugwe Badu, and I must accept you, all of you, no matter what. It took me a long time to realize the same about my mother and by the time I realized this, too much damage was done. I went to Dad's grave a couple of days ago. As I stood there, it occurred to me how much damage the living causes to each other and then it's too late. I don't want that to happen to us."

I was about to tell him I was sorry. But I changed my mind.

I had not confirmed this with the doctor yet, but I had a certainty that the baby was there and an equally strong conviction that this one would be carried to term—Ghanaian, Rwandan, American. A baby for our times.

"You are going to be a father," I said, "the father of a very special baby."

He put his hand over my belly. Because this was not my first pregnancy, Juju could very well have expressed skepticism, worried that it would not be carried to term. He didn't. "I know," he said instead without explaining himself. I didn't need an explanation, just that we were in accord. I was about to thank him for returning. He hushed me once again. And then I realized he was no longer looking at me but at the TV screen and that he was grinning. I turned to look at the TV, ignored when he entered the room.

By a margin of fifty-two to forty-eight, I had won Senate confirmation as Chief Justice of the Supreme Court of the Unites States of America. The phone began to ring. "Don't' answer, Chief Justice Badu," Juju said, as he reached for my dress. "This is the moment when we celebrate our baby."

And as I moved him closer and closer to the couch and the phone continued to ring, as if in endorsement, I thought how fortunate I was that I stood to be the supreme interpreter of the Law of the land, its top judge; how I was being offered an opportunity to impact millions. As they say happens when you are about to die, my life seemed to flash before my eyes—Papa and Mama, Placide, Jean Pierre, Auntie Shama, even Anan... Butare, the foundation of fortitude, my struggles and my triumphs; Chicago and the accumulation of strength; and then Washington DC, the need to perdure through the valley of hellfire and taste the fruitage of that perseverance, and then the trajectory ... But this time, the death that flashed before my mind's eyes was a form of rebirth, a rebirth that is also a form of death, a death of the old that begets the new, a newness that trumpets a future of hope. And as I embraced the son physically, I was also affirming the father and his words: Mate... Checkmate....

The beginning is a beginning.

## Note

I consulted a range of books in writing this novel, although I need to emphasize that this is a work of fiction and any shortcomings are entirely mine. In particular, Dante's words at the cemetery are taken from Robert Pinsky's *The Inferno of Dante* (Farrar, Straus and Giroux, 1996). A small portion of the novel was previously published as a short story, *The Fools Tomatoes*, in Worldview magazine (Winter 2003).

## About The Author

Benjamin Kwakye was born in Accra, Ghana. His first novel, *The Clothes of Nakedness*, won the 1999 Commonwealth Writers' Prize, best first book, Africa. His second novel, *The Sun by Night*, won the 2006 Commonwealth Writers' Prize, Best Book Africa. His third novel, *The Other Crucifix*, won the 2011 IPPY Gold Award for Adult Multicultural Fiction. He is also the author of a collection of novellas, *Eyes of the Slain Woman* and the collection of short stories, *The Executioner's Confession*. A graduate of Dartmouth College and Harvard Law School, he presently practices law and is a director of the African Education Initiative.

Printed in the United States
By Bookmasters